Dea[d]

Rachel Lynch is an author of crime fiction whose books have sold more than one million copies. She grew up in Cumbria and the lakes and fells are never far away from her. London pulled her away to teach History and marry an Army Officer, whom she followed around the globe for thirteen years. A change of career after children led to personal training and sports therapy, but writing was always the overwhelming force driving the future. The human capacity for compassion as well as its descent into the brutal and murky world of crime are fundamental to her work.

Also by Rachel Lynch

The Rich
The Famous

Helen Scott Royal Military Police Thrillers

The Rift
The Line

Detective Kelly Porter

Dark Game
Deep Fear
Dead End
Bitter Edge
Bold Lies
Blood Rites
Little Doubt
Lost Cause
Lying Ways
Sudden Death
Silent Bones
Shared Remains

RACHEL LYNCH
DEAD END

CANELO CRIME

DK | Penguin Random House

First published in the United Kingdom in 2018 by Canelo

This edition published in the United Kingdom in 2025 by

Canelo Crime, an imprint of
Canelo Digital Publishing Limited,
20 Vauxhall Bridge Road,
London SW1V 2SA
United Kingdom

A Penguin Random House Company
The authorised representative in the EEA is Dorling Kindersley Verlag GmbH.
Arnulfstr. 124, 80636 Munich, Germany

Copyright © Rachel Lynch 2018

The moral right of Rachel Lynch to be identified as the creator of this work has been asserted in accordance with the Copyright, Designs and Patents Act, 1988.
All rights reserved. No part of this publication may be reproduced or transmitted in any form or by any means, electronic or mechanical, including photocopy, recording, or any information storage and retrieval system, without permission in writing from the publisher.
No part of this book may be used or reproduced in any manner for the purpose of training artificial intelligence technologies or systems. In accordance with Article 4(3) of the DSM Directive 2019/790, Canelo expressly reserves this work from the text and data mining exception.

A CIP catalogue record for this book is available from the British Library.

Print ISBN 978 1 83598 291 4
Ebook ISBN 978 1 78863 021 4

This book is a work of fiction. Names, characters, businesses, organizations, places and events are either the product of the author's imagination or are used fictitiously. Any resemblance to actual persons, living or dead, events or locales is entirely coincidental.

Printed and bound in Great Britain by Clays Ltd, Elcograf S.p.A.

Look for more great books at
www.canelo.co | www.dk.com

Chapter 1

Ullswater's visitors had packed up for the day, and the lake was still. The water kissed the pebble beaches along her northern shores, and the cars that normally choked the lay-bys and car parks were gone. The steamers had finished their hourly chugging up and down, and the only onlookers were the bowing trees, gently swaying; until tomorrow, when it would all start again.

Hidden away from prying eyes, whatever the time of day, concealed beyond a private driveway, lay an old stately pile, proudly dominant for two hundred years. Wasdale Hall, home to the Fitzgeralds since the Domesday Book, sat in darkness for two reasons: one, the current earl, Xavier-Paulus II, baulked at the electricity bills; and two, his grandson, Zachary, had been out fishing all day. There was ample light, though, from the mid-May sun as it dipped further behind the Helvellyn range to the west of the lake. In the driveway sat three old Land Rovers, one still containing Zachary's kit from his session at Aira Beck. He'd pulled out a three-pound beast of a trout that morning, and the kitchen still smelled of cooking. Linda, the housekeeper for almost thirty years, had cooked it the way Grandpa liked it: with plenty of butter, and parsley from the herb garden at the rear.

Zachary stayed in the kitchen by the Aga, which beat out the only heat in the house, and forked chunks of dog food into two feeding bowls. He'd long since pulled off his boots, and his belly was full; now it was the turn of the dogs, who eyed him greedily. There wasn't a sound; they watched TV rarely, and not even a radio broke the hush, while Grandpa was long for his bed and Linda had washed up and gone to her home in Watermillock hours ago.

Samson and Delilah hovered hungrily but patiently; they knew their turn would come. The two great lumbering dark brown Labradors licked their lips in anticipation. Zachary stood up and the dogs padded over from their baskets and began to eat. He put the fork in the sink and the tin in the dustbin and watched them gobble their dinner. Fatigue gripped him and he yawned. There was little more to do; only have a shower and climb into bed. The season was heating up nicely, and there would be plenty more fishing days to come. He knew that as soon as he left the warmth of the kitchen, he would be hit by the icy blast of the rest of the old windy mansion, until he jumped beneath his duvet and generated his own heat. Grandpa was adamant: the heating went off on 31 March, and came back on again on 1 November, every year without fail.

Zachary lingered a little longer. The kitchen was his favourite room: it was where he talked to Linda, and Brian the gardener, and it was where he could put his feet up on a chair, muddy boots drying by the Aga. It was where he talked about his paintings, and the best places to catch perch; it was where he gutted his fish, and it was where he listened. It was also where he preferred to eat. Grandpa ate in the dining room, alone. It had always been so. Zachary preferred to sit with Linda and Brian. Not because he didn't love his grandpa; nothing could be further from the truth. It was simply because Grandpa had certain routines that would never change. He was a creature of habit.

Zachary allowed the dogs to finish, and let them out to roam around in the garden for the last time before bed. They always stayed close and he never worried about them wandering off. But tonight they didn't seem to want to go. Samson whined and looked up to the ceiling, as if he wanted Zachary to take him upstairs. Zachary laughed and stroked the dog. Delilah copied and refused to go out.

'Have it your own way then,' he said affectionately. 'In your baskets.' They reluctantly obeyed, and stared up at their master with huge eyes. Zachary almost felt like curling up beside them. He shrugged his shoulders and yawned again, flicking off the light. No one locked doors around the lake except the tourists, even after last year, when that woman had been found by Watermillock church. He shivered.

As he climbed the stairs, he thought about his grandpa's weakening health. It wasn't that he suffered from a malady or a dangerous infection; more that he was simply old. He was ninety-five and was beginning to show it. He grew weaker by the day, and it pained Zachary to see him like that. He'd always been strong, independent and steady, but now he was frail. There was no one else, and it had been like that for a very long time. Something inside Zachary ached, and it was a familiar feeling: Grandpa was not going to be around forever.

His thoughts were interrupted by a faint thud overhead, and he stopped on the bottom stair and looked up to the ceiling.

He heard the noise again.

The great hallway was freezing, and he felt his way up the grand staircase lit only by the moonlight coming through the window, reflecting off the lake. He could easily find his way in much darker corners – after all, he'd lived all nineteen years of his life here – but he still held onto the banister and watched for anything illuminated or out of place. He dismissed the noise and carried on.

He paused at the impressive window on the first landing, overlooking Ullswater. The lights of the Peak's Bay Hotel could be seen across the lake, and Zachary was thankful for the peace and quiet afforded by their isolation. He imagined couples dancing and friends drinking in the bar until the early hours, and thought that Grandpa must have enjoyed that life a long time ago, but not now.

He continued up the stairs, but halfway up, he stopped. He thought he'd heard the sound again. This time it concerned him, as it was an unfamiliar noise, and he tried to work out what it was. He listened carefully in case it happened again, but there was nothing. He made a decision to check on Grandpa before he retired to his own bed. He didn't usually do it, but it wouldn't hurt. The noise could have been Grandpa dropping something, or even falling, and he couldn't risk leaving it till the morning. Grandpa might need him.

There was a light under Grandpa's study door, and Zachary wondered if he'd fallen asleep at his desk. Maybe the thud he'd heard was his grandfather tumbling from his chair. His steps quickened, and he went to the study door.

'Grandpa,' he said, quietly at first. No answer came back. Maybe he'd just forgotten to turn off the light.

'Grandpa,' he said again, louder this time.

Even as he turned the handle, he knew that something wasn't right. A whiff of something in the air, a creaking noise…

He swung the door fully open, and sank to his knees.

The smell of shit stung his nostrils, and Zachary buried his face in his hands and sobbed. Covering his mouth, he crawled towards the middle of the room, where a stool lay knocked over on the floor. Above it, the body of his grandfather swung to and fro.

Chapter 2

Kelly jumped from the top of Kailpot Crag into the freezing water below and screamed. She didn't reckon there was anyone else on the planet who would dare push her over the edge, and as she emerged from the lake below, she squealed at Johnny in mock horror. He laughed out loud and jumped in after her, making his body into a bomb. She wasn't offended when he pretended to be laddish, because she saw straight through it. It was a relief to be with someone who expected nothing from her apart from what they already had.

The water would have stopped the heart of someone from a warmer climate, but for Kelly and Johnny, it was luxuriously refreshing. They were alone, because it was May, and too cold for tourists to venture here. But the cold bothered neither of them because they knew that this was the best time to visit; when they both needed to cool off after equally taxing days.

They swam towards the middle of the lake, and Johnny caught Kelly's leg. She wriggled and they both went under the surface. The cold stung her eyes as she searched underwater for him. He'd swum beneath her and grabbed her leg once more. They broke the surface and caught their breath. The water was a deep turquoise, and they could see fifteen feet below them. Kelly was a confident swimmer in the Lakes, but not in open water: she hated swimming in the sea. Here, only the odd ugly pike lurked beneath, and the experience didn't leave a sticky residue of salt and sand.

They swam out further and got used to the temperature. The tensions of the day melted away and Kelly felt free.

'Race!' Johnny shouted. She was as competitive as he was, and he knew she'd take the bait.

'Where to?' she asked, treading water. She was used to the cold now, though she could feel her body was covered in goose bumps.

'Back to the beach,' he called. They were about a hundred metres away from the shore, and Kelly wondered if they might spot a steamer puffing around the bend, to the left or right of them. But there was no sound.

'Go!' she shouted, and dived beneath the surface. She knew Johnny would grin broadly as he held his breath and took his first stroke. But he'd still win.

He pounded the water back to the shore, coming up only every six strokes for air. Kelly had to take a breath every four. She could feel his body pushing through the water only feet away from her and knew he was overtaking her. She pushed harder. By the time they were in less than three feet of water, he was close enough for her to grab his shorts and pull them down. He stopped and clutched at them, but it was too late; Kelly swam past him and was officially the winner.

She strode out of the water, pulling her hair back and wringing it out over her shoulder. Laughing to herself, she turned around to watch Johnny pulling his pants back up. He grinned and came towards her. She expected a kiss, but at the last moment he slapped her firmly on her backside. Technically that was a victory too; he knew she hated it.

Well, she pretended to. The first time he'd done it, on a run around the lake, she'd gone to berate him, delivering the full extent of her indignation, but he'd smiled and defused her mood without saying a single word.

They were both short of breath, and sat down on their towels on the tiny shingle beach. It was the type of place you saw in a magazine, empty, hidden and private; but come summer, it would be rammed, noisy and annoying.

'So, was it broken?' Kelly asked as she pulled a sweater over her bikini and lay down on her side, propped up on an elbow. A light breeze began to stir the trees, and they moved from side to side, like elders nodding their consent. Johnny rubbed himself roughly with his towel; goose bumps covered his body. Kelly watched him. Maybe it was time to get dressed after all.

'Yes, in three places. It was pretty bad,' Johnny said. He was talking about a woman he'd brought off the mountain this morning, who'd fallen down a gully on St Sunday Crag. Luckily her boyfriend's mobile phone had a signal, and the helicopter had managed to get Johnny up close enough to reach her within two hours. She was now tucked up in the Penrith and Lakes Hospital, awaiting complicated surgery. 'It must have hurt like hell,' he added. For Johnny to say that, it must have been bad.

Kelly's day hadn't been anywhere near as exciting, but it had been challenging nonetheless. Her superior at HQ, DCI Eddie Cane, was doing his best to get her to commit to a desk there, pen-pushing reviews and cold cases. Technically it was her next step – a promotion, and an honour indeed, but not one that Kelly wanted bestowed upon her. Reappraising cases and crunching paperwork at HQ had never been her intention; she was an operational officer, made for the outdoors, and she couldn't desert her team, not now.

–

'You can't avoid promotion forever, Kelly,' DCI Cane had said to her this morning, catching her out.

'Why not? I'm doing the constabulary a favour,' she'd said. 'I'm not ready to stare at the wall; when I am, I'll let you know.'

Cane would have a job convincing her, but the powers that be wanted to acknowledge her contribution, which was not insignificant. Since moving back home, Kelly had put herself in a few tight spots that had perhaps been unnecessary, but that had led to convictions. On paper, she was worth the extra letter before her name, but Cane knew that she saw HQ as a graveyard of crusty old men, ploughing through data and cobbling the odd press release together. They were both aware that was not the case at all, but that wasn't the point. Kelly Porter was a risk-taker, which was precisely the reason they needed her at HQ, but it also meant that she'd only be satisfied cracking cases rather than handing them out.

'Don't you think you need a break, Kelly? Let some young blood get their teeth into cases.' DCI Cane never gave up. 'What about Will Phillips?' he'd asked.

'Young blood? Christ, I've only just turned thirty-eight! Will is a good operator, Eddie, but he's not ready. You know that.'

Kelly could feel the thrill of running a case threatening to leave her behind as a young upstart filled her shoes. It bugged her. It was nothing to do with Will. She had a solid relationship with him that had been tested many times. But the same was true of the whole team, and she wasn't ready to let go yet.

'Strictly speaking, Eddie, it should be Kate Umshaw who becomes the next SIO.'

'So is that a no?' DCI Cane had asked. Kelly had taken her hands off her hips, where they'd sat defiantly the whole time she'd been in his office, and folded them together. She'd said enough. Cane had smiled. She was off the hook. For now.

'Can I take the increased salary but be a senior operational officer at the same time?' Her head had tilted to the side and her eyes shone cheekily.

Eddie Cane had known it was coming. Hell, if they were in a bigger force, she'd have no choice, but here things were slightly more… fluid. Besides, Eddie had to admit that with Kelly as the go-to SIO for serious crime in the northern Lakes, they would do well to keep her there.

'Do you ever sit down, Kelly?'

'You know the answer to that, Eddie. Sir.'

–

'It's the same in the army,' Johnny said now. 'The better you are in the field – allegedly – the higher you go and the further away from the real troops. You end up getting a bunch of muppets sitting behind desks in Whitehall, making decisions for the boots on the ground and risking their lives. They get out of touch. It's like teaching or the NHS: top heavy with honour-seeking egotists. It's crazy but unavoidable.' He never had to explain army jargon to Kelly, because it was so close to the language used by coppers. It was one of the things they loved about each other.

'And that's exactly what I don't want. I joined to be a copper, not a document-handler. Paperwork doesn't excite me, Johnny.'

'I know, but there are benefits too: you'd have the authority to get other people to do stuff on your behalf,' he pointed out. 'Isn't that what always frustrates you? When you know what you've got to get through, when you should be concentrating on connecting the dots rather than drawing them all first? I've seen it, I've seen you doing it, and you hate it.'

'I know, but if I'm not there at the beginning, then I'm playing catch-up. It's Hobson's choice,' she said. She stood up and pulled her jeans over her wet bikini bottoms; she'd rather do that than hang around and get colder. They started to pack up.

'What about the money?' he asked.

'You don't strike me as the type to bother about that kind of thing,' she said, and smiled.

'I only don't bother about it because I have enough of it. Stop evading the question. No one refuses promotion, Kelly.'

'Well I do. I'm happy where I am, and I've built a cracking team that works.'

'Can't you take the title and stay where you are?' he asked.

'I already asked that. They're thinking about it.'

Johnny shook his head. She'd been sitting on the information all along.

She slipped on flip-flops and picked up her things, wet hair dripping down her sweater. She didn't mind; she wasn't the type to get prissy about it. He slapped her bottom again, probably half because he knew it pissed her off, and half because he wanted to touch her. She rounded on him and stuck her chin out.

'I love that face,' he said.

She turned around and marched away, with Johnny bringing up the rear. She knew he was watching her swing her hips from side to side, as she did when she was making a point.

When they reached her house in Pooley Bridge, she went straight to the fireplace to start a fire. The evening air still had a pinch in it, and besides, Kelly liked to take advantage of the open fireplace in her new home whenever she could. She could stare at the flames lapping over glowing logs all evening. Johnny opened a bottle of wine, and Kelly flicked on the news. They were growing more comfortable with each other, and moved around like a couple. Occasionally Kelly considered making things official, but more often than not she dismissed the idea straight away.

The TV had been left on full volume for some reason, and the noise assaulted them.

'Concerns are growing as to the whereabouts of two young women in Cumbria,' said the reporter. The man stood ten minutes from Kelly's door, at Howtown campsite. Both Kelly and Johnny were aware of the drama unfolding close to where they lived; Johnny had been a part of the initial search for the girls, which was still ongoing. They watched the report intently and Kelly sipped her wine. It was full-bodied and herby, just the way she liked it. She'd put one of her junior officers in charge. These types of cases usually ended up the same way: with the unfortunate hikers being found stuck on some crag somewhere with piss poor equipment and no phone. Kelly laid her head on Johnny's chest, and he moved so that he could put his feet up with hers. He probably wouldn't be going anywhere tonight.

'The two women were last seen at around six o'clock on Sunday evening, two days ago.'

Kelly's eyes half closed as she allowed herself to relax. She was trusting Rob Shawcross to investigate the case; unless something major changed to elevate the file beyond missing, she wouldn't need to become involved. Now, however, photographs of the missing girls appeared on the screen, and she sat up.

'What is it?' Johnny asked.

The missing persons' case had been just that to Kelly: a report containing data that needed to be classified, and that was all. It wasn't necessary for a detective of her rank to delve further unless it was elevated to suspicious, and that didn't normally happen for forty-eight hours, by which time they'd surely be found. She hadn't seen the girls' photographs. Until now.

The two young women were in their late teens. They attended Lancaster University together and had been on a camping trip to Howtown, near Ullswater, when they disappeared. Initial enquiries had unearthed ordinary profiles; nothing that raised alarms. The girls seemed to be sensible, skilled and used to the mountains, with no history of rash decisions or risk-taking. Rob had contributed the details in the team brief this morning, and mountain rescue was working round the clock.

Kelly fiddled with her hair and looked at the photographs again. Johnny watched her.

As she studied their faces, she bit the inside of her lip. Both girls had striking blonde hair, and were also extremely pretty. It was something in the shape of the faces, as well as the hair colour and age, that made Kelly reassess the status of the inquiry. In February, another young woman had gone missing and there'd been a medium-scale hunt involving local TV and radio, but the case had been passed to Lancaster when it was revealed that the last sighting was Carnforth train station. Now, alarm bells were ringing.

'They look just like Freya,' she said.

'Who?' Johnny asked.

'Freya Hamilton. She went missing just under four months ago. We got a call from Humberside Police – that's where it was reported, by her sister – saying she was working in the Lakes at the time. We took it on, but it quickly became clear that there'd been a sighting of her since then in Lancashire, so we passed it to them.'

'You never mentioned her,' Johnny said.

'I know, the case was off my desk as quickly as it landed really. To be honest, I never gave it a second thought after it went to Lancashire Police.'

'So you've no idea if she was found?'

'No.'

'But now you want to know?'

She looked at him and nodded, biting her lip.

'Yes, I do.'

Chapter 3

As Kelly drove out of Pooley Bridge the following morning, the hamlet had yet to wake up. The first steamers in May didn't land at the jetty until gone 9 a.m., and the pubs and B&Bs had yet to fill up to their peak season capacity. She left Johnny in bed, envying him his shift work. He wasn't due in until this afternoon. Her hope was that by the time he woke up, the two girls would have been found safe and well.

Only last winter two men had gone missing on Scafell Pike. In such severe conditions, after four days' searching, the consensus was that they had met with tragedy; however, after another two days, they'd been found, dehydrated and with a few broken bones, but dug in and warm – and most importantly, alive – in a snowy insulated hole. So it was early days yet and no one was reaching any hasty conclusions.

Recently Johnny had begun to leave more clothes at her place, and when she thought about it, it didn't bother her. More than that, she liked it. When he was there, he made himself at home, cooked meals, ran baths for her and washed her clothes. She'd moved out of her mother's for some freedom, and to get away from her sister, and it could be said that she'd replaced their needs with someone else's, but she didn't see it like that. This was different.

Part of her missed her mother, but it had been the right move for both of them. Wendy now had to fend for herself and not rely on either daughter, and it had done her good. She was more independent and both of them could breathe. As for Kelly's sister Nikki, she'd become more of a burden in ways that no one could have foreseen.

Kelly pushed thoughts of her family firmly to the back of her mind as she strode into Eden House. She never tired of the red-brick facade and the anticipation of briefing her team. She'd built a solid squad and couldn't imagine that changing. DCI Cane would have to work a lot harder to split them up; for now, none of them were going anywhere.

It was looking like the beginnings of a hot day, and the plain-clothes shuffle, as she liked to call the awkwardness detectives exuded in their suits, would be more uncomfortable than normal. This was the kind of weather that made Kelly want to get her running kit on and follow Johnny up a mountain. They all felt it; it was like some kind of itch, and by the end of the day, ties were pulled low, skirts were fiddled with and shoes kicked off. That was the order of Kelly's office, and it suited them. If they could get away with coming to work in casual shorts and flip-flops, they would, but it was out of the question.

She made her way upstairs to her team, ready to listen to Rob's brief. Today was day three of the girls being missing, and questions would be asked. There were several factors that could elevate the hunt to something more sinister – telephone use, bank card use, anything flagged up around friends and family. Kelly kept the latter to herself. She'd have no idea, until she spoke to Lancashire Police, whether Freya Hamilton had turned up alive and well. She also wasn't sure what she'd do if it turned out that she was still missing.

The news about the girls was still local; they were adults after all. But that would soon change if they didn't turn up soon. A standard holding statement had been issued by HQ, but as Kelly walked into the office, she looked around for Rob, keen for an update. DC Will Phillips was already at his desk and he waved to her as she walked into the briefing room.

'Rob's gone for coffee,' he said.

'No worries, it's early yet. I've got something to catch up on, so we'll start when he gets in,' she said. Will nodded and went back to his screen. They'd worked together for a year now, and were familiar with each other's habits. Kelly was known as no-nonsense.

There was a pleasant waft of Ralph Lauren in the office, as there always was when Will was on shift, and it reminded Kelly of her father: always immaculately turned out, no matter the weather. If Will struggled to juggle work and home with a new wife, he didn't show it. She remembered the number of cold plates of food that had been thrown into the bin by her mother when she'd got fed up of waiting for Kelly's father. To Kelly, that was all her mother ever seemed to do: sit by the window waiting for John Porter to come home and be looked after. It was her reason for living; and Kelly's reason for remaining unattached — that was, until Johnny.

At her computer, she searched for the closed file on Freya Hamilton and wrote down the number for the detective in charge of the case in Lancashire. It was a start. She tapped her pen on her desk, toying with what she might say. She felt a little foolish; the girl had probably been found happy and well months ago, but she still knew that she had to make the call.

By the time she walked into the briefing room, Kelly had her answer, and it wasn't the one she'd been hoping for. Freya Hamilton was still missing.

–

At 8.30, those on the day shift filed into the meeting room and sat down with notepads. Kate Umshaw, fresh from a ciggie outside, brought the familiar pungency of tobacco with her, while Will and Rob nursed coffee. It was just the four of them. Kelly was keen to start and kicked things off bang on time. Her colleagues noted her knitted brow but didn't comment; Kelly Porter was the type of boss who let you know if she wasn't happy.

There was a smattering of check-ups on a burglary, two domestics, and an assault on a teacher at the local school, then Kelly got to the point.

'Rob, can you bring us up to date on the missing girls, please.'

Rob Shawcross had joined the team last year and was proving to be a valuable asset. He was Kelly's ideal colleague: he didn't say a lot, but what he did say was worth remembering. He and Will were a good match, and Kelly reckoned that in a tight spot, they'd be her first two choices to have around.

Rob tapped on his laptop and brought up a diagram on the whiteboard. The simple family-and-friends tree was used for all standard profiles, only this time there were two of them.

'Have we had any sightings yet?' Kelly asked.

'No. Not one. Mountain rescue are scratching their heads,' Rob said.

'Is the site secure?' Kelly asked.

'Yes, guv. We've done a search of their tent, and the manager of the park is collating a list of visitors for the past two weeks, as well as the girls' routines.'

Kelly made a note. 'What about the families? Have liaison officers been dispatched? Any secrets there?'

Rob looked at his notes. 'Only one red flag, and that's the ex-boyfriend of Sophie Daker, Garth Cooke. He's been staying at the same campsite. He's been questioned and told to remain in the area. He's a scumbag, but nothing has jumped out so far. Apparently Sophie dumped him and he's not happy about it.'

'Why was he staying at the same campsite if he'd been dumped?'

'He says they were going to get back together but she needed time.'

It sounded lame to everyone in the room.

'So, he's pissed off that he was dumped but not that she's missing?' There was a ripple of mirth around the small group.

'How many statements?' Kelly knew that uniforms at the site would have taken detailed statements, and she hoped there was something to go on.

'Forty-three so far. If it's all right with you, guv, I'd like to coordinate a larger search from the campsite, including local volunteers. We've had over a hundred enquiries offering to help. I think it's time we drafted in some more uniforms too.'

'I agree, we're on day three and I don't like the way it's going. Do we know of any bank account or phone activity?'

'One mobile phone was found in the tent, so it looks like they only had one with them when they left the campsite. No bank transactions, and no activity on the other phone since a Facebook post on Sunday.'

'Saying what?'

'Hashtag friends.' Rob flicked a key and a photo flashed up on the whiteboard. The photo was a selfie of the girls outside their tent, beaming faces close together.

'Nice. They're attractive girls.' Kate Umshaw spoke for the first time. Her colleagues looked at her and agreed.

'What's this Garth Cooke like?' Kelly asked. 'Is he worth speaking to again?'

'A bit of a twat, to be honest,' Rob said.

'Bring him in. OK, let's use this photo as a media lead. It's a good one, it'll get sympathies flowing. Are the parents up for a TV appeal?'

Televised appeals often helped. They were also good for ruling out the family. Plenty of cases had taken unexpected turns after a public appeal. For one, she'd have a body-language expert and a criminal psychologist watching. And for two, it would give her an insight into the girls' relationships with their nearest and dearest.

'Can we liaise with Lancaster Police and get some statements from friends at the university too, please?' There was always the possibility that the girls had taken off and were in a different county by now.

Was that what Freya Hamilton had done?

'I spoke to Hannah's pastoral head at Grizedale College and also Sophie's at Furness College. They both hold the girls in high esteem, and gave portraits of polite, conscientious but private members of their communities. They're model students,' Rob said.

The case bugged Kelly. People went missing on the fells all the time, but seldom for this long. It was incredibly rare for someone to get lost and not be picked up by mountain rescue. Johnny and his fellow volunteers knew the fells like London cabbies knew the streets of the East End. They came from all over the world and had probably notched up thousands of peaks between them, some at competition level. They knew all the popular walks, as well as those doing the rounds on social media for being unorthodox and even dangerous. Websites boasting secret crags and base jumps were becoming more and more prevalent, and Kelly wondered if the girls were thrill-seekers. She needed to work out the motivation behind their trip: were they adrenalin junkies looking for kicks, now at the bottom of a hidden ravine? It didn't sound like it. They weren't members of extreme rock-climbing or unusual sports groups, plus they'd grown up round the fells; they were both local girls. And that begged another question: had they made a pact to disappear for some reason?

'I'm assuming everything was bagged and tagged from the tent and sent to the lab?' She didn't look up. It was standard procedure; she was just ticking off her to-do list. 'Anything unusual?'

Rob tapped his pen.

'Rob?'

'I just thought it was too tidy for two teenage girls.'

'Explain?'

'I've got a sister, and her bedroom is a nightmare: make-up, perfume, books and clothes everywhere. Their tent looked as though it had been tidied up before we got there.'

Chapter 4

Xavier-Paulus Fitzgerald, the 7th Earl of Lowesdale, lay on the slab of senior pathologist Ted Wallis. Ted had been told that the suspected cause of death was suicide, but it was his job to decide whether this was supported by his findings. That was all. He wasn't a judge and he wasn't a detective.

But many things bugged him about the corpse lying sprawled in front of him. Not least because Ted remembered the earl in his prime, hosting grand balls in his tuxedo. He could have opted to pass the autopsy to a junior colleague, but his curiosity had got the better of him. The old goat was ninety-five years old, and Ted wanted to know whether he'd taken his own life. He had plenty of questions, and he wanted to find his own conclusions, not trusting anyone else to do so. His biggest query was how a ninety-five-year-old man had got himself up on a stool and balanced there long enough to tie a complex knot, get the noose round his neck and step to his death.

He'd read the gossip. The earl was said to be a virtual recluse these days, excepting his grandson, and the fact that the nineteen-year-old had found the body disturbed Ted. The boy was no doubt in line to collect a lot of money; relatives had killed before for less, but he didn't want anything to cloud his judgement at this stage and pushed the thought away. Perhaps the answer would lie in the earl's brain; he could have been riddled with Alzheimer's or dementia. Ted doubted it. Looking at the statements from the grandson and housekeeper, it seemed the earl had still possessed all his faculties.

The earl's once grand estate, reaching from the ancient hunting grounds of Little Mell in the north to Haweswater in the south, had been reduced to one old pile on the shores of Ullswater. Nobility no longer paid. Wasdale Hall was a shadow of its former self, he'd heard. But he hadn't heard that the earl was crazy; just fiercely private. With good reason.

Ted paused. The old man looked in good shape, and the distinctive Fitzgerald nose and high brow struck him. He hadn't really changed. Ted had been invited to the hall on several occasions. There was no doubt that Xavier-Paulus Fitzgerald knew how to throw a good party, and having a senior pathologist brushing shoulders with the guests seemed to add kudos and legitimacy, something the earl craved in spades.

The lofty hall and drawing rooms had echoed with dancing and singing as local society enjoyed behaving itself badly. Ted also remembered the couples who stole embraces in the garden by the fountain, and wondered if it was still there. It was that fountain that had led to the eventual disintegration of his own marriage. He never found out who told Mary, but it didn't matter now. Images came back to him and he closed his eyes. They'd been drunk. They'd giggled like children as she flicked water at him and he'd kissed her for the first time.

He opened his eyes and steeled himself for the job at hand. Even the old earl had been at it; they all were.

With no legitimate heirs, the title would die out now, and who knew what would happen to the house. Maybe it would pass to the earl's illegitimate grandson, Zachary, though no doubt distant relatives would emerge, lured by the scraps of what was left. Ted didn't believe that Xavier had only ever sired two children – there had to be more. A virile old dog like him must have been screwing beautiful women for decades. And there'd been plenty of that going on at Wasdale Hall.

Turning to the body, Ted pulled his overall over his head. His hands were elegantly steady as he tied the strings behind his back. His nails were short and clean, although no scrubbing-up was done for an autopsy. He adjusted the glasses perched on his strong nose and switched his head torch on before saying a silent apology to the man who'd been the perfect host but had met such a desperate end.

The eyes showed obvious signs of trauma associated with asphyxiation, though strangulation was not always the cause of death in a hanging. The blood vessels had exploded and there was severe bruising on the neck. The pattern of the rope was clear, and Ted thought that it must have taken the old man some time to tie a knot strong enough to hold him; despite his age, he must weigh a hundred and eighty pounds.

The event had not been unplanned. Perhaps he'd had help. He looked back to his notes. Allegedly the housekeeper had not been there – the grandson had called her after making his discovery – but the gardener had been on site, outside in his shed. The name was familiar, and he quietly tutted to himself; Brian Walker must be getting on in years himself, but old habits died hard, and Xavier liked to surround himself with those he trusted. Ted moved on.

He photographed and measured the contusions on the neck and noticed bruising on the forearms as well, which might be consistent with the effort needed to get the noose satisfactorily around the neck. The old man must have been determined. He'd come to the heart later and look for evidence of vagal inhibition leading to cardiac arrest, another possible cause of death with hanging. He'd need to examine the vagus nerve in the earl's neck closely.

He spoke into his microphone as he worked, and his assistant awaited instruction. The earl had tied a slip knot, which was particularly efficient at tightening under gravity. The bruising around his neck confirmed that the knot tightened to the side, above the right mastoid process. From a fairly low ceiling, as in this case, it was harder to decipher between hanging and manual strangulation, as the familiar V shape common from greater heights wasn't there. From a substantial height, such as a tree or a high beam, depending on where the knot was placed, deep contusions were left in a V shape, with the apex underneath the Adam's apple and each arm ascending up behind the ears. The marks on the earl's neck were less severe, indicating either a very slow death or a gentle impact. Both would have been excruciatingly painful. Ted had seen similar marks before but they were always accompanied by scratches where the victim had tried to save themselves, having changed their minds.

'Facial congestion, purple protruding tongue with black tip.' Ted spoke rhythmically. 'Lividity in feet and hands, but also anterior.' Blood pooled at the lowest point available, and it was obvious that the earl had been hanging for a short while after death, sending his blood south, then to his back after he was cut down. Pretty standard so far.

He looked into the ears and amongst the shaggy grey hair. The earl's scalp had yet to start thinning.

'Aural haemorrhage,' he recited into the microphone.

He lifted the arms and looked at the armpits, as well as under the nails, using a scraper to gather possible evidence, then worked his way down to the belly button, legs and finally between the toes. An assistant bagged and labelled every piece of matter: hairs, the scrapings from under the fingernails, and a ring worn on the earl's wedding finger. Ted examined it, turning it over in his fingers. It had an inscription on the inside: *Forever, Boo, 1977.*

The assistant helped to turn the earl over, and Ted examined his anus. He remembered that Boo was the earl's pet name for his lover, Delilah Mailer: intoxicating, cosmopolitan, enchanting Delilah, hostess, and tease. She'd disappeared from Wasdale Hall shortly after Zac was born, taking his mother with her. The frivolity stopped. There were rumours that the earl had since named a dog after her.

'Spontaneous faecal drainage,' he said, adjusting his mask.

Happy with the external examination, Ted could now eviscerate. He placed a glove on each hand – one couldn't be too careful: cadavers carried thousands of hazardous germs – then took a scalpel in his right hand and made an incision under the clavicle to the belly, revealing the inside of the chest. Some used a Stryker autopsy saw to get through the ribs, but Ted preferred shears, as he could control every snap. With the ribs broken, he could now get to the heart and lungs, and he sliced through the neck muscles with his scalpel, enabling him to remove the sac from gullet to anus with one yank. It made a squelch as he laid it next to the earl. He inspected the cavity but found nothing of note. He'd examine the organs later and then replace them, so the body could be sewn back up to resemble a human.

Next, he made an incision from behind the left ear all the way around to the right and pulled the skin covering the earl's face back over the top of the head, revealing the skull. He levered the skull apart with a surgical stainless-steel T-bar and removed the brain. It would be sliced into 1 cm pieces and sent to the lab for testing. Samples of blood, urine, bile and vitreous humour from the eyes were all extracted, and Ted took care to replace the fluid from the eyes with exactly 2 ml of water to prevent their collapse.

He looked at his watch: 1.35 p.m. He'd been working for over two hours and he was hungry. He removed his gloves and instructed his assistant to clean the slab once the earl was bagged, ready for release to the undertaker. The report could wait. The brain pathology would take another couple of days, maybe less if he hurried it along.

Ted never had a problem eating after an autopsy. He was ravenous, and when he got to the canteen, there was a meat goulash on offer. It looked delicious.

Chapter 5

Kelly left the office at 9.30 p.m., her head buzzing with facts, but she couldn't go home yet. There was nothing she wanted more than to drive to Pooley Bridge, open her front door and settle on the sofa with a beer, but she had no choice.

The evening was black already, and she thought wistfully of the long summer nights ahead. In May the nights were still surprisingly chilly, even after a sunny day, and she shivered, hoping that the two lost girls were safe and warm somewhere together.

The drive was a short one. Her sister still lived in Penrith, as she had done all her life. She and Matt had bought a house close to Mum and Dad, and had raised their three children in the same tiny terrace they'd lived in since getting married. Kelly remembered the wedding, and recalled treading on eggshells even then, trying to melt away into the background lest she be accused of stealing Nikki's limelight on her big day. As if that had been a possibility, with her sister looking like some kind of chandelier cum pageant queen.

Kelly wondered idly why a woman would allow herself to look like that for a day, just to be presented to a man as a kind of gift from her father. Of course it was tradition, but being a cynic, she questioned even the most sacred traditions. She had her own favourite joke about weddings and she shared it with anyone who'd listen: 'Why do brides smile so much on their wedding day? Because they've given their last blow job.' Boom. Clever.

Nikki didn't think it was funny.

Nikki called her scared. She said that Kelly hadn't got married because she thought herself above it; too selfish to care for another person on the level it took. It was only an opinion, but it stung.

Move on.

She knocked on the door, and Matt answered. Ria, the youngest, clung to her father's leg. Matt smiled weakly. 'Hi, Kelly, come in.'

Despite Kelly's problems with her sister in the past, Matt never seemed to get involved. Sure, he benefited from the cash that flowed nicely from their mother's purse, but he never showed Kelly any animosity. He was an ordinary, simple guy. He was thinning on top and expanding in the middle, but he worked hard and he was a devoted dad.

The girls were closer in temperament to him than to Nikki, except perhaps Charlie, the eldest, and Kelly decided that this was a good thing. Ria came to her auntie, and Kelly scooped her up and gave her a kiss. The other two were watching TV and far too big for kisses. Charlie was now fifteen and often eyed Kelly suspiciously, as if Nikki had briefed her and she felt the tension between her aunt and her mother. It annoyed Kelly, but she wasn't playing that game; dragging a fifteen-year-old into their petty squabbles wasn't her style. Charlie could think what she liked.

'Hi, girls.'

They were glued to an American teen soap and Kelly received a couple of grunts in reply. The place smelled of neglect, and judging by the lines around Matt's eyes, he'd been trying his best to keep working as well as run a household. She put Ria down.

'Isn't it bedtime?' she asked Matt. He seemed caught out, and Kelly suspected that since Mummy had become ill, bedtime had perhaps slipped to something a little more fluid. He shrugged.

'I'll make you a cuppa, Kelly, or do you want something stronger? I've got wine.'

'A glass of wine would be nice. I've just finished work.'

'Shut the door,' he mouthed. She did so, and they were alone in the kitchen.

'Where is she?' Kelly asked.

'Where do you think?'

'In bed?'

Matt nodded.

'You know, it's completely normal, Matt. She may never get over this.'

He looked at his feet. The doctors had all told them as much. The trauma was too great: the fear, the pain, the sheer terror. Last summer, when the Lakes had found itself in the grip of the serial killer known as the Teacher, Nikki had become the fifth and final victim – and survived. Sometimes Kelly believed that her sister might have been better off not being found. They all might have been better off. It was a savage conclusion to draw, but sometimes rehabilitation after such an experience was more harrowing than the event itself. It was not just Nikki who was struggling; the whole family was imploding.

At first, Kelly could have been forgiven for daring to believe that the horrific events might put an end to their feud; after all, it was she who had found Nikki. But recently Nikki had hinted that it was all Kelly's fault in the first place: her job, her proximity to weirdos, even that Kelly should have found her sooner. The hints had turned into accusations, and Kelly had thought more than once that she should simply walk away, blood relative or not. Enough was enough.

Matt handed her a glass of wine and she took her first sip, savouring its succour. They'd drawn up a rota designed to make sure there was always someone here to look after the kids. Nikki knew enough people to help out, and at first they queued up at the door. But as time had passed, people became less willing, and suddenly busy. It would seem that Nikki's friendships were not quite as solid as she'd once assumed. And so it was left to Matt to juggle the delicate pieces of a household that was quickly tumbling down around him.

Charlie was skipping school, Donna was bed-wetting, and Ria had stopped talking. Kelly tried to pull strings at the hospital, via Ted Wallis, but not even the senior pathologist could conjure mental health staff where there were none. There was simply no money in it, and Nikki and her damaged family were not a priority for stretched resources.

'She's lucky to have you all around her; many don't have that,' they'd been told.

'Matt, you look knackered. How about paying someone to help? I know Mum would help with the money,' Kelly said, gulping another mouthful of wine.

He looked at her, and she could see the shame behind his eyes. Working-class people didn't pay for help; they offered it to one another. He looked down and drained his beer. Kelly wondered how much he was drinking. He looked rough. His cheeks were red, his nose swollen, and his belly pushed against his clothes. She sighed and went through the motions, as she did every time she came.

'How is she?'

'She's been muttering on about those missing girls. She wanders round in the middle of the night and wakes the kids up, asking them questions about the door locks, and who they've been talking to.'

Kelly supposed that was normal. Anything reminiscent of women in danger would trigger it. She drained her wine and opened the kitchen door. She walked back through the lounge, where the girls were still glued to the TV, and out into the hallway. Making her way up the stairs to Nikki's bedroom, she knocked very gently on the door. There was no answer, so she went in.

Nikki was sitting upright in bed, staring into space. It was as if she could see something through the wardrobe opposite her. Kelly didn't know if her sister was aware of her presence, and walked slowly to the bed.

'Nikki,' she said.

'What do you want?' Nikki asked. It wasn't accusatory, or aggressive, just a question.

'I came to see how you are.'

Nikki began to smile, and Kelly knew what was coming. 'I'm good, thanks,' she said.

When her sister's behaviour had first become worrying, Kelly had expected nothing less than fireworks. There was no way that Nikki Morden, seeker of attention, carrier of gossip and holder of a whole small country full of bitterness, could possibly not cause a scene. But she'd been wrong, and it had thrown them all. This quiet, contemplative Nikki caught them off guard, and they didn't know what to do with her. She no longer wore make-up, she had lost interest in celebrity reality shows, and she wasn't glued to Facebook any more; all she did was sit here in bed, locked away in whatever world she'd created for herself to cope. Every professional who'd been roped in had said the same thing: it was normal. The mind could only cope with so much until it shut down, and would only recover once it had processed enough to make room. It was a bit like coma.

'Nikki, the girls need you.' Kelly appealed to the mother in her.

'The girls!' Nikki's face changed to a look of panic.

'Yes, they're downstairs. They're safe. They need putting to bed, and they'd love it if it was you who put them there.'

'No! Hannah and Sophie! She has them!' Kelly's heart sank as she realised that Nikki was trapped inside her mania. They needed help. The family couldn't go on like this.

'No she hasn't, Nikki. The Teacher is in prison, remember? You're all safe.'

'Are you sure?' Nikki's eyes darted around.

Kelly nodded. 'Really sure.'

'So who's got them?' Nikki gasped. She stared at her sister and clutched her arms. Kelly hadn't realised how strong she was until she'd grabbed her the first time, months ago. She had bruises to prove it. She tried to wrest herself away from the vice-like grip.

'Nobody has got them, Nikki.' She lied easily. She had no idea if the girls were dead or alive, but she wasn't about to tell her sister that.

She looked around the room, searching for anything that was connected to the outside world, anything that might be feeding Nikki news stories that she didn't need right now. An iPad sat closed on the end of the bed. Kelly took it. Nikki didn't notice.

'They have! They're tied up!' Nikki grabbed Kelly by the arms again.

Kelly winced. She couldn't cope with this. It was one thing dealing with nutters behind bars, but someone close to you – your own flesh and blood – was a different challenge altogether, and she was no professional.

'Stop it!' she snapped.

Nikki stared at her, and her hands dropped to her sides.

'Fucking stop it! You have a husband, you have three gorgeous kids who desperately need you.' Kelly searched her sister's face for any sign of cognisance, any whisper of registering what had just been said. There was none. She had no choice; she had to ring the hospital. If she didn't get anywhere, she'd drive to A&E herself and not budge until mental health was involved. Fuck their budget. Everybody was overstretched.

The slap came before she could react, stinging the side of her jaw. Every instinct inside her body wanted to retaliate and teach the aggressor a lesson; she'd have done it to anyone else on the planet. Her fists balled and her nails dug into her palms. She locked her jaw. Nikki rocked back and forth.

What Kelly wanted to say was: *You won't get a chance to do that a second time. You're not crazy. You're fucking lazy. Get a grip.* But she didn't. Maybe one day she would, but one thing was for sure: if Nikki ever struck her again, she wouldn't hold back. Her heart pounded and she swallowed her adrenalin. Some people were just impossible to care for, she thought.

'Get out of bed, Nikki. You need a shower. Then we're going to put your kids to bed.' Her voice was deadpan.

Nikki did as she was told and stood up, allowing herself to be led to the en suite.

'You weren't there,' she whispered.

'Yes I was,' Kelly said through gritted teeth. 'The fear you felt is normal, the dreams you have are normal, the depression… it's all normal. But you have to do something about it.' She glared at her sister. 'If you ever hit me again, I'll knock your fucking head off.'

Nikki blinked and looked down.

'Get in the shower. I'm going to fetch the girls.' Kelly left.

Downstairs, Matt looked questioningly at the red mark developing on her jaw, but Kelly turned the other way.

'Right, guys, Mummy's up, and she's going to come and say goodnight to you, so off to bed now,' she said.

Charlie started to complain. 'Do as you're told,' Matt said firmly.

Kelly looked at him, surprised. Charlie threw her a look that could freeze molten rock, but she stood her ground. The TV was switched off, and the three girls made their way to the stairs. Kelly held Ria's hand.

-

By the time Kelly got home, it was gone midnight, but she couldn't sleep. Instead, she opened a bottle of wine and flicked on her iPad. She had a load of reading to do.

It was 4 a.m. before she fell asleep, fully clothed, still on the sofa.

Chapter 6

Rob Shawcross stood in a field, piss-wet through, directing scores of uniforms and close to three hundred volunteers. In winter, a search in the Lakes might be pursued for up to ten days, and walkers had been found without food and water, surviving just on melted snow, after that long; but in May, there was no acceptable reason why, if the two missing girls were still in the National Park, they hadn't been found. Pressure was mounting, and a few camera crews had turned up from Manchester and Glasgow. It was, as yet, still a northern story. They all hoped it stayed that way.

The rain slashed in sideways, and Rob struggled to keep his hood up, speak into his radio and keep civilians contained. Their excitement and eagerness was reaching fever point, understandably, but he couldn't let them loose on the hillside until he was happy with their grid reference, so he could tick off each square as they went.

—

Kelly waited in the prefabricated office for Garth Cooke. From the window, she could see Rob, and it reminded her of all the shit assignments in British weather that she'd notched up before she earned the privilege of staying inside with an electric heater. The manager of the campsite, Jack Sentry, had made her a mediocre coffee, and she perched on the edge of a table and eyed him up. He was the nervous type, and appeared defensive when she asked about the two girls. Perhaps he was edgy because they'd commandeered his site and were allowing hundreds of feet to ruin the grass.

'Maybe they went for a walk,' he was mumbling.

'Well, we'll hopefully find that out,' Kelly said. She got the distinct impression that Jack Sentry didn't like being beholden to a woman.

Even inside the cabin, the damp air smelled of the lake; it was the same smell that woke her each morning, when she'd rather stay in bed with Johnny than face the world. She'd got into the habit of not wanting to get out of bed, wanting to stay there next to him, listening to him talk. He too was an outsider, and it was perhaps no coincidence that they'd found each other. He understood how it felt to be on the fringes.

She took comfort from the fact that her team appreciated her; without them, her job would be a whole lot harder. As a result, she didn't feel as though she needed to go charging out into the middle of Rob's search and take over; she trusted him.

Outside, Rob shouted through a loud hailer, trying to control the mob. It was time to go, and Kelly watched as they trudged metre by metre towards the fells. Uniformed officers in high-visibility vests kept the crowds in team-like formations, and spoke into their radios.

The searchers ambled slowly forward in three directions: one group to the lake, the second to Martindale, and the third to Loadpot Hill. Kelly had ordered police dogs to be brought in and they'd gone crazy around the tent and then headed off towards the fells. It wasn't an exact science that was admissible in court, but the whole force would rather trust their dogs than any human testimony. The three canines involved in the search were each a unique mix of Labrador and pointer, with a smattering of hound, and they'd trained with the police since they were pups. Their handlers struggled to keep them back, and Kelly watched from the cabin as they pulled ferociously towards the Loadpot Hill trail.

She had instructed that the dogs be allowed to go ahead and the foot search bring up the rear; it wasn't feasible to contain both. The three handlers kept in contact with Rob and were over two hundred metres ahead when they disappeared out of sight. Kelly turned back to Jack Sentry.

'Did the girls pay up on time?'

'Ah, no, actually. It was a bone of contention. They were tardy even by holiday standards. It seems trivial, but it's not when they're using water and electricity paid for by everyone else.'

Kelly found his irritation disproportionate to the subject: a few days of showers and heat wasn't enough to get worked up about, was it?

'So they weren't up to date?'

'No. They owed the last day.'

'The last day? Had they told you their plans?'

'Erm, no. I assumed...' Sentry moved to the window. 'They must have found him by now; his tent is only in field two.' He was talking about Garth Cooke and the PC who'd been tasked to bring him to the office. Kelly waited.

'Did you find anything about the situation unusual?' she asked.

Sentry smiled. 'Well, Garth wasn't best pleased that his girlfriend preferred girls, let's put it that way.'

Kelly processed the nugget of information and looked outside once more. The weather had eased slightly and she hoped that the rain hadn't dampened the dogs' abilities.

–

Outside, Rob's group trudged slowly forward, as was their brief. He'd instructed all volunteers to look at the ground carefully, holding up a hand if they spotted anything that didn't belong on the mountainside. They were looking for anything at all: cigarette packets, litter of any kind, personal belongings or maps. As the weather cleared a little, he could see steam rising off the swarm of people around him. They carried plastic sticks: singularly inoffensive and beneficial when searching for evidence but not wanting to contaminate the area.

When they reached the stile that led directly to Loadpot, with the dogs long gone, Rob halted the group and instructed them to carefully clamber over the drystone wall to either side. He himself went first and waited until everybody had been helped over. Straight away, someone shouted and held up their hand. It was a young man who'd drawn attention to himself, and now he was embarrassed as all eyes turned to him. Rob walked across to him and they exchanged words. The young man pointed at a cigarette packet on the ground. Rob was already wearing two layers of plastic gloves, and he removed an evidence bag from his case, bent down and retrieved the item, dropping it into the bag and sealing it.

They carried on.

As they began to ascend, they slowed even further and came upon a wide clump of ferns. They'd been instructed to move the plants with their feet – mindful of adders –

and look under the wide leaves. The foliage was rough, and they were stuck there for a good half an hour. Another voice carried on the wind. Again Rob went to them and bagged an item. The third person to raise the alarm was less embarrassed, and by the time they reached the foot of Swarth Fell, seven more items had been bagged.

Everything would head off to the lab to be checked and swabbed. The Lakes National Park was relatively free of litter, but the search was proving fairly productive, and Rob was eager to begin properly logging and photographing the items. He'd carefully noted each location, and back at Eden House, he'd add them to the map.

Another voice punctuated the wind, and he went across with a bag. This time he bagged a discarded cider bottle, drained and thrown away; a brazen flouting of National Park authority.

After a good forty-five minutes, Rob was starting to feel the cold. He rubbed his hands together. He could see that the searchers were beginning to chat, as they were prone to do when their attention lapsed after a while. He decided that another twenty minutes and they'd be done. He had a wealth of booty, and it all needed to be sorted and labelled: that would tie up the rest of his day.

A crackle caught his attention on his radio and he halted the group. It was one of the canine handlers. Rob had chatted to all three of them before they'd set off, and he remembered the dark brown mutt called Trooper and her handler, an officer called Doug. Now he learned that Trooper had led her master off the beaten path towards the drop-off that led to the Fusedale Pike route. She'd gone insane over something and refused to budge.

'We've got a bag, sir.'

Rob knew that Doug wore gloves and could be trusted to have a cursory rummage inside.

'And?'

'There's an ID card belonging to Hannah Lawson, as well as a mobile phone. That's not all. It's difficult to tell without chemicals, but there's a dark brown substance on the outside in a definite linear pattern.'

Rob knew what Doug was thinking. It could be the remnants of Hannah's last meal at McDonald's, it could be make-up, it could be rust. Or it could be blood spatter.

'Sorry, mate, you're gonna have to stay up there.'

'I know, sir. I'm sealing the area now. I've called the other two over; they turned up nothing.'

'Give Trooper a pat from me.'

'Will do, sir.'

'I'm on my way.'

Rob radioed Kelly. Times like these were the best and worst moments of a case. Their first clue was in, and that was a fact to rejoice at. However, it was a sign that all was far from well with the girls, and the case had just elevated itself to something much more alarming.

Chapter 7

The news made it imperative for Kelly to speak to the person who seemed to know most about the two girls on the whole of the site: Garth Cooke.

'Did anyone go inside the girls' tent before the police arrived?' she asked Jack Sentry.

He didn't answer straight away.

'Well I can't guarantee that, can I?' he said at last. 'I mean, it's a tent.'

Kelly didn't appreciate his attempt at cleverness; it struck her more as derision, and it was tasteless. He didn't seem to be responding in the way one might expect when two lives were at stake. She hadn't informed him about the bag, and he hadn't perceived her change in mood.

A knock on the flimsy door caught her attention and Garth Cooke was escorted in by a uniform. He was scruffy, evasive and uncomfortable. But he'd stuck around.

Kelly saw a fleeting glance from Sentry to the young man, and noted that neither had expressed, as far as she was aware, much concern for the girls; only disparagement.

'Hello, Garth, please will you sit down. Mr Sentry, would you leave us alone?'

Sentry nodded, got his coat and left.

'You reported Hannah and Sophie missing?' she asked. Garth nodded.

'I've already told loads of coppers what I know,' he said. His eyes settled on anything around Kelly rather than her face and she didn't trust him, but they had a long way to go yet.

'What made you suspicious?'

He sighed loudly. Kelly jotted notes.

'I couldn't find them on Monday morning and I thought they'd gone off somewhere – you know, for a walk. But I couldn't find them on Tuesday either, and I asked around and nobody had seen them. I tried Sophie's phone but it went to voicemail. I thought I'd better tell someone then.'

'Were you here together on holiday?'

'Kind of.'

'What does that mean?' Kelly asked. She noted his attire; his jeans were hardly suited to a walking holiday in the Lakes. She watched as he looked around the room. His hands were firmly in his pockets and his shoulders hunched over. He wasn't relaxed.

'Dunno.' He shrugged.

'Did you come here together or not?'

'No. I wanted to speak to Sophie, but she got pissed off when I showed up. I only wanted to talk to her.' His eyes widened and Kelly felt a little sorry for him.

'So you did talk, then?'

'Huh?'

He wasn't concentrating, instead peering around the room, distracted. But she had noticed one thing. If she'd blinked, she'd have missed it, but it was there, as clear as day: a distaste when he mentioned his ex-girlfriend's name.

'You said you're Sophie's boyfriend?' she asked.

He winced. 'Not any more.'

43

Kelly nodded and wrote a note. 'When was the last time you saw her?' she asked.

'I've already been through all of this.' He was getting frustrated, and Kelly watched him carefully.

'You said in your statement that it was Sunday lunchtime,' she pressed on. Garth nodded.

'So what were the three of you doing that day?'

Garth was caught off guard. His mouth opened but nothing came out.

'What made you come here? Wasn't the relationship already over? Wasn't it a little… crowded?'

Anger flashed across his face. She'd hit a very raw nerve.

'Did they spend too much time together for your liking, Garth?'

Again she saw indignation and rage bubbling just beneath the surface.

'They were always together, joined at the fucking hip. Sophie followed Hannah round like a little puppy. It pissed me off.' The anger spilled out of him, the emotion palpable. He had just given Kelly evidence of a motive: jealousy.

'Were they lovers?' Kelly pretended nonchalance.

Garth's mouth fell open. Kelly looked him dead in the eye, but he glanced away, not used to the scrutiny. 'Garth?'

'They were fucking bean-flicking sluts,' he spat.

Kelly winced: it was a sentence that was so barbed, it almost jumped out into the space between them. She watched as the young man's demeanour changed and he grew more confident and cocksure, as if the whole world would sympathise with his predicament: the fact that his girlfriend had left him for another woman.

'That's harsh. So you were ashamed?'

He looked down at his hands and she could see his cheeks burning.

'Tell me, Garth.' She paused. 'Did you harm the girls?'

He shook his head vehemently.

'No.'

'Come on, you're hurt, degraded, ashamed – and it's all Hannah's fault. I bet you hate her.'

'They wandered off. Good riddance, I say. I'm done.' His chin jutted out, but then he realised his mistake. Kelly pounced on it.

'They wandered off? You mean you saw them?'

He put his head in his hands and rubbed his eyes, then slowly nodded.

'They were giggling and stuff, and they went off for a walk with a backpack and everything. I wanted to follow them, but you know what? I'm not doing that any more. She can do what she wants.'

'Where did they go?'

'Up towards Loadpot Hill. It was late. It was dark.'

She was transfixed by his cool; he'd just turned the investigation potentially on its head.

'Do you realise that you've probably wasted four days of police time?'

He bit his dirty nails, then took a packet of cigarettes out of his coat and lit one. Kelly didn't bother stopping him.

'What you've just told me makes you the last person to see them, do you understand? I'll need corroboration of your statement, else you're in some deep shit. You've just made yourself my prime suspect. Why the hell didn't you share this information before now?' She hadn't even stopped to challenge his story; she'd heard only ten minutes earlier about the bag, and its location fitted with what he'd just told her.

Garth tutted and rolled his eyes. Kelly got the impression that he had no idea of the seriousness of what he'd admitted. He was too immersed in his shame at being dumped.

'What have you been doing since Tuesday?'

'I've been in my tent.'

'Did you go in Sophie's tent?'

'No, but I know who did.'

'And who might that be?' she asked.

He thumbed over his shoulder to the door. 'That fucking pervert out there.'

'Mr Sentry?'

Garth nodded.

Kelly got up and walked to the window. She could see the crowds of people getting back into their cars after coming down from the search. She also saw Rob, who was speaking animatedly with a dog handler; no doubt the one who had found the bag. She turned to Garth, who puffed hard on his cigarette; he'd almost finished it, such was his need for the calming effects of the drug.

'Garth, have you heard of a girl called Freya Hamilton?' It was a long shot. Garth looked at her and shook his head.

'No, I haven't. Why?'

'No reason.'

He sniggered and rolled his eyes. They both knew that police officers never asked irrelevant questions.

In Kelly's experience, the young man before her was telling the truth, despite how distasteful he might appear. There were certain facial signals that couldn't be controlled by will alone; they went back to when apes communicated with signs and minuscule movements of tiny facial muscles; they were still there if you knew where to look. Kelly had seen plenty of people try to override their instincts and fail miserably. Garth was transparent, and it showed. He didn't have the intelligence to be anything else. Sure, he had motive, but she was more interested in what he'd just told her.

'Let's go back to when you watched them leave their tent,' she said.

'Yep.' He licked his fingers, pinched out his cigarette and placed the stub in his pocket. Kelly was reminded of Johnny telling her that that was what they did on patrol so the enemy couldn't track them. Garth looked anything but the savvy soldier.

'Did you follow them?' she asked. Silence. 'Garth, did you follow them?'

He began to nod. 'Yes, I did.'

'Your story has changed three times: first you say you last saw them at lunch time, then you say you saw them leave for Loadpot Hill, now you're telling me that you followed them. You see my problem here?' She stared at him and he blinked. He gave the impression that he was unaware of his predicament, and Kelly seethed with frustration.

'Where did they go?' she asked.

'They headed up Loadpot, like I said. I can't remember much because I was… I was drunk. I'd drunk a whole bottle of cider.'

'OK, let's get back to where they went. How far did you follow them? Did they see you?'

He shook his head. 'No, they didn't see me.'

'How do you know?'

'It was obvious, they only had eyes for each other.'

'I see.' Kelly did a quick replay in her head of possible scenarios. Garth would have had a difficult time overpowering both girls, if he was telling the truth and he'd been drunk. She looked at his hands: no injuries. She'd read that Hannah Lawson was a black belt in judo; she'd take some pacifying.

'Can you take your coat off, please?'

'Why?'

Kelly sighed. 'Just do it.'

He stood up and removed his stained jacket; it would need bagging. 'I have to eliminate you from my inquiry. Is there any reason why you might have Sophie or Hannah's DNA on you? Let's say, in any of those brown-looking stains?'

Garth looked down. 'No! That's cider. And gravy. I had chips!'

'All right, calm down.' Thankfully he was wearing a short-sleeved T-shirt and Kelly noted that he had no marks on his forearms. Anyone who had restrained two grown women would have a few telltale marks on them. Garth had none.

'Do you own a car?' she asked. He shook his head.

'How did you get here?'

'Train and bus.'

As Kelly dismissed him, she'd already made up her mind that Garth Cooke wasn't someone they needed to be spending time on. Their answer was elsewhere.

She watched him go back to his field, hood up, shoulders hunched over, protecting himself against the rain with his hands deep in his pockets.

Rob came into the cabin.

'Tell me about the bag,' she said.

'We did a fingertip search of a seven-square metre area; there was nothing else. The bag is in the back of my car ready for the lab, and we should have some results in a few days. Will is going to take charge of the two phones.'

'Good job, Rob. The ex-boyfriend just told me that he saw them leave towards Loadpot on Sunday night. He was pissed and emotional. He also told me that the site manager went into the girls' tent.'

'Christ.'

'I know. Let's get him back in.'

'Is there something wrong with your face, guv?'

She touched the swollen area where her sister had hit her and kicked herself for not applying more make-up. 'No, I don't think so. Do you want to call Sentry in?'

By the time Rob came back with the site manager, Kelly had had just enough time to grab a concealer out of her bag and touch up her foundation in a cracked mirror that hung on the wall.

'Mr Sentry, we won't keep you much longer. A witness statement has come to my attention. It mentions a sighting of you going into the girls' tent after their disappearance.'

Sentry looked between Kelly and Rob.

'He must be mistaken. That kid's always drunk or high.'

'What kid? I never mentioned a name. Did you or did you not enter the girls' tent?'

'No.' He stood firm and his gaze never wavered. Kelly could smell his deceit, but her concern wasn't the lie, it was the reason behind it.

'So to be absolutely clear: you never entered the tent of Sophie Daker and Hannah Lawson?'

'No.' There was no hesitation.

Kelly didn't care. She knew that, as surely as the sun rose and set every day, if they found any link between

Jack Sentry and the girls' tent, then he was fucked in the eyes of the law. It was all she could get for now.

Chapter 8

Johnny parked his Jeep Grand Cherokee and went to the boot to grab a waterproof and some water; they might be out for a good few hours. He was to meet Kelly at the hospital helipad in Penrith; as he made his way around the building, the yellow chopper stood ready with its blades turning. An air search with the Cumbria Constabulary was a rarity, and it was a privilege to be asked along. He hoped it hadn't been a decision that Kelly had deliberated on for long. He was accomplished as a mountaineer, he was an excellent map-reader, his instincts were sound, and there was a fringe benefit that he knew she couldn't deny: it was an opportunity to see him.

Kelly was ready and waiting in the helicopter. Her face was straight, serious and a little irritated. Johnny was fifteen minutes late, and he knew tardiness was one of her pet hates. She was dressed in casual gear, appropriate for their outing, but it didn't hide her body language: language that he hadn't seen for a long time. It was her game face, and he was unused to it. Perhaps something had happened at work. He decided to cut her some slack; after all, when he'd returned from a long deployment in some godforsaken country of sand and parasites, he'd been a miserable bastard to be around. Maybe he could cheer her up.

They shook hands because professionally that was their only choice. There were rumours about the two of them, of course, but in front of colleagues they behaved appropriately. If he could steal a moment and touch her hand, he would, but for now he sat in his place and nodded to the others in their company. He had heard the news: the case had been elevated to more than a missing persons and the spokesperson allocated by HQ was now using language that Johnny knew meant they believed the girls had met with foul play. They'd managed to talk over the phone briefly, and Kelly had filled in the details.

He saw an opportunity and brushed her hand, and her eyes met his. She tensed, as he knew she would, and he smiled at her. She couldn't say anything, or allude to the affection in any way, but the passion in her eyes was all he was after. He wanted her to know that he was there for her regardless of what it was that was irking her.

That was why she was different and it was why he had taken to staying over at hers so often. She didn't suffocate him and she was as passionate about her job as he was about his. He just wished he'd met her ten years ago.

'Ready?' she shouted over the noise of the chopper. He was still smiling.

The pilot nodded to Johnny; they knew each other. Many police pilots were also mountain rescue volunteers. The fourth member of their team was a photographer who'd been requested by Kelly, and she introduced her to Johnny.

Once the doors were closed, the noise lessened and the wind was shut out, making the space feel claustrophobic and expectant. Kelly looked out of the window and put on her headset so she could hear the pilot. Johnny did the same. They fastened seat belts and listened as the pilot radioed the control room. Satisfied with flight checks and weather reports, he now addressed them directly.

'Right, folks, we're about one minute from take-off; please make sure you're fastened in and the refreshment trolley will be round shortly.'

Johnny smirked; these guys all cracked the same terrible jokes. Even Kelly smiled. She hated flying, especially in helicopters, and the pilot clearly knew it.

Kelly's stomach churned and she willed herself to concentrate on the job. She'd flown in choppers three times in her life before: once from Scotland Yard to Luton Airport in pursuit of an armed drug dealer; once across to the Isles of Scilly; and the third time in a mountain rescue chopper, at night, flown by the same pilot who was flying them today. She'd hated every flight. There was something about the way a helicopter lunged and dived that made her stomach produce uncontrolled waves of nausea, and she hoped that today's ride would be smoother. There was no rush; they were just charting territory and noting anything that looked out of place. It was another dimension to the search for the girls. Rob and the team were working with every single statement, trying to produce leads, but as the hours ticked by, optimism was waning.

One of their last hopes was that Sophie and Hannah could have pitched another tent deep in the National Park, looking for privacy. The Lakes were full of hidden coves and crags, and without access to media or phones, the girls could be blissfully unaware that they'd caused a fuss. It was still possible that one of them had simply misplaced their backpack. Unlikely, but possible.

'Any news?' Johnny asked.

'Apparently Sophie Daker's father threatened to kick her out if she carried on her relationship with Hannah.'

Kate Umshaw had been given the unenviable task of interviewing Sophie's parents, and Geoff Daker had emerged as a bully who saw Hannah Lawson as a troublemaker. It hadn't taken Kate long to work out that the parents had realised that their daughter was in a lesbian relationship and it wasn't welcome.

Johnny raised his brows. 'Jesus, wasn't he bothered that she's missing?'

'I think the fact that she's in a same-sex relationship is more upsetting to him.'

'What an idiot.' Kelly knew that as a father himself, Johnny couldn't comprehend such an attitude. To him it only meant one thing: that Sophie's father obviously didn't love his daughter. 'Why would he do that?'

'Not everyone is OK with same-sex partners, I suppose.'

'But she's his kid.'

'I know. Apparently he's the total opposite of Hannah's father.'

Kate had met both sets of parents and reported back that Hannah's parents were gentle and slightly bohemian, and, more importantly, sick with worry. They were staying at the Crown in Pooley Bridge and Kelly was hoping not to bump into them.

'Do Hannah's family know that the girls are lovers?'

'Apparently yes, and they treated Sophie like their own. They also said that Hannah would never run away willingly; she had too much going on in her life and had a completely open relationship with her parents.'

'That's what they say. You never know.'

Kelly nodded in agreement. It was at times like this that she was thankful she didn't have kids of her own; she imagined it was times like this that made Johnny wish he spent more time with Josie, his daughter.

The blades spun faster and louder, and the chopper fought between tarmac and sky. Gradually it lifted, and Kelly's belly inverted. They were up. They hovered for a few seconds, and then lurched sharply to the left and gained height at a rapid rate. Kelly's hand involuntarily grabbed the seat, and she held onto her notepad and pen with a vice-like grip.

She could tell that Johnny wanted to hold her hand but knew he couldn't. He was staring at her, but she avoided his gaze, though her cheeks were pink. She'd told him about Nikki's blow and knew he could see evidence of it under her make-up. Her patience was wearing thin. There was no point in talking to her mother about it; she was like a referee at a heavyweight showdown, too scared to call the shots and eager to let the punters decide. It was hard to believe that Kelly and Nikki had the same parentage.

'Look at the lake, Kelly.' Johnny pointed out to the front of the chopper as they flew west. She followed his hand and it distracted her. She'd never seen Ullswater from the air during the day, and she'd never seen it not pulsing with activity. It was deserted. The jetties had been closed and were manned by uniforms. Kelly had ordered a dive team in, and the mammoth task would take a few days. The tourist board was pissed off, but at least it wasn't peak season. She didn't much care for their objections; the lake needed to be searched, and sooner rather than later. Local boat owners and divers had already generously offered their help.

As they reached their flying altitude, Kelly tried to settle and focus on the job. The fells were still busy and she could make out the dots of fluorescent jackets crawling over them. She had to raise her voice to brief the photographer on what she wanted. They were aiming to produce a grid that they could overlay onto a map back at Eden House. Between herself and Johnny they might have done it from memory, but the third dimension, from the air, was an opportunity for a new perspective.

Kelly's brief was simple. Most of the buildings down there they'd recognise from their time on the fells – and this was why she'd brought Johnny along – but some they wouldn't, and these were the ones she was interested in. If neither she nor Johnny recognised a dwelling, then it would be photographed, mapped and checked out as a point of interest. Sophie and Hannah could have taken shelter somewhere and might be injured.

They were also looking for telltale distress signals, like items forming symbols, as well as evidence of a tent in a secluded spot.

'There's my house.' Johnny pointed it out. Pooley Bridge looked asleep, like the lake. They talked about various ramshackle structures they'd used for shelter over the years, and found that they'd both retreated to many of the same ones. Occasionally Kelly indicated a point of interest to the photographer and instructed her to take several images as the pilot circled, then she logged it on her map and Johnny noted coordinates. They flew over Wasdale Hall, which looked splendid from the air. Kelly had always wondered what it was like inside; the family was terribly private, but rumours abounded about the goings-on there, and only recently, the earl had committed suicide. The death appeared as sad as the family legacy.

She instructed the pilot to fly low over Gowbarrow and only now appreciated the vastness of the fell. It was easy to forget the immensity of the National Park, and they couldn't cover all of it. The area around Ullswater probably made up a tenth of it, but that was where Kelly was focusing her search today. Time in a chopper was money, and they didn't have much. They headed south over Place Fell, concentrating on the area around Loadpot Hill, and followed the ridge all the way back to Pooley Bridge.

So far they'd catalogued twenty-seven dwellings, some large and some that looked like wrecks. Only the ones they agreed they knew nothing about made the list. If Hannah and Sophie had decided to run away, they might be hanging out in a disused barn or something similar. It would take masses of man hours to log the coordinates, and then perhaps weeks to check them all out.

'Where would *you* go, Johnny?' Kelly asked. The photographer looked at him, and Johnny looked out of the window in thought.

'Further west,' he said. 'It's quieter and more impenetrable.' He was right; the western fells were still relative wildernesses. Both girls were confident hikers and campers, and they could be anywhere. But Kelly had to establish the likelihood of the scenario before they called off the current search, and so far she was undecided. Had they left of their own accord, or was there foul play? They flew south-west, leaving Ullswater, towards Helvellyn, circling over St Sunday Crag and back over Great Dodd.

Their time was up. They'd seen nothing out of the ordinary, but they'd collated vast amounts of information that might prove useful later. Once Kelly cross-referenced the information with a two-dimensional map, it would be clearer in her head what the possibilities were for the girls.

–

As they approached the helipad in Penrith, a call came through to Kelly's personal mobile.

'Kelly Porter,' she said. Johnny looked at her and knew that he might not see her again tonight; she was throwing herself into work just like he would if it were him. He could wait. He was going nowhere, and she was worth it.

Once they were back on the ground, Kelly unstrapped herself, still with her phone under her chin, and went to open the door, ignoring the pilot. Johnny stared at her and the photographer looked away. Kelly jumped from the chopper and bent over to avoid the spinning blades.

'She did this last time,' said the pilot.

'I'm not surprised,' said Johnny, getting out after her.

By the time he reached Kelly's car, she already had the engine running and was ready to leave.

'I can drop you home if you like, I've got to check on Mum, and then something's come up at work.'

He smiled and nodded. 'I'll cook something and leave it for you.'

'You really don't need to.'

'I know.' He fastened his seat belt. 'What's up?' he asked.

'That was the coroner's office. He's not happy to put suicide on the Earl of Lowesdale's autopsy report, and there's been a burglary at Wasdale Hall. The late earl's safe is missing.'

Johnny whistled. He was used to her sharing her cases with him; the information never went any further, and he often saw a different angle to Kelly, who found herself fully immersed and unable at times to step back.

'Gold-diggers, no doubt. He was worth a bit, wasn't he?'

'I have no idea.'

Chapter 9

Linda Cairns scrubbed the carpet for the third time.

It would have to be replaced. Not because of the stain – she would get that out – but because of Zachary. He hadn't come into the study since finding his grandfather. No matter how much scrubbing Linda did, Zachary would forever see his grandfather's faeces dripping onto the Axminster below.

She'd come as soon as he'd called – it was only five minutes from her cottage in Watermillock – but the ambulance had taken forty-five minutes as a lorry had broken down on the A592 and blocked its path. By the time she eventually found Brian in the garden and asked him to help cut the earl down, he'd been hanging for a good hour. His body had hit the floor with a thump, and Linda had instantly regretted asking Brian to do it. His head had banged on a chair and Zachary had reached out to comfort him, only to recoil again.

She'd finally managed to get the boy out of the room, and Brian had sat with him in the kitchen. Linda herself had waited with Xavier. She couldn't leave him. Too many had left him already. The stench was toxic, but her nose became quickly accustomed. She sat slightly to his left so she didn't have to look at him. She'd seen his tongue, and the bulge in his pants. He'd been still when she got there with Brian, but Zachary had, between his sobs, told her about the convulsions and how he'd tried to hold his grandfather's legs.

Linda had finally left the earl when the police arrived. She had to. The room had to be treated like a crime scene, they said.

'Crime?' she asked.

'Routine, Linda,' said the policeman. Linda had known Paul Gaskill since he was a lad in short trousers, getting caught stealing boats from Glenridding to go fishing on the lake. She still saw his mother. Paul gently explained that an inquest would be held to determine cause of death.

'Well it's obviously suicide. Are they idiots?' Linda said.

Paul was patient with her.

'It doesn't work like that, Linda,' he said gently.

The medic left the room after confirming life extinct, and made his way to the kitchen to inform the family. It was ludicrous, but procedure. Zachary walked out of the house, followed by the dogs.

'Cup of tea?' Linda had asked Paul weakly.

'Yes, thank you. A forensic team will have to work their way through the house, Linda, and take away anything they need. It might be prudent to get Zac to move in with you for a while.'

'He'll never do that,' Brian said.

'He's right,' Linda agreed.

Paul's radio had fizzled into life and he spoke into it.

'Affirmative. Subject has been confirmed life extinct, Sarge. I'm not going anywhere, I'm with the family now.' The radio went dead again.

'The undertaker is on his way. I've got to seal off the room and a forensics team will come first thing in the morning. I know it's hard, but we need to preserve the room as it is, so I'm afraid no one can go in there for now.'

'But why? It's crazy. He killed himself.'

'It's procedure. Any unnatural death goes to the coroner's office. I'm sorry.'

Linda had bent her head and squeezed her eyes between her forefinger and thumb. She had a headache.

Now, as she scrubbed, the vision of Xavier's body kept coming back to her. She hadn't heard any gossip in Watermillock, or further afield, and was confident that Paul Gaskill had kept his mouth shut. That must have killed him, she thought.

Zachary hadn't come back until one o'clock in the morning, and neither she nor Brian had asked where he'd been. By then, Xavier's body had been removed from the house in a tough black bag. The undertaker and his assistant had worked silently and Linda had watched tight-lipped as the earl departed his house for the last time.

The weekend had gone by in a blur of police cars and people wearing plastic suits and overshoes. Linda watched helplessly as they removed boxes full of items, including the rope and the stool. They could have been precious or personal, she didn't know, and she had no right to ask. She was an employee, and that was all. It was Monday morning before the last uniform left Wasdale Hall and she was allowed in again. Her first job had been to tackle the stain on the carpet, but three days later, she was still working on the damn thing.

She'd opened all the windows, but the smell still lingered. The carpet was an arrangement of black and beige checks, and she'd worked furiously on the huge stain. At first she merely created a gloopy mess of stinking soap suds, but on the third attempt it was becoming easier. She'd changed the water twice again today.

She stood up to assess her work and decided to leave it for now and have another go this afternoon. Deep down, she knew that her effort was merely nominal. A photograph caught her attention. Before last week, it had been a long time since she'd been in this room. She usually left the earl's tea outside the door.

The photograph was the only thing left on the desk. It was framed in silver, and upon closer inspection must have been left by the police because it was dusty. They wouldn't need an old photo. She cleaned it and put it back. The woman in the photo was beautiful, that was undeniable. Xavier could go to her now, after all this time.

As she gathered up her cleaning equipment, Linda shook her head.

She hoped that he was finally at peace.

Chapter 10

'The brain pathology shows two separate events, ten minutes apart. Unconsciousness from strangulation can occur within minutes, but death takes much longer.' Ted spoke into his phone. Kelly sat alone in her office, having dismissed the day shift. She was in no mood to go home just yet and would have to visit Wasdale Hall anyway. DC Emma Hide was due in to work the late shift and Kelly had plenty for her to do.

She closed her computer and waited for Ted to continue.

'The first incident lasted approximately one minute and produced unconsciousness; the hypoxy… sorry, oxygen starvation in the brain wasn't sufficient to kill, but it knocked him out, so he would have been unable to induce the second episode, which was fatal.'

'So someone staged it to look like suicide?'

'Yes.'

'How sure are you?'

'It's absolute. The first thing that niggled me was that Xavier suffered from arthritis in his hands; he simply couldn't have done it.'

'If he was strangled to unconsciousness beforehand, are there any physical signs? I'm thinking long-term, Ted, you know, like court appearance.'

'No, I'm afraid it doesn't work like that. Strangulation or choking to make someone pass out requires less violence than you might think, and rarely leaves obvious marks, especially when the neck is a mess anyway. It also might not have been done with a tourniquet-type item; it could have been simple suffocation with a pillow.'

'So, he'd be unconscious but still breathing?'

'Yes, he would also have been weighty and cumbersome. I would wager that it would have created a fair amount of noise getting him into position.'

Kelly had scanned the report quickly and noted that the grandson had been the only one in the house at the time, while the gardener was outside. None of them had reported anything unusual – aside from the earl's death – until the grandson found that the earl's safe was missing.

'Could he have tried to hang himself twice?'

Ted exhaled. 'If he was forty and fit, determined and organised, yes, I suppose so, but the actual hanging was extremely effective, so why get it so wrong the first time round? In any case, the brain pathology shows that he didn't regain consciousness in between the episodes. Manual self-strangulation isn't humanly possible because you'd pass out and regain consciousness before you died. There were none of the claw marks common in ligature strangulation cases, so my money is on suffocation followed by hanging when the victim was still unconscious. The rope mark is above his Adam's apple, whereas in ligature strangulation it's usually below it. The hyoid bone was also broken.'

'Homicide.'

'I'm afraid so, Kelly.'

'Poor old bastard.'

'Indeed. I knew him a long time ago; he was a good chap. There are plenty of rumours about the family that you might want to check out, although, I'm sure most of them are hogwash.'

Kelly loved Ted's old-school jargon and she realised that she missed him. It had been a while since they'd enjoyed a pint.

'Thanks, Ted. Take care. I'll call if I need any clarification. Are you down this way any time soon?'

'I was just thinking the same thing.'

'Give me a bell when you're coming.'

'I will.' They hung up.

Emma Hide was busy inputting data and knew to contact her boss should anything develop, and Kelly still needed to visit her mother. She had her laptop with her, and any automated updates would pop up instantly. She was hungry and realised that she hadn't eaten all day. She couldn't just turn up at her mum's and expect food after not seeing her for almost a week, so she planned to grab a pasty or something quick at the small Co-op round the corner.

Penrith wasn't busy and she left the one-way system behind, driving past the red-stone castle and heading to the suburbs. The tourist season hadn't really started, but a steady stream of walkers milled around, blocking pavements and generally getting in the way. Kelly was glad that she was driving in this direction, and she was glad that she'd chosen to live in Pooley Bridge.

She parked her car and entered the Co-op, heading for the convenience aisle. She noticed a woman in the same aisle who seemed stressed and in a hurry. The woman moved closer, searching for something in particular, and

Kelly stepped out of her way. That was when she realised that she looked familiar.

'Michelle?' She wasn't a hundred per cent sure, but it looked like Michelle Hammond, who'd she'd gone to school with.

The woman stopped. She blushed a little, and brushed her hair off her face.

'Kelly?'

'I thought it was you. Are you living in Penrith?' It was a banal question, but Kelly didn't know what else to say. It happened a lot. Whenever she found herself in this kind of situation, face to face with an old pal from decades ago, it threw her. Michelle looked worn out, as if life hadn't been as kind to her as it had been to Kelly.

'Er... yes. You look well, Kelly. Have you been on holiday? I heard you'd moved away.'

'I worked in London for a bit. I've been back for almost two years now, though. You look... er... well too,' Kelly lied. 'Are you still with Tony?'

Michelle laughed. 'No! God! He pissed off when the first one arrived, bastard.'

'Oh, I'm sorry.' Kelly felt awkward. She wanted to reach around Michelle to get to the sausage rolls, but the two of them were stuck there, in some time warp that didn't fit.

'What are you sorry for? He's a twat. I think he's shacked up with someone down in Manchester,' Michelle said.

Kelly didn't know what to say next. Since she'd been back, she'd had a smattering of conversations just like this one where she simply had nothing in common with somebody she'd gone to school with.

'How's Dan?' she asked. Dan, Michelle's brother, was actually one liaison that Kelly wanted to forget, but she felt the need to make conversation and lighten the atmosphere. She'd had a drunken one-night stand with him after their sixth-form prom night. They'd staggered outside behind the soccer club, and he'd propped her up against a table. It had been rushed, fumbled and unpleasant. She'd fancied him since third year. The fumble never led to anything, and she'd realised that her affections had been misplaced. Still, it would be interesting to know how he'd done since then.

Michelle's mouth twitched at the corner and Kelly got the impression that she'd said something wrong.

'You never heard?' Michelle said.

'No, what?' Kelly asked.

'He's dead, Kelly. He was run over leaving the Rush Club one night after a skinful. He wandered into the road, and… Well, it was about five years ago now.' Michelle looked at her feet.

'Christ, Michelle, I'm sorry. I didn't know.'

'Well, I suppose you were busy in the big smoke, thinking you were better than the rest of us.' The swipe came from nowhere and Kelly was caught off guard.

'What?'

'Oh fuck off, Kelly. Everyone knows you left because you thought yourself a cut above.' The anger was palpable, Kelly could touch it, but she didn't understand it.

Michelle had already turned away. Kelly felt smacked across the face. This was the girl she'd giggled her way through maths with; they'd spent Saturdays buying sweets and make-up from Woolworths; writing lists of boys they fancied, scoring them out of ten; sharing secrets. She stood in the middle of the aisle, other shoppers walking around her, wondering what she'd done to offend someone she hadn't seen for possibly twenty years.

And Dan was dead.

She felt like an impostor. In London, she'd been free; free from parochial nonsense about who fitted in and who didn't. Here, time had passed but some people had stood still. Kelly felt assaulted by her old friend's bitterness, and it hurt. Perhaps that'd been the real reason she'd left: because she'd never fitted in in the first place. From the age of thirteen she'd talked about wanting to go to London, and now she remembered Michelle pretending to be posh and intimating even then that Kelly would somehow betray her tribe if she left. And she had. She'd forgotten all of them and now expected to waltz back and make a success of it.

Maybe she couldn't just return to her old life after all. Nikki had said the same. She'd fooled herself into thinking that after two years she was beginning to belong. But now she felt the outsider again, like a nomad with no roots and no homeland. She became aware of her surroundings and she saw that people were staring at her.

Her feet began to move forward and she hastily grabbed a pie that she didn't want and took it to the checkout. She couldn't see Michelle. Her mood was oddly depressed, and she felt naked and exposed. Suddenly she wanted to cry, but she pushed the thought away as foolish. She swallowed hard. What had started out as a busy and perhaps exciting day had lost its lustre. She felt mortal, and she realised that she didn't feel that way very often. Her life wasn't usually punctuated by negativity and criticism, and she realised that this was another reason she'd left. She hadn't been able to quantify it, or even vocalise it; she just knew she wanted to go. Nikki called it selfish, and Michelle called it getting above her station. If she hadn't just heard it for herself, she'd laugh. She wondered if more people spoke about her like that. She badly wished Johnny was there.

She didn't hear the checkout operator ask for money; she just blindly entered her card number on the machine and walked out.

Hannah Lawson and Sophie Daker entered her head again: they were friends, buddies – *besties* they called them now. Kelly realised that apart from Michelle, she'd never had a bestie or a buddy. Her best friend – her only friend – was work, and that had been her choice. Even Johnny was a loner: an anomaly, a drifter on the fringe, hiding from something; that was why they got on.

She bumped into someone on her way out and dropped her bag. Without looking up, she muttered her apologies, scooped the bag up and rushed blindly back to her car.

Chapter 11

'But she said you were hard on her, Kelly. It's only been a matter of months.'

Wendy Porter delivered her weekly lecture on the fractious nature of her daughters' relationship. To Nikki, Wendy appeared to take Kelly's side, and to Kelly, she appeared to take Nikki's. Kelly sat on the arm of a chair in the lounge, a position she regularly assumed if she was uncomfortable or about to leave.

'Mum, I get it, I really do. But it hasn't been a few months, it's been almost a year, and anyway, that doesn't mean anything to her kids, who are really struggling. She needs to…' Kelly hesitated.

'What, Kelly? Just take it on the chin and move on? She's not like you. She needs help.'

'I know! But she won't accept it; she'd rather complain about not getting it than go looking for it,' Kelly said. She was frustrated and tired. She knew she was being hard on her sister, but twenty-odd years of bickering wasn't going to go away overnight just because Nikki had been through a tough time.

'I'm trying to be honest with you, Mum. I really am doing my best with her, but it doesn't come easily. Just because—'

'Just because she was nearly killed by a lunatic! Listen to yourself!'

Kelly got up and paced up and down. She hadn't come here for this. Nowadays their conflict seemed to escalate before she even got through the door, and it was always about Nikki: was she getting the help she needed? Had Kelly called a specialist? Had Kelly called her friends? Had Kelly checked on the children? Christ, it was as if Nikki had got herself kidnapped on purpose so she could milk it.

Kelly breathed.

She still had to drop by Wasdale Hall. She looked at her watch: it was 9.45 and she decided it could wait until morning. Forensics had searched the place and statements had been taken from the family. The earl was stone cold in the morgue. He had been dead a week. She was behind the power curve already.

'Are you itching to go, Kelly?' Her mother knew her well.

'No, Mum, I'm sorry. I'm tired.'

'You're always tired. I'm going to trial a new drug,' Wendy announced suddenly.

'Really?' This was something to be buoyant about, and Kelly's interest was genuine. She sat on the sofa next to her mother. 'That's great news, Mum.'

'Well, it's early days, but they say I could get a few more years yet out of the old carcass,' Wendy said. Kelly shook her head. The candour was positive but, like most children, she wasn't quite ready to admit that her mother wouldn't be around forever.

'I told you, Mum, you're bombproof. Does it have any horrible side effects?'

Heart cancer was effectively a death sentence, or so they had thought, but Wendy's last tests had shown less indication of spread, and even some signs of retreat in several sections of tissue. The doctors talked, talked and talked some more, and Kelly tried to keep up, for the sake of her mother, who asked incessant questions later. But she always missed something, or forgot to clarify a certain point. She found herself phoning the oncologist at the Penrith and Lakes Hospital on a regular basis to run through things with him. They were on first-name terms. He didn't mind, he said, and they'd known each other already anyway, through a previous case. Now, he was almost part of the family. Kelly made a mental note to grill him about the new drug. Her mother wasn't a guinea pig.

'Mum, you shouldn't be worrying about me and Nikki when you're battling this.'

'You can tell you haven't got children of your own, Kelly Porter; until you do, you'll never understand why we mothers worry. I'll never stop. One day you'll both realise that it's not worth hating each other.'

'That's not fair, Mum. I've always tried with her, but she's just so critical, so... toxic about everything.' She was back on the sofa arm, Michelle Hammond's words stinging in her head.

Thinking you were better than the rest of us...

'I don't know what I did wrong,' Wendy said.

'Mum, you did nothing wrong. We're different, that's all,' Kelly lied. The fact was that their mother sided with Nikki as a default setting, or at least that was how Kelly saw it. Sometimes she failed to comprehend how she was related to any of her family members. Her drive, her attitude, her ambition: she had no idea where it all came from.

'It's as if we're not even sisters,' she said. She was thinking out loud, and her directness took Wendy by surprise.

'I don't know what you mean!'

Kelly knew she'd gone too far. Why couldn't she just keep her opinions to herself? A clock ticked in the background, and she looked at her mother. Wendy seemed miles away. Kelly followed her gaze, and it landed on an old photo in a frame that had stood there for perhaps thirty years. It was of Kelly and Nikki. They wore brightly striped tank tops over blouses with huge collars that swooped down over the wool. They both had missing teeth. Their haircuts were worthy of the Bay City Rollers. They didn't look alike even then.

'Mum?' Kelly said.

'I'm so tired suddenly,' Wendy said. She stood up, but faltered a little, and Kelly went to her.

'I'll get you into bed. Have you had your tablets today?'

Wendy nodded towards the kitchen. 'Check my drawer.'

Kelly left the room and found the tray that was set out each day with her mother's pills; it was empty.

'Looks like you have,' she shouted from the kitchen. She went back into the lounge. 'Can I get you anything to take upstairs, Mum? Have you eaten?'

'I'll have that nice sausage roll in the fridge, and a cup of tea, please.' Kelly was alarmed; her mother was distant, withdrawn almost. Perhaps she'd be able to get hold of the oncologist tonight.

She made a cup of tea and placed the sausage roll on a plate. By the time she'd tidied up and checked the fridge for milk, Wendy had fallen asleep. Kelly stood looking at her for a long time, and finally went back to the kitchen to make a note of the name of the new drug. A second check confirmed that her mother was still asleep and so she shook her gently awake and helped her upstairs, taking the snack up to her and leaving it on a side table. She did a final check of lights and windows, then left, locking the door behind her.

As she headed to Pooley Bridge, she phoned the hospital on speaker. The oncologist wasn't due in until tomorrow, but his secretary said she'd get him to call first thing. Next, she phoned Johnny.

'Sorry it's late,' she said.

He yawned. 'I was asleep.'

'Sorry.'

'What's with all the sorrys? Where are you anyway, still at work?'

'No, I'm on my way home after seeing Mum. She had a bit of a funny turn, but I got her into bed.'

'You want to come here?' She closed her eyes in relief; that was exactly what she needed.

'Yes please,' she said.

'I'll open the door.'

Chapter 12

Zachary chose a damsel nymph he'd made himself to attach to his lead line. The forests behind Wasdale that led up Little Mell Fell were full of deer that had roamed there since ancient times, and their hair was an excellent buoyancy aid for his flies. There was also a constant supply of pheasant tails around the lanes, if one knew where to look, and these added colour to his booby traps. The indigenous wild brown trout loved them, but he wouldn't share his secrets with his fellow anglers competing on the lake, even when asked directly.

Grandpa preferred perch, and occasionally Zachary would land one for him.

But that no longer mattered.

The brown trout season was short, lasting only as long as the mayfly: March to June. He was fishing off the shore, and no one else was about. The mouth of Aira Beck was the best place to go, and only serious anglers started as early as he did. There was a steady swirl of water on the surface of the lake generated by the wind, which kept it oxygenated.

Zachary didn't bother to fish on hot, airless days, as the trout stayed at the bottom, unwilling to venture out if not even flies could be bothered. Today he already had three good-sized trout in his bag: one weighed around a pound and a half, and the other two close to two pounds. They would fillet nicely.

Something tugged at his line, and his rod bent firmly downwards.

He pulled resolutely and gave a little line at the same time as reeling it in, repeating the action until he saw a struggle near the surface. It was a perch, and it looked a decent size. The familiar razor-sharp spines on the back and the orange colouring confirmed it, but they were notorious fighters and wouldn't come in easily. He remained steadfast and repeated the strict operation of bending and reeling every five seconds or so. Finally the whole fish leapt out of the water, and Zachary knew that the hook was embedded; the damn thing had probably swallowed it and it would be impossible to remove. Never mind, a quick blow to the head would sort that out, and then he could retrieve his hook. Perch made good eating; Zachary liked them baked with slices of lemon inserted in the cavity. Nothing else was needed, apart from butter.

As he pulled the fish towards him, he took care to avoid the spine, and grabbed the head at the same time as abandoning his rod and catching hold of the tail. A spike caught him and sliced into his hand. It stung like hell but he was not about to let this prize go; it looked a good three-pounder. He held it firmly and found a rock to bash its head. A beauty.

It had rained lightly after lunch, but now the sun had returned and the wind had dropped, stilling the water. There would be no more fish today, so it was time to head home.

Force of habit made him gut the four fish at the lake edge; he threw the mush back into the water to nourish the others that had fared better today. He could have done the gutting back at the house, as now there would be no more tuts of disapproval from Grandpa. His heart sank as he remembered his loss; it stung more than his hand ever would. He cleaned the fish, wrapped them in a cloth and popped them into his bag along with his lunch box and flask. He washed his hands and packed away his rod and collapsible stool. As so often happened when he was out on the lake by himself, he found himself shivering, sensing that he wasn't alone. He looked around sharply, but shook his head when no one was there.

It was Grandpa who'd taught him to fish, though it had been many years since the old man had been able to come down here with him. Zachary's earliest memories were of sitting on a boat, passing Grandpa pieces of cockle or prawns to feed onto his hooks, and learning how to slice a fish from the anus up to the throat without catching the bowel. He imagined the old man's lifeless body on the pathologist's slab, being gutted from throat to anus, and he wondered if the surgeon would miss the bowel.

The image came back to him; it never left him alone, and it was always accompanied by the smell.

Shit dripping onto the carpet.

Grandpa's lifeless body.

Trying to support his legs thinking him still alive, in with a chance. Revulsion. Loss.

His tongue.

It had taken a while for Zachary to realise that the screams were his own: shouting for Brian.

The interminable wait. Brian running up the stairs, Linda sobbing when she arrived at the house. Finally the thud as Brian had cut Grandpa down.

Why?

Everybody who'd ever meant anything to him was dead. Memories of his mother played in his head on a canvas he'd created as a child. Those shapes were two-dimensional, but the ones of Grandpa were not.

He'd seen his grandpa laugh. He'd also seen him cry, but it was the chuckle of an old man who everybody said was reclusive and strange that would remain with him. He knew better. He knew the love that had resided in his heart, a love that had enveloped him as a boy, and then a teenager, and then a man.

The pain was visceral.

The weekend had been a blur of police and forensics, apart from when he'd gone fishing, and then he'd been able to clear his head and find some escape; some solace. But always the same questions plagued him.

He'd overheard Linda talking to Grandpa about money, and Zachary also knew well the pain he carried because of his grandmother and his mother. But Grandpa had survived this long without them. *He waited until I was old enough to cope.* People said suicide was cowardly, but Zachary knew they were wrong. If only he'd walked into his grandfather's study an hour earlier; even ten minutes earlier.

He'd yet to find out if he'd be able to stay at Wasdale Hall. Linda and Brian talked frantically about who from the noble and far-reaching past of the Fitzgerald legacy still survived. Zachary wasn't aware of Grandpa ever mentioning anyone else, but that didn't mean they weren't out there.

He cared little. It wouldn't irk him greatly to move on. He might have to drop out of college, but he'd pretty much done that already. He could find work elsewhere; any farm in Cumbria would employ a strong, healthy lad such as him, with his knowledge of fell and dale, and the wildlife therein. As long as he could stay close to the lake and mind his own business, he could supplement his existence with fish, deer, game and hedgerow plants. And he'd continue to paint.

Linda and Brian were worried about their own futures, of that he was sure. If only Grandpa had married Delilah, then Zachary would now be heir and rightful owner, and in a position to give the pair security. But he knew the world enough to understand legitimacy and nobility, and how important one was for the other.

His young brain, though witness to the worst of what people could do to one another, struggled to comprehend why, and that brought him to the other question burning in his head: why was Grandpa's safe missing? Yet more police were expected to dig and delve around, asking more questions, and Zachary sighed as he got into the Land Rover to head home. They'd enjoy a supper fit for an earl tonight, and then they'd wait for the lawyers and vultures to tell them their future.

Chapter 13

Delilah had given birth to the sounds of Fleetwood Mac.

It was a punishing labour. Her contractions had plagued her all through the night, and Xavier rushed round like a terrified hen about to be slaughtered. It made Delilah more anxious.

'Xavier, please calm down!' she'd said. His hands shook, and he willed her to get into the car so he could drive her to the Penrith and Lakes Hospital.

'I knew we should have gone to London,' he said.

There had been talk of delivering the twins by Caesarean section, but Xavier would have none of it.

'Well I'm here now, so we'll have to be satisfied. Everything will be all right,' she soothed him.

At 3 a.m., she could take the pain no more, and she finally allowed him to help her to the car. She heaved her huge body, ravaged by pregnancy, into the Land Rover, and Xavier drove like a lunatic.

'Xavier!' Delilah shouted breathlessly. 'I assume you want your children born alive!' It made no difference, and Xavier swung the car round the lanes to the A592. The roads were deathly quiet. It was a good time of year to give birth, or so said the ward sister. September was the busiest time.

It was Delilah's idea to have music. Xavier propped her upright – or semi-upright – as they were escorted to a birthing suite. She no longer cared who examined her, or where they prodded.

'Eight centimetres dilated,' the sister said. 'Nearly there,' she added, and smiled at Delilah, who now gasped for air in between contractions. She'd never felt pain like it. Her abdomen tightened like a vice around her pelvis, knocking the wind out of her, and she held her breath. The music helped a little, but it irritated Xavier.

'It's better if you breathe,' said the sister.

Delilah was given a mask and sucked at it hard. Her body was drenched in sweat and she didn't know whether to sit up or lie down. The sister kept looking between her thighs, and Xavier eyed her with suspicion. But the pain prevented her from scolding him further.

'Can we turn that damn thing off?' he said. The sister looked at him and then to Delilah.

'Shut up, Xavier.'

The twins were born naturally, ten minutes apart. Delilah was exhausted, and Xavier was ushered out of the room. She needed to sleep, and to eat.

Strikes and IRA bombs plagued the Callaghan administration, inflation crippled the country, the Yorkshire Ripper slew prostitutes, Marc Bolan and Elvis died, and Queen sang 'We Are the Champions', but neither Xavier nor Delilah cared.

'Oliver and Trinity,' Delilah whispered when she woke up. Not even the forlorn realisation that her stomach was disfigured and her breasts were the size of balloons could distract her from her babies. They sucked hungrily, and she gazed at them. Xavier daren't touch her as he watched her feed his children.

'Come here and sit with me,' she said. He perched carefully on the bed. He hadn't expected this. He'd been in control of everything that touched their lives for so long, and now he simply didn't know what to do.

'Hold them, Xavier,' she insisted. Initially he could only manage one at a time, but soon he got the hang of holding both together.

They stayed at Wasdale Hall with their babies, in a cocoon of extra waiting staff and so much help that Delilah felt stifled. Xavier didn't even smoke around them, and he insisted that she remain in bed, until, fed up and bored, she wandered out into the sunshine with the twins sleeping in their Silver Cross coach.

From day one, they were inseparable. They snuggled up together, sucking each other's thumbs, and they cried together, ate together and learned to sit up together. They couldn't be parted, else they would wail and fling their arms around until reunited. Delilah suggested allowing them to be left to cry, but Xavier gave in to their every demand. A father for the first time at fifty-five, he became terrified if the twins made an unusual noise, or if they didn't wake up when they were supposed to.

The parties stopped for a while.

Delilah grew more bored and stifled. At first she put it down to the novelty, and explained away Xavier's obsessive nature over them. He wouldn't allow the children to be alone, and he hung about the nursery, dismissing the maternity nurses and their opinions built on years of experience: he knew better. He was always there, checking to see if they were warm enough, or if they had eaten the right amount. One by one, the nurses walked out.

'Leave them be, Xavier!' Delilah grew more and more exasperated with her lover – the father of her children – as he became increasingly paranoid and gripped with fear lest something happen to the twins. He sacked five nannies who in his opinion took unnecessary risks.

Delilah tried to placate him and make him see that they weren't dolls to be cosseted and cooed over; they were growing toddlers, strong and wilful, and that was a good thing. Delilah didn't want precious darlings; she wanted bright, strong characters, like her lover had once been.

But nothing could appease him. With the twins becoming the new focus of his life, he followed them everywhere, and Delilah watched him. Matters came to a head when Xavier couldn't find them one day. He looked stricken, and his brows sat high on his large forehead. He banged his fist on the table.

'They've gone to the lake to play,' Delilah told him calmly. She was growing tired of his overprotection.

'On their own?' He was horrified.

'Of course not on their own!' Delilah screamed back at him. 'Trudy is with them.' Trudy, their seventh nanny, had a gold-plated reputation and a library full of references, but nothing was good enough for Xavier. He ran to the lake, panting like an old man, screaming for his children.

He found them in the water, because that was what they loved to do. They frolicked and squealed as they played, until their father called them in. Trudy rolled her eyes, and resigned three weeks later.

Neither child understood why one would have a lake at the bottom of one's garden and not play in it; it didn't make sense. And neither child could understand why their father was so angry with them for having fun. And so they learned to keep secrets.

They made up codes for certain activities, and Delilah and the subsequent nannies were complicit, all tired of the straitjacket Xavier had made for them. Delilah grew distant and out of love.

By the time the twins were teenagers, it had become a part of their fibre: making up stories and scenarios to avoid detection. By the time they were adults, they were very good at it indeed.

Chapter 14

Sophie's eyes twitched as she slept fitfully. The skin on her eyelids quivered as she withdrew from deep sleep and into the period before waking when the brain's movie camera went into overdrive, creating ten-dimensional neon kaleidoscopes of colour and action.

She was sitting on the top of Loadpot Hill with Hannah. The love between them burned with an intensity that almost woke her. Almost. They huddled underneath the blanket they'd packed, jumpers acting as barriers to the damp cold trying to seep through from the dewy ground. Their breath came in clouds and mingled together as it hung in the air in front of their faces, facing east as they waited for the sunrise.

This was what they'd come for. They'd just been waiting for the perfect clear night. The stars, which only twenty minutes ago had spread across the black sky like thousands of spilled crystals, were dimming as the sun made its way around the planet and brought daylight to Europe. The canopy keeping them safe slowly disappeared and made way for an endless sky of orange and grey.

She wore Hannah's blue Jack Wills sweater, which was too big for her and covered her hands with the excess material. The wind dropped and a silence descended that was so pure they could hear their own breaths. Hannah fumbled around in the bag and produced a silver hip flask;

she sucked from it greedily, then passed it to her lover. Sophie gulped at the liquid, which burned at first but then softened and generated gentle heat that warmed her face. Her cheeks contrasted with her white hair, which, even contained by her woollen hat, blew in the rising and falling breeze. She pulled a strand from her mouth and passed the flask back to Hannah.

They sat in a cocoon – or that was how it felt – under a rock face, protected from the wind when it came, perfectly wrapped on all sides by nature, except to the east, where the orange and grey sky was slowly turning to dark blue and purple. Then, as if someone had poured molten rock onto the horizon, a blob of bright silver spread across where the land met the sky over Yorkshire.

They smiled.

Hannah delved into the bag again and pulled out two Snickers bars, and they gobbled them hungrily, relishing the sweet caramel and salty nuts. Ullswater lit up as the rising sun cast enough light down the valley to pick out the glistening reflection of the surface. Up here, they didn't have to fit in, they didn't have to follow anybody's social media account: their latest live videos on Instagram or their stylised moody selfies on Snapchat. Up here, they could forget about what society expected from them and imagine a different life, far away from everything.

The rock fall was unexpected.

At first they didn't understand what was happening, as Hannah lay on the ground, blood gushing from her head. They weren't high up, and they weren't on an unsteady ledge, so the event puzzled them and disarmed their senses.

Sophie woke up.

Her waking brain opened her eyes automatically, but she shut them tight again as fast as her muscles had levered them wide. She didn't want to see what she'd become used to in the dingy room. It wasn't the cold that was the worst; it wasn't the dark, and it wasn't the pain in her stomach as she craved food. It wasn't her cracked lips that yearned for water. It wasn't even the fact that she had no idea if Hannah was alive or dead.

No, what paralysed her most with dread and horror was *him*.

Chapter 15

Kelly pulled in to the long gravel driveway and looked up at the house. Wasdale Hall was all that remained of the Fitzgerald fortune, and it was clear that its glory days were behind it. The house itself was grand enough, with its castle-like walls and modern additions here and there. But its most attractive feature was the view. Ullswater sat seductively in plain sight. She could smell the lake, and a light breeze wafted up towards the house.

She slammed the door of the Audi and took a deep breath. Her conversation with Ted Wallis whirred around her head. Homicide. Without a doubt. The most important task was creating a sketch of the earl's life and who was in it. She wanted to get a framework of his last twenty-four hours; Ted had confirmed time of death at around eleven on the Sunday evening. Linda Cairns, the housekeeper, had left to go home around nine, leaving only the earl's grandson and his gardener on the property.

Framing the driveway, trees and bushes fought for space, and two battered Land Rovers were parked in front of the house. Somewhere a dog barked, or maybe there were two. There was no sign of the press. The earl's death had made quite a stir in the local news; he was highly regarded and of noble stock. That always caused a ripple; there was nothing quite like gossip when it originated amongst the rich and famous, and the Fitzgeralds were like royalty in these parts. She had a head start, though: only she and her team were privy to Ted's theory that it wasn't suicide. After the initial flurry of excitement surrounding the hanging, the journos had gone back to covering roadblocks caused by flocks of sheep, and tourists stuck on the fells.

Kelly had googled the newspaper articles on the earl's death and found herself engrossed. Xavier-Paulus Fitzgerald was an upright, noble man with a strong nose and an air of pomp. Reading the family history had taken her well into the night, and she'd opened a bottle of Argentinian Malbec to bring along for the ride. Johnny had fallen asleep beside her and she herself had eventually nodded off in the small hours. They'd talked about how similar their professions were, the only difference being that he'd dealt with murder and misdeeds on a world scale. They discussed it often: what human beings were capable of doing to one another. To other people it might sound grim or fatalistic, but to them it was the ultimate question: what turned kids into delinquents? And they frequently concluded that presidents and prime ministers were just power-hungry criminals in charge of armies. Wasn't it Moors murderer Ian Brady who had said that he was no worse than any world leader who waged war?

She shuddered and glanced up at the windows, which looked dusty and neglected. The curtains were closed. Plump pendulums of wisteria hung around the door, and the aroma was potent as they blew gently from side to side. Like the lineage, the house had seen better days.

Kelly wondered what sort of a kid Zachary Fitzgerald was. Was all well with his relationship with his grandfather? If not, was it motive to kill? Always. She couldn't help but feel a sense of sadness at the neglected facade:

the mighty had indeed fallen, and fallen hard. She pushed the romanticism from her brain and shook her head as she remembered her latest letter from the Teacher, the serial killer who'd terrorised the National Park last year. The lunatic still hounded her from prison with poetry and rumination about the fall of mankind into despair and savagery, and sometimes she agreed.

She gazed at the lake. It was a stunning setting, and Kelly understood why, despite his long-term partner deserting him, the earl had never left. She remembered her own reasons for going, the pull of London irresistible. She shook her head, reminding herself that the elusive and elegant Delilah Mailer had never been the earl's wife, and that made Zachary illegitimate: he might stand to gain nothing. She spotted the exclusive Peak's Bay Hotel across the lake, and wondered if the earl had minded the intrusion of tourism on his patch. He'd sold the land for a hefty sum, getting him out of a financial scrape. She wondered how much was left; surely the house alone would fetch a million. It amused her: in London, it would go for twelve times that.

She pressed the doorbell and stood back.

A woman in her sixties answered, immediately looking suspicious. And so she might: they'd been hounded by journalists in the immediate aftermath of the earl's death. The woman looked beyond her guest towards the gates and Kelly recognised her as Linda Cairns, the housekeeper, and she was exactly what she had expected: a proud but frumpy woman who'd given her life to serving the earl's family. She looked tired, and hardship was etched into her deep wrinkles, as if pain was a constant visitor in her life.

'No press. No one is home, thank you. Goodbye.'

She went to close the door, but Kelly showed her badge.

'We've had the police here already,' Linda said.

Not for the first time, Kelly felt unwelcome at the beginning of an investigation, but she persevered. This woman must know all Wasdale's secrets, and Kelly wanted her to share them. She was no stranger to the initial responses of witnesses: they either fought, ran, froze or simply lied. This woman was potentially closer to the old earl than anyone, except perhaps his grandson, and Kelly needed her on side.

'Good morning, ma'am, I'm Detective Inspector Kelly Porter and I'm here to ask you a few questions about the late earl. May I come in?'

'Like I said, we've already had the police,' said Linda. It was like a mantra: monosyllabic and well-practised.

'I know, ma'am, but the case has been passed to me to take further.'

'Why?' Linda asked.

'Sorry, this is not a very good start, is it? I know you've seen several officers already, but I have to satisfy the coroner that the details of the earl's passing correlate with his findings,' Kelly said gently.

'He committed suicide,' Linda said, still blocking the doorway. Kelly nodded.

'That's why I've been assigned the case, ma'am. It's my job to speak to anyone who knew the earl well, and I believe you to be one of them, Mrs…?'

Linda's shoulders sagged, and Kelly waited patiently as the woman processed her options, which were rapidly disappearing. She was touched by the housekeeper's loyalty, but it didn't change the fact that she needed to get on with her inquiry.

'Cairns. I'm the housekeeper. I've been here for twenty years. I'm…' Overcome, she began to cry, finally cracking under the strain. She wiped her face and shook her head. Kelly moved closer to the door, knowing this was her chance. She put a foot on the great stone step and Linda moved back.

'It won't take long. I know it's a very difficult time for you all. I have a letter here requiring me to gather as much information as possible from those living here, and from the earl's possessions,' Kelly said, stronger now. Before Linda realised it, she was fully in the doorway and now standing in the hall. It was cool inside and she quickly scanned the place. Her earlier sense of wretchedness lingered: it was no cheerier in here. Paper peeled off walls, and damp patches decorated the high ceilings, under which hung the antlers of stags who'd met an untimely end. It was dark and dreary, and smelled of neglect. It was now clear that more than one dog lived here, and Kelly could hear somebody calming them down. A male.

'Call me Linda, please.'

Kelly waited. She was in, and she needed to take charge, but not yet. Linda, back in housekeeper mode, led her into what might once have been a splendid reception room but was now a functionless place, unused and unloved. The fireplace was pristine but she noticed a thin layer of dust on an occasional table. Briefly she wondered how Linda Cairns earned her title.

'Could I get you a drink? Maybe some biscuits?' Linda managed a weak smile.

'That would be lovely, thank you, Linda,' Kelly said. The woman nodded and disappeared.

Kelly looked around and picked up a photo from a table. It was of a young man, handsome and smiling but at the same time distracted by something. She knew at once that she was looking at Zachary Fitzgerald. The photo had none of the dated colours that would match the earl's younger life, but all the characteristics of the lineage. She heard exchanged voices.

Linda came back with a tray, and set about pouring tea and offering biscuits. She was the kind of woman who, Kelly thought, soothed everything with tea and biscuits. Kelly remained standing, suspecting that if she sat, great clouds of dust would choke them.

'Please sit down.'

She now had no choice and obliged. Predictably, a plume of particles billowed out of the cushion on which she sat and danced around in the one shaft of sunlight that pierced the room. Linda didn't seem to notice and sat down facing her, fiddling with her apron.

'Do you live here, Linda?' Kelly asked.

'No, I live on my own in the village,' the housekeeper responded.

'Watermillock?'

'Sorry, yes.' Linda coughed, her throat no doubt irritated by the grime.

'Do you work here full-time?'

'When I'm needed, so full-time during the week, and some weekends.'

'But you weren't here when the earl's body was discovered?'

Linda looked at her hands.

'No. I wasn't. I wish it had been me, you know, that found him, but... Poor Zachary. It's not right.' Tears flooded her eyes again.

'Is Zachary at home? I'll need to speak to him too.'

'He's already gone through enough! He was questioned by a policeman that night. Isn't that sufficient? Can't he be left in peace? He's nineteen years old.' Linda was bereft once more. Kelly moved on, letting the subject of the young man go for now.

'Apart from you and Zachary, who else comes and goes?'

Linda composed herself.

'Well, there's Brian, the gardener. Erm... The postman comes every day, and we get milk and eggs delivered.'

'Did you notice anything out of the ordinary in the days or weeks before the earl's death?'

'No.'

'Were there any changes to his routine?'

'No.'

'Did he have any unexpected visitors, or anyone you didn't know?'

'No.'

The whole time, Linda looked down at her knees and fussed with some imaginary thread.

'Could you check to see if Zachary is around, please?'

'He's likely off fishing. He's been doing that a lot since...' She fell silent and stopped toying with the material. At last she got up and left the room, not once making eye contact with her visitor.

When she returned, she was alone.

'Brian said he went fishing at six this morning. He's usually out all day.'

'Right, when he gets back, will you have him call this number?' Kelly handed over a card. 'I'd like to see Brian now, please.'

Linda nodded and wiped her eyes again. Kelly looked at the woman's hands; they were red and angry and looked as though she'd been scrubbing with caustic soda for twenty years. She followed her through to the back of the house, and into a magnificent kitchen with a huge inglenook fireplace, inside which hung old metal pots and pans. Something bubbled on an Aga and it smelled good. A man around the same age as Linda sat at the table but stood up quickly to offer his hand. Two dogs approached her, one with enthusiasm, the other less so.

'Get down, Delilah. Morning,' the man said.

'Brian, I presume? Brian Walker?' said Kelly, petting the more confident dog.

The man nodded his confirmation and walked across to Linda, standing beside her protectively. The quieter dog followed him, and he bent over to stroke its ears. They made a simple, homely couple, and straight away Kelly detected more than just friendship between them. Her hand left the dog and it padded away.

'As the earl's surviving next of kin, it's important that Zac gets in touch as soon as he returns,' Kelly said, aware that it wasn't just the two dogs protecting the young man.

Brian folded his arms and stared at her.

'Mr Walker, I believe you were on the premises the night the earl passed away. Were you aware of anyone else who might have been around? Does anyone else visit?'

Brian rubbed his chin, thought about saying something, then changed his mind.

'Isn't it time to leave the kid alone?' he asked.

'I appreciate your concern, and your desire to protect Zac, but—'

'It's Zachary,' he said curtly.

'Sorry, forgive me. The safe…'

'Zachary told us about that. We don't go in the earl's private rooms.'

'Indeed. Is anything else missing?'

'No.' Kelly noticed that Linda had become mute, happy, it appeared, to let Brian answer for her.

'Were either of you aware of what was in the safe?'

'No.' It was emphatic from both.

'I'll look around now, if that's OK. Could you show me where it happened?' Kelly asked.

Linda glanced at Brian, who nodded almost imperceptibly.

'I'll take her,' Linda said quietly.

'You cut him down?' Kelly asked as Linda began to walk towards the kitchen door. Brian nodded.

'Aye.'

She eyed him and noticed that underneath his shirt, his forearms must have measured the size of her own biceps.

Chapter 16

Upstairs, the study was cold and dark and Kelly noticed that, out of the presence of Brian Walker, Linda visibly relaxed. The housekeeper walked over to the window to draw the curtains. The walk up the stairs and along the hall had confirmed what Kelly already suspected: that the rest of the house probably hadn't seen much of Linda Cairns' housekeeping talents either. The carpets had obviously been expensive once but were now dull and worn, the door frames were badly in need of paint, and the corners of the windows were dark with mould. If someone wanted to get hold of the earl's money, Kelly wasn't seeing much evidence of any. She needed to know what was in the safe.

The room smelled sweet and she instantly recognised the pungency of death.

'Linda, can you tell me exactly what happened,' she asked gently.

Linda took a deep breath. She'd probably been over it a thousand times. Civilians often thought that the police made them go over and over facts and chains of events because they were somehow incompetent, but it could prove very handy if it turned out that those details changed, however slightly, from statement to statement. So far, Linda Cairns had stuck to her script.

'Zachary called me. He was in hysterics. I calmed him down and he told me what he'd found,' she began. Her arms were folded tightly across her chest and her voice was emotionless. 'It took me about five minutes to get here, and I found him… there.'

Kelly looked at the discoloration on the floor. It had been scrubbed to within an inch of its life and she figured that Linda's hands hadn't fared well. She had studied the photos and she knew where the stool had been, the position of Xavier's body and what else had been in the room. She glanced around. 'And Brian, when did he arrive?'

'I called out for him – he was in the garden, in his shed. He brought a knife and cut him down,' Linda said, looking at the floor. This time her voice shook, and she wiped her eyes again.

Kelly knew that Linda and Brian's prints would be all over the place, and hoped that they were stored in the safety of the lab in Carlisle. Soon she'd know if anyone else but the earl had left any trace in here too.

'It was gone eleven o'clock at night, Linda; what was Brian doing in the garden?' Kelly asked. Linda's cheeks flamed.

'He often works late, in and out of his shed; he spends more time in there than at home, fixing things, building things, listening to his music.'

'And where's home?' Kelly asked, guessing the answer.

Linda blushed. 'He stays with me.'

Kelly nodded and glanced at the housekeeper's ring finger. It was bare. 'Didn't he hear Zachary scream? He heard you when you called him.'

'The police have already asked all these questions. He was listening to music. He likes it loud, and the earl never complained.' Linda avoided eye contact.

'Is it just the two of you, in your cottage in Watermillock, I mean?' Kelly visualised the pretty collection of holiday lets and private stone houses where last year a woman's brutalised body had been found in the churchyard. In a macabre twist, tourist attention was on the up for the little hamlet.

'My son comes and goes,' Linda said quietly.

'And what's his name? I'll have to speak to him.' Kelly flipped open her pad. Her list of statements to gather was growing.

'Dominic,' Linda said.

'How old is he?'

'Why do you need to know that?'

The question caught Kelly off guard; she wasn't used to being challenged over an innocent enquiry.

'For my notes.'

'He's twenty-three.'

Kelly added the information. 'Surname?'

'Cairns.'

'Father about?'

Linda opened her mouth. Kelly had been abrupt on purpose. 'That's none of your business!'

Kelly smiled. 'I'm afraid it is, if he's also local and knows where you work, and for whom.' She waited.

'No. He scarpered years ago.'

Kelly held Linda's gaze. 'You can leave me now.' She could tell that Linda desperately wanted to say something – to object, to stand her ground, anything to regain some form of order in this sad old house, order that had disappeared with her boss. But she retreated without a word, and Kelly heard her footsteps going down the hall.

Her mobile buzzed. It was DC Emma Hide, telling her that the earl's will had been faxed over to Eden House by a solicitor's firm in Penrith.

'Most of the estate is left to Zachary Fitzgerald. But there is also a bequest to his housekeeper, Mrs Linda Cairns. He left her a hundred thousand pounds.'

Kelly whistled and wondered if Brian Walker or Dominic Cairns knew about the posthumous gift. She also wanted to know why the housekeeper was worth so much to the earl.

'Did he have that much to leave?' she asked.

'He was cash-poor but asset-rich; there's stacks of it squirrelled away in bonds and accounts. The solicitor reckons he's worth over a million.'

'The house is in a shit state.'

'My grandad's the same,' Emma said.

'What?'

'He's loaded but wears the same trousers all week.'

'Did the solicitor mention anything about valuables left in the house? Old people do that all the time, don't they?' Kelly was thinking about the safe and who knew it was there.

'He said that there were some discrepancies and he did suspect that the earl kept cash on site.'

'Thanks, Emma.'

Kelly hung up and looked around. She could take her time to a certain extent. The initial inquiry had left the study sterile but untidy, and she wondered where to begin. She took off her jacket and laid it across the back of a chair, then walked to a large sash window and struggled to get it open. Once in the fibres of a place, the smell of death was difficult to rub out. A waft of lake-rich air drifted in, making the atmosphere a little more bearable.

She looked at the large stain on the floor; it saddened her that a nineteen-year-old boy had been the one to discover the body. Unless he was the one who'd strung his grandfather up in the first place. A million quid was now firmly on the table and up for grabs. Zachary Fitzgerald was made for life.

Along one wall, glass-fronted oak cabinets displayed stuffed animals, and Kelly peered at them. A squirrel stared back at her with surprised eyes, and she screwed her face up. It reminded her of school trips to Holker Hall as a child, and walking round museums full of butterflies pinned mercilessly to cloths. It was both charming and repulsive. She wondered why the earl had never opened his house to the public, like many noble families in need of income, but she already knew the answer: he had been an intensely private man.

Another wall contained books, floor to ceiling, and against a third sat a huge oak partner desk. It might once have been used by two people, but not any more, as it was pushed right up to the wall, concealing one side. Kelly tried to move it, but it wouldn't budge. Upon closer inspection, the drawers on the room side were all unlocked and contained various papers, which she rifled through. There were newspaper cuttings from the 1950s, housekeeping notes, and some guest books.

An old photo in a silver frame sat on the mantelpiece. The processing, hue and fashion of the subjects placed it in the seventies. It was of the earl and a much younger woman. She was seated on what looked like a bar stool, and he stood close behind her with one arm draped casually around her shoulders. They smiled comfortably into the camera. Kelly undid the frame at the back and slid the photo out. On the back it read: *Xav and Boo, Cannes, 1978.*

A ring found on the earl's hand had been released by the coroner's office and Kelly had it in her pocket. Perhaps now was the time to show it to Linda. She popped the photo in an envelope, along with several documents, and went back downstairs.

She found Linda and Brian in the kitchen, much as before. Not much gardening or housekeeping seemed to be happening today, and she wondered how much the pair were paid for doing nothing. They were drinking tea and eating fruit cake, and looked so comfortable one could be forgiven for thinking the kitchen theirs. The dogs lay under the table, now used to their new visitor. Kelly coughed.

'Sorry to disturb you both again,' she said. They stiffened. 'I wonder if one of you could clarify something for me. The earl was wearing this ring when he died.' She reached into her pocket and held it up, watching the couple closely. They glanced at one another. 'Could either of you tell me who Boo is?' She thought she already knew the answer. What used to take investigations weeks to find out was now available on Wikipedia in one swipe.

Brian spoke first.

'The love of the earl's life. Mother of his children, Oliver and Trinity. Grandmother to Zachary. The only ones who ever loved him, and who won't see a penny of all of this.' He waved his hand in the air, impassioned.

Linda threw him a look of fury. Kelly was surprised by his response, which was unexpectedly lyrical from the man she'd got to know so far. It made her think he was either a bullshitter or overcome with grief.

'Name?' she asked.

'Delilah Mailer.'

'Where is she now?' asked Kelly, though again she already knew the answer. Brian tutted quietly, almost imperceptibly. Almost. Kelly was satisfied; every reaction from the odd couple now could be useful to compare later, and she stored it.

'Dead.'

'Oliver and Trinity?'

Again it was Brian who spoke. He seemed to be enjoying the limelight.

'Dead.'

A picture of a family history marred by tragedy was emerging. Kelly had read into the small hours of the legacy that undoubtedly sat heavily on the shoulders of young Zachary.

'I'm aware that Trinity was Zachary's mother. So who is his father?'

Linda and Brian looked at one another. Again it was Brian who spoke first. Linda looked away.

'I'm afraid Trinity kept that to herself, Inspector. I don't even know if the earl knew. Zachary's the only one left.'

Kelly noted that Brian had suddenly become the fount of all knowledge, and articulate with it. He hadn't moved from his feet-up position on his employer's chair.

'With respect, by all means come back, but I think we've had enough for today,' he added.

It was a curious statement.

'With *respect*, Mr Walker, this is an affair for the family. Does Zachary possess a mobile phone?'

Brian's face reddened. 'Aye. It'll be switched off.' He reverted back to a harmless member of staff and took his feet off the chair.

'I'd like to see your shed, Brian.'

He nodded, then got up, pulled on his boots and left by the back door, not saying a word. Kelly followed. He led her across a pretty courtyard and down a long path to a large gate. Beyond it, she could see the lake, and beautifully tended gardens: perhaps Brian was a valued employee after all. He took her past vegetable and fruit plots and finally to a large outbuilding. Kelly followed him inside.

The place was well ordered and the equipment clean and tidy, and as Linda had said, he had many projects up and running. In the middle of the floor at one end stood a complete weights bench. But what she noticed most of all was the various hanging animals. It was the end of the season. She saw plenty of game birds there, but a large deer caught her attention. It looked sorrowful and helpless.

'Good hunting?'

'The earl's lands are plentiful. He was a fan of game pies and Linda is a great cook.'

'Is that yours?' Kelly asked, nodding at the bench.

'I like to keep fit. I'm not getting any younger.' Kelly saw the first signs of warmth at the corners of his eyes; she could have been wrong, but his expression seemed flirtatious. The tiny hairs on her arms stood up.

'Thank you, I think I'm done for now,' she said.

'After you.' He gestured to the door.

On the way back to the house, Kelly felt Brian's eyes on her back. She was thoughtful. The weights on the end of the bar set up on the bench had totalled sixty kilograms on both sides; that was an impressive lift.

'How long have you lived with Linda Cairns, Mr Walker?' she asked. She turned around; his face had dropped.

'Few years now.'

'And you get on all right with her son, Dominic?'

'He's not a bother. I look after his mother, that's all. Lad's got a temper on him; he comes and goes.' Brian was cagey; it was obviously a touchy subject.

'Children of your own?'

'No.'

Back in the kitchen, Kelly found Linda stirring something on the Aga.

'Please get Zachary to contact me as a matter of urgency,' she said to the pair. They nodded. 'I'll see myself out.'

She left via the back door and walked into the garden, where she paused and looked back up to the house. The earl's study was easily visible, and it was clear that a scream would carry down here to the garden. There was also only one way out. Would a young man shouting over the dead body of his grandfather really be drowned out by music?

Chapter 17

'I don't like her.' Brian paced up and down with the dogs following him, trying to work out if he was about to fetch the treat tin.

'You were too cocky,' Linda said.

'She's got no business here.'

'Of course she has! She's the police.'

'Nothing better to do. You saw him, Linda, he killed himself. I'm surprised he didn't do it years ago.'

'Stop it! He was tortured to death, God rest his soul.'

'Oh stop your talk about God. The earl didn't believe in him and neither do I.'

'What did you know of Xavier? I'll tell you what: nothing. Now go and do what you're paid to do, unless you've given that up as well?'

'You're not the lady of the manor yet, Linda.'

They glared at one another, until the familiar chug of a knackered Land Rover broke the attrition.

'That'll be Zachary. Get your dirty boots out of here.'

'Never bothered you before, m'lady.' Brian gathered his jumper and the packet of sandwiches that Linda had prepared and walked out, slamming the door.

Linda wrung her hands and sat down heavily at the table. The chair creaked and she closed her eyes, reminiscing with affection about how Xavier refused to buy new ones, despite her asking him for years to do so. The huge kitchen table was made of ancient oak and it would last another lifetime should it need to. She placed her hand on it and it felt warm. The patina was dated and beautiful from years of welcoming guests through the back door. It had been there as long as the house. Dirt clung to the supports and spiders hung from beneath the wooden bolts.

She didn't need to keep her hand there for long before the memory came back, as it always did. Her skirt up around her waist, her feet supporting her weight on a couple of chairs – they were creaky even then – and Xavier heaving on top of her. He smelled of booze, as he did each time he came to her, and cigarettes.

She'd wanted it. She'd wanted him.

She'd known all along that he didn't love her, but it didn't matter. Brian didn't love her either and that was the way of this world. Men took what they wanted and women gave it.

She forgave him, as she always did. He begged her to hate him, but she couldn't, and she'd never told a soul. She had thought that Xavier had kept their dirty secret to himself too, but no, he couldn't even do that.

She blushed as she thought of how many people had sat at this table, tucking into one of her hotpots. An expert would have said that the sheen on top was from the provenance of the thing: its age and history. It was its history all right, but not the history one might think. Years of her arse sliding back and forth, Xavier grunting his need into the night, was a provenance not usually advertised at the auction house. It wouldn't fetch much of a price anyway, not even if people knew the truth; especially if people knew the truth.

The memory vanished as suddenly as it had appeared. He came to her no more and all she had left was this table and what she'd done on it. Her hand moved around in a circle, caressing the soft wood. It felt more like silk than oak. She knew that Brian had guessed. That was why he stayed around. The lure of something so palatable to an earl, no less; that and the money. He knew it was coming. It could be explained away right enough: she'd been a loyal servant for close to thirty years.

The door banged open and she jumped. Zac plonked three huge fish on the table, blood oozing from their gills, leaking over the place where she'd gently rested her hand.

'Zachary!'

He laughed. 'What do you think?' He was proud of his catch.

'I'm sure you're pleased with yourself, and they'll make good eating, but I've just cleaned the tabletop. Now look!'

Her indignation didn't concern the young man; he laughed and took off his boots, leaving the beasts where they lay. He loved to get a reaction from Linda and she willingly took on the role of grumpy aunt. She tutted and removed the fish, leaving a trail of blood between the table and the sink.

'We've had a visitor, Zachary.'

'Really? Who?'

'A detective. She wants to speak to you. She wouldn't tell us what it was about; all very shifty if you ask me. I think it's to do with the safe.'

'Why do they need a detective to find a safe? That's a bit grand. What if Grandpa got rid of it before he…'

Zac stopped what he was doing. His head lowered and he sighed.

'When is she coming back?' he asked.

'She wants you to call her.'

Chapter 18

Sergeant Steve McKellan had dived with Cumbria's Police Underwater Search Team for eight years. Jobs in the Lakes soothed him, and it beat grubby canals or abandoned mines any day. Visibility was usually good, and there was relatively little hazardous rubbish compared to what they might find in an urban waterway. Hypodermics, glass and toxic chemicals made those dives both perilous and unattractive. However, no one could predict the amount of silt and mud stirred up at the bottom of a lake, and it still called for prudence.

Crowds gathered on the shores of Lake Ullswater; his team always caused a stir if the dive went ahead in daylight. Police dive searches caught the public imagination, and everybody knew about the missing girls. Tourists and locals alike had pieced together the link between the dive team's presence and the news. Two national crews had got as close as possible to their entry point, and no doubt they'd have the latest ultra-zoom cameras. Steve turned away from them, busying himself with his kit, not wanting to appear on the evening bulletin.

It was a warm day and he let his drysuit hang around his waist until after the brief. Three divers would enter the lake, linked together by a guide rope held by another officer on shore. Four more divers would patrol the surface; two on board the RIB. Thirty years ago, divers went in without radios or guide ropes and Steve held his predecessors in high esteem.

The brief concentrated on the search area. The lake had a bottom of fifty-one metres and this would be the most dangerous part of the dive. Every diver knew that once twenty metres was passed, everything became more complicated and dangerous. They weren't in open water but the safety brief was the same. Their biggest enemy was the cold and the dark. Beneath ten metres, they'd need torches, and it was unlikely that the temperature on the surface was much above four degrees Celsius; that would get colder with depth.

Steve wore leggings and a jumper under his drysuit. It would be a long dive. The grid they worked on was in a square formation, and each square had to be picked through by hand. He'd got used to feeling his way rather than expecting to see stuff, although today he might be pleasantly surprised; the lake looked inviting and clear. They all knew they were looking for bodies. He'd seen the photos. The girls were the same age as his daughter.

Nothing gave Steve more satisfaction than finding a deceased. It gave the family closure and occasionally solved a homicide. They were also looking for personal items: rucksacks, clothes, phones, wallets and the like. They carried torches, but light had very little to do with visibility. If the silt stirred up, he'd have to use instinct instead.

Steve wore his wife's wedding ring on a chain around his neck, and he kissed it as he always did before a dive. He believed she protected him and kept him safe, as she had done when she was alive. He was prepared mentally for what they might discover, and his determination built as they finalised their strategy.

Kelly parked her car and put on her sunglasses. Things were beginning to move; they had to catch a break soon. She finished the last of the sorry excuse for a sandwich, bought in haste from a shop in town, and made her way over to the dive team. She'd worked with these teams before, and she knew that if there was anything down there, they'd find it.

A ripple of excitement flowed through her as she approached the team leader. He was broad and fit and had a wide smile. She extended her hand and he shook it, introducing himself as Steve McKellan.

'Nice day for it,' he said.

'You received my notes?' she asked. Steve nodded.

'We're working off a standard grid. Visibility should be good today,' he said.

'Good luck,' said Kelly. 'I'll be on the shore.'

'You can stay in radio contact over there,' he told her, pointing to several people surrounded by equipment and aerials.

'You've got quite an audience,' she commented, nodding to the crowd.

'Usual,' he said. 'At least we're out of the way.'

It was true: the beach they'd chosen had been closed off, and no one could reach them. Kelly knew that it was different in a city canal, where the press could bribe apartment owners for the best line of sight around the intended dive. The last thing they wanted was to bring up a body and for a family member to see it on the evening news.

The team checked fins, buoyancy, weight belts and pressure, then spat into their masks to test their head gear. They were using full masks today, equipped with radios. The divers looked clumsy on land, but Kelly knew that as they entered the murky gloom of the lake, they'd become weightless and lithe. The line was checked by all three officers, and they signed the 'OK' signal. The divers submerged.

Kelly went to the communications team and introduced herself. She was given a headset. Steve checked in with the other divers on his radio.

'Karen, John, good comms?'

'Roger, Steve.'

They were starting from the Howtown side and planned to work towards the middle this morning. This afternoon, they'd go west.

On the RIB, an officer manned the side-scan sonar, from which signals and readings were sent to the truck on the shore where Kelly waited.

–

Steve felt warm and settled into the dive. He checked his buoyancy and hovered just above the lake bed. Divers who couldn't control their buoyancy, drifting up and down, kicking up silt and scaring wildlife, irritated the hell out of him. Visibility was good at about twelve metres, but all three divers knew that it would reduce rapidly the deeper they went.

There wasn't much to see. The lake bed was mostly made up of rocks and pebbles. Steve spotted the odd anchor, and a few beer cans. Under water, tin and litter gradually turned brown, like everything else. They were looking for anything that stood out; that shouldn't be there.

Strong currents swept them from side to side, and Steve's ears were filled with the magnified sound of rock tapping on rock. The deeper they swam, the more silt surrounded them. He flicked on his torch. His ears adjusted as they passed twenty-five metres, and he became aware of the temperature dropping. They moved little, apart from forward, and it did nothing for the cold.

After bottoming at fifty-one metres, they were on their way back to shore when Karen stopped and held up her hand.

'There,' she said into her mouthpiece; she'd spotted something. The other two halted, and one of the team on the surface signalled to the RIB to stand by.

They hovered over a sandy area dotted with rocks. Steve checked his depth: they were at fifteen metres. Pondweed above them prevented the sun's rays penetrating this far down, but their torches lit up the area as long as they stayed fairly still. Their movements were slow and deliberate. Steve adapted his buoyancy and sank a foot, taking him to just above the pile of rocks in question.

To the side of one large rock, a canvas handle sat in the sand. Karen had a keen eye; it could have been a plant or a fish. It was neither. He lifted the rocks very carefully, one at a time. They were light underwater and he moved them easily, but he took care not to discard them roughly and so disturb the lake bed. Karen and John took it in turns taking the rocks from him until they'd removed eleven in total. Silt had kicked up, and they waited for a minute while it settled again. They didn't move.

It was a large holdall. The torch beam revealed it to be a royal blue and black Head bag. Steve tried to lift it, but it was too heavy. He made a decision not to open it. He suspected it had been weighed down with something, but forensics would want to go over every item, including whatever had been used to sink it to the bottom of the lake.

The truck on the shoreline was equipped with a portable winch, and the RIB collected it. Steve was running out of air. If they didn't get a move on, he'd have to surface. Karen and John both gave a thumbs-up, signalling that they were going up. They'd been under water for forty-five minutes. Steve spoke into his radio.

'See you at the top. I'm staying.' Someone would have to tie the winch.

Karen and John swam ten feet away from where Steve waited on the lake bed with the bag, to keep silt to a minimum, and began their ascent.

Finally the RIB arrived and the winch was lowered. As Steve tied it to the bag, he checked his air. It was dangerously low. He finished tying and the bag lifted gently from the bed. As he watched it rise, he noticed that there was something on one end. He shone his torch as the bag moved away from him.

Two large initials had been written in black marker pen: F. H.

Chapter 19

Kelly arrived at Eden House with her stomach churning. Finding Freya Hamilton's bag changed everything. Of course they would need to wait for definitive results to confirm ownership, but with the Head bag listed among Freya's belongings, as well as the initials, it made for a morbid atmosphere in the incident room, and rightly so. Kelly had assembled her whole team. It didn't occur to her that it was Saturday. It didn't matter.

—

Outside, DS Kate Umshaw stubbed out her cigarette and decided again that this was not the week to quit. The cloud of toxic fumes followed her inside, but no one commented. She pressed the button for the lift rather than take the stairs, knowing that it would only add to the exertion already forced upon her clogged lungs. As she walked out of the lift and along the corridor to the incident room, she was thankful that she'd avoided promotion again: Kelly Porter would have to face this one.

DC Rob Shawcross sat back on a chair with his feet up and studied his computer screen. DC Will Phillips stared pensively out of a window, glancing occasionally at the door, expectant for the moment of Kelly's arrival. DC Emma Hide read poetry. Kate walked past them and sat down.

'What time is it?' asked Kate.

'Eight twenty-two,' replied Will.

Kate nodded and fiddled with her laptop, wishing she'd squeezed in one more smoke.

—

Kelly entered the room and walked straight to the whiteboard. She opened her Toughpad – they all had them; officers were notoriously clumsy and too many had been damaged. Cost-cutting was at the forefront of everyone's mind.

Three photographs appeared behind her on the white screen: Sophie Daker, Hannah Lawson and Freya Hamilton.

'Three women, similar appearance, disappeared into thin air. Let's start with Hannah and Sophie. What have we got?'

Will Phillips was the first to speak.

'Guv, the bag found on Loadpot Hill has been identified as Hannah Lawson's; the mother confirmed it. The mobile phone is being downloaded, though it'll take some time. There was a silver hip flask – that's being tested for DNA. The stains on the bag tested positive for human blood and we got a quick result on it: it's confirmed that it's Hannah Lawson's. That's not all. The blood spatter at the scene where the bag was found also matched Hannah's. We retrieved and cast a single tyre track at the scene, and some trainer prints. None of the prints are in our databases; the track is from a bog-standard Land Rover – they're fairly common round here, used by pretty much every farmer from here to Barrow. It's a generic model.'

'So we're looking at abduction for sure.' Kelly made notes on her Toughpad. Every computer in the office was hooked up to the HOLMES 2 system, and the information updated their working model instantly. The dynamic reasoning engine was like an extra officer in the room, but one who didn't need to sleep, eat or think. It made sure that no detail was missed, but then the details had to be inputted first; if there were no details, then there was nothing to compare, and comparisons built investigations.

'Yes, guv. But to take two women is no easy job, and Hannah is a judo expert. It must have been pre-planned.'

'Or they were disabled somehow. Right, Freya Hamilton?'

'Lancaster has sent the file; the case is back to us now. The bag contained personal stuff: a toilet bag, various items of clothing – including a grey sweater, official merchandise from her sixth-form college in Doncaster – and some electrical goods. No phone or ID. The sweater and the bag were positively ID'd by her sister, who lives in Cleethorpes.'

Two investigations – one of which they'd thought was on Lancashire turf – had just potentially become one, but they needed to find links, and so far all they had was the fact that the girls were of similar appearance and last seen in the Lakes.

'Why is the sister Freya's next of kin?' Kelly was curious.

'The parents washed their hands of her a few years ago. Cocaine addiction. From what I can make out, it was assumed at the time that Freya had wandered off in search of a score and a party weekend getting high. She'd been in and out of jobs in the Lakes, including the Peak's Bay on Ullswater, so no one except the sister seemed to miss her. Lancaster closed the case when the leads dried up.'

'Because they were in the wrong place,' Kelly said. 'But we've still got no body, and all three girls could still be alive. I want the photos re-released to the press, as well as last sightings and everything we know about their movements.'

'Freya's last movements were quite erratic,' Will said. 'She'd been missing a lot of work. It sounded like she fell in with the wrong crowd, and spent more time trying to scrape enough money together for drugs rather than at work. It was no surprise to anyone when she failed to turn up for her shifts. She wasn't even reported missing until three weeks after the last sighting in Carnforth.'

Kelly nodded: she'd known her team would have done their homework.

'We've also had the results back from Garth Cooke's clothes. No other DNA was found apart from his own,' Will added.

'So there's nowhere near enough for an arrest. He's not our man,' Kelly said. 'Our MO has changed. If we're going with abduction, Garth has no transport, he's a wet weekend and couldn't overpower two women in my opinion, and he was drunk and stoned in his tent for three days. A scuffle would have left something. Also, if they're linked – and it's a big if – Garth Cooke had nothing to do with Freya Hamilton. We'll keep him as a POI and notify Lancaster police to keep an eye on him.'

'Are we upgrading the investigation, guv?' Emma Hide made her first contribution. Kelly looked at the whiteboard. The three girls could have been sisters: around the same age, with the same beautiful blonde hair and wide smiles. All three had taken very little with them in terms of personal items when they disappeared, as if they'd simply gone for a stroll and never returned.

'I'm ruling nothing out, let's put it that way. We'll investigate them as two cases but I want everything cross-referenced as we go. The chances of three young pretty women going missing innocently with the evidence of foul play we've got sitting in the lab is about as likely as Kate giving up her cigarettes.'

Kate Umshaw took a half-bow from her seated position.

'The proximity bothers me too. Hannah and Sophie were last seen on the shores of Ullswater; Freya worked in the area and her bag now turns up at the bottom of the lake. From Freya's mobile phone records and bank activity, we're looking at three months missed while the case sat in Lancaster. It's a hell of a long time. When the press get hold of this, they'll tear us apart.'

Kelly stared at the board. 'How did a drug addict get a job at the Peak's Bay Hotel?' The Peak's Bay was arguably the most exclusive resort in the Lake District. Everybody looked at their screens. 'We'll need to pay them a visit. They should have CCTV and up-to-date files on employees.' She paused as notes were jotted on pads.

'Turning our attention to the Earl of Lowesdale,' she said. Eyes bobbed up. Kelly knew they'd all wanted to visit Wasdale Hall and were eager to find out what she had seen, but each acted professionally and waited patiently.

'It's big. A bit unloved, but my bet is someone wants to get their hands on it. The housekeeper is set to inherit a hundred grand; the grandson gets the rest. Any takers for interviewing Zachary Fitzgerald with me?'

Their nonchalance deserted them and hands flew up. Kelly went to the end of the table and picked up a file. She plonked it in front of DC Emma Hide and smiled.

'There you go. Have a look through that lot, and as soon as I hear from him, I'll let you know.' Emma was a slave to detail, and the rest of the team knew that if anyone could scour a pile of papers four inches thick by the afternoon, it was her.

'Am I looking for anything in particular, guv?' she asked.

'Financial affairs mainly. Payments or gifts. Any skeletons: usual stuff.' Emma nodded. Kelly continued. 'I need someone to give cold cases a real thorough going-over – dating back at least five years. And Rob? Put some pressure on Jack Sentry, will you? I don't like him. Find out his background and get back to me. Right, everyone, let's meet again at the same time tomorrow. And let's hope we get to the bottom of this before your holidays kick in.'

They packed away their things and turned to their screens. Emma took herself off to a quiet corner and Rob left the room. Kate said she'd be happy to trawl through cold cases, Kelly assumed it was because it involved leaving the room and going downstairs, creating an opportunity for a trip outside into the sunshine to smoke.

Chapter 20

Hannah shivered in the dark. The place was a hovel. And it was freezing. Her only companions were the spiders weaving busily in corners and behind beams. When light did come in, it was through shutters that remained closed, and any warmth from the sun's rays never penetrated deeply enough into the small room in which she found herself. Her head pounded. She'd thought she'd known hunger when she'd given up bread for Lent, but now the knowing emptiness in her gut, alongside a thirst that stuck her lips together, made her realise that she'd never been deprived of anything in her short life, ever. She'd even licked the dried blood from her hands, but now that had gone too.

Her tongue felt swollen in her mouth and she counted the rhythm of her breathing... one two... in... one two three... out. With her faculties of taste and sight diminished through malnutrition and an endless dark, her others went into some kind of hyper-drive. She heard the tiniest sounds – a mouse scraping, a fly buzzing or a tap running – but she never heard Sophie. She smelled everything too, including herself. She closed her eyes and tried to imagine flowers, perfume, Sophie's clothes, but one smell kept creeping in above the others, even stronger than the burger she craved: *him*. His smell was all over her.

She'd fought, but quickly realised that the only thing to attack was the rags around her and the cable ties holding her hands together. He wasn't stupid. And she knew he'd done it before. She went over and over in her mind how stupid they'd been. Sitting on the ridge line with Sophie, watching the rising sun in the east, she'd felt a blow to her head, heard Sophie's gasp. He'd appeared from nowhere, offering to help. They were confused and Hannah was momentarily dazed; of course that was the plan all along. He hadn't given them any indication that he was a fucking raging lunatic, but then she guessed they never did. That was why she felt stupid. If only she could turn back time. People said it all the time, but Hannah knew what it really meant now.

He'd told them he had a first-aid kit in his car, but they hadn't questioned why he had a car up there at that hour; they hadn't questioned anything. She'd been so wrapped up in what Sophie had said minutes before. Finally the wait was over. Sophie wanted her. She wanted to be *with* her, not like a friend any more, but like a partner. It made her dizzy. And weak.

Now she was angry, but it was too late. Her questions counted for nothing and there was no going back on the foolish decisions they'd made. He'd helped them to his car (how the hell he'd got it up there in the first place was another fucking mystery that she'd overlooked in her befuddlement), promising first aid and shelter nearby. He'd seemed nice. Normal. They'd got into the car and she remembered very little after that, apart from a banging head and this dingy, grime-infested room. And his smell when he was on her, breathing on her, touching her, laughing at her, choking her.

She'd tried to keep track of the days, but her muddled brain wouldn't allow it, and days merged into nights in one long torment. She thought she'd known fear. Like when she almost got struck by a speeding car on a zebra crossing: her heart jumped into her mouth, her gut froze, her skin prickled and she couldn't stop shaking. But this was different. This was menacing, visceral, all-consuming fear, and she felt constant pain as a reminder. She knew that he must have drugged them shortly after getting into his battered old Land Rover, but how? And more importantly, why? She'd never met anyone with whom she couldn't reason before – well, apart from Garth. But Garth was stupid; this guy was not.

She'd tried to work out why he was doing this to them, but each time it made her head ache. And now she'd worked out that he didn't have a reason, and he didn't need one. He was just an evil bastard. The frustration flushed adrenalin through her body and she kicked the wall, hurting her swollen foot. She had injuries all over her body and had stopped counting them or worrying about them. Nothing else mattered apart from getting out.

It hadn't taken long for her to begin to do as she was told.

She fought at first, but she'd underestimated him. Her martial art meant nothing here in this hellhole. She tried desperately to keep her wits about her, and to hope. She needed her sanity to see her through. He'd only been there in the room with her twice, but that was enough to confirm that he had no intention of letting them go.

Maybe they wouldn't make it out – Sophie might be dead already. But she couldn't give in to negative thoughts. Sophie must be somewhere else, and she had to believe that she was still alive. From minute to minute, hour to hour, Hannah didn't know if he would visit, and, if he did, whether it would be for the last time. She stank. She repulsed herself, but he didn't seem to notice or care. Occasionally she heard him moving about, or a door banging, but try as she might, as much as she strained her ears and closed her eyes tight to help them along, she never heard a whisper of another soul.

She felt like she was turning into an animal: that was what he'd done. In the periods of long absence, she rubbed up against the grimy bedding, or wiped her face on her forearms; anything to mimic grooming, as if that would cleanse her. It didn't. She checked her discarded water bottle again, as she had done a thousand times before: it was empty.

The floor was brick and it chilled her bones. She made it to the door and reached up with her restrained wrists to try the handle. It was just something that she did to occupy her mind. It was a normal thing to do, trying a door handle, and so she did it. Every hour. It was still locked. She rattled it, but not too hard. She had no idea where he was. She didn't even know where *she* was. Her mind played tricks on her; it was the lack of water. Her brain felt fried.

'Sophie,' she whispered. She placed herself prone on the ground and put her lips to the crack under the door. 'Sophie,' she whispered again. She heard nothing. The skin on her lip split anew and it stung. She licked the fresh blood and tried to swallow. Not even tears came any more.

She crawled back to the bed on her knees. It was the only furniture in the room apart from a chest of drawers. There was no bedding, but she had a stained blanket and wriggled under it as best she could without the use of her hands, trying to get warm. The cold was maddening; it taunted her as she tried to fall asleep – anything to make reality go away. But her brain wouldn't allow it; she was to be ready for the next time, if and when it came. Maybe he'd moved on somewhere else and they'd die here from hunger and thirst. Hannah didn't know which scenario was worse. She'd do anything to survive.

She curled up tighter on the bed and rubbed her fingers together, blowing on them. There wasn't a sound and she had no idea where they were, only that it was in the middle of nowhere. She wondered if anyone was searching for them. Surely they'd have been missed by now? She imagined people crawling all over the National Park looking for them, and somebody stumbling upon this place. She envisioned her salvation and rescue, together with Sophie, who would be unharmed. Sleep came momentarily, but instinct woke her joltingly.

Think.

She looked around again, half hoping that it had all been a dream. It wasn't. She'd tried the window. The shutters were locked, preventing her from getting to the glass. She'd tried levering them open but they were sturdy. There was nothing in the room that could be used as a weapon and she'd found out the hard way that she didn't have the strength to go head to head.

The same thoughts whirled around her brain.

Then the front door banged.

Chapter 21

The voice had been polite and gentle, with a hint of maturity that hadn't quite emerged in his nineteen years but was beginning to. Zachary Fitzgerald had called Kelly's personal mobile and they had agreed to meet at Wasdale. Kelly was keen to finally meet the young man who'd endured the ordeal of finding his grandfather in his final humiliating state.

Emma sat in the passenger seat, reading. Kelly enjoyed the peace and quiet; it allowed her to recycle her thoughts. The drive along the north shore of Ullswater was uneventful, and she took a minute to absorb the beauty: a few boats chugged lazily along and the water beckoned any passer-by to park up and dip a toe in. She could drive the route all day long, but sadly they soon pulled off towards Watermillock and her stomach knotted again. The Fitzgerald estate wasn't quite as far as the church where they'd found the Teacher's first victim last year, but it still made her tense.

She pulled in to the private road and Wasdale Hall loomed close. Emma stopped reading and looked up at the house.

'I wished I was a princess living here when I was a little girl,' she said, taking Kelly by surprise.

'Really?' She laughed. 'If it was ever that grand, it's long gone now.' But Emma never took her eyes off the property, and Kelly realised that nothing could dim the younger woman's romantic notion of the place.

Mrs Cairns answered the door and was cool. It was no surprise. The last thing Kelly expected was a warm welcome, and she'd briefed Emma earlier. After they'd finished here, they were going along to Linda's cottage to meet her son, Dominic. Perhaps that was why she was anxious; more likely it was just her usual demeanour.

'Morning, Linda,' Kelly said brightly. She barely got a smile in return as she introduced her colleague, but at least Linda opened the door to let them in. This time, they were led to a different room, and it was well kept. A fire burned and Kelly remembered that it was still only May. Some effort had been made and she wondered who had instigated it.

'Wait here, please.' Linda disappeared. Neither Kelly nor Emma sat down. Instead, they looked around. The room was cosy and well furnished, if a little sparse. The armchairs were worn, but in a pleasing way, and Kelly wondered if the room had been used by the earl until very recently. A grand painting of a hunting scene hung over the great stone fireplace. Kelly looked closely at the characters: a nobleman on a horse surveyed his land, surrounded by trusty hounds, as a gentlewoman and her daughter sat on a grassy bank. It was dated, ephemeral and a little disconcerting. It belonged in a museum, not a home, and reminded Kelly of the earl's study: a snippet of a bygone era.

The door opened and a tall, shy young man with dark floppy hair walked in with his hands in his pockets. His fringe was long enough to give his eyes somewhere to hide, and he was slim but well built, like his grandfather had been. His face was chiselled and his shoulders broad;

there was no doubt as to his lineage. He wore a maroon jumper with a grey shirt underneath, and a pair of worn black jeans. He had slippers on his feet and walked silently towards them, only looking up when he was a metre away.

'I'll stay, Zachary,' Linda said, following him in.

'No. I'm fine.' His voice was gentle but firm, and Linda looked annoyed. Kelly wondered if she wanted to stay not only to protect the boy, but to listen to their conversation so she could relay it back to Brian and who knew who else. The dogs sneaked around her and Linda went to shoo them out. Clearly they weren't allowed in this part of the house. But lots of rules had been broken lately.

'Leave them,' Zac commanded, his voice deliberate. Linda shot him a momentary glance of surprise, but then left and closed the door. Kelly watched as the older woman did as she was told, and was surprised at the authoritative nature of this young man.

'Zachary, I'm Kelly Porter, and this is my colleague Emma Hide. It's a pleasure to meet you. I'm so sorry about your grandfather.' Kelly held out her hand. Zachary went towards her to take it, but his one glance up was towards Emma.

'Hi, it's Zac. Please call me Zac.'

'OK, Zac, may we sit down?' He was too tall for her and she wanted an even playing field.

'Yes please.' Zac sat too, stealing another glance at the younger detective.

'I'll get to the point. You reported your grandfather's safe missing, but that's not the only reason we're here. There's no easy way to put this, but the post-mortem has concluded without doubt that your grandfather's death was staged to look like suicide.'

Zac looked at Kelly now, fully concentrating on the detective in charge, with Emma forgotten.

'What?' His face, bereft as it was before the blow, now crumpled, and he placed his hands either side of his head. His foot tapped uncontrollably, making his knees jolt. Kelly gave him time. She'd delivered shit news many times over, and there was no way to dress it up and make it soft and bouncy; the only way to do it was to be blunt and deal with the fallout.

'So you think the safe has something to do with it?' Zac's voice was steady but higher-pitched than before. Kelly nodded.

'It could well be, and it could indicate a motive. Zac, this is now a murder inquiry. We need you to help us paint a picture of your grandfather's world: who was in it, who he trusted and, more importantly, who he didn't trust and why. I appreciate that he was a private man. Were you two close?' Kelly reckoned she already knew the answer. Zac nodded, and now the tears came in streams down his face.

'How can you be so sure? I saw him…'

'I know you did. And I want you to try and cast your mind back and tell me everything – every tiny detail – about what you found. Take your time.'

Zac got up abruptly and paced towards the fireplace. He appeared deep in thought. He brushed away his tears and composed himself, and Kelly got the impression that here was a young man wise beyond his years. She'd read that neither parent had stuck around for long – not that they knew who his father was – and his grandfather had raised him. If his only pals were Linda Cairns and Brian Walker, Kelly surmised that the lad's day-to-day life must have been pretty dour.

'I heard a noise.'

'What sort of noise?'

'A bang. I guess it was the stool.'

'Could it have been anything else?'

Zac closed his eyes and screwed his face up. 'It could have been a window.'

Kelly looked at Emma, who made notes.

'How long was it from the banging noise to when you went in?'

'Ten minutes, no longer.'

'Was the window open when you did go in?'

Zac thought intently.

'Yes, it was open.' It was this kind of tiny detail that Kelly was looking for. Now she could instruct forensics to examine the window frame as a potential entry and exit point.

'Would you have known if anyone was in the house?'

Again Zac concentrated. 'Not really. It's an old house; it creaks and things rattle. The dogs would have sensed it, though, if anyone had got in.' Zac petted them. Both animals sat protectively at his feet and had nuzzled their snouts into him when he'd cried.

'Do you know anyone who was harassing your grandfather, blackmailing him, perhaps, or bothering him in any way?'

'No,' Zac said.

'Did he tell you of any particular worries before he died?'

'No.'

'Do you know what was in the safe?'

'No, I never asked, and I never saw him use it.'

'How did you find out it was gone? Where was it kept?'

Zac reddened slightly. 'It was in his wardrobe. I saw it arrive, a couple of years ago, and helped Brian put it in there. I went in to look at his clothes…'

Kelly understood. She'd done the same with her father's shirts. They still smelled of him six months later when they were sent off to the charity shop.

'It might be a good time to tell you that we've spoken to your grandfather's solicitor, and apart from a gift to Linda, you're the sole beneficiary of the estate. I think there is debt, but that is for the executor to discuss with you. I thought you might like to know.' Kelly waited.

Zac bent his head and sighed. 'He'd said I was, but I didn't expect…'

It was a tender moment and Kelly couldn't help but feel maternal towards the young man. 'What is your relationship with Linda and Brian?'

'Erm… she's always been here. She does everything. She was close to Grandpa. Brian comes and goes. Grandpa rarely let him in the house. He thought there was something going on between them, but he never asked. Everybody else knows they've been living together for years. My Grandpa didn't. He was old fashioned.' He blushed a little, and Kelly warmed to this good-natured young man even more.

'Can you take me to your grandfather's room and show me where the safe was?'

'Sure.' The three of them stood up and Zac stole another glance towards Emma before leading the way out of the room. He commanded the dogs to stay at the foot of the staircase as he went up. Kelly and Emma followed him along the landing and into a dark bedroom. Zac tutted and drew the curtains. He looked at the bed for a moment; it seemed to Kelly a hugely private gesture.

A grand mahogany wardrobe stood against a wall, and Zac went to it and opened the left-hand door. He pointed inside.

'In there.'

'When was the last time you saw it?'

'Grandad asked me to fetch a jacket. That was about two days before he died.' Zac looked at his feet.

Kelly went over the route to the bedroom in her head. She'd never known a lightweight safe – that would defeat their purpose – and so moving it would be a professional job. It was possible that the earl had ordered it removed before he died.

'Thank you. When you said you helped get it up here, do you remember what it looked like? Even the model perhaps?'

'Brian will know; he ordered it.'

Chapter 22

Linda Cairns' cottage was a pretty stone structure with a small, well-tended front garden and an archway that led to the main entrance at the side. Kelly had insisted that Linda need not accompany them, and the news had resulted in even poorer manners from the housekeeper. They knocked on the small red-painted door and stepped back. The smell of spring flowers was heady, and early wasps and bees buzzed around.

The door was opened by a tall young man in swimming shorts and nothing else. His body and hair were wet and he'd left footprints behind him on the tiles. He smiled confidently and stood back.

'Kelly Porter?' he asked. Kelly nodded, held out her hand and introduced Emma. Dominic Cairns, it appeared, had similar taste to Zachary Fitzgerald, as he couldn't stop staring at the pretty young woman. Kelly watched in amusement as Emma returned his gaze and he looked away.

The kitchen was ordinary and small. A loaf of bread and a bread knife sat on the counter, as well as jam and cream. Dominic folded his arms. 'I'll just get a towel,' he said.

'Been for a swim?' Kelly asked.

'I'm training for my first Ironman.'

'Well, you've got much in common with my colleague, then,' Kelly said, looking at Emma, who smiled pleasantly but didn't say anything. Dominic raised his eyebrows and disappeared, coming back rubbing himself with a blue towel.

'Mum said to expect you. I didn't know the earl, by the way, I wasn't allowed up to "the big house" much. He didn't like commoners – apart from those who worked for him, of course.'

His smile was wide and mocking as he used his fingers to indicate speech marks in the air. It was incredibly disrespectful and Kelly noted with interest that he emphasised the word 'commoners' with disdain.

'So when *did* you go to Wasdale Hall?'

They watched as Dominic continued to dry himself casually. He seemed to enjoy his spectators.

'I hung out with Zac a bit, I was allowed in the garden and the kitchen. I haven't been there for years, though. The earl was a rude old bastard – excuse me. I don't know why Mum put up with him.'

'So when exactly were you there last?'

Dominic stopped rubbing. He turned his back to them and carved a slice of bread. The muscles along his naked back rippled. He was deeply tanned. A scratch, perhaps two inches long, marked his otherwise perfect skin from his scapula to his armpit.

'Oh, I'd say about six months ago.'

'Do you work, Dominic?'

'Nope. Work's for losers. I've got better things to do.' He dolloped jam onto the bread.

Kelly clenched her fists. His arrogance was startling but not grounds for arrest. She let it go.

'So you're supported by your mother?'

Dominic put the jam spoon down and picked up another, plunging it into the cream. He took a bite of the laden bread and turned around, chewing.

'You could put it like that.'

'How do you get along with Brian?'

He snorted. 'We leave each other alone. He fucks my mother when he thinks I'm out.'

'What's the scratch on your back?'

'No idea. Bush when I was swimming. Dunno.' He continued to chew.

'Where were you last Sunday evening?'

Dominic now used the towel on his head. 'I was at a party in Kendal, with friends.'

'Can we take the names of those friends, for verification?'

'Sure.' He read them out as Emma scribbled. He supplied phone numbers as well.

'Thank you for your time. We'll be in touch.'

They went towards the door and Dominic made no effort to assist, so they let themselves out.

'Twat,' said Kelly. Emma nodded. They put their sunglasses on and got back into Kelly's car.

Chapter 23

Linda walked out into the sunshine and stared towards the lake. She hoped that her son was being polite to the police officers.

Fat chance.

She shook her head and her mind wandered back to a memory long hidden in the recesses of her brain. She'd left through the back door then too, looking for the boys. It must have been a good fifteen or sixteen years ago, because Zac was a mere toddler. She closed her eyes.

–

Dominic had taken little Zac down to the lake, and they were late. The earl had instructed that Zac needed to be ready for their fishing trip at 9 a.m. sharp. It was now 8.42 and she couldn't see the boys. She left the pots in the Belfast sink and wiped her hands on her apron. Brian had been tasked with getting the boat ready; the engine had needed servicing and he'd taken it to the jetty to test the motor. Dominic had been told firmly that they were only to play for twenty minutes after breakfast, but he never listened.

She slammed the back door and headed towards the lake. Her sandals crunched on the gravel and she peered left and right, half expecting them to be hiding in the rhododendrons.

'Dominic! Zachary!' she shouted again. She still couldn't see them.

Everybody was on edge. The earl had only left his room once since the news, and that was to take his grandson fishing. Zachary was only three years old, but the earl treated him as a son. After all, they only had each other now. Her head filled with regrets and unwelcome thoughts. What a mess! The day that Delilah had left, taking Trinity with her, was bad enough; now Oliver was dead.

The vision of Oliver's coffin, covered in lilies – her own choice – sitting at the altar before it disappeared behind the curtain, never left her. The earl hadn't attended, damning his only son to the flames of the crematorium without a final word. Only she and Brian had accompanied Oliver on his final journey, sitting in an empty chapel listening to the vicar's empty words of commiseration. She'd since taken to watching young Zachary like a hawk, and him disappearing for a minute more than was expected drove needles into her stomach.

Her stroll turned to a jog as she headed to the shore of the lake.

The family had fallen apart and Linda couldn't recall when it had begun to unravel. She could make no sense of it. Only two years ago, Wasdale Hall still echoed with constant music and chatter, brought to it by the particular tastes of Delilah Mailer. Her favourite was Motown. Linda cleaned, polished, cooked and rocked cradles to the background of Smokey Robinson and Marvin Gaye.

Not any more.

Silence rang in her ears, as well as her own shrill cries as she neared the lake and searched for the two boys – her own the older, and in charge.

'Dominic! Zachary!'

A plastic sword lay discarded next to the path, and she picked it up, panic rising in her chest. She heard splashing and clenched her fists. She'd specifically ordered Dominic not to let Zachary in the water. It was only by the earl's good grace that he was invited to play with his only grandson, and Linda could see that privilege ebbing away too.

Suddenly she spotted them. Dominic was holding Zachary by the feet as the younger boy splashed around frantically, trying to keep his head above the surface of the water.

'Dominic!' Her shriek caught the seven-year-old off guard, and he dropped Zachary's feet, sending him under the water. Linda waded in, heedless of her shoes and tights, and grabbed the little boy, who coughed and spluttered. Dominic stood knee deep in the water, glaring at his mother as she held the younger boy up and cradled him, bouncing him up and down on her hip in an attempt to stop his tears. Zachary coughed water and swallowed hard.

'What in God's name do you think you're doing?' she spat at her son, who trailed his hands in the water beside him, shamefaced at having been caught out.

'Teaching him to swim,' he said quietly.

'Drowning him more like!' Her own words surprised her, and she marched out of the lake, dripping wet. Dominic remained standing in the water, sulking.

'It was only a game,' he said defiantly. Linda scowled at him.

'Get out of there! I'll be sacked!'

'What's sacked?' the boy asked. Linda didn't answer, simply tutting and tending to the toddler in her arms.

It was only years later that Zachary told her what Dominic had done next.

As she had fussed over the little boy, her son had raised his hand and drawn it across his throat in full view of the toddler. Zachary didn't say a word, but began to shake. 'He's in shock!' Linda cried, hitching him higher on her hip and starting to run back to the house. She had less than ten minutes to soothe him before the earl expected him ready for his trip.

Dominic stayed at the lake as his mother scurried back to the house. He spotted a fat frog making a racket in the mud. It sat proudly taunting him, and he waded across to the shore where it guarded its patch. Quick as a flash, the seven-year-old grabbed a rock and brought it crashing down on top of the amphibian, splattering its guts and severing its head. He glanced up at the big house and sniffed as the small ripples of a wave caused by the morning steamer washed away the frog's entrails.

Chapter 24

Kate Umshaw drove to the drab building on the outskirts of Penrith where the cold case files had been moved five years ago. A statement had been released to the press and it was becoming near impossible to smoke outside Eden House. Usually, missing persons' cases saw the odd journo harassing the offices of the local mountain rescue, but the news of the reopening of the Freya Hamilton investigation had sent the media into a frenzy.

Already, details of Freya's drug abuse and promiscuous past had been reported, and the press were trying to do the same to the reputations of Hannah Lawson and Sophie Daker. The photos of the three girls had been published side by side, and a trickle of national correspondents had appeared, asking questions. It was a good time to get out of the office, despite the fact that it was a Saturday and normally Kate wouldn't be there in the first place. She'd left her girls home alone, squabbling over hair straighteners, and slammed the door behind her.

She parked in an empty spot on the street and stubbed out her cigarette. It would take her all afternoon to trawl through the paperwork that hadn't yet been transferred to the database. Cumbria certainly didn't see the volume of cold cases that other constabularies did, but it was a loose end that needed tying up, and no matter how insignificant the entries seemed upon first glance, she needed to make sure that their missing trio weren't masking a precedent they'd missed. It was a long shot, but if Freya Hamilton could slip through the radar of two constabularies, then there might be more. Everybody knew about the head that had been found by an amateur diver in Wast Water ten years ago: who knew what else there was. It was high time that the files were sorted out anyway.

A bored uniform sat at a desk and sipped from a dirty mug, no doubt pissed off to be working on Saturday morning, and no doubt hung-over, judging by his eyes. Kate nodded and introduced herself. Her ID was checked and she was given free rein to roam in the two box rooms containing the archives yet to be inputted on a twenty-first-century system powered by electricity rather than manpower alone. The task suited her. She took off her jacket and began with the nearest box, planning to work her way through until her watch said five o'clock. She'd packed a sandwich, and settled down to an afternoon of peace and quiet away from the office. The bucket she'd passed on the way in, crammed with cigarette butts, told her that she could pop out for a quick break any time she pleased. She felt as though she had been given a day's leave.

The severed head case from Wast Water had its own box, and she flicked through it slowly. The identity of the man – Asian descent, in his late forties, rest of body never found – had never been established. *Machinery Accident* was written in red across the top of the case file, and Kate wondered if the senior investigating officer had been satisfied with the outcome. Everybody had heard of the case and there were plenty of quarries and mines around the place where a labourer could get into bother. The inquiry was ten years old, and every year, the DNA profile was inputted into the updated pool of results in London, with no joy.

It didn't fit her MO, but that wasn't the point: she'd learned over the years that only methodical and deliberate searching ruled anything, trivial or not, out of a case. She glanced at the grisly remains in the glossy photographs and thought about the head resting in a freezer somewhere in a Carlisle lab. She hoped that one day, a family somewhere would get the answers they craved.

On her fifth box, she stopped and rubbed her neck. She was quickly making her way through her flask of coffee, and thought about asking the uniform at the front desk if there was a kitchen where she could fill it up. She put the box back on the shelf and looked around: there was more here than she'd thought. She'd narrowed it down somewhat – or Kelly had – to females of a certain age, possible origins outside the Lakes National Park, and inside a five-year window working back from present day. As she stretched, she scanned the file names and reached into her handbag for her pack of Marlboro Gold. A label caught her attention: it read in bold, on the front of a box file, *Cold: Bones – Hartsop*.

Hartsop was a tiny hamlet next door to Brothers Water on the way to Kirkstone Pass. Kate stopped looking for her lighter. She rarely saw the tag 'bones' on anything. It was extraordinary, and so piqued her interest.

She pulled the box down and opened it.

It was a sparse enough file, only a few pages thick. The victim's name was Abi Clarence, and she'd last been seen five years earlier, at Edinburgh Waverley train station, reportedly on her way to start a job at the upmarket Peak's Bay Hotel on the southern shore of Ullswater. Kate scanned the information and found a statement given by a Mr Roger Morden: the man who'd found the remains in a glade near Hartsop three years ago.

Mr Morden had been out with his wife. It was a wet, miserable day and they'd walked the perimeter of Brothers Water, deciding to eat a picnic by a pretty bridge near Pasture Beck that they'd read about in a Wainwright guide. Roger Morden was clearly a talker. He detailed in the transcript how soggy their sandwiches had become in the downpour, and how sodden their socks had got on the flooded path round Brothers Water. All was redeemed, though, when they sheltered under a glade to dry off. That was until Roger had taken a closer look at some debris under the trees.

Roger Morden coached junior football and, as a result, had trained and taken an interest in anatomy and physiology when he was studying first aid. It was this that made him take a more scrupulous look at what he'd spotted. If he hadn't, then the remains of Abi Clarence might have lain there for years to come, undiscovered still. Mr Morden's keen eye had identified part of an iliac crest as well as a sacrum, and it was lucky he knew the difference between the skeleton of an animal and that of a human being. The report detailed the painstaking description that he had given on the differences between the two, and how he'd known he'd found something more sinister than simply a few scattered bones from a roadkill or a hunt.

To the horror of his wife, he'd handled the bones and held them up to gauge the width and breadth of the sacrum in particular. His wife had scolded him but couldn't stop him delving further and popping the items in a bag to take to the nearest police station. It turned out to be Keswick. A sceptical police officer had filed a report and sent the bones off for analysis. When it came back that they were indeed human, Roger Morden had been thoroughly investigated as a person of interest. The star witness was exonerated fairly quickly, though, and proved to be a stellar help to the investigation. But it wasn't Roger Morden's tome of a statement that made Kate Umshaw reach for her chair and discard the cigarette she'd intended to smoke.

It was the photograph of Abi Clarence. She'd been identified from DNA extracted from the sacrum and matched with a hit from a drug rehabilitation programme in Edinburgh: the girl was an addict. The image had clearly been taken before her preferred mind-altering substances took hold, because she beamed into the camera, a mere seventeen years old, with fresh skin and bright eyes. Kate searched the file and found another photo, which was dated two months before the last sighting on CCTV in Edinburgh: in this one, her eyes had sunk and her cheeks had grown gaunt, clear signs of the grip of addiction. Kate wondered how on earth the girl had managed to land a job at the Peak's Bay. Like Freya Hamilton.

She read on. Without evidence of cause of death, the coroner had ruled it inconclusive, and so the case hung suspended between accidental drug overdose, death by misadventure and natural causes, any one of which could have resulted in the girl's decomposition under a bush. Homicide wasn't suspected.

Besides, Abi Clarence had never even been reported missing.

Chapter 25

'If you don't want to meet the guys, then what about a training run with me?' Johnny was trying his hardest to distract Kelly. It was pool night, but Kelly couldn't be bothered. In the whole time she'd been back in Cumbria, she'd missed only a handful of Saturday nights with her old school pals, Andy and Karl. Three had quickly become four when she'd introduced Johnny. But tonight she couldn't be moved.

It had been a long time since she'd forced her team to work at the weekend, so Johnny knew that her cases must be weighing heavily. Two missing girls was enough to lose sleep over; he should know, he'd searched for plenty of young walkers in the fells. The difference was that for the most part, the latter showed up alive and well. These girls had been missing for almost a week, and now Kelly was telling him that there might be more.

He massaged her back. She sat between his legs with her head down, mumbling about the idiots who lived at Wasdale Hall. He'd never heard of the place, but then an outsider wouldn't have. Johnny had only lived in Pooley Bridge for five years, after selling up in Salisbury following the divorce from Carrie. Ancient gossip passed him by, and he kept himself to himself. That was why he'd chosen the Lake District: anonymity suited him.

Kelly groaned. Johnny had found a stubborn knot near her scapula and pressed his knuckle into it. She winced but didn't stop him.

'What'll relax you more? A pint or a run?' he asked. 'I know you're knackered, but that's an excuse to do nothing. I can tell that you want to sit here all night and read about work, but I'm not going to let you.'

Her notes were strewn all over the floor of the lounge, and they would probably stay like that for the coming weeks. He'd seen it before. They'd be like an extra piece of furniture. He'd once tidied her files from the exact spots where she'd left them, and she'd gone ballistic. He hadn't made the same mistake again.

She tutted. 'I want to sulk, and drink wine,' she said.

Johnny laughed. 'Right, I get it. We can do that later. Come on, come for a run with me. It's amazing out there, and it'll clear your head, you know it will.' He stopped rubbing and she lifted her head, turning round to look at him. 'Tell me what to read – I'll read anything,' he said. 'We can go over it when we come in.' He wasn't giving up. He knew he was right.

She looked through to the patio doors, where late-afternoon sunlight filled the small terrace, and sighed. He'd won.

Kelly got up and went into her bedroom. Ten minutes later, she'd pulled on her running kit and tied her hair back. Johnny knew that apart from exercise and alcohol, until recently she had done little else to relax. Only a swim in a cold lake, or a climb to the peak of a fell – along with the bottom of a glass – took away the incessant need to chew over facts and check her laptop. Nowadays, an evening with him, spent walking, talking or next to him in bed, also did the trick. She texted Andy and Karl, telling them of the change of plan.

She'd introduced Johnny to her two old school pals four months ago. Andy had been warm and welcoming, keen to get to know the man who was taking up so much of Kelly Porter's time, but Karl had been less so. It was obvious that he still hoped Kelly would fall for him one of these days. Johnny found the game amusing, and watched Karl with interest when he tried to impress her with a new joke or his physical prowess.

They drove to Buckholme Wood and parked next to the tiny River Lowther that ran through it. It was on the very edge of the National Park, and a hidden gem. Johnny was in training for the Lakeland 100, which he'd vowed to do before his fiftieth birthday. The event was unique because it didn't go over the famous peaks, instead meandering through stunning valleys, challenging bridleways and some of the most beautiful areas within the park. Johnny had done most of the Wainwrights. He wanted something different, and coming in at a cool hundred miles, with no breaks, the Lakeland 100 was a mammoth task.

Buckholme Wood was a perfect training ground. They ran through forest and across tracks, and it felt as though they were in the middle of nowhere. They didn't see another soul. For the most part, they remained silent. Johnny knew that Kelly would speak when she was ready.

He had never had a girlfriend he could run with. Carrie had never shown any interest, and no one else could keep up with his pace. He always ran on his own, or with men. Kelly was different. She not only kept up, she also didn't mind getting dirty, and they jumped over becks and bogs, never slowing much at all. They'd decided to go for a fairly steady ten miles, and they were halfway in when she began.

'We told the families of the two girls that we think they've met with foul play,' she said. It was a big deal and wasn't lost on Johnny. He'd never notified a family of a loved one's death before, but he'd been to plenty of funerals. Mud splashed up their legs, and their breath billowed out in front of them like smoke; it was soothing, and with every step, Johnny could tell that Kelly felt a little less stressed.

'What made you come to that point?' he asked. He'd lived through serious investigations with Kelly before, and he knew how she worked. He also knew that the more she talked, the more she wound down.

'Injured walkers don't normally disappear, especially when there's more than one of them, and they don't leave mobile phones and half-filled hip flasks behind.'

'Injured?'

'There was blood on a bag belonging to one of the girls, and minute traces where it was found. No emergency call was logged. It's been almost a week with no bank transactions.' Kelly listed her reasons as she jumped over some boulders.

'Have you got any good leads yet?' Johnny asked. She was opening up to him and he could see that her shoulders had given up some of their tension and her arms were moving more freely.

'My team are working their arses off, but it's early days. We've got a few leads but they're not major.'

'What about the other missing girl?'

'Tenuous, but I'm not happy about it. Something stinks. I asked Rob to look into the background of the campsite manager where the two girls were staying, and he found out that the man was working at the Peak's Bay at the same time as Freya Hamilton. He's an oily character. I don't trust him.'

'Enough for an arrest?'

'Don't be silly,' Kelly said cynically. 'If I arrested everyone I didn't trust, London would be a pleasantly quiet place to live.'

'But then you wouldn't be here,' Johnny said.

'Sometimes I think that still might be a good thing.'

'Why?' She'd taken him by surprise.

Kelly stopped and bent over, taking in air. They'd come to a branch in the track and she would let Johnny decide which way to take: over the top to make their lungs scream, or around the long way for stamina. He chose the former.

'I bumped into an old friend of mine the other day and she basically called me a stuck-up cow. She said I'd gone away because I thought I was better than everyone else, as if I looked down on my old mates.'

'What a bitch.'

'I know, but…'

'She's got under your skin?'

'Yes.' The incline made talking difficult. Kelly bent slightly as Johnny held a branch up over her head. She ran beneath it and he ducked under too, letting it fall behind him. He loved watching her run: her body twisting from side to side as her legs powered her forward, her auburn hair flicking from side to side in its ponytail. Johnny stayed behind her and she looked over her shoulder.

'Have I lost you?' she shouted.

'No, I'm just enjoying the view,' he called back. She laughed, basking in the compliment.

Johnny knew that Kelly sometimes felt as though everyone around her – her family especially – was quick to find fault, and it was an indulgent pleasure to treat her the way he did, never criticising anything about her: not her dress sense, her choice in music, or the amount she ate.

'You wouldn't run here alone, would you, Kelly?' he asked.

'I haven't thought about it,' she said. The sky was getting dark, and she visibly shivered. 'I can look after myself.'

'I know you can, that's not my point.'

'I don't like doing these runs on my own.'

'Good,' he said.

They paused at the top of the hill and jogged on the spot to keep warm.

'So, which of the idiots at Wasdale Hall knocked off the earl, then?' Johnny asked, changing the subject back to her job. He could tell from her face that her old school pal had touched a nerve and she needed distraction.

'There's always assisted suicide. He could have paid someone to do it,' she said.

'Why would he have done that?'

'Why would a ninety-five-year-old go all the way to Switzerland when he could get a loyal servant to do it in his study? Let's go, it's nearly dark,' she said.

They ran back the way they'd come, and by the time they reached the car, it was fully dark. They wiped off with towels, and pulled on jumpers.

'Are you still determined to work tonight?' Johnny asked.

'Yes, but I can do it in front of the fire with a glass of wine.'

'Can I borrow your shower?' He had begun leaving clothes and toiletries at Kelly's a few weeks ago. It wasn't something they'd made a fuss about. She left stuff at his place too.

She smiled. She had a big shower.

Chapter 26

Two hours later, as Kelly dozed on Johnny's chest in front of some banal reality TV programme, her mobile rang: it was her brother-in-law.

'Matt,' she said quietly.

'Kelly, I'm sorry. I don't know who else to call,' he said. Kelly thought this an ironic statement, given that it was she who was held to be the source of her sister's breakdown. She gritted her teeth. He always said the same thing. Poor bloke, it wasn't his fault. Must be pretty bad if he was calling this late on a Saturday.

'Matt, Nikki has made it clear she doesn't want me involved,' she said as she swung her legs off the sofa and took a swig of wine. Johnny carried on watching TV, but she knew he was keeping one ear on the conversation, which could at any point go royally tits-up.

'I know, Kelly, but that's bullshit. It's pride. She hasn't got the balls to say she needs somebody, not even me.' Kelly was tempted to say that her sister needed no one, and even if she did, Kelly wasn't the person to ask. Past insults flared up in her mind, and she was close to giving in to her damaged pride.

'What do you want me to do?' she asked. She looked at Johnny and mouthed, *Sorry*.

'She won't get out of bed again. It was the same last week.'

'What did the doc say?'

'He's upped her drugs,' Matt said forlornly.

That'll help, thought Kelly: a patient presents with mental health issues, so the doctor prescribes drugs; the drugs don't work, so he prescribes stronger ones. If only therapy came in a pill, there'd be no depression in the UK. Everybody loved pills: magic pills to help evade the real problem. What Nikki needed was trauma therapy, but they'd applied, and the waiting list was up to a year.

'Last time I spoke to her, she told me she didn't need to talk to anyone, and to mind my own business. There's only so many times I can offer to help, Matt, before I get sick and tired of being told to fuck off.'

'I know. I live it every day,' he said.

Kelly rubbed her eyes. Her tank was empty. She looked at Johnny again and put her hand over the phone.

'Will you come?' she asked him quietly. He nodded.

'I can be there in about an hour, Matt.'

'Thank you.'

She heard a mixture of relief and torment in his voice, and couldn't imagine how he was holding everything together. At least the girls were probably in bed by now; it was gone ten o'clock. She hung up.

Johnny allowed her to vent.

'She blames me, she fucking hates me, and yet I'm the one they all fucking call.'

'She's suffering from post-traumatic stress,' he reminded her gently. 'She went through a terrifying ordeal.'

'She wasn't harmed, Johnny. I know she was scared, but she was taken to get at me.'

'I know, but just because you're not scared of the bogeyman doesn't mean that other people aren't.' His tone was strong, and Kelly prickled.

'You don't know my sister.'

'I know PTSD.'

'Don't take her side.'

'I'm not. All I'm saying is that it affects everyone differently, and I don't think she's faking it.'

'I didn't say she was faking it, just that she needs to snap out of it.'

'You can't snap out of PTSD.'

—

They arrived, and Kelly parked outside the terrace. Matt opened the door and looked at Johnny.

'Matt, this is Johnny. I asked him to come. He's got experience of this sort of thing.' She looked at Johnny and smiled breezily. He ignored the jibe and held out his hand, which Matt took.

'I'm sorry, Kelly, I couldn't call Wendy again.' He moved back and they entered the house.

The place was a mess, as usual. Piles of clothes littered every surface, dirty crockery and cutlery lay forgotten on tables and sofas, an old bike blocked the hallway. Kelly tripped over a doll and bent to pick it up; it belonged to Donna – the middle girl. Kelly had bought it for her. The place smelled unloved and neglected. It was also very dark. She went to a window and opened it, allowing fresh air to rush in; the atmosphere was instantly clearer. She also found a switch and flooded the place with light. Matt shaded his eyes. He looked like shit.

'I didn't know who else to call,' he said again, and Kelly softened.

'It's all right, Matt. I'm glad you called me. How did it get so bad?' She'd only been there less than a week ago. She was dismayed, and angry. She willed herself to calm down. 'Look, it'll take us half an hour to get things straight.'

Matt began to say something, but Kelly interrupted him.

'Matt, there's no point in standing on ceremony. That's why I'm here, right? Not to talk to my sister.'

Matt bent his head. 'She's not seeing anyone.'

'No one at all?' Johnny asked.

'Just the doctor.'

'I'll go and talk to her,' Johnny said. Kelly and Matt stared at him, their mouths open. Finally Matt spoke.

'She doesn't know you.'

'Well introduce me, then.'

Kelly watched them as they headed for the stairs. When Matt came back, she expected Johnny to be with him, having been kicked out by Nikki. He wasn't. Matt shrugged.

Kelly looked around. She went into the kitchen and shook her head. It might take them longer than half an hour. She cleared the sink and ran some hot water, to which she added bleach and soap. It was therapeutic in a way, and took her mind off her cases. She rolled up her sleeves, found black bin liners and went around tipping anything into a bag that wasn't pinned down or semi-clean. It didn't leave much. She worked silently, and soon the pile of dishes seemed to be getting smaller. She glanced up from time to time at the ceiling above her head, and wondered what the hell Johnny was saying to her sister. He was taking a long time. She heard nothing.

When she next looked at her watch, it was almost midnight.

She checked in the fridge for wine. It was disgusting. She ran some more hot water and began emptying it so she could clean it, discarding anything mouldy or out of date.

'Aunt Kelly? What's wrong with my mum?'

Kelly jumped and spun around to face Charlie, standing in the kitchen doorway.

'You should be in bed.'

'Bullshit, I'm fifteen, not three,' the girl said. She had a point.

'Your mum's… a bit poorly,' Kelly said lamely, and instantly regretted it.

'Who's in her room? Is it another doctor?'

'Kind of, he's a specialist.'

'In what?'

'Post-traumatic stress disorder.'

'Is she an alcoholic?'

'Why do you ask that?'

'I found a vodka bottle in the washing basket, and she stinks of it and talks shit.'

'She needs time, Charlie. The… accident left her really tired and unwell, and she needs to rest,' Kelly said.

'Was it when she went missing?' Charlie asked.

'Yes, that's it. But she'll get through it, I promise.' Kelly closed her eyes and silently kicked herself for promising anything when she had no idea what the coming months would bring. Promises couldn't always be kept.

Johnny startled them both when he walked into the kitchen.

'Sorry, Charlie. This is Johnny, he's my really good friend, and he went to chat with your mum.'

'Friend with benefits?' Charlie asked, smirking.

'Charlie!' Kelly was indignant, but Johnny laughed.

It was only later, once they'd cajoled Charlie back to bed, and Matt had passed out on the sofa, that Johnny opened up about his conversation with Nikki. It was only then that he also explained that before he'd left the army, he'd trained as a counsellor, gaining a degree in psychology.

His speciality was PTSD.

Chapter 27

Sophie drifted from sleep to waking, and back again. Parts of her body felt numb. She'd gone beyond hunger and the thirst was crucifying. She dreamt of all types of drinks: Coke, Fanta, juice, and plain old water. Anything. She'd drink anything. She'd lost count of the days and nights and only counted the number of times he visited her. She'd compiled a list of characteristics in her head, not because she thought she might get out of here alive, but because it gave her mind something to do other than panic; it kept her sane.

The strength was slowly draining from her body and the last time she'd taken her own pulse, it was down to fifty-seven beats per minute. Hannah had taught her how to do it. She didn't know when, but at some point – when it was dark – she'd heard a noise and strained her head towards it. It was a voice other than his. The sound had been a whimper, and Sophie was sure that it came from a female. She'd read about hellholes just like this in Belgium, or was it Germany? Where girls like her were chained up and abused for months, if not years, before succumbing to the lack of sustenance.

Why?

Psychos. She studied them.

She'd chosen psychology because it fascinated her. She wanted to become a criminal psychologist specialising in body language. She knew weirdos at university; they shuffled around the corridors in their goth gear, never looking you in the eye, off to their next screening of *The Evil Dead* or *Zombie Dawn*. Or there were the ones who dressed smartly, but asked freaky questions in lectures about the world's most prolific killers. Fetishes, fantasies, mystery voices and imaginary spectres: they were all the same, purely the product of a screwed-up mind, fucked in childhood, playing out the roles they'd been taught.

But *he* was different. He looked... normal.

She'd once had a screen saver on her phone that read: *Normal is not something to aspire to, it's something to escape from*. She'd thought herself intelligent and witty. But now she didn't feel either of those things; she felt a fool. Hiding in plain sight was a concept she'd studied time and time again, but now she'd seen it first-hand. He was clean, articulate, ordered and, dare she say, handsome. It made her feel sick. She would have thrown up had she anything in her tummy, but it was empty. This was a quandary. He was diminishing her physical attributes, making her weak, ill and animalistic, yet he kept himself in fairly good shape. He mumbled to himself, and talked of the mountains, current affairs and pop songs. Her great fear was that despite listening intently to his voice, she couldn't pinpoint one thing that made him psychotic apart from what he did to her.

It didn't necessarily hurt, and he washed her and brushed her hair afterwards, but perhaps that was the point: his fetish was pedestrian; he craved power not to maim, but to direct. He had created a world where he controlled everything, and as long as he kept her, he was in charge of the show. She'd thought that she recognised him, perhaps from the campsite, but she couldn't place him.

Staying alive had become a pastime intertwined with concentration and order. When she'd heard the woman whining – and she was convinced now that it wasn't Hannah – she'd also heard him angry. The woman was playing a different game to hers: she was resisting, reasoning, appealing, and ultimately fucking up his script. She wouldn't last.

She'd seen his anger, and it had appeared suddenly and sadistically when she too had tried to reason, to ask him why. It was as if she'd spoken a foreign language. He'd looked at her as if she were mad, as if he could do whatever he wanted. Which he could. But it didn't seem to occur to him that he was doing anything wrong. He wanted something, he took it, and that was all.

'You don't have to do this. If you let us go, I won't tell, I promise.' She'd tried bargaining. 'You'll get caught eventually. Lots of people know we were coming up here.' Or: 'Think if you had a sister, how would you feel?' But none of it worked; her pathetic mumblings were only rewarded with violence. That was when he ticked the psychopath box: lack of empathy, culpability or any sense of right and wrong. She remembered all the long, hot, airless lectures that she'd sat in, daydreaming about being on a beach in Ibiza, or in a beer garden by the Lancaster Canal, and wished that she'd paid more attention, because she had a prime specimen right here before her. Her lecturers would never believe her.

Now she heard another noise, and sat upright, though the dizziness forced her to lie back down straight away. It was a banging and scraping noise, and she tried to figure out where it came from and what had made it. There was another female voice, but again it wasn't Hannah's.

A short cry pierced the space between the walls and then stopped. Sophie held her breath. There was another thud and a slammed door. She strained her ears, longing to hear Hannah's voice, but nothing else came. She slumped against the bed and thought about asking him for some food, or a sugary drink: she'd been well behaved and hadn't caused a fuss.

She thought about the night on Loadpot Hill again, as she did a thousand times a day. It was totally her fault that they were in this mess. It had been her stupid idea to go trekking in the middle of the night. It was she who had forgotten to grab Hannah's bag when she was injured, only to remember much later that their only phone was in that bag and could have raised an alarm. It was her idea to go with him to get Hannah's head looked at. It was she who had convinced Hannah that he was simply a concerned individual out on the fells, just a walker who couldn't possibly cause them harm.

She'd told Hannah they'd be fine. They'd let their guard down: Hannah because she was injured, and Sophie because she was too fucking trusting – the person who studied psychos. They'd been duped because they were cold and high in spirits from their dawn vigil. They'd never imagined it would lead to this.

The place fell silent once more and Sophie let her imagination choose her daydream. This time, she was a fish. She swam around a reef, mesmerised by all the colours; they were bright, vibrant and real. The water above her was perfect azure and she was warm. And she had a full tummy.

She closed her eyes.

Her body ached, but the vision took her away from the physical pain and into a parallel world where she felt safe. She curled her knees up to her chest and lay in a tight ball on the bed. She pulled Hannah's sweater tightly around her and wondered if she'd get water today. It could be day or night, she had no idea. And she no longer cared.

She was back on the reef, and she floated into a deep sleep, jerking from time to time as her world disappeared and reappeared. In her semi-conscious fluid state, she sensed movement around her in the deep water, and the colours began to darken. She spun around, gasping for air, coming face to face with a giant shadow that blackened the whole reef. She fell deeper into her slumber, and gradually the inky black enveloped more and more of her, until finally there was nothing left.

Chapter 28

The Peak's Bay Hotel was a vision of luxury and style, tended immaculately and standing pristine in the Ullswater sunshine. The fact that Freya Hamilton had worked there, and Abi Clarence had been hired, even though she'd never started, pushed it up their priority list of lines of enquiry. Kelly parked the Audi and Rob looked around, impressed. It was all pillars and whitewash, like something from a colonial era, buffered by decades of history from the outside world.

'Christ, you need some money to stay here, guv.'

'Sure do. I can barely afford to bring my mother for dinner – it's a surprise, she doesn't know yet.'

'Nice, I need to get myself promoted.'

Kelly smiled. They slammed the doors of the car and walked together into the foyer. It was airy and spacious, framed by a huge glass lantern. Sunlight spilled in, illuminating the few couples lounging on the sofas reading the papers, or taking coffee and afternoon tea.

Rob had called ahead and arranged to meet the day manager, Harold. He was in his mid fifties and looked every inch the loyal and spruce front-of-house man. His suit was cut and pressed beautifully, and his shirt gave the impression that ten ladies of the establishment had starched it for hours, causing aching backs and damp brows. He wore a gold signet ring and flashed white teeth when he smiled. He was short, but made up for it with copious hand gestures as he ushered them into an empty conference room where they could talk discreetly.

'I believe you were after some old employment records, yes?' He spoke as if he were arranging a piece of musical theatre, complete with tetchy thespian queens eager for the starring role. His hands flapped and he didn't sit down.

'We're enquiring after three employees: Freya Hamilton, who worked here last year, Abi Clarence, who was due to start working here in June 2013, and Jack Sentry, who—'

Harold interrupted. 'Sentry?'

'Yes,' Rob said. Kelly watched Harold with interest.

'Are you familiar with the name?' she asked.

'Of course. He was let go under unfortunate circumstances. We thought him a model employee at first, but it was discovered that he was…' Harold coughed and covered his mouth, as if about to share an enormous secret. 'He was earning money on the side.' He looked at the two officers, expecting them to understand exactly what he was telling them. They didn't. He rolled his eyes.

'He was entertaining ladies.' His eyebrows arched, and he winked. Kelly and Rob remained stony-faced. Harold tutted. 'In their rooms.' He lingered on the word 'rooms' and his intonation made it quite clear that the ladies in question were willing to pay for the sexual services of Mr Jack Sentry. It made him promiscuous and rather entrepreneurial, thought Kelly, but that was all. If anything, it confirmed that Jack Sentry was a memorable character.

'When was he let go?' she asked.

'I should think around Christmas time. I don't know where he went; I couldn't tell you that, I'm afraid.'

'How long was he in employment here?'

'Let me see, I've been here for eighteen years, and he came along… yes, it was the year of the London Olympics – so 2012, correct?'

Kelly and Rob nodded. It was a fair old stint, and it put Sentry here in the same time frame as both Freya and Abi. Rob produced the photographs of the two girls. Harold recognised both of them.

'*She* never started here; utterly unreliable, I told them, and I was right.' He was pointing at Abi.

'But she was offered a job?'

'Yes, in fact it was Jack who interviewed her.'

'So he was fairly senior then?'

'He was a conference and banqueting manager, minor role really,' said Harold, straightening his tie.

'And this one?'

Harold looked at the photo of Freya. 'Hmm, nice girl. She didn't last long, though. At the time, the gossip was that she was dealing in illegal substances, if you know what I mean?' He held a fastidious finger to one of his nostrils and snorted.

'What's your staff turnover like?' Kelly asked.

'Well, it's the hotel industry; we try and retain them, but there's no pride in it any more. These girls come and go.'

'Thank you for your time, Harold. Perhaps we could take a look at their employment files, if you keep records?'

'Of course, though we might not have anything on the girl who didn't officially start.'

'We understand,' Kelly said.

As they left, with copies of Freya Hamilton and Jack Sentry's employment files, Kelly and Rob discussed Abi Clarence.

'Didn't her file say that she'd worked in the Lakes the previous summer?'

'Yes, her parents used to visit regularly; she knew the area fairly well.'

'She must have stayed somewhere when she came for interview. I wonder what Mr Sentry has to say about it.'

The Howtown campsite was on their way back to Penrith. As they pulled in through the entrance, Kelly considered Sentry's fall from grace: going from a manager in one of the Lakes' most prestigious hotels, to a campsite.

The place was pretty deserted. A few tents were erected, but there was no evidence of the campfire smells that indicated holiday homeliness: stoves brewing tea, bacon sizzling, or smoke billowing across with the wind. The police tape had gone, and Hannah and Sophie's tent had been removed in its entirety as police evidence.

They walked to the office and knocked before going inside. Jack Sentry sat at a desk with his head in his hands, studying paperwork. It was a sorry sight. Rob did the talking this time.

'Business slow?'

Sentry cracked a half smile, recognising the officers. He closed a ledger and sat back in his chair.

'Good afternoon, Mr Sentry,' Rob said. It was an unannounced visit, but that was Kelly's intention; it was always more productive when a person of interest was caught unaware, and Sentry had been pushed to the top of their pile since they'd delved into his past. Kelly had learned that he had also applied for a job with mountain rescue, and she'd asked Johnny to ask around to see if anyone remembered him; they did, and reported him as an arrogant man who cracked jokes about lone women in distress on the fells. The decision not to employ him, even on a voluntary basis, had been unanimous.

Kelly leaned against a filing cabinet and watched. Rob was her bouncer. He was six foot four, and solid muscle. He didn't throw his weight around, but he gave the impression that he could if he wanted to, and that was all Kelly needed. She was glad that she'd tasked him with the foot search, and that he'd met Sentry before.

Sentry stood up, but stumbled over a chair leg and tripped, gathering his footing just short of Rob.

'Ah,' he said, straightening. 'Sorry about that. You caught me... off guard.'

'We've got a few things that we need to clear up. We could do it at the station, but perhaps you might like to answer a few questions before that's necessary,' Rob said.

Sentry shifted and looked from one officer to the other. 'Of course, anything you need. What's this about?'

'Sit down,' Rob said.

He did so, slowly. The officers remained standing. 'Am I in some kind of trouble? You look... very serious.'

'We were hoping that you could help us decide that. We've just paid a visit to the Peak's Bay Hotel and had a chat with Harold, the front-of-house manager.'

Sentry rolled his eyes. 'God, that old pervert. I can imagine what he told you.'

'We're interested in the period of your employment there. Do you recognise either of these two girls?' Rob handed him the photographs of Freya Hamilton and Abi Clarence. Sentry took them and looked at both intently. Kelly saw flashes of discomfort pass over his brow, and his eyes darted from one to the other.

'I think one of them worked at the hotel for a time. The turnover is unusually high in the hotel industry, you know; they come and go.'

'Indeed. We need your absolute concentration, it's important.'

'This one, I think, yes. I seem to recognise her face, but not this one.' The affirmative was for Freya.

'Freya Hamilton?'

'Ah, yes, that's her name.'

'What was your relationship with her?'

'No relationship. I barely remember her.'

'Why did you leave the Peak's Bay?' Rob asked.

'It was time to move on. I'd been there too long.'

'That's not what your file says. In fact, it states quite clearly that you accepted money from certain female clients for extra services not advertised by the establishment.'

'Now I can't help it if some of those lonely ladies gave me generous tips. The rest of them were jealous. I should have declared it, for sure, but it was innocent enough at the time.'

'So you didn't earn the money; it was purely tips?'

'Absolutely.'

'But your employment file states, and I quote, "unsuitable for the hotel industry at this level, due to indiscretions of a sexual and amorous nature not in keeping with the standards upheld by this establishment".'

Sentry turned red, but Kelly assumed it was more out of anger than embarrassment. Anger at having been caught out. He obviously hadn't expected this level of digging. Still, it proved nothing.

'When was the last time you saw Freya Hamilton?' Rob asked.

Sentry swallowed. 'I haven't seen her for months,' he said.

Sentry's body was giving off the telltale signs of a liar, but they didn't yet know why. He pointed his foot towards the door, his arms were folded, his brow furrowed, and he blinked rapidly; all responses beyond his control, and all revealing.

'Jack...' Rob used the informal address, and sat down, equalising the height difference. Kelly didn't move. 'We've got a problem. These two girls are both missing; in fact one of them is dead.' He let the news sink in. Panic appeared in Sentry's eyes.

'Freya?' he asked.

Rob shook his head.

'No, Abi.'

Kelly watched his reaction carefully and thought that a trip to Penrith station might not be a bad idea; it was time they read him his rights.

'You worked with both of them,' Rob continued. 'Now we have two more missing girls – both very attractive and young – and you were in a position of power over both of them, in that you managed their accommodation, similar to your position of dominance over Freya Hamilton and Abi Clarence. It doesn't look good, does it?'

Sentry stood up and went to the door. Rob watched him. Kelly decided it was time to set out what they had.

'Mr Sentry, we can take you in and conduct a formal interview, at which, as you probably know, you're entitled to have a lawyer present.'

'Am I charged with an offence?'

'No.'

'Are you arresting me?'

'No.'

'I've told you everything I know about all of these women; women I have absolutely nothing to do with.'

'You are categorically stating that you are not aware of where any of these women are now?'

'Yes.'

'Do you live alone?' Kelly asked.

'Yes. I live in the static home behind the site.'

'Can we say, for the record, that you willingly gave a DNA sample?'

It was a gamble. There was no evidence that Freya Hamilton was dead – she could have sunk her own bag in Ullswater – and there was no evidence that Abi had come to a grisly end other than by her own hand. There was also flimsy evidence about what had really happened to Sophie and Hannah, but the photos had rattled Sentry. He knew the girls and he was unwilling to elaborate, and that was always a red flag.

'What do you mean?' he said.

'It means I take a swab from inside your mouth. If you've got nothing to hide, then it shouldn't be a problem. You can see why we need to eliminate you from our enquiries.'

Sentry paused for a moment, looking between the detectives.

'Of course I consent, I've got nothing to hide,' he said.

Kelly removed a swab kit and some gloves from her bag. Rob watched carefully as Sentry opened his mouth and she took the sample.

'Thank you,' she said when she was done. 'I wouldn't go anywhere in a hurry if I were you.'

'I've done nothing wrong! These girls think it's funny to go around making false accusations. Men don't stand a chance. You always side with the woman!' It was quite an outburst.

'What makes you think anyone has made allegations?' Rob asked him.

'All right, I knew Freya well. We had a… thing.'

'A thing?'

'We hung out. It was nothing. I genuinely thought she'd just taken off, like they always do.' Sentry was sweating freely.

'And Abi?'

He paced up and down. 'It was years ago. She was only around for a few weeks and she never officially started. What happened to her?'

'We're not at liberty to disclose that information. Where did you hang out? At the hotel, or somewhere else?'

'I dunno. Sometimes there. Sometimes on the fells, you know?'

'I'm not sure I do,' Kelly said. 'Can you elaborate?'

'Outside.'

'Did you have a favourite place?' Kelly's mind was whirring. She was thinking of her helicopter ride with Johnny when they scoured the fells from above, looking for abandoned buildings – buildings that would be perfect for young lovers and more.

But it was too late. Jack Sentry had clammed up. If they needed to speak to him again, it was very clear that it would have to be under formal conditions, with a lawyer. They'd reached his limit.

'We'll see you again soon,' Kelly said. 'Don't go far.'

Chapter 29

Wendy Porter sat in an armchair and heard the key turning in the door. She smiled to herself: she was getting used to having Kelly around so much, but also enjoyed the fact that she'd moved out. Kelly was never a great cook. She wondered how Nikki was, as she hadn't heard from her lately. Kelly always avoided explaining exactly what it was that was wrong with her sister, and Wendy decided that if it was important, someone would tell her. Well, at least that was what she hoped. It was satisfying what one could achieve when one was dying. Her oncologist, Mr Yanni, was more than happy to suggest a psychologist who might be able to squeeze in a visit to her daughter.

-

Kelly went to her mother and kissed her cheek.

'Hi, Mum, how are you today?' She threw her coat over a chair and Wendy tutted. Kelly ignored her; the tut was habitual rather than circumstantial, and nothing Kelly did reduced or prevented it.

'Good! I'm not sore at all. I'm looking forward to our trip out. Can you tell me where we're going now?'

Kelly stopped fiddling with the TV controls and looked at her mother.

'I'm taking you to the Peak's Bay for dinner, Mum.'

The Peak's Bay Hotel was where they'd scattered her dad's ashes. The hotel didn't know this, of course; they'd go mad if they did, but Wendy had been adamant. It had been their favourite place for afternoon tea. They couldn't afford to stay there, or even to have dinner, but afternoon teas often came on special offers, and John Porter would wait until they were advertised to surprise Wendy.

'Tonight?'

'Yes.' Kelly was apprehensive after her visit there earlier today, and had thought about changing the reservation, but it had been booked for months. She wasn't keen on places that tried too hard, preferring little pubs in the fells that boasted nothing but delivered everything.

'Oh Kelly, you have surprised me.'

Her mother looked well, and without getting too optimistic, the new drug seemed to be working. She had more energy, and hadn't needed a blood transfusion for several months. Sometimes Kelly had to remind herself that her mother was gravely ill, because judging by her manner most of the time, no one would know. But at this stage she daren't hope for the best; they'd just take each step one at a time. She wondered when the first question about Nikki would make an appearance, and hoped that the surprise might dampen the interrogation.

Wendy got up out of her chair, and Kelly watched, astonished at the transformation. It was only when her mother turned to the light that Kelly noticed she'd applied her make-up beautifully. It touched her. Mum had probably been looking forward to this trip all day, not knowing where she was going.

Kelly helped her to the car, and Wendy looked up at the sky briefly.

'It's a lovely evening, Mum.'

She was spending her life in the car, but she didn't mind. It was normal. They drove out of Penrith, through Pooley Bridge, and Kelly wondered if Johnny would be waiting for her when she got home. They needed a holiday. They'd talked about it, but every time they seemed on the verge of booking something, some crisis – usually to do with her family – popped up and they postponed.

'How's Johnny?' her mother asked, as if reading her thoughts.

Kelly smiled.

'Come on, Kelly, you're not going to let another one go, are you?' Wendy was mischievous.

'Mum! For God's sake! I don't need a man to make me complete like…' Kelly stopped.

'Like Nikki,' Wendy finished for her. 'How is she?'

Kelly scolded herself. She'd scored an own goal, just like that, without even thinking.

'Erm, I think she's good, Mum,' she lied. She didn't want to burden her mother further, but also knew she was treading on shaky ground. Her mother could tell when she was hiding something. That was how she'd found out about Johnny. She'd said that Kelly looked different, and it must mean she had a man. Kelly had been ostensibly horrified but eager to tell her mother about him, and they'd met a few times.

'He's very dishy,' Wendy had said after their first meeting.

'What's dishy, Mum?' Kelly asked.

'You know, he's terribly handsome.'

Since then, Johnny had won her mother's heart every time they'd met. And now it appeared he was doing the same with her sister. Kelly didn't want to admit what everybody else could see as clearly as the lake in spring. Johnny was becoming part of her; part of them all, and she wasn't sure about it. The prospect of him playing happy families with her made her feel claustrophobic.

Michelle Hammond popped into her head again. Kelly felt unusually tense, and couldn't decide whether it was her mother, her sister or just bloody Cumbria, where everybody knew your business and finding some escape from it all was impossible. Maybe she didn't belong here after all.

Kelly drove and Wendy stared out of the window. Each knew the other's body cues without having to watch; they could tell by their voices. Kelly knew that her mother was aware of her holding onto the steering wheel tightly, sunglasses firmly over her eyes and jaw clenched, anxious to avoid conversation about her sister. She knew that her mother would have a faint smile at the corners of her mouth, her hands crossed on her lap, and that at any minute she'd brush her skirt for imaginary crumbs, desperate to talk about Nikki.

'I'm the last person she wants to see,' Kelly said finally. Wendy brushed her skirt.

'How do you know if you don't try?' she asked.

'I do try!' Kelly snapped and felt instantly selfish. 'Are you looking forward to dinner, Mum?' She wasn't ready to tell her mother that she'd spent three hours at Nikki's yesterday.

'Isn't it very expensive?' asked Wendy.

'I don't know, let's find out. It's my treat.'

They drove on in silence.

The Peak's Bay Hotel sat tucked away behind tall alpines, low junipers, ferns and rhododendrons, just as Kelly had left it that afternoon, though coming here for pleasure rather than work made it feel less stuffy. The gardens gave off the whiff of a natural approach: they embraced the fauna of the area, but behind the apparent relaxed efficiency, a team of gardeners ploughed away every day of the year to produce a haven of peace and tranquillity, with a touch of the luxurious. As soon as they entered the great gateway, Kelly and Wendy breathed easier. Birds twittered and hopped between branches, and swooped over the car as it slowed on the gravel. Kelly pushed thoughts of the missing girls out of her mind as much as she could.

The car park was full of Range Rovers, BMWs and Mercedes. Here, guests could pretend that they could still reach an untouched wilderness, despite their real lives being shackled to traffic, chaos, pollution and noise. Some came for one night only, all the way from London, just to breathe. Others came from further afield, from the USA and Europe, as they did every year, hiring the same suites for weeks at a time.

Kelly understood. Some nights in London – usually in summer – she'd thrown her bedroom window open to suck some air, only to be met with a sauna-like mix of petrol, pavement and piss. Disappointed, she'd closed it again and switched on a desk fan. This evening as they got out of the car, the air from the lake assaulted her, and it resembled pure wet rock, cooling and fresh. Wendy didn't notice, not having ever been without it.

The day they'd scattered Dad's ashes, they hadn't dressed so smartly. They'd posed as walkers, casually checking out the shoreline and grabbing a coffee. Non-residents could pop in any time for lunch, dinner or simply a drink, but only those wearing suitable attire could enter the dining room. That had suited them. The beach was private, and because they'd paid for coffee, they were left alone. They found the bench that Wendy and John used to love, overlooking the lake, and sat for a while, Wendy in the middle of her two daughters. After a while, she took the urn and disappeared behind a rhododendron bush. She was only gone for minutes; when she returned, she nodded and they left. The deed was done. Dad was at peace. Secretly.

'This is nice,' Wendy said now.

They had a table by a window overlooking the lake. Kelly was itching to check her phone, but she'd have to wait until she went to the toilet; now was not the time. A steamer chugged slowly on the lake, heading west to the Howtown jetty. It'd be the last of the day; it was only when the summer season kicked in that they ran until sundown. She wondered if Hannah and Sophie had used the steamers, and realised that if they'd caught one to Glenridding from Howtown, they could have gone much further afield. But Garth had told her they'd left at night, way after the steamers stopped. The two girls were striking, and there was a good chance that the amorous young lads who came and went, working the steamers from now until September, might remember them.

Wendy coughed.

'Sorry, Mum, I'm...' Kelly started to say.

'Thinking about a case,' Wendy finished for her. Kelly smiled.

'You've got me there, sorry.'

'I was wondering if you'd managed to contact any of your old friends,' Wendy said. It was a strange thing to say, though not entirely unexpected. Apart from her Saturday pool nights with Andy and Karl, she hadn't really bothered to look up old acquaintances. Partly through fear of rejection – she was the one who'd left – and partly through nonchalance. She'd pushed her run-in with Michelle Hammond to the back of her mind.

'I think they're all busy, Mum,' Kelly said weakly. It was true. She'd bumped into a few old school chums casually, and everybody knew she was back, but after the obligatory 'Good to see you!', 'You look so well!', 'How was London?', 'You have how many children?' it became tedious. She wasn't about to tell her mother what Michelle had said.

She was aware that Wendy thought her aloof, but that had been years ago. She'd been mortified when her mother set up play dates for her with her friends' kids. All had ended in disaster. Kelly preferred listening to music, cycling to the lake; and later, smoking cigarettes and playing pool, none of which was on her mother's agenda. Now she felt the same disapproval. Well, at least she had a boyfriend. Kind of.

Her mind turned to Johnny, and she softened. She'd been unkind. He'd done nothing wrong in trying to help Nikki. Not only that: her sister had agreed to see him again. He kept surprising her and she liked that.

'Mum, I'm happy as I am. I don't need loads of friends. You know that. Gaggles of girls is Nikki's thing.'

'And look, they're all there for her, right when she needs them,' Wendy said. Kelly had no idea where her mother got her information from. She flicked her ponytail absent-mindedly.

'And that's great, Mum. I'm pleased for her. I really am.' Wendy clearly had no idea that Nikki's so-called friends had one by one slowly abandoned her.

'But what would you do if…' Wendy began.

'If what, Mum? If I was hurt or in trouble? I'd cope,' Kelly said.

The menus arrived. Wendy's eyes were drawn straight to the prices. A starter of scallops and caviar with pea and mint puree and cauliflower spray came in at twenty-four pounds.

'Mum, have what you want. It's a treat. We won't get to do this often. I was given a pay rise recently and this is my celebration,' Kelly lied. 'You love crab, don't you? Look, there's a crab ravioli.' She could see Wendy noting that the crab ravioli in question, floating on a lake of lobster bisque, came in at thirty-two pounds as a main course. She took the menu off her mother.

'I'll order,' she said.

The waiter returned and Kelly gave their order. A sommelier came to the table and enthused about a Sancerre. Kelly asked to try it, and Wendy simply nodded. She'd clearly seen the eye-watering price.

'You've got to admit it's good, Mum.'

'How do you know so much about it, Kelly?'

'London is full of restaurants like this, though they're not so much up their own arses. Besides, I have nothing else to spend my money on – you know, like kids.' She'd expected to get some kind of maternal pull plaguing her by thirty, as had happened to her friends, but she never had. Now, at thirty-eight, she doubted she ever would.

Their starters arrived. Kelly had ordered the scallops for her mother and lamb croquettes for herself.

'Isn't that Wasdale Hall?' Wendy asked. Kelly followed her mother's gaze across the lake. She wondered what Zachary would be dining on tonight. She couldn't imagine him in a place like this, but she'd also wager that he'd have no problem holding his own.

'Yes, it is,' she said. 'I was there yesterday.'

'Really?' Wendy stopped eating and put down her fork. For a woman who'd baulked at the price, she was doing a good job of cleaning her plate. She took another gulp of wine, and Kelly thought she'd have to order another bottle. It came in at sixty-four pounds; the sommelier would be only too happy to oblige.

'Why were you there?' Wendy asked. It was a strange question. The earl's death had been all over the news, as well as the coroner ruling it suspicious. Surely it was obvious that someone would investigate it.

'It's my case, Mum.'

Wendy's mouth remained open.

'Mum?' Kelly said.

Wendy gulped another half-glass of wine. Kelly was becoming concerned that she wouldn't be able to get her back to the car. She wasn't even sure if it was all right for her to drink on the new drug.

'I knew him,' Wendy said.

Chapter 30

The autopsy had been carried out sixteen years ago, but it was still fresh in Ted's mind.

The corpse was a mess. The propellers had ripped his skull apart, and there was tooth and bone embedded deep in the brain and the chest.

A kayaker had made the discovery. He'd alerted a local angler, who'd recognised the boat with its outboard motor still running beneath the surface, churning the bloody water, making it look like beetroot soup. The body had floated away and was making its way into the middle of the lake, and the police had to move swiftly to close it for the day. They'd faced angry steamer owners, swimmers and anglers, but it was non-negotiable. By the time a boat crew fished him out, he'd been nibbled by carnivorous perch, greedy for breakfast. One of the officers had vomited, only adding to the fish's grim meal.

It took them three hours to perform the autopsy, and they'd taken over three hundred photos.

So when Ted received the call at the coroner's office in Carlisle, he remembered the case straight away. He also remembered the sensationalism surrounding the death of a well-respected local man, and how the media ran the story for weeks as the Cumbria Constabulary deliberated its verdict. It was eventually decided that the death had been an accident. A particularly nasty accident. But not everyone believed it.

—

Oliver Fitzgerald had been a congenial man. He was an award-winning angler at only twenty-three, a keen golfer, and a regular fixture at the Pooley Bridge Inn, where he played snooker and chatted up barmaids spending their summers earning money for their next term at university. Like his father, he was tall, strong and imposing, and he regularly waited until closing time to take young students to clubs in Penrith, or back home for other activities. He had free rein at Wasdale Hall. His father didn't complain; it pleased him that his son was so virile.

Xavier-Paulus had waited fifty-five years to sire children, and when Delilah gave him twins in 1977, he'd pushed anew for a divorce from his estranged wife. To no avail. Alas, Delilah would never be his legally betrothed, but she'd brought renewed glamour to Wasdale Hall as friends from London encamped for weeks at a time, sending the Lakes' social circle into a whirl. It was after one of those summer balls that Delilah had conceived, down by the shore of Ullswater, as the water lapped her ankles and the shingle scraped her back.

—

'So was it a straightforward boating accident, in your opinion?' Kelly asked the pathologist over the phone.

'I was never convinced, if I'm honest,' Ted replied.

'Really? Why is that? It was ruled an accident at the time.'

'I know but there were a couple of things that were odd.'

'I'm listening,' said Kelly.

'Firstly, Oliver was an accomplished sailor. He was only twenty-three, but he grew up on the lake. He had a string of Royal Yachting Association qualifications. Secondly, there were no signs he had tried to save himself, and that was unusual.'

Kelly moved her ponytail to one side and sipped her coffee. She had five minutes to herself in her office, and the door was closed. She calculated that sixteen years ago Ted would have been a more junior pathologist, and that was why the signature on the post-mortem report was from another coroner, now deceased.

'So if it wasn't an accident, then what do you think it was?' Kelly valued Ted's input. She respected him and spoke to him like an inquisitive daughter asking for help with her homework.

'Suicide,' said Ted.

'Seems to run in the family,' Kelly commented. 'Why wasn't this taken into account at the time?'

'I wasn't in charge back then. I was still learning. I was experienced for sure, but seniority in the world of pathology comes late, Kelly. It's a bit like being a high court judge; you have to be geriatric before anyone respects your judgement taken on its own.'

'Did you vocalise your dissent?'

'Yes, but I was overruled.'

'But everything you've just told me makes absolute sense. I don't care how senior the coroner was, how could he be so obtuse?'

'The service is more – how shall I put it – transparent today. A few high-profile litigation cases have brought liability to the forefront.'

'So the coroner fucked up – excuse me – and got away with it?'

'Nothing was proven, you have to remember. There was evidence that Oliver was highly emotionally unstable at the time, but the family didn't even question it. In this case, I can't give you a definitive opinion. It's a science, Kelly; there are facts and then more facts – the way they're interpreted is your job.'

'Thanks.'

'It was a bit of a media circus, I remember. The family has such a sad history. There was some argument – and there's only gossip to fill in what it was about – but Oliver's sister and mother left and never came back. I read they died in a road accident. That was when the earl shut himself off.'

'And the raucous parties stopped,' Kelly said.

'Who told you about all that?'

'How come you know so much about the Fitzgerald family, Ted? Don't tell me you attended all those debauched parties as well, or are you just a keen historian?'

He fell silent.

'Ted? Are you there?'

'Yes, sorry. I think we were momentarily cut off.'

'So, did you?'

'Did I what?'

'Party at Wasdale Hall?'

His silence said it all.

'Ted! My mother told me last night that she'd been there too. God, you lot! Dark horses. Did you meet her?

I know you met my dad. People say I look just like her when she was my age.'

'Oh, I'm not sure, Kelly. I definitely remember meeting your father; he was very tall, wasn't he? Everybody knew about the parties. The Fitzgeralds were our celebrities. Tittle-tattle about them was nothing out of the ordinary. Besides, I'm a bit of a boffin when it comes to Cumbrian heraldry. You know we have some of the oldest families in the UK up here in the sticks?'

He'd changed the subject and distracted her with the word 'boffin'; she hadn't heard it in years and it amused her.

'Are you down in Penrith any time soon? I could do with going over both reports with you, and perhaps reminiscing about some of the goings-on at Wasdale Hall,' she said.

'Erm… actually, Kelly, I've got a very important meeting on Monday, which I need to prepare carefully for. I'm happy to look at my diary after that, though,' he said.

Ted Wallis had never needed to consult his diary so carefully before, and Kelly was taken aback.

'That's absolutely fine, Ted. You let me know. Bye, then.'

'I will,' he said, and hung up.

Kelly stared at the phone. Her thoughts drifted to her mother, and what she'd told her about one summer evening in 1975.

Chapter 31

Delilah Mailer sprayed Amazone by Hermès onto her clavicles, watched keenly by Xavier, who hung about at the foot of their bed smoking a Players No. 6. The scent was a new release, and she'd had it decanted into a turquoise and rose Victorian atomiser at Harrods. The top notes were of hyacinth, shrouded with jasmine and just a hint of lily, and finished with cedar. Xavier was fully dressed, but he was waiting for Delilah to fasten his tie, as she always did. She knew it wasn't that he couldn't do it himself; more that he enjoyed being close to her.

She was wearing claret: his favourite. The silk gown clung to her body, and her skin, kissed by summer, glowed toffee-like, framed by her golden hair. It had been pinned up and bejewelled with garnets. She took his cigarette and puffed on it. She was ready.

Downstairs, music played and staff busied themselves with the final preparations. Food was laid out on tables covered in white cloths, and wine from the cellar had been decanted. Delilah had taken care of the guest list, as she always did, and Xavier had no idea who was coming. They came up here for the summer, to escape the smog of London, but Delilah soon became tired of the local accent and the lack of finesse. Throwing an annual ball was her way of relieving the boredom, and occasionally she'd find someone to rouse her interest.

There were some familiar faces, and some new ones too. Delilah worked hard at getting to know the who's who of the north-west, and it was usually a smattering of doctors, lawyers, bankers, army officers, Yanks obliging their wives with a trip to little England, and the odd politician. It wasn't London, but she always pulled it off.

As Delilah tied Xavier's black silk tie – he never wore anything with colour – his hand wandered to her hip and he looked her in the eye.

'Xavier, we haven't time,' she said.

'There's always time,' he said, undoing her handiwork.

—

They wafted downstairs as the first guests arrived; people invariably turned up on time in these parts, unlike London where everybody was late. A few seasoned regulars acted as chaperones to others, less accustomed to Xavier Paulus II and his elegant mistress. Guests were usually brought to Xavier; Delilah, on the other hand, needed no introduction. She moved around the room looking for someone to make her laugh, someone to light her cigarette or pour her another brandy. She was equally generous to female and male guests, as she found them all fascinating, but it was the gentlemen who lingered around her longest.

No matter how many times John Porter had told his wife that she was the most beautiful woman in the room, when Delilah Mailer walked towards her Wendy felt a mixture of unimportance, awkwardness and featurelessness, as if all her shine had been sucked away in one turn of blonde curls. John soon forgot his promise to stay by his wife's side, and no one noticed her make her way out to the garden to get some air. Her jaw ached from smiling when she didn't want to. Her emerald dress felt tight and her skin clammy. She lit a cigarette and walked through the garden towards the fountain. No one else was around, and the noise of laughter, music and clinking glasses faded the further away from the great house she went.

There was no doubt their hosts were generous. She'd eaten smoked salmon pâté, sausages wrapped in delicate pastry, the softest beef on tiny rounds of bread with a tartar sauce dabbed on top, strawberries with pink cream, avocado mousse and oysters. She'd suffer tomorrow, she thought. Her head was woozy too. She'd opted for the cocktails rather than the wine, thinking this to be the wiser choice, but whatever was in the pink liquid with flecks of gold in it had gone straight to her head, and she needed to sit down. No one sat down in the great hall; they all stood talking and laughing, or else dancing and spinning until they fell over. It seemed she was the only one tired of it all.

She sat down on the edge of the fountain and put her hand in the water. It was beautifully cool, and she touched some to her forehead. Her auburn hair was heavy and hot and she lifted it up to let the cool air circulate around her neck. It was peaceful out here, and she looked at the lake, wondering what it might be like to live here every day. The Fitzgeralds packed up at the end of each summer and went back to London. Nobody seemed to care that they were lovers. That was what it was like in London, she supposed.

A noise startled her and she turned around. A man came from behind a bush and blew cigarette smoke out of his mouth.

'I do apologise,' he said. 'I needed some air, and it looks like you did too.' His smile was warm, and Wendy didn't feel vulnerable at all; he was just another guest. His dinner jacket was open and his tie hung loosely around his neck. After a pause, he finally came forward and introduced himself. He held out his hand, and Wendy took it.

'I'm Ted. Ted Wallis.'

Chapter 32

The Land Rover screamed along the narrow lane, pushed to the limit set by the parameters of the 1970s factory that had built it. The interior rattled, bashed by the rain from above and the unseen potholes beneath. The driver was unconcerned: the performance of the vehicle wasn't his priority, only the fact that it got him there quicker.

The deer in the back stank of fresh blood.

A glorious snap of three weeks' sunshine had turned sour and the Lake District had returned to its status quo: rain, and more rain. Even before the sun disappeared behind the mountains, headlights were needed to see ahead in the flat dark grey canvas that afforded little natural visibility. The rain lashed in through the open windows, soaking the occupant. He drove the lane like a local, navigating twists and turns before they appeared: he could have done it blind.

He gripped the steering wheel in anger and forced the vehicle closer and closer into the bends, ramming it into bushes as it cruised past, creating another dent to add to the mosaic of damage already on it. He hadn't meant to do it, but it always happened that way, and he couldn't stop. His fingers felt slippery from gutting the deer there where he'd felled her, in the heather. It was high up and he hadn't been expecting such a large one to appear in his sight. It was an opportunity, and he never missed an opportunity.

The policewoman thought she knew, when she looked at him and at his shoulders and hands. She thought she knew strength when she saw it, but she had no idea what it really looked like. His power wasn't a gift, it was a craft, years in the making. But there was lots she didn't know too.

He should have taken more care, but when they whined like that, and didn't understand that he was there to look after them, he had no choice. The girl had been a mistake from the very start. He was learning. He hadn't come this far for nothing. He'd always known the rules: not too young or fragile, because they didn't last; not too old, because they tricked and deceived; not too familiar, because that was too obvious.

Weak. That was what she was. And now he had to hide her. He sniffed as he thought of her sharing her final journey with the deer. She didn't really deserve such a prestigious reservation, but he had no choice. He couldn't have missed the deer, and it was a detour worth the wait.

Now, with the deer ready for hanging and the clouds darkening across the canopy above him, it was time to get on with why he'd come in the first place. It had been a good afternoon for a hunt and it wasn't all the time that he got so lucky.

The tension in his body began to loosen as his thoughts turned to the last time he was up here. That kill had been unexpected too, and that was what had made it both exquisite and disappointing all at the same time. That was when he'd first had the idea, given to him, he believed, by something divine and bigger than himself.

Keep her.

He smiled and nodded his head ever so slightly, sending his appreciation to the woman on the hill. It seemed a lifetime ago. The rush of pleasure had been too much, and he too inexperienced, and it had been too quick. He smirked at his innocence and lack of moral fibre, remembering when he'd jumped at every knock and every police appeal. He needn't have worried: she'd never been found.

And neither would this one.

The sky was properly black now and he switched off his lights, turning off onto a farmer's track, only used during the hours when sheep were counted and gates mended. He drove through two fields, using only instinct and ingrained knowledge as his guide, and parked behind a dry-stone wall, though not so dry tonight.

The noise of the water soothed him and he got out, slamming the driver's door shut. The deer was still warm, but the girl wasn't. She smelled worse by far. Disgusting.

He dragged her by her feet and she hit the ground with a slap. He didn't look around. No one came here. He had thousands of feet, hundreds of fields, millions of sheep and an eternity of sky to cover his tracks. His only question was, how close to the beck? Too close and he risked her drifting downwards towards tourists and farmers; not close enough and he risked exposure by a curious sheepdog. He couldn't be bothered to dig; what was the point? He dragged her a short distance to the water and dumped her by the beck while he found various bits of detritus and foliage to make a hideout good enough to aid and mask her decomposition.

Even before his job was finished, excitement mounted in his stomach as he anticipated what awaited him at the ruin. They were both magnificently perfect, but not so pretty now. He didn't want to lose them too quickly, but one was more compliant than the other.

He worked faster and heaved the body into a hollow. She was heavier in death and he was sure that the body wouldn't move from the pit he'd found. He covered the shallow hole with branches and mud, then waded into the beck and stripped. The water was bracing but invigorating, and he splashed it over himself, washing away the stench.

He had work to do.

Chapter 33

The chapel was quiet.

Zac had invited Kelly.

The only other attendees were Linda Cairns, Brian Walker, a man Kelly recognised as the solicitor in charge of the will, and Zac himself. Kelly hadn't expected the invitation, and she felt foolish as she walked to the middle of the chapel, watched by five sets of eyes, including those of the vicar. The body had been retained by the coroner's office at the mortuary but had finally been released.

Zac had told her that his grandfather wasn't religious at all, but a ceremony was protocol, and no one knew what else to do. He smiled at her, and she smiled back, grateful for one ally at least. He wore a suit and looked more than his nineteen years. He waved her over, and for a moment she wavered before going to the front and sitting next to him. The vicar coughed and they stood up. Kelly could feel the disapproval on her back from Linda and Brian. Their heightened state of anxiety, no doubt at her presence, might come in handy later when she followed them back to Wasdale. She had some questions for them.

The organist began playing something doleful and gloomy that Kelly didn't recognise. The notes rose and fell like soldiers being slain on a battlefield, and she felt depressed as hell. She'd been to plenty of funerals – more than she'd like to at her age – and usually the family made some attempt to capture the life of the loved one in song. Not today. Not unless the earl was the most morose and wretched creature to have been brought into the world, and this Kelly doubted. The way Zac talked about him, as well as her own mother's account of him as a host, would indicate the opposite. Poor bastard.

The service was wooden. The vicar stumbled nobly through snippets of the earl's charity work, his preservation of the flora and fauna of the estate, and his love of his only surviving heir. This was the one moving element of the affair, and Zac looked down at his shoes. Kelly felt a warmth off this young man that was unexpected, and she wondered who he'd got it from; certainly not the housekeeper, and not his mother, who'd disappeared when he was a tiny boy. Trinity Fitzgerald had never told a soul who Zac's father was, and he'd been brought up at Wasdale Hall without parents. Even his uncle had disappeared from his life when he was only a toddler. Ted was right: it was a tragic family.

As the coffin was wheeled away, Kelly took Zac's lead and followed him out into the aisle. She was aware of the solicitor leaving, and of Linda and Brian loitering, uncomfortable in their smart black clothes. Zac asked her to accompany him to the house.

'Of course. I need to speak to Linda and Brian anyway.'

'Why?'

'Some questions regarding the safe.'

'Do you think you'll catch who did this?'

'I don't know, Zac, but I can promise to try.'

'Are you any closer to finding out?'

'I want to be honest with you: no. But investigations take time.'

They drove in silence. Kelly allowed him his own thoughts. Brian and Linda were behind them. When they reached Wasdale Hall, Zac turned to her. 'Will you walk to the lake with me?'

It was a simple request, and utterly disarming. Kelly couldn't work out if he saw her as a mother figure, or a pillar of justice seeking answers on his behalf: probably a bit of both. She nodded.

Brian and Linda got out of their car as Zac led Kelly round the back of the house to a pathway that led to the shore. She'd worn heels for the funeral, and they sank in the gravel. They walked through the gardens, and she imagined them in all their glory. There was a beautiful old stone fountain sitting at a crossroads in the path; Kelly wondered if Delilah and Trinity had wandered down here to share secrets.

'It's beautiful, Zac,' she said. He smiled and nodded. 'A wonderful place to grow up.'

He nodded again and stared at the lake.

'Do you want to talk, Zac?'

'I just miss him,' he said. They walked slowly, and Zac picked leaves from the bushes and tore them apart.

'I know, I can see that. Zac, do you think it's possible that your grandfather asked someone to help him get rid of the safe and then stage his own suicide?'

Zac looked at her and his eyes pierced her own. He didn't make eye contact often, but when he did, it was as if he saw into her soul. 'Do you think that's what he did?' he asked.

'The removal of the safe and the hanging: they're both pretty demanding – and noisy – undertakings, and we've found nothing indicating a break-in or evidence of force.'

They stood at the shore of the lake, which spread out in front of them; Kelly could see the roofs of Watermillock, with its spire at the centre.

'But who would do that for him?'

'I don't know; do you?'

Chapter 34

Brian had loosened his tie and sat with his feet up in his usual spot. Linda put the kettle on the Aga.

Kelly came in through the kitchen door. She'd left Zac at the lake, and when she'd turned round to check, she'd seen him sitting down with his shoes off, skimming stones.

'Afternoon, both. Let's get straight to facts, shall we?' she began. Linda kept her back to the room and Brian folded his arms.

'Zac tells me that you helped get the safe upstairs, Brian. He also said you could confirm the model, because you ordered it.' She waited.

'I can't really remember; it was years ago.'

'Right. My trouble with all of this is that you've both worked here for years, the place runs along simple routines – you guys know who comes and goes daily, if not hourly – yet here we have a safe weighing perhaps a hundred kilograms disappearing silently, and the murder of a man who sheltered you for most of your careers and paid your wages, and I can't seem to get any answers from you. None of this is random, yet you're not willing to help, either of you. Linda, will you leave the kettle!'

Linda jumped and turned around.

Kelly's phone buzzed and she looked at the screen and tutted. It was Will Phillips.

'Excuse me, I'll be two minutes.' She walked outside. 'Will?'

'I've got an update for you. How did it go?' He was referring to the funeral.

'Next question. I'm just talking to the housekeeper and gardener now; they're holding out on me. What have you got?'

'We've got a girl called Cheryl Gregory who used to work with Jack Sentry, willing to talk, sounded a bit nervous. She works at the Sunnyside Guest House in Pooley Bridge now. I sent Emma down there. Turns out Sentry was her boss at the Peak's Bay. She was more than happy to verify that he was on the take for extracurricular activities; he used to boast about it apparently. Emma said she was scared of him. That's not all, guv.'

'What?'

'Turns out Sentry bedded both of the victims for an advance on their wages.'

'Christ.' Kelly took her hat off to Emma Hide: she had a way with witnesses that no one else matched.

'Anything else?'

'She told Emma about a ruin they used to use up on Place Fell.'

'Thanks, Will. I'll be in shortly, I'm just finishing up here.'

'Are you going to be online for the TV appeal?'

'Of course.' Kelly had completely forgotten about it. Hannah Lawson's parents were due to give an appeal, live on TV at three this afternoon. She closed her eyes; she'd told Johnny she'd meet him at Nikki's.

'Oh, and guv? Turns out Dominic Cairns' alibi checked out, but when Emma was going through those papers, she found out he was expelled from an expensive school down in Surrey. The earl was paying for it.'

'Why was he expelled?'

'It didn't say, but I called the headmaster and he said he'll talk to you.'

Kelly hung up and went back into the kitchen.

'So, Linda, can you tell me about Dominic's private school in Surrey, paid for out of the earl's pocket?'

Linda dropped a teacup and it smashed on the stone floor.

Chapter 35

'Is that my mummy?'

Zac holds his grandpa's hand. He's six years old.

'Yes, I told you it was.' They are walking through daffodils near Aira Point, where Wordsworth escorted his sister Dorothy, and Xavier is telling Zac about the way fish think. Zac finds it funny. Whatever his grandpa tells him is the truth. Grandpa's hand is warm, as always, and Zac's is tiny inside it. Linda has made them a picnic, and Xavier has carried it from the car, which is parked in the small car park off the A592. Only Grandpa can find these secret places, and he finds a new one every time he brings Zac fishing.

Xavier holds the worn photograph in front of the little boy.

'And that is Grandma,' Zac says triumphantly.

'Yes, it is,' Xavier says.

'But they got dead.'

Xavier squeezes his grandson's hand and wishes with all his heart that it was not true. But it is.

'How do you get dead, Grandpa?' asks the boy.

Xavier has to think about the answer. The picnic rug is laid out near the lake and they have come for a walk between eating their sandwiches and a treat for dessert. Linda has made lemon drizzle cake, and it is Zac's favourite.

'No one knows why, Zac,' he finally says.

'I said how, Grandpa, not why.' Zac is earnest in his correction. Of course, Xavier thinks, wanting to know why is such an adult pursuit. Children are simpler.

'They stop breathing,' he says.

'Just like that? Fish take a long time to stop breathing, and they wiggle about. Unless you bash them over the head,' Zac says. Xavier thinks his philosophy is a solid one.

'It's a little bit more complicated with people. They can have an accident, or they can get a disease.' They make their way back to the rug, and Xavier puts away the photo.

He's never lied to Zac, and he's never smothered him in stories to mask reality. However, he's also never told him exactly how his mother died. He can't face it, and he doesn't know the words.

'So did Mummy and Grandma catch the same disease?' Zac asks. Xavier thinks a little while. His breath is short, but they soon reach the blanket and he sits down.

'Yes, they did,' he replies.

'Why didn't I catch it?' Zac asks.

'Because you're strong, and it's not your time,' Xavier says.

'So everyone has a time? And weak people die?' Zac asks.

Xavier laughs. 'You're hurting my head! Let's eat some cake!' Zac claps his hands and sits next to his grandpa.

'How is school, young man? Linda tells me that you won a prize.'

'I did! I won a voucher,' Zac says.

'A voucher! For what?'

'A book. I won it for painting a picture.'

'And what book will you buy?' Xavier asks.

'A big one!'

'And what did you paint?'
'Mummy and me.'

—

The coolness of the air after the storm last night made the ground damp, but Zac didn't notice as he tried to hold on to the memory. He lay on his back, feet in the water and his hands over his face. His eyes were wet when he opened them, and he sat up staring out to the lake.

It's not your time…

Zac thought back to a few weeks ago.

'It's soon my time, Zac. You're ready to be a man,' his grandfather had said.

'Don't talk like that, Grandpa,' Zac had complained.

They had been sitting in front of the fire because the evening was cooler than expected. Linda had left for the evening and Brian was off on one of his walks. Legal quarry was growing scarcer, but Brian always managed to find something on the estate, and rough shooting was at the earl's discretion. They'd eaten Linda's venison pie and sat quietly, sated with food and wine.

'You'll understand why you need to make plans for your end when you're old and puffed out like me,' Grandpa said.

Zac knew that he never would.

To his mind, there was only one person his grandfather would trust to do the job.

Chapter 36

The press conference was filmed at a hotel in Kendal. Journalists packed the room and Mr and Mrs Lawson were due to arrive in less than two minutes.

The appeal was closely watched by a body-language expert as well as a criminal psychologist, both from the comfort of their own home. Live streaming and connectivity were at least one way in which the force had moved forward, and SIOs like Kelly no longer needed to assemble their teams in one room to watch the events unfold; they could all comment and update in real time, no matter where they were, as long as they had access to the closed channel. Kelly watched on her sister's TV in the lounge.

The house was quiet, as the girls were at school and Matt had gone to work to plead his case for more time off. If he lost his job, it would only add to the family's hardship. Johnny had been upstairs with Nikki for twenty minutes.

Kelly watched as Hannah's mother and father were led into the conference room by a DCI from HQ. As with most investigations of this calibre, the SIO made contact with the families but rarely to communicate major developments. The family liaison officers usually did that.

Hannah's mother grasped a tissue and her eyes were red and puffy; she never looked up at the cameras. It was always about the mothers, and the pain etched into their faces: that was what brought in the phone calls and galvanised the public to scour their memories. The fathers – if available – were there merely to show that grief wasn't just a female preserve, and men could cry too. It helped.

Kelly bit her nails and fiddled with her hair. Her mind wandered. The photographs of Freya Hamilton and Abi Clarence had been released, but today was all about Hannah Lawson. Sophie Daker's parents had declined to take part.

The DCI said some words but Kelly didn't hear them, then it was the turn of Mrs Lawson and the cameras went into a frenzy. Her husband held her hand tightly and kept his eyes down.

'Please, someone knows where my daughter is… She's such a kind girl… She means nothing to you and everything to us…' Mrs Lawson choked and stopped speaking. The cameras flashed mercilessly.

Kelly had had enough. She paced up and down, her stomach knotted with adrenalin. She wanted desperately to be in several places at once, and least of all here, but she'd promised Johnny. She picked up a photo of their family, the four of them: Mum, Dad, Nikki and herself. Dad was sitting in his armchair and his two girls took a knee each. Wendy leant over behind and peered into the camera. Kelly tried to remember who'd taken it. It didn't matter. Melancholy washed over her and she studied her sister's face. They were more different than alike. Her sister had the distinct Porter nose and hairline. Kelly realised that her own was different. Everybody always said that she was more like her mother. Maybe that was why they'd never got along, her and Nikki; it was destined from birth. She snorted and replaced the photo, wondering why Nikki would have it on display in the first place.

Johnny came into the room, and Kelly spun round. Nikki was standing behind him. The sisters looked at one another.

'We're going for a walk,' he said.

'Right, I'll get my coat,' Kelly said.

'I don't want you to come.' Nikki's voice was harsh.

Kelly looked at Johnny, who turned to Nikki.

'This isn't the time, let's go,' he said. But Nikki held her ground.

'No, this is all her fault. If that lunatic hadn't been after you, he'd have never come for me.' Her neck turned red and Kelly knew well enough that this was a sign of acute anger; she'd seen it before. Her face screwed up like their father's used to when he was tired and prickly.

'Nikki, Kelly is trying her best…'

'You!' Nikki took a step towards Kelly, who moved backwards against the TV screen. She couldn't think of words, stunned into silence by the sight of her sister's face, red and full of hate. 'Who do you think you are?' Nikki screamed.

Johnny sighed and caught her arms.

'I'm sorry, Kelly.' He turned to Nikki and urged her backwards.

'Get off me! She's never been like us!'

Kelly stood rooted to the spot, Michelle Hammond's words echoing in her head again, unwelcome and damaging. *Like us…* Anger flushed her body and she see-sawed between blaming Johnny and then her sister. In the end, she glared at both of them and stormed out, slamming the door behind her.

She had no idea where she was going, but she drove away, heading for the fells. Accusations and pictures flooded her brain and she wondered if indeed she had made the biggest mistake of her life coming back here. No matter what she tried to do, who she turned to, she couldn't fit in. She even looked different to them. It was pathetic, she knew, but she couldn't help the thoughts flowing now they'd begun. Her hair and eyes were her mother's, but it was as if everything else about her was alien and didn't belong. Even now, Nikki had Kelly's boyfriend's sympathy, and it made her blood boil. She held the steering wheel tightly and watched her speed.

She drove round for a while, changed her mind, drove back the way she'd come and finally ended up at the end of her mother's street. No one was around, so she turned off the engine and caught her breath. She put her head to the wheel and closed her eyes tight shut.

Who do you think you are?

She's never been like us…

A car drove past and she lifted her head. It was a gold Jaguar and she'd seen it before. It parked outside her mother's house, and Kelly watched in disbelief as the driver got out and straightened his tie. He held a bunch of flowers, a large bunch of flowers, and looked down at his feet before knocking on the door.

Kelly slouched in her seat and held her breath.

The door opened, and he smiled and was let straight in.

The car belonged to Ted Wallis. Ted and her mother had both lied to her.

Chapter 37

'Guv, there's been a sighting reported of a Land Rover up at the Boredale Hause route near Place Fell last weekend.'

The TV appeal had produced several lines of enquiry that all had to be chased, and the team knew that the majority of them would turn out to be just that: lines of enquiry. However, now and again a public appeal threw up a nugget and so was worth it.

Kelly only knew one way to escape personal stress and that was to spend more time at work. She was ignoring Johnny's calls and had yet to decide how to confront her mother.

The appeal had been slick and accompanied at appropriate moments by photographs of Hannah's clothing, the hip flask, her bag, Loadpot Hill, the Howtown campsite and a generic Land Rover. The tyre track hadn't given them a break, but Land Rover had said that the model that used those tyres must pre-date the year 2000.

'Can we dispatch someone to take a statement?'

'Done.'

'How many Land Rovers do we have registered in Cumbria?'

'One hundred and thirty-five, guv.'

'And how many models before 2000?'

'We're still working on that.'

'Was there a decent description of the driver?'

'Male, Caucasian.'

'Great, that narrows it down.'

She went into her office and sat down heavily.

It had been almost a week since the two girls had been reported missing, and just over a week since the earl's death. It felt like four. She needed a run to clear her head but she had too much to do. Another dive had been approved by HQ but had turned up nothing, and she was spending too much money. She yearned for the sunshine of last week, but the grey cloud had refused to lift, and it made everything bleaker, including her mood. She doubted she'd be any further along in the earl's case if it had been ruled homicide straight away; they were playing catch-up, but all leads on persons with access to Wasdale Hall had been checked.

She picked up the phone and dialled the number for the headmaster of Dominic Cairns' school in Surrey. She could easily hide in here all day, catching up with phone calls and updating the files on her computer, essentially moving paper from one imaginary pile to another, though nowadays it was a case of shifting data from keyboard to keyboard, and possibly scribbling something on the whiteboard in the incident room. But none of that would give her any answers. At some point, she'd have to face Johnny and her mother.

The number rang out.

She could call Ted directly and ask him why he was bringing her mother flowers – a stranger according to his own admission. It could have been a courtesy call to the widow of John Porter, but she'd never seen Ted in such a fine suit, and so worried about his collar. Something didn't sit right with her.

Will knocked on the door and peered around it, checking to see if she was busy. It was too late to pretend, and he caught her staring out of the window, looking at the rain.

'Guv, we've found CCTV of Abi Clarence at Waverley station.'

'It went back that far?'

'No, it was filed under the original search.'

Of course it was; what a dumb question, she thought.

'You all right?' Will asked.

She shook herself and turned to him. She'd created this dynamic team that had proved itself to HQ several times, and she was stupidly proud of them all, so why did she feel different? Why did she feel like a fraud? Burnout. It was lethal. She admitted that she was tired, and counted backwards. She'd worked eight days straight, well into the evening, and she hadn't slept well.

'Can I get you a coffee?' he asked.

'Yes please.' She smiled. 'Is the CCTV uploaded?'

Will nodded. 'Oh, Emma has the model of the earl's safe, too: it was a Chubb DuoGuard Grade 1, if that means anything.'

Kelly flicked on her computer and found an email from Will with the CCTV footage and a series of stills. They captured a young girl waiting on a platform. She had a large bag next to her and was looking at her phone. Kelly couldn't see the girl's face, but the image had been positively ID'd by Abi's sister. She wore a bright red hoody, clearly emblazoned with the Gap logo. Kelly wondered if her bone fragments would ever yield anything other than the fact that she had lain in a glade for two years. She also wondered if anyone but the sister cared.

Will came back and placed a mug beside her.

'I'm trying to get through to the headmaster. Is Cheryl Gregory here?'

'She's waiting downstairs.'

'Right, I'll try this number again and then we'll go down.'

Will left her and this time her call was answered. The man sounded stiff and proper, what one might expect from a headmaster of a reputable establishment. He was officious and direct.

'So Dominic Cairns was expelled when he was seventeen?' she asked.

'Indeed. It was, I'm afraid, an accumulation of matters we simply could no longer accept here at Hodds Hall.'

Kelly appreciated the man's sense of propriety. 'Could you explain?' she asked.

'We finally accepted co-education status in 2010, against my express wishes, but the governors have the ultimate say, you understand. Cairns was an impertinent child. He never fitted in.'

The words stung Kelly, and she felt a chink of sympathy for the boy who was being denigrated in her ear.

'His housemaster warned the earl personally that if standards weren't upheld, the boy faced expulsion.'

'And why weren't these concerns raised with his mother?'

'We never had correspondence with the mother, only the earl.'

'Was he his legal guardian?' Kelly asked.

'Of course.'

Kelly wrote this down and underlined it. 'Sorry, carry on.'

'The boy was a nuisance; he took great pleasure in bullying his way through the school, and then things went too far.'

Kelly waited.

The headmaster coughed. 'He was accused of indecent assault. I must stress that no charges were ever brought, but if it had been my daughter…'

'I understand. Do you have the details of the girl involved?'

'I'm afraid that's confidential.'

'But, sir, the Children's Act specifically states that when a child is at risk, the duty to share information is absolute, with agencies such as ourselves in particular.'

'The parents withdrew the matter.'

'Your duty to the child comes first; it overrides the parents' consent. Surely you know this.'

'Indeed I do, but when there's no record of it, and neither the child nor the parent acknowledges the event, there's nothing to investigate, is there?'

'So why are you telling me?'

'Because the girl committed suicide.'

Kelly was dumbfounded.

'Over what happened?'

'That's my belief, and it always has been, but when the parents got their hands on upwards of two hundred thousand pounds after her death, it had the effect of sealing their lips.'

'And you're going to tell me that the money came from the late earl?'

'I couldn't possibly say.'

When Will came back into Kelly's office, her coffee had gone cold, untouched.

'Guv? Cheryl Gregory is still here. Are you ready?'

Kelly sprang out of her chair and grabbed her Toughpad, following him to the lift.

'I just had the strangest conversation with Dominic Cairns' ex-headmaster.' She told Will the details as they descended to ground level. The element of police investigation that elicited snippets of human behaviour surrounding their persons of interest in an inquiry was the most fascinating aspect of the job, but also the most frustrating. If one could prosecute using the examples of deviancy, poor character and a bent moral compass, then the streets would be safer for sure, but the negative press surrounding anyone's past was inadmissible for good reason: people were complex creatures, with many faults, but only a minority committed serious crimes. If they'd lived through a witch hunt in Salem, then Dominic Cairns might have been the first on the bonfire, but a taste for bullying vulnerable girls, even into taking their knickers off, didn't make him their guy.

That said, he had just become more interesting. She tasked Emma with finding a paper trail for the money; the next time she spoke to Linda Cairns, the earl's kindly generosity wouldn't cut it for why he had paid thousands for the boy's education.

Cheryl Gregory was a slip of a girl. She was a nervous wreck and probably weighed a hundred pounds wet through. Visiting a police station was no ordinary outing, but she had volunteered. Kelly and Will went into the interview room and acted pleasantly to calm her nerves. Cheryl's hands were thin and red, her nails short and bitten.

'What can you tell us about Jack Sentry, Cheryl?' Kelly kicked off the interview.

'He was my boss at the Peak's Bay.'

'How long did you work together?'

'About five years.'

'And what was he like to work for?' Kelly eased in with some housekeeping. It was quite obvious that Cheryl Gregory was someone who wanted to stay on the right side of the law, but she was extremely anxious. They ran through her employment history and her various positions in the hotel, gradually working towards the nature of her relationship with her boss. Cheryl had opened up to Emma saying that she was afraid of her boss and Kelly wanted to know why.

'Did you ever go with Mr Sentry to the location on Place Fell?'

Cheryl looked at her hands and eventually nodded.

'What did you do there?'

Cheryl reddened and Kelly felt regret that she had to make the girl so uncomfortable, but it was vital.

'Did you go there for sex?'

Cheryl nodded again and closed her eyes. Her cheeks were the colour of deep summer raspberries.

'And Freya and Abi went up there too? Can you identify them for the record?' Kelly placed the photos of the girls on the table. 'Did you ever go together?'

Cheryl confirmed the identities.

'Sometimes.'

'And what did you do?'

'We played music and...'

'Illegal substance use?' Kelly waited. 'I can't arrest you retrospectively, you're not on trial; I'm building a picture of what happened to Freya and Abi. Cheryl nodded again.

Curiously, Kelly had never seen the place in question; it must be well tucked away. Even on the helicopter ride with Johnny, they hadn't spotted a ruin near the fell. So far, things weren't looking good for Mr Sentry, who at best was a liar.

'Mr Sentry has played down his relationship with the two girls. Would you be willing to contest that under oath?'

Cheryl swallowed and Kelly knew that she made a risky witness, simply because of her fear, but that could also go in their favour.

'Abi is dead and Freya is still missing. What would you want them to do for you if the roles were reversed?'

'Tell the truth.' Tears spilled over in Cheryl's eyes.

'Do you think you could point the place out on a map?'

'Yes.'

Chapter 38

Days of heavy rain had whipped up the mud, and diving had been suspended for three days. The dive schools around Ullswater had made so many cancellations due to the police search, and now the weather, that they were keen to resume: time was money, and tourists paid well for dive lessons.

Ullswater was no Red Sea, but it attracted its fair share of leisure divers. The PADI centre was run by a jovial Aussie called Jayden. At twenty-two, covered in tattoos, ripped and undeniably masculine, Jayden was a hit with the ladies. He spent his summers in the Lake District and wintered in France as a ski instructor. Both venues offered a string of college girls, wanting to hike and swim in the summer and ski in the winter.

But it wasn't just the girls. He was attracted to the spirit of a place too. The serenity of the Lakes charmed him and made him feel at peace. It was the same in the Alps, or back home on the water. Of course, deep-sea diving with great whites was something for adrenalin junkies only, but here he could appreciate nature on a smaller scale, and he noticed details. Besides, it was a good lake to learn in, and it would help him towards his goal of dive master. Students here looked for a gentle swim and a photo opportunity. Occasionally, in July or August, if it was warm enough, he would risk a half-wetsuit, but only if he had his eye on a particularly hot girl in his class.

He had one here today. She wasn't the sharpest tool in the box, but her butt looked great in neoprene, and when they got back to the centre, she peeled it off, revealing a tiny bikini more suited to Bali than Cumbria, though he wasn't complaining.

He'd given the brief. It would be a straightforward navigation dive, and with a bit of luck they'd see some interesting fish. The pike always raised the most gasps: they were butt-ugly and vicious. The kit was counted onto the RIB, and the divers climbed in one by one. He held his hand out to steady them, and the small boat rocked. Some of the girls giggled, and he winked at them. Including two seasoned divers notching up dive time, he had a total of seven. They were put in buddy pairs; the remaining one would be partnered with him. He also had a driver and a guy helping with kit. Getting out of a RIB into the water was easy; getting back into it in full kit, even with an empty tank, was the tricky bit.

As they headed for the middle of the lake, the surface looked calm and clear. The silt had settled after the huge storm, and it promised to be a good day. They cleared their masks with spit and lake water, and in turn read out the pressure level in their tanks. They checked buoyancy aids, weight belts and itinerary, and they were ready. Jayden went through dive symbols; he liked to finish with a straight palm on top of his head to signal 'shark': it always got a laugh.

'Ladies and gents, I'll go in first and bob around until you're all in. Don't make me wait too long. It's a nice day but it's still England, right?'

Another laugh.

He sucked on his mouthpiece and lowered his mask before rolling backwards and disappearing for a few seconds. He equalised his buoyancy and waited for the others. One by one they plopped in, cleared ears and sucked air. When they were all ready, he began his descent. Today's dive would be a steady twenty metres, with a deepest point of twenty-four metres. It should take them forty-five minutes, by which time they'd be freezing.

He watched them all carefully.

Once on the bottom, he signalled 'OK' to every diver, and each replied in turn. So far, so good, he thought. The lake was quiet, and the sun shone through from the surface in great shafts of colour. On a shallow dive such as this, most colours could be discerned, though here in the Lake District the view underwater was chiefly green and brown.

Twenty-five minutes into the dive, Jayden saw something flash and turned to where he'd spotted it. He held up his hand to stop everyone and wrote on his plastic board: *Wait here.*

He swam ten feet to where he'd seen the flash, well within visibility for his team, and looked around. Every now and again, stuff turned up in the Lakes that was found to be worth something, and Jayden was always on the lookout. He turned around and gestured for the others to come over carefully. Once the silt had cleared, they took it in turns to admire his find. He held up his diving GPS, knowing that the coordinates might be required for any salvage work, and gave the thumbs-up. He might very well have just discovered a bounty. There was no way they could take the find with them, but Jayden was excited. He had something to tell the girls later.

They completed their square route, and made their way back to the RIB, where they'd decompress at six metres. Any dive deeper than fifteen feet had to include safety stops on the ascent to avoid the bends. They took it in turns hanging off the lead rope, looking up at the bottom of the boat. The view was pleasing but also sinister. Jayden had once seen the underbelly of a shark on a dive off South Africa, and it had taken him fifteen minutes to pluck up the courage to swim up to the final six metre safety stop. It had been the longest four minutes of his life, as he stared into the blue abyss waiting for Jaws to strike.

They handed their tanks up to waiting hands, and took it in turns heaving themselves into the boat. It was a strange sensation, going from weightlessness to land, and they would feel peculiar for a few hours.

'How old did it look?'

'Have you seen it before?'

'Did you try the lock?'

'How will you get it up?'

They bombarded Jayden with questions, but he knew he'd have to report his find, rather than hiring some lifting gear and going it alone. There was little point getting excited about what might be in it. It had looked pretty new to him, and it was only thanks to the heavy storm that its hiding place had been disturbed.

They'd know soon enough.

He'd taken note of the make as well. It was a Chubb DuoGuard Grade 1. There was a three-way handle next to a security knob. It was around fifty centimetres wide, and the same deep and tall. It hadn't been dropped by accident by someone out walking, or testing their microlight. It'd been dumped in there for a reason.

Back at the shed, the talk was focused on the unfolding intrigue, and everybody had a theory. Jayden laughed as he listened to them. The closest big town was either Pooley Bridge, or Glenridding, and he didn't know if either boasted a police station. All police phone numbers were standardised now, so he guessed he'd be put through to a generic switchboard, from where the information would eventually find the right person. He didn't know anyone with the necessary lifting equipment, but he was sure the police would, or at least mountain rescue.

It was only eleven o'clock. He asked if anyone fancied an early lunch, and the student with the nice arse said she'd get a sandwich with him. The day was getting better by the hour. Jayden nodded to her and she looked away coyly. The potential of becoming the hero of the hour, with possible media interest, had just elevated him from exotic foreigner with some interesting tattoos to local celebrity, and it didn't hurt one bit.

Chapter 39

'I'm sorry. I had no idea Nikki would do that. She just flipped.'

Johnny put his hands on Kelly's shoulders and looked into her eyes. The thought of resisting was more exhausting than simply telling the truth, and Kelly realised that she'd never felt that way before about a man. The fight had always excited her more than the armistice. Now, she wanted to be vulnerable. She wanted Johnny to say sorry and mean it. She needed him.

'I don't know if I want to do this any more,' she said.

'What? Us?' He came closer.

'No. This.' She swept her hand around her. They stood in the hallway of her house in Pooley Bridge, almost in the exact spot where he'd first pressed her against the staircase, ripping her clothes off and making her sweat with anticipation. She bent her head and leant on his shoulder. He smelled of fresh air mixed with Ralph Lauren and she wanted nothing more than to forget her job for a couple of hours, but he was due on duty soon.

'I came back like fucking Poirot, waltzing in and solving everything, expecting Mum to make this huge adjustment to her life and me to just fit in where I'd left off.'

He held her tighter.

'It's not working.'

'That's bullshit. Pick it all apart: is this about Nikki or is it about your job? Because from where I'm sitting, you're nailing it. So what if your sister is falling apart, so what if your mum is narrow and parochial, so what if your old school friend insulted you? So fucking what?'

He took her face in his hands and forced her to look up at him. He kissed her eyes and allowed her tears to wet his lips. One hand went to her neck and brought her face closer; the other massaged her scalp through her hair, sending tingles down her back.

'I thought you needed to go,' she whispered.

'I do.'

He took her by her hand and led her upstairs, laying her gently on the bed and starting to undress her. She closed her eyes and pretended that this bed, and what was happening on it, was the only thing that mattered in her world right now.

'I love you, Kelly,' he said.

She put one hand over her face. A tiny demon from her past murmured softly into her ear: *Don't believe him*, but it was easily batted away.

'I love you too.'

When she took her hand away, he was looking at her. His face was set in concentration and she realised that it was just as hard for him to say. He didn't fit in either, but he fitted here. She leant gently to one side as he undid her skirt and slipped it off.

—

Once she'd closed the door after watching him go, she decided to get a shower and make herself some food. She flicked on the radio and looked at her watch. She'd only popped home for an extra jumper, having found that she hadn't put one in her car this morning. Johnny had been waiting for her. Now she figured that she had time to make a decent sandwich, grab a bottle of Coke and take a moment to reset. She smiled. All she'd needed was a moment's intimacy. If only you could bottle it: *shagacetamol*. It didn't make any of her problems go away, but it had definitely changed her perspective.

The news report on the radio focused on the discovery of the safe in the lake. It was an unusual find, and it wasn't public knowledge that one was missing from the local stately home, but the salvage of it had made headlines. Kelly listened as she sliced cheese. It was a local channel and still played music that she'd grown up to: Blur, the Stereophonics, the Macarena. It was comforting. It struck her that she'd grown used to the provincial charm of her surroundings, and she realised that Johnny was right. She'd caused a rift in the mighty status quo of a little corner of Penrith, but she'd achieved a hell of a lot more than that.

Fuck 'em.

Nikki blamed her for not finding her sooner when she'd been held in that shitty garage by The Teacher; she blamed her for everything anyway, so *plus ça change*. Her mother had some explaining to do, and not the other way around. Michelle Hammond had remained inside her cage since primary school, and not leaving it was her own fault. As for Kelly's job, she only had to look around the office at Eden House and see how much effort her whole team put in to know that she was worthy of it. She shook her head, surprised that she'd let things get to her.

She happily finished making her sandwich, and left the house with her extra jumper and bottle of Coke. As always when she was in the car, which was a lot of the time, she ticked off an imaginary list in her head. It didn't take long for the post-coital elation to wear off and reality to creep back in, surely and steadily as she approached Eden House. But that didn't stop her from breezing in with a smile on her face and Kate commenting on it.

'Good news, guv?'

Kelly made a note to herself to meet Johnny more often at her house for a lunchtime break.

Chapter 40

Hannah checked under the corner of her mattress.

At first, the scraps of food he gave her – the odd half a sandwich, a bowl of dry Cheerios, a chicken drumstick – were gobbled greedily as her body craved calories. At university, her training regime was brutal. Judo was an explosive sport and required strength, suppleness and stamina, and she combined cardio fitness with weights. Three times a week she'd run six miles around the campus, and three times a week she hit the gym. She changed her weights routine every four weeks, concentrating on the largest muscles in her body: her glutes, quads and chest. Her diet consisted of high-quality protein and nutritious fats, and the lack of them had made her first angry, then weak, and finally lethargic. Her dreams were dominated by steak, butter, avocados and cheese.

After a few days – she had no idea exactly how many – a plan had formed in her mind. Instead of consuming the tasty treats thrown to her as if she were an obliging dog, she'd decided to hoard them. The morsels were carefully wrapped in her baby-blue knickers, and stored in the secret corner, underneath the grotty bedding, and it took all her willpower not to cheat and have a bite. It became her new obsession, and she approached the project like any athlete would. So many times she'd counted and arranged the nibbles, even sniffing them to calculate how many calories they contained. She knew each food group and its nutritional value off by heart, and looked at her cache, reckoning she had enough to trick her body into thinking that she'd been on some stupid cleanse, and that she was about to embark on normal eating again. She knew that the time she'd spent in the hovel wasn't enough to cause serious damage yet, and so her body was storing and preparing for a famine. A good meal would restore her vitality, not permanently, but perhaps long enough to enter a fair fight.

Some of the meat items smelled, but she no longer cared. In her mind, she saw the best plate of food that a sports nutritionist could possibly produce, and she began taking bites, bit by bit, masticating them thoroughly so that she could properly digest and absorb the goodness. She had to check herself and not swallow too enthusiastically, because her brain was telling her that she was starving.

She wasn't.

She was simply deprived. She had water, and that made all the difference.

Part of her plan was to acquiesce. The first few times he'd entered her room and approached her, she'd fought like a wild animal, but it made no difference because he overpowered her every time. A woman tied and bound was never a match for a man with a plan. She hated his smell, she detested his body, and she despised his clever talk. Christ, it hurt at first. It stung and burned, and she lay for hours afterwards, degraded, desperate and weak, hating herself and longing to be free. The overwhelming fear that he was doing the same to Sophie was the thing that almost tipped her over the edge.

Then she'd heard the girl. And it definitely wasn't Sophie. Whoever it was had displeased their captor, and Hannah was left in no doubt as to what he was capable of. She'd listened to the sickening punches, the grunts and the slaps. She had held her head against the adjoining wall and cried as another girl had succumbed to his rage. Perhaps that was what happened after he simply grew bored, or perhaps she had done something wrong. Whatever the reason, Hannah couldn't wait any longer. The same fate might already have befallen Sophie. She'd sat, shaking with fear and disgust, as he dragged something out of the adjoining room and into the hallway. It sounded heavy. Hannah guessed that the girl would no longer feel the pain, and she wasn't coming back.

She heard the key in the lock and closed her eyes. Her gluttonous feast had been hours ago, and she could feel her blood sugar level surge and her brain come alive. That was all she needed.

He was a man of predictable taste. He also left the door ajar, presumably in his haste, or excitement, she knew not which. And the last three times, because she'd become a welcoming wretch, he'd cut her cable ties. It aided his comfort, and no doubt convinced him of her subjugation.

She continued to pretend to sleep. Her heart beat faster and her stomach churned. Doubts assaulted her mind. She knew he was strong, that was certain, but was he as angry as she was? Was he as determined? One thing was for sure: she had the element of surprise.

She stiffened as he came close to her and shook her shoulder.

'Hannah,' he whispered.

The sound of his voice revolted her. He knew their names because they'd exchanged pleasantries when he'd been doing his Good Samaritan act on Loadpot Hill. Hannah knew now that it had all been part of the stage production: names were important. A name could be used to praise, to love, to encourage and to ingratiate. It could also be used to taunt, to bully, to demean and to diminish. It was a clever detail, well rehearsed.

He turned her over and pulled her cable ties, then cut them. She played along with the game. He didn't speak, but he smiled and lifted her hair up and away from her shoulders. He did this a lot, as well as forcing her to brush it. Hannah found herself idly wondering if the other girl had long blonde hair too. Perhaps this was his thing; all psychos had one. Sophie had told her about it after one of her long lectures on murder.

Hannah held her breath and waited for his arousal. That was when he'd be most vulnerable. He turned his back and began to take off his jeans. She sat up and watched, silently, waiting until he had one leg in and one leg out, no doubt salivating over what was to come.

As he balanced precariously on one leg, she pounced, springing off the bed, charging towards him and ramming her shoulder into his back as forcefully as she could. He gasped and toppled forward, bashing his head against the chair, which clattered underneath him. She sprinted out of the room and down the hall, desperately searching for a weapon. A kitchen was what she needed, or a fireplace, or a hefty ornament.

She found none of those things. Just a corridor with two more locked doors and a dead end. There was absolutely nothing that she could pick up, break off or fashion into a blunt instrument capable of causing harm. Nothing.

She turned and faced the way she'd run, only to find him standing in the hallway, smiling at her. To get out, she needed to pass him, but now they were equals in the arena, and he blocked her way.

'Help! Help!' she screamed. She lowered her shoulder and charged at him, but this time he was ready. As she flew into him, he brought up his belt and slapped it down onto her head, buckle first, with such force that it stunned her and she fell to the ground. Her vision went misty as her head hit the wooden boards, then he kicked her in the gut. The impact forced the remnants of her last, carefully planned meal upwards and she spewed liquid out onto the floor.

Before she could engage her brain and produce another last attempt at fighting back, her wrists were forced together and a fresh cable tied tight; tighter than before. She gasped as the plastic cut into her skin.

He dragged her by the legs and she left a trail of bloody saliva along the floor as freedom slipped away from her and she was dumped back into the room. He walked out and slammed the door, locking it.

Only one thing kept her from giving up.

When she'd screamed, a faint echo had reverberated around the bleak corridor; but it hadn't been an echo, Hannah was dead certain of that.

It had been Sophie, replying to her call.

Chapter 41

After one of the driest months of May on record, the afternoon saw angry, black clouds gather over the northern fells and torrential rain battered the thirsty hillside. Brilliant sunshine gave way to a tempestuous downpour and turned the dusty tracks to mud, and the withered waterfalls to cascades. From the warmth of Kelly's bed, Johnny listened to the flood bouncing off roofs and pouring down street drains. He was on call and it never ceased to amaze him how many walkers remained determined to hike in such shit weather. What was the point? It was as if they enjoyed pitting themselves against a giant opponent, to see if they could triumph over it.

The thought of Kelly beneath him in her bed would keep him warm as he and his colleagues in mountain rescue braced themselves for the night ahead, knowing that anyone caught in such a storm would likely find themselves in trouble. On days like this, Cumbria became a canvas paused. Boats stayed attached to their jetties, ice cream shops closed, outdoor furniture remained stacked against walls, and the hills fell silent. In late May, the rest of the country were cleaning their barbecues, but in the Lake District, shops sold out of cagoules.

Plenty of walkers had remained optimistic right up until midday, determined to plough ahead despite the surprise warnings. But by two o'clock, no one began any new walks, and hikers spilled off the mountains into pubs to steam-dry walking gear and eat hot meals. Red noses and ruddy cheeks glowed in the bars and restaurants, and walkers shared stories of when the rain had hit.

Beda Fell wasn't a particularly hard hike, but in weather like this it was easy to become disorientated. When the call came in from two walkers up there unable to see which way they'd come, Johnny was the first to be reached by radio. He showered quickly and gathered his things.

From Pooley Bridge, the drive to Boredale would probably take him twenty minutes, if the roads were clear. Dusk had begun to fall, and he called in to the operator for an update. She said the walkers were getting cold and couldn't find shelter. She'd advised them to find a rock and shelter from the wind.

'Have they got waterproofs?' he'd asked.

'No.'

'What?'

'I know, Johnny, you just can't tell these numpties. They think, a walk in the hills, how romantic, then *bang*, they're lost; no water, no whistle, no food and no map. Idiots.'

'Any landmarks?' he asked.

'They started at St Martin's Church and took the usual route, but the weather came in before they summited, so they could be anywhere.'

'How far do they think they wandered?' he asked.

'An hour.'

'Great, they could be in Grizedale by now. OK, give me their number.'

Johnny could smell north from south, but he took a whistle and compass everywhere with him. Before mobile phones, it could take days to find someone; this couple were lucky.

He called the number on speaker as he drove along Ullswater's eastern shore. He knew that was where he was even if he couldn't see it. He couldn't see anything. He'd have to rely on instinct tonight. He felt the anger of the lake, and hoped no one was out on it.

He parked at St Martin's Church. The car park was deserted as expected, except for one other car, which he assumed belonged to the lost walkers. He peered inside and noticed waterproofs and a map on the passenger seat. He shook his head.

He began the ascent quickly, wasting no more time.

Howe Grain Beck was a rapid, swirling mass of angry water, and Johnny assessed it as he crossed Christy Bridge. Within thirty minutes, he was on the summit of Winter Crag. The couple had described a place of large scattered rocks, and he figured this was where they were. He shouted into the grey bleakness and heard voices.

'Help! Over here!'

He dialled their number again, and it worked, thank God; it could be hit-and-miss up here.

'On three, both of you shout as loudly as you can,' he told them. 'One, two, three.'

'HELP! HERE!'

Johnny closed his eyes. They were to the east. He dropped down a few feet and listened again.

'HERE!'

They were closer. He shone his torch, and the wind stopped briefly, allowing the noise to travel easier. There they were, behind a boulder, waving their arms. He walked over to them and introduced himself.

'Johnny Frietz, mountain rescue. How are you? Anyone injured?' he shouted over the wind.

They were uninjured, but cold and thirsty, as well as terrified. There was nothing like getting lost on the fells to give amateurs a healthy respect for nature and her capabilities. He opened his backpack and gave them water. Next he got out two large waterproof jackets and two Tracker bars, which they devoured hungrily.

'It's all right, we'll have you down soon,' he said.

The helicopter was busy on Skiddaw. A hiker had fallen down a gully and broken his leg. His friend had tried to reach him, only to fall too and break his foot.

The night closed in and the sky grew darker. The couple shivered and held onto one another. Johnny instructed them to follow his every step, and tied a guide rope to both of them. Eventually they found lower ground and the gradient began to even out. They heard rushing water, and the light from Johnny's torch made Howe Grain Beck look like an oily slick of waves.

'Jesus!' He halted. 'Wait here. Don't move. I just need to check the bridge.'

The couple sat down and cradled a torch between them. This would be a story they'd share many times over from the safety of their flat once they were home.

Johnny couldn't be sure what it was, but he'd spotted something. Whatever it was, it didn't belong here. He approached cautiously and saw it again. His heart raced, and as he shone the torch around, he saw a flash of red and white.

It could be a mannequin. But mannequins didn't have eyes like that. And they didn't bloat like that. It was stuck under the bridge on the other side, and seemed to be wedged in by branches. Had it come from downstream?

The wind changed and he caught the smell of rotting flesh. He'd smelled it in Iraq. It was sweet, and stuck to the inside of his nostrils.

He called the desk.

'Julie. Phone the police. The walkers? No, they're OK. But I think I've found a body. A woman under Christy Bridge. No, I'm not fucking joking.'

He made his way back to the shivering couple, and guided them across the bridge to St Martin's and back to their car, taking care to keep them facing away from the corpse. They remained oblivious to what he'd just discovered.

'You can follow me back down. Where are you staying?' he asked.

'Penrith.'

'Well come back to the centre with me and we'll get you checked over, then you can have a shower and something substantial to eat.'

The last thing Johnny wanted to do was babysit, but he had a duty. He needed a stiff drink. He'd drop the walkers off at the centre and knock off for the night.

But first he needed to call Kelly.

—

The nearest on-duty constable to St Martin's Church received the call at three minutes before ten. He waited for a medic and they left Pooley Bridge together. Blues weren't required on the narrow lanes, but a break in the weather would have been helpful.

It was a hell of a storm. The constable parked at St Martin's, and they grabbed torches and macs out of the boot then followed the path to Christy Bridge. They'd only gone ten yards and they were wet through.

'Haven't seen rain like this for a few years,' said the constable, who'd just been about to knock off shift. His girlfriend would be pissed off.

'Was it a genuine call?' asked the medic. He'd seen plenty of cases of dead bodies being sighted under bushes and in lakes, only to find them either hoaxes or bits of plastic.

'Mountain rescue guy called it in, so it sounds legitimate.'

The sky was oily black and the water loud. They were close. The constable's radio crackled, but he barely heard it. He knew the area and was familiar with the bridge but they couldn't see anything from this side. As they crossed the bridge, they spotted her. She was trapped inside a tangle of branches.

The medic would have to get close enough to pronounce her dead. They had waders in the car, and the constable went back to get them. He also radioed HQ in Penrith. They wouldn't be able to touch the body until forensics came. He prayed that someone was on shift, otherwise he might be shafted with staying with the body for hours. He needn't have worried; he was told that DI Porter was almost there.

He returned to the beck and they both put on waders. The water was fast, but not too deep, and so they found a footing easily. When they reached her, it was clear that the body was human, and that she was very dead. It wasn't the first dead body the constable had seen, but it was the first victim of murder. He wasn't being fanciful, nor was he jumping to conclusions: she had deep wounds around her wrists, and a large amount of bruising to her face. She was naked apart from a grubby sweater that was half hanging off her body. She hadn't gone for a late-night swim and drowned, that much was clear. He didn't want to look, but he couldn't keep his eyes off her.

The medic pronounced life extinct, and they made their way back to dry land. Back in the car, they filled out paperwork and waited. The vehicle steamed up and the constable wished he'd thought to bring coffee. He kept the car running so they could listen to the radio, and stay warm.

In the distance there was the familiar flash of an ambulance car, followed by an unmarked car, making their way to the car park. A medic and a forensic officer jumped out and strode across. Behind them, a plain-clothes officer got out of her vehicle. Blimey, that was quick, thought the constable.

'Night shift is on its way so you can go home soon. We'll make a start.' The officer flashed her badge. DI Kelly Porter. 'Have you got waders?' she asked the medic and his forensic colleague.

'Yup.' They carried large boxes full of equipment for processing a crime scene, and though much could be done by torchlight, they'd have to come back tomorrow. Pity the poor sods who got to guard her tonight, thought the constable. He'd had a lucky escape as he'd only finished nights two days ago. Result. Which was more than could be said for the deceased, who was going nowhere.

DI Porter asked for a pair of waders.

'Ma'am, do you think that's a good idea?' He looked at her skirt.

She held out her hands. One of the medics walked to the back of the vehicle and handed her waders and a waterproof.

'Thank you,' she said, slipping them on over her skirt suit.

They waded into the water. Even through the thick insulated plastic, Kelly could feel the piercing cold of the rushing water.

They'd have to wait until daylight to free her, and forensic information would be difficult to collect. Collecting crime-scene information on dry land was bad enough, but from water it was a nightmare. Kelly doubted there'd be anything left at all. But she wasn't here to see a factory operation of bagging and tagging for the lab. She was here to see the face of the victim.

'Jesus,' one of the officers said quietly. Even hardened investigators were capable of shock.

'She's badly swollen,' the other said.

Close behind, Kelly got her first glimpse of the body and sighed when she saw the state of it. The dead, staring eyes and the contrast between the girl's naked white flesh and the soiled sweater made her clench her fists. They'd need DNA and family ID, but there was no doubt in Kelly's mind: she was looking into the face of Freya Hamilton. The top she wore had once been red, and she could make out the familiar lettering where it was folded and smeared with mud: *GAP*.

Chapter 42

The Howtown campsite was shrouded in darkness.

Jack Sentry had got rid of his last campers this morning, and he knew it wouldn't be long before the detectives came back with a warrant for his office, if not his own arrest. They'd worked out his connections with the Peak's Bay and it wouldn't take much digging to find out just how much time he'd spent with Freya Hamilton and Abi Clarence. It had started as a bit of fun. All these girls were the same: desperate for more money to spend on fake nails and hair highlights. The drugs were a fringe benefit. Christ, they'd got higher than Helvellyn in that place, and he was sure the uniforms would soon be breathing down his neck.

He'd had a feeling it might end like this.

He packed quickly and checked his passport. He'd cleaned up, he was sure. But he regretted the fact that he'd snooped around in the girls' tent and taken a few keepsakes. The odd bra and pair of panties wasn't enough to nail him for their disappearance, but the British judicial system had a nasty habit of favouring little girls who were exploited by sexual predators. Not that he was one of those! But he was taking no more chances.

A box underneath the desk containing cash deposits he'd hidden from HMRC over the last three years had around three thousand pounds in it. His hands shook slightly. He looked at his computer: he needed to destroy it. He decided he'd break it down and throw the parts into motorway café bins.

He took a final look around, wiping prints from any smooth surface as he went, then heaved a large rucksack onto his shoulder, making sure his hunting knife was where he'd packed it. He left the office and looked up at the black sky. It was time to move on. The phone call from Cheryl Gregory had been the last warning. She hadn't called him in months. He no longer had any use for her – she was a dull shag anyhow – but there was no doubt in his mind that they'd got to her.

He started his car and pulled out of the car park as slowly and quietly as he could, without any lights. The road that led to Pooley Bridge was deserted, and soon he'd be on the M6, heading south from Junction 40. His thoughts had been of only one thing since DI Porter and her sidekick thug had last interviewed him: where he should go.

He'd come upon the ruin one beautiful sunny afternoon. It was off the beaten track, and had probably been there for a few hundred years. It was perfect. Hidden amongst millions of years of rock formation and glacial shift, noise muffled easily and they'd partied hard. Too hard perhaps, but ecstasy came at a price. He thought about Cheryl again. He'd grown bored of her quickly; she wasn't really his type, but she'd been convenient at the time, when he'd had a dry patch. He knew where she worked now, and he'd seen her a couple of times in Penrith. She still looked nervous. He toyed with the idea of driving over there just to make sure.

As he pulled away, his thoughts turned to Freya and Abi. He'd taken them both up there. Whacked on volumes of substances that made even his toes curl, they'd both been fit for nothing but a few high-stake games. The place was warm and remote, and he'd taken hotel bedding for their comfort, not that they noticed. No one seemed to lay claim to it, but the fireplace was clean and the chimney stable, and he'd built a fire. They'd got loaded in front of it and he'd got carried away.

Not his problem. Any girl already hooked on smack was a disaster waiting to happen, and they should have taken more care. The photographs shown to him by the detectives were a revelation: both taken way before the drugs had wreaked havoc. A less keen eye wouldn't have spotted their addiction as easily as he, but he was an old hand and knew what they craved.

Now, he had two options: hide or be caught. He couldn't afford the latter.

There was no choice.

The M6 was quiet. He hated it normally. It was the longest and dullest road in Britain; no wonder people fell asleep at the wheel. The odd lorry with foreign number plates hugged the middle lane, and he overtook them, gesturing a wank as he passed. At this rate he'd be on the M25 before breakfast. He considered his options, running through countries in his head and thinking about the ones that had poor relations with the UK, or dodgy extradition agreements: Turkey, Egypt, Argentina. Fuck the Middle East; he dismissed that outright. He also had to balance it with who would let him work. He had to survive, after all. With his knowledge, he could disappear into any wilderness, but it would be tricky in a foreign country, and he would struggle to avoid detection. He wasn't a spy, and he only had one passport.

He slowed the car. He was being stupid; he was leaving the place he knew better than anywhere in the world. He could easily hide in the Lakes and keep himself going. He knew enough farms, dairies and fishing lakes to stay alive, and he could butcher. A motorway café was advertised for a mile ahead. He'd pull off and think it through. He'd grown his beard, and his hair was shaggy; he wore bulky clothes to hide his athleticism, and glasses with clear lenses. Mr Ordinary.

He ordered coffee, bought a prawn-mayo sandwich and sat with his back to the seating area. His computer lay in pieces in the bin in the car park. Next, he'd have to dump his car. If he left it near an airport, they'd think he'd gone abroad, and that would give him more time. He wasn't far from the Manchester junction. He could hitch from there.

He felt calm now he had a plan. As long as he stayed ahead of the detectives, he could remain safe and anonymous. He would love to be around to see DI Porter's face when she found out she'd missed him. That would be almost as satisfying as going back and doing it all again.

Chapter 43

Zachary couldn't sleep. He was scared to.

He got out of bed and took his dressing gown from behind the door. The house was cold. As yet, he had no idea as to the state of his finances. He'd never got involved, and why would he? Grandpa had taken care of all of that. He had still been as sharp as ever at ninety-five, and showed no signs of slowing down. The solicitor in Penrith had called and asked Zac to come to the office, but he hadn't gone. That would be an acknowledgement that Grandpa was never coming back. Then there was the funeral.

Grandpa hated religion.

'Pack of hypocrites!' he'd rant if the subject ever came up. Linda went to church regularly, and Grandpa constantly goaded her, for the fun of it.

'Would you believe me if I said I could fly?' he asked one day as Linda served them both lemon drizzle cake after a fishing trip.

'No, of course not, Xavier,' she answered, clearly knowing what was coming.

'No hard evidence, right? So why do you believe in bloody Jesus?'

On occasions like this, she smiled at him broadly and warmly, refusing to be drawn into an argument that she would lose every time. Zac liked to listen to them bickering; it was as if he had parents. Grandpa and Linda bickered over most things, but it was affectionate and habitual. They'd stopped in the weeks leading up to his grandfather's death. Grandpa had spent more time on his own in his room. Zac should have known something was wrong.

He got out of bed, opened his door and walked along the hall to Grandpa's room. It was just as the old man had left it. He didn't turn on the lights; the moon gave all the glow he needed, illuminating the room in pre-industrial romanticism. He made out the urn that Brian had placed on the mantel this afternoon, after a blazing row with Linda. He'd overheard them. He hadn't caught everything, but it had been enough for him to send them both home.

They'd been discussing the female detective, and it hadn't been favourable.

'She can sniff something, Brian. She's not going to let go,' he heard Linda say.

'There's nothing to sniff.'

'The safe?'

'He asked me to do it. It'll never be found.'

Zac had guessed all along that his grandfather had ordered Brian to get rid of his belongings; no one else could have done it.

'I don't like the way she knows things,' Linda said.

'She knows nothing. It's her job to snoop. There's been no crime here, Lin.'

'She said that if she finds out I've withheld anything, I'll be in trouble. I should just tell her everything.'

'There's nothing to tell. It's private stuff; family stuff.'

'Why did he have to go in such a spectacular fashion, the selfish old bastard? He's left a hell of a mess.'

Zac had entered the kitchen silently, the way he had been taught to stalk a deer.

'I think I've heard enough, and I think both of you should leave.'

'Zachary!'

Linda's face had gone purple and Brian had stood up, using his brawn as he always did to intimidate, but it didn't work on Zac.

'How much of our conversation did you hear, Zachary?' Linda asked quietly.

'It doesn't matter. They've found the safe, so I'll know soon enough what's in it.'

Brian took a step forward, but Zac stood tall. 'You don't intimidate me, Brian. You might have been my grandfather's lackey, but you're not mine. Get out. Both of you, get out!'

His voice had boomed, startling the dogs, and they'd scurried to their baskets.

'I'm surrounded by liars! I always have been!' His face crumpled and Linda moved towards him. 'Stay away from me!' he cried. 'Give me your keys, I know you have spares. I want you out. From now on, I'm locking the doors. You're no longer needed.'

He held out his hand. Linda and Brian looked at each other, then back at Zachary, knowing he was serious. They each retrieved their spare key from coats that hung behind the door. The kettle began to whistle.

Now, Zac touched a finger to the urn. It was cold, like a dead body. He hadn't looked inside. A tear slipped down his face and he wiped it with his dressing gown sleeve.

'I miss you, Grandpa,' he whispered.

He walked to the wardrobe and opened the doors. He looked at the space where the safe had once stood, then glanced up and touched a jacket. He parted some clothes and peered beyond. There was nothing on the floor, but above was a cupboard, and he opened it. Inside was an old cardboard box that looked sealed. There was also a black hat box and a small suitcase.

He took down the box and slid his fingernail underneath the tape. He left it on the floor while he walked to the lamp by Grandpa's bed and flicked it on. His eyes took a little time to adjust, then he settled on the floor again with the box.

Inside, he found packets of photos and baby memorabilia. His own first shoes were labelled carefully, and there was a silver hip flask with his initials engraved: ZOF, Zachary Oliver Fitzgerald. He popped it into his dressing gown pocket and opened a sleeve of photos.

His mother stared back at him.

Grandpa had removed all photos of her from the house when she left, or so Zac had thought. His breath caught in his throat. 'Why did you leave me?' he whispered.

She was laughing in the photo, arm in arm with his grandmother. Their blonde hair shone brightly. The next one was of him as a baby, with Uncle Oliver cradling him. Oliver was beaming, as he always did, and Zac could hear his laughter echoing through the house, even now. He had brought love and laughter wherever he went. The next one was of Zac and Grandpa on a fishing boat. He was about nine years old, his mother and grandmother long gone, but he looked happy enough.

A large photo in a cardboard frame caught his eye, and he turned it over. It was Delilah, his grandmother, in all her glory: party-ready in black and white. Colour had been added by an artist, and it looked synthetic and impossibly old-fashioned. Her lips were red, her jumper pink and her hair golden, but the rest was sepia. It must have been the trend back then. He flicked through the rest, but they were all similar. All depicted Grandpa's life in various stages of euphoria and collapse.

Then he spotted an open envelope. It contained a letter, and he thought about leaving it alone; it looked private. Indeed, everything in here was private, and he had no business snooping around. But snooping was the only thing that would get him answers.

One look couldn't hurt, could it?

He opened it.

2 January 2003

My dear Xavier,

The pain I suffer is beyond measure. Always know that I love you and am with you every day and every moment. I take all the blame for our children's folly. If I could turn back time, I would, but we reap what we sow.

There is nothing that I want more than to come back and sleep in our bed and walk in our garden, but we both know that cannot happen. We agreed that there had to be a clean cut or no cut at all, and that was unthinkable.

I think about you day and night. I know that Trinity wishes she could make everything better, and slowly she is accepting what she has done. I worry for her health.

Zachary is such a lucky boy and he will, under your supervision, thrive like the angel he is.

We will meet again.
All my love,
Boo X

Chapter 44

Xavier was even more protective of the new baby than he had been with his own. Delilah never would have thought it possible had she not witnessed it with her own eyes.

It wasn't quite the scandal that he had fretted over. His daughter becoming pregnant out of wedlock was, he had to be reminded, the same thing he himself had celebrated not so long ago. It was true that he and Delilah felt married, but that wasn't the point.

Trinity endured a long labour, and they were too far away from the hospital when her waters broke. Xavier point-blank forbade an air ambulance to Penrith, and so Delilah delivered her own grandchild.

Zachary.

She knew that as soon as Xavier saw him, he'd fall in love, and he did. The Fitzgerald nose, the wide, strong hands and the quiet self-assurance of one so tiny was intoxicating. There was no question that they'd stay at Wasdale Hall.

But, like her mother, Trinity soon became bored of the endless hills, the empty sky and the chirp of birds on the shore of the lake. Delilah took her daughter to London more often and Xavier assumed the role of parent for the second time in his life, and this time, he was good at it.

Not even Oliver could snap his sister out of her sulk.

'She's got everything she could possibly want right here,' Xavier complained of his daughter's selfishness and her blatant neglect of her son. Now they had two children who seemed to wander through life relishing the trappings of their father's cash but doing little to seek the maturity that Xavier expected.

'They're spoilt!' Delilah snapped during one of Xavier's rants about the laziness of his offspring. She'd had enough of his self-delusion. After all it was his fawning that had turned the twins into brats in the first place. But, instead of staying at Wasdale to heal the gaping wounds caused by too much money and idleness, she took off to London whenever she could. Now that Xavier had his grandson, Delilah concluded, her time at Wasdale had come to an end, and she planned her escape.

It was a mere second, a blink in time, that eventually made up her mind. It wasn't the fact that their romantic relationship had died years before, or that she was well aware that Xavier had the odd mistress — no, that was to be expected from a man like him. It was one glimpse, one word and one look that finally caused her to leave.

The sky over Wasdale Hall had turned grey, and the windows had all been closed and the fire lit. Oliver was nowhere to be seen, no doubt sleeping off a hangover after bedding one of the summer volunteers at the lake, who all seemed to find him charming and, most importantly, generous. Delilah had closed the door to the nursery and checked that Zachary was fast asleep, before making sure that Xavier had his final dark, rich espresso, which he took nightly before bed. She wondered that he ever slept, but it was what he did.

Accustomed to the ancient noises of the house, she was taken by surprise when she heard a gentle giggle coming from Trinity's room. At first she dismissed it as a late-night phone call and none of her business, but it irked her. If her daughter was entertaining in her room without her knowledge, it really was the final insult.

She went to investigate, muttering under her breath, seeing visions of herself and Xavier raising their grandson in their twilight years, when they should be retired on the Amalfi coast. Nothing had gone to plan.

As she went along the hall and turned left onto the main landing, she heard the definite whispers of a hushed conversation, followed by the distinct tones of her daughter shushing someone to be quiet. One unplanned pregnancy was quite enough, she thought; another would be downright rude – and using her house to do it! She clenched her fists. She'd had enough.

She approached the door, and the giggling became brazen. Her daughter seemed to believe that illicit sex wasn't invented until 1990, but she was about to be taught otherwise. Delilah hadn't given Trinity permission to host a guest, and definitely not one in her room, late at night, that she'd never been introduced to.

She toyed with what to do. Should she barge in? Or give Trinity a chance to explain?

She heard moans.

That was enough! She turned the handle and opened the door.

Trinity was completely naked and sitting on top of a man, whose hands clenched her buttocks. It was a most confident display, and it left Delilah in no doubt that it was a regular occurrence.

Trinity spun round, and the look on her face was something that would haunt Delilah from that moment forward. Beneath her, being satisfied by her daughter, was a man whose face she knew well.

She'd watched him grow up, she'd supported him, protected him and nurtured him. Her own face crumpled in horror as she sought words to express the revulsion welling up inside her.

The face she stared into, and couldn't free her mind of, was that of Oliver, her son.

But worse was to come, as Delilah turned slightly to her left and saw Xavier rushing along the hall.

'What is it? Is everything all right? What's happened?'

She had been unaware of the howl that had escaped her body as she'd recognised her daughter's lover, and the significance of his identity became clear. How long? When? Why? And her thoughts turned in an instant to the secret paternity of her grandson, Zachary.

'No, Xavier, don't!'

But it was too late.

Xavier stood in the doorway, gaping at his children.

Delilah and Trinity left for London the following day.

Chapter 45

One week after the earl's autopsy, in a lock-up on a council estate on the outskirts of Penrith, his safe was forced open by a certified locksmith in sterile conditions. Will Phillips was present, and Kelly waited for the phone to ring. She had other things to attend to so couldn't be present for the opening.

Fingerprints would be long gone, and if what Zachary Fitzgerald had told Kelly about Brian Walker getting rid of the safe on the express orders of the earl was true, his prints would prove nothing anyway. However, they now had a sighting of Brian's boat pushing out from Glenridding marina late on the afternoon of Friday 13 May, two days before the earl's death. The witness specifically recalled the boat because it sat low in the water, and he'd waved to Brian to ask if he was all right. The man who'd come forward after the appeal around the lake was uncomfortable at dobbing in a local, and a loyal one at that, but it had stuck in his head. The circumstantial evidence was adding up.

Brian had now been formally asked to come to the station in Penrith to record an interview. He'd waived his right to a lawyer, saying he didn't need one. That was why Kelly had stayed put. She'd done some digging on Brian Walker. He'd left school at fourteen and drifted around between labouring jobs until he'd been taken on by Delilah in 1970. He'd been at Wasdale ever since. He had no record, no family and no mortgage. He stayed firmly where his bread was buttered. Linda, with her own property – a gift from the earl – a secure job and her connections to Wasdale, must be an attractive prospect to him, especially now that she was to inherit a cool £100,000.

Kelly thought about Brian's weights bench, and how strong a man in his sixties needed to be to lift the earl's safe. It made her shudder. She remembered what Ted had said about the hanging: someone would have had to lift the earl into place. The assisted suicide theory was looking more and more unlikely; why knock him out if he was willing, or had it been done to save him unnecessary pain? After all, Brian was a loyal servant. If he'd been tasked with something, he'd want to do it right.

She tapped her pen on the side of her mouth and looked at her phone every ten seconds. Finally it rang.

'So?' she asked.

'It was all dry; it's a bloody good safe.'

'Thank you, I'll remember that next time I buy one,' Kelly said.

'Sorry, guv. So I've logged twenty-five items. I've had a quick look and they're mostly papers relating to the earl's private assets, letters from family, or legal documents. His World War II medals were also in there, as well as some photographs.'

'But you haven't read them?'

'I thought you'd want me to get them to the lab for processing first, to see if we could establish who handled them apart from the earl.'

'I do, Will, thank you, but I need you to read them before we lose them for six weeks.'

'OK, I'll call you back.'

Kelly hung up, then called Johnny. She'd asked him to check out the location of Jack Sentry's secret hideout on Place Fell. All he'd found was a battered old ruin that had seen better days and was locked up and abandoned. It was disappointing. It couldn't even be used as a bothy.

She took the stairs for exercise and to work off some energy. Her adrenalin was pumping, and she was desperate for a run. She peered out of the windows as she went down the three flights of stairs, and stopped by one overlooking the car park at the rear of the building.

Amongst the usual Fiats, Audis, Fords and Toyotas was an old Land Rover that reminded Kelly of the three she'd seen parked outside Wasdale Hall. She looked at the plate; it was a Y registration and to her recollection, that dated it sometime in the 1980s. She carried on down.

Kate Umshaw was already in the interview room, and Kelly smelled the familiar whiff of Marlboros and realised that she fancied one. She greeted Brian and the interview got under way.

'How did you get here today, Brian?'

'One of the Land Rovers. The earl let everyone use 'em, it's no bother.' He was defensive. Kelly noticed a scratch on the side of his head and asked him how he got it.

'Sheep got stuck in a fence and didn't like me bothering her. They've sharp hooves if you take your eye off 'em.'

Despite Kelly's instinct, as the interview went on she couldn't help warming to the man. She had to constantly remind herself that the sixty-year-old sitting in front of them could easily be a murderer.

'Does Dominic, Linda's son, ever drive the earl's cars, Brian? He seems to come and go as he pleases, and the earl was generous to him, after all.'

This caught him out.

'I don't know.'

Brian had a habit: when he was telling the truth, he embellished and elaborated; when he was nervous and unsure, or plain lying, he resorted to 'I don't know', and that was all you got. It was as predictable and watertight as any theory Kelly had had. She asked him about where he'd gone to school and how he'd come into the employment of Delilah Mailer and Xavier Paulus Fitzgerald. Sure enough, Brian had endless stories to tell. But as soon as she asked about the earl's safe, he replied, 'I don't know.' It would show up on tape and was easily argued in court.

'How is it that Dominic has means to live? Does his mother support him, or perhaps his father?'

'I don't know.'

'Did you kill the Earl of Lowesdale?'

'No! That's damn slander right there!' Brian stood up and his chair fell backwards. The uniform standing behind him politely placed a heavy hand on his shoulder and he sat down again. It had been quite a response and, given Kelly's test theory, probably the truth.

'Where is Dominic Cairns at the moment? Is he home, do you know?'

'He's probably off on one of his drives. He disappears for days on end. Generally comes back with the odd deer, mind…'

Kelly watched him. He'd tripped up.

'What does he drive? I thought he didn't own a car.'

Brian didn't say a word.

Kelly finished the interview and released Brian Walker. He was by no means eliminated, but they hadn't enough to keep him in a cell or charge him.

Her next stop was Jack Sentry, but when she went to the desk to see if Rob had checked him in, she found him white-faced.

'Guv, Jack Sentry has disappeared.'

'What?'

'His trailer's been cleared out, as well as the campsite office. He's gone.'

'ANPR?'

'We're checking. We've got a hit at Manchester airport.'

'Christ. Check all flights for the past two days.'

'Yes, guv.'

She took the stairs again up to her office and watched from the window as Brian Walker got into the earl's Land Rover. She needed a warrant for those cars, and she thought she had a good chance of getting one. She called Will.

'Have you anything for me?' she asked.

'Plenty,' Will said.

'I'm listening.'

Chapter 46

Cheryl Gregory bit her nails and watched the staff TV with her colleagues. The room was airless, and there was space for perhaps five of them.

'This is Chantel Dean, for Sky News, in Ullswater, the Lake District, Cumbria.'

A map of Britain flashed onto the screen, with Cumbria highlighted in red, and the spot where Freya had been found in yellow. A photo of Freya appeared in the bottom left-hand corner. A missing person case had just turned into a murder inquiry, and it was a quiet news day elsewhere: there were no politicians currently fucking each other, no celebrities avoiding tax, and no terror attacks. A murder would do nicely, even a murder in Cumbria, despite no one south of Nottingham knowing where the hell it was.

'Detectives have confirmed that Freya was the victim of a homicide, and have warned locals and tourists to be vigilant. Freya went missing four months ago, but it was thought that she'd been spotted in Lancashire and the case was transferred. Two other girls have been missing here in the Lakes for over a week now, and concern is growing for their safety in light of this recent discovery. Hannah Lawson and Sophie Daker were staying at the Howtown campsite, and Sky News has learned that the manager of that campsite has been questioned by police. I asked a police spokesperson what she thought was the likelihood of finding the girls alive now, but officers are being deliberately cautious, not wanting to panic the public.' Chantel Dean smouldered on camera, evidently conscious that this could be her career-defining moment.

The camera switched to a recorded interview, set up inside Cumbria Constabulary HQ. A senior officer read from notes, looking up and down, as they were taught, to get as much eye contact in as possible.

'We can't jump to conclusions, and we're doing our utmost to find Sophie and Hannah.' The officer paused. 'We're urging anyone with information to come forward, no matter how insignificant it may seem.'

'And I believe you've set up a website and dedicated phone line?' asked Chantel Dean.

'Yes, we have set up a phone line, and we have a large team working round the clock, as well as continued searches for Sophie and Hannah.' The officer humanised the girls, using only their Christian names.

The website, email and phone number flashed across the bottom of the screen, along with the relevant Facebook and Twitter information, before the bulletin flicked back to real time. Chantel Dean had clearly preened herself whilst the VT played.

'So, what is seen as one of the most beautiful places in the country has been shocked by the horror of finding a young girl murdered and her body dumped. And police now face the hunt for two more women who are still unaccounted for.' Chantel Dean looked fleetingly pained. The camera zoomed out, and as she was framed by the lake, she smiled. 'Back to the studio.'

Bulletins rolled every few minutes, and Chantel Dean's next stop was as close to Christy Bridge as she could get. It was swarming with police, but she managed to find a good vantage point. In the distance, clouds boomed and rain began to fall; lightly at first, but by the time Chantel went live again, she was reporting from inside an unflattering raincoat and utterly pissed off, though she didn't show it.

'Do we have anything else from Cumbria, Chantel?' asked the newsreader in the warm, dry studio.

'Yes. Police have just released this photograph of Jack Sentry, the manager and owner of the site where Hannah and Sophie were camping. They're calling him a person of interest, and concern is growing for his whereabouts.'

'Is he a suspect, Chantel?'

'The police aren't confirming that at this stage.'

'And just who is Jack Sentry, Chantel?'

'Well, this is what we know so far. He's unmarried, and an accomplished climber, and he worked for many years at the exclusive Peak's Bay Hotel, here on Ullswater, not far from where I'm standing.'

'Do the police think he's left the area, Chantel?'

'They seem to be unsure about that, but the story has affected people deeply here in Cumbria. Flowers and candles have been left outside St Martin's Church, which is near to where Freya's body was found. You can see them behind me. I've read some of the messages, and they're outpourings of grief and sadness for the girl and her family.'

'And what have the police had to say about the mistakes made over Freya's last known whereabouts?'

'Well, questions need to be answered, that's for sure. For now, they're staying tight-lipped, and we're hoping for a new statement tonight.' Chantel beamed.

'Thank you, Chantel Dean, in rainy Cumbria. We'll keep you updated on our main story as the news unfolds, here on Sky. Now, Victoria Beckham is saying that she won't be joining the Spice Girls reunion...'

—

Cheryl's pulse quickened. A flurry of excitement rippled through the tiny room. Colleagues swapped theories and a few shared gossip about Jack Sentry. Many knew him. The drama allowed Cheryl to slip out of the room undetected. Her shift had ended twenty minutes ago.

She went outside for a cigarette and lit it with shaking hands. She stood under a huge hydrangea bush, to shelter from the worst of the rain, and sucked in the chemical cocktail greedily. It was time to move on, she thought. She'd been here for five months, and she'd saved the majority of her pay. Hotels up and down the country were desperate for seasonal staff. She needed to get as far away as possible, and considered the south coast; there must be thousands of hotels down there. She exhaled and inhaled rapidly, and it felt good. The toxic mix hit her bloodstream and calmed her nerves.

She'd asked herself if Jack was capable of murder.

She'd never thought so before tonight. He was rough, he was amoral and he was arrogant, but murder was in quite another league. She hadn't seen him for weeks, and struggled to believe that he could do something so terrible. But the police seemed desperate to speak to him. And *someone* had killed Freya.

He'd been in Cheryl's bed, he'd kissed her and done things to her that she wasn't proud of. She couldn't go to the police. It would come out. She couldn't live with her parents knowing. No, she'd move instead.

She flicked her cigarette-end under the shrub and made her way round the back of the hotel towards the staff accommodation. A noise startled her, and she turned quickly. A hand wrapped around her mouth, and she was dragged into a bush. She fought hard, but quickly realised that it was no use: the man was much stronger than her. She recognised his smell. He always wore the same cologne. She stopped struggling, and after a while, he let go.

'What the fuck are you doing? You're wet through, where have you been?' She hit him and he cowered.

'I've been walking,' he whispered.

'The police are everywhere, looking for you.' She tried to whisper and shout at the same time.

'I didn't do it, Cheryl. I swear.'

'Fuck off. Why are you here?'

'I need you.'

'Me? Why the hell would you need me? I thought you preferred Freya. Maybe you killed the others as well.'

'No! I swear I didn't touch any of them. I didn't even know that Hannah girl.'

'Fuck off! She was at your campsite, you moron. She's your type, Jack. Blonde, slim, pretty; looks like she'd cry if you touched her.'

'I'm sorry. I didn't know you'd hate it so much. You gave me the come-on, moaning and shit. I thought you wanted it.'

'No, Jack, I didn't want it. Not like that.'

'I'm sorry. Cheryl, I need to hide. Once they find out who really did this, it will all be over.'

'Jack, you're crazy! I can't hide you.'

'I can stay in your room. I won't make a sound, I promise. I won't touch you. I'm scared, Cheryl.'

She felt herself softening. He seemed genuinely terrified. He didn't look like a cold-hearted kidnapper and killer of women.

'Just for tonight, OK? Wait there.'

She checked the back of the hotel, then picked up a rock and threw it at a security light.

'Where d'you learn to aim like that?' he asked when she returned for him.

'Doesn't matter. Come on.'

They took a private stairwell, and Cheryl prayed they wouldn't bump into anyone. They made it. She closed the door and stood behind it, panting.

'You can sleep on the floor. Are you hungry?'

'Starving.'

'Wait here. I need some smokes. I'll grab some food on my way back. I'm locking you in.'

'Cheryl?'

'What?'

'Thank you.'

Chapter 47

Ted Wallis's thoughts were not of the dead girl in front of him, but of Wendy Porter.

Kelly stood opposite him on the other side of the body, and even though her mouth and nose were covered by a blue mask, he could still see her eyes; could still see that she was Wendy's daughter. He regretted waiting so long to summon up enough courage to go and see Wendy. But now he had, and the woman before him was a constant reminder.

He turned his attention back to Freya Hamilton and tried to work out from his first cursory glances if she'd been out in the elements for some time, or freshly dumped. She was in a bad way, but she hadn't been butchered, though the water could do even worse things to a corpse than a weapon. That and the creatures within the icy depths. A familiar stench rose from the body and Ted noticed Kelly put her hand to her nose.

'Do you need a moment?' he asked.

'No, I'm fine.'

Ted had been on tenterhooks since she'd arrived. Something was bothering her, and he got the distinct impression that he'd done something wrong. It was possible that she'd been sent here by a senior officer against her will, and was simply not looking forward to witnessing the dismembering of an already rotting corpse. It wasn't for everyone. There was no doubt that once the operation got under way, Freya would let off plenty of foul-smelling gas, and Kelly might need to leave.

Ted placed his own mask over his face and pulled on a pair of latex gloves. The external check would give him clues as to how long the girl had been dead. Bodies pulled out of fresh water were in better shape than those taken from the ocean: salt, sea creatures, temperature and lack of entomology all derailed investigation, and time of death was rarely established for such corpses.

Freya had been missing for four months, but she hadn't been dead that long, that was obvious to both of them. It was possible that she'd been wrapped in something and buried, only for the heavy rain to wash the grave away. So she might not have been in the water very long. Her head and orifices were fairly intact, and that supported his theory that she'd been wrapped up, and only exposed to the elements as she'd been washed down the beck. The body had gone beyond lividity, and blood pooling was consistent with the victim being laid on her back. Putrefaction had begun, and Ted knew that when he cut her open, the room would be filled with the vile stench of hydrogen sulphide, carbon dioxide, methane and nitrogen; a heady mix, and one never to be forgotten. He doubted he'd be able to extract foreign DNA.

There was an absence of maggots; to Ted, this confirmed that the body had been wrapped in something before being dumped. She was well preserved. He estimated her time of death as up to one or three days ago, but he'd have to check the body thoroughly for blowfly pupae. He cut away the once red sweater and bagged it.

'That belonged to a girl who went missing five years ago,' Kelly said. Her voice was emotionless, and Ted wondered if that was the source of her irritation: too many dead people.

'The sweater?' he asked. Kelly nodded. 'This changes everything, does it? Have you any idea who you're looking for?' He was trying to keep the conversation strictly within the boundaries of work, but he was keen to ask her how she was, if she was happy, if she wanted dinner sometime. His visit to Wendy had made him realise that he needed to stop dithering and make the most of the time he had left. He thought about her cancer and how he'd avoided her all these years, only to pluck up the courage now and find out she was dying. His hand slipped and he tutted. Kelly looked at him oddly.

'I've got an MO and a profile, but nobody to compare evidence to,' she said flatly. There was nothing like a dead brutalised body to strip the joy out of a day.

'Deep purple welts in the skin around the ankles... Skin has some slippage, but not advanced.' Ted spoke into his microphone.

'Restraint wounds?' asked Kelly.

'My guess,' he said. 'Did Freya Hamilton have any distinguishing features?' He was trying to confirm identity, for procedure, before he moved on.

'In the notes it said that she had a large birthmark next to her left nipple.' Kelly looked at him.

He could see a mark next to the left nipple but had assumed it was a leaf stuck to her chest from the beck. He tried to wipe it off, but the mark remained: it was a large birthmark, and he asked for it to be photographed.

It was obvious that Freya had once been pretty. Even after the elements – and something else besides – had ravaged her, she still looked semi-alive; asleep even.

'You're still hoping to find the other girls alive?' Ted asked. Kelly nodded.

'If you're right and Freya died approximately between two and three days ago, then that means she was kept alive prior to that, probably in restraints. I'm thinking that wherever that was is where I'll find Sophie and Hannah.'

'What about the other one? The one whose sweater this is?' Ted pointed to the bag.

'We'll never know; she's a pile of bones. Found by walkers near Hartsop.'

Ted whistled. 'Crikey.'

'Was she raped, Ted?'

'I can't say for sure. That's the water, I'm afraid. There is evidence of sexual activity, and… let me see.' He went closer. 'Yes, healed abrasions. My guess is yes, she was, over a prolonged period.'

'Thoughts on cause of death?'

'Judging by her eyes, I'd say the beating around the head did it, but I won't know for sure until I see the brain.'

'Sure.' Kelly nodded.

'Let's turn her over.' Ted summoned his assistant, then spoke into his mic again. 'Any of these wounds could have caused a rabid infection, and she could well have died from septicaemia. Let's look inside.'

As Ted made his first incision, there was a long release of trapped air caused by her body consuming itself; nature's bin collectors had moved in. She was way past rigor, but was still in the grip of bloat – although that could have been slowed by the cold water.

'Thank God for that rain,' said Ted. Kelly nodded. In hotter weather, Freya might not have fared so well, though pathologists were hardened to it.

Freya's insides looked frothy and gloopy, like some kind of organ soup, but he could still make out each separate element. The cadaver sac was intact, and he was able to remove it completely. Kelly looked away as he did so. Ted kept an eye on her as well as the task at hand. He felt her unease keenly and wanted to comfort her.

'The rest is purely scientific, if you want to head off. I'll write a full report tomorrow and email it to you,' he said.

'No, I'm staying. I'm all right,' she said.

He looked at her and nodded.

'I think she died of septicaemia, Kelly. I think the marks on her skin are not just bruising from the beck – or something else. Now that I've seen her organs, I'm pretty sure. Her heart is enlarged with the effort, her spleen is hard and her lungs are congested. I think the bruising is consistent with petechiae. Having said that, I'm pretty convinced that it was only a matter of time before the beating killed her.'

'I have no idea what petechiae is.'

'It's the small purple marks all over her skin. Indicative of blood poisoning.'

'So she had a raging infection. Someone didn't look after her very well,' Kelly said.

'I think that's an understatement. I think you've got a sadist on your hands.'

'What about the guy? Wouldn't he get it too? The septicaemia.'

'I'm afraid it doesn't work like that. Septicaemia is internal. It only takes one type of bacteria to get into her bloodstream and multiply and travel. Even if he was still having sex with her, he might be free from bacterial pathology, because he kept himself clean, just not her.'

Kelly shivered. It was freezing in the mortuary, and she pushed her hands deep into her pockets as she watched Ted finish up. She was still standing in the same position as he washed down the slab with a hosepipe.

He looked at her.

'Don't you think it's time to go, Kelly?'

'I'll wait for you. I need some hot coffee,' she said.

'What about something stronger?' He always kept a nip in his office, but he was thinking about taking her out.

'I'm on duty.'

'Coffee it is, then.'

'I'll meet you outside. I can't wait to hear all about why you're so interested in my mother.'

Ted's mouth fell open. Kelly walked out.

Chapter 48

They walked into town and found a quiet bar that served coffee.

'Don't you think that, with all the women living in Penrith – or the whole of Cumbria for that matter – you could have avoided my mother?' Kelly asked.

They walked slowly; it was more of an amble. Kelly had dabbed more perfume on, but still couldn't get the smell of the mortuary from her nostrils. Her skin felt chilly from the bowels of the hospital, and she knew she'd sleep badly tonight, even in Johnny's arms.

'I haven't seen her in years, Kelly. Like I told you, I met her at Wasdale Hall. She's very easy to talk to,' he said. Kelly rolled her eyes.

'And you met my father too. You already told me that. Why, when I asked you originally if you'd met my mother, did you say you couldn't remember?'

'Oh Kelly, I don't know. Maybe it brought back memories. Does it bother you? It's only a catch-up, and the odd meal here and there. Has she said anything?'

'No. She doesn't even know that I know yet. I saw you knocking on her door, taking her flowers. Seems a little over the top if you barely remembered the woman. And now you're telling me it's more than once. Are you seeing her, like properly, then?'

Ted stayed silent under Kelly's interrogation.

'Anyway, it really doesn't matter what I think. My mother isn't about to take relationship advice from me. God, she'd see more of you on purpose if I told her I didn't approve. Listen to me! I sound just like my mother!' she said.

They ordered drinks and took them to a table. Kelly kept her jacket on.

'How do you work in the mortuary all day? I'm freezing.'

'Well I don't. I work in the lab, and I sit at my computer writing reports for more hours than I'd care to admit. It's the basic science, Kelly. Since da Vinci's first sketches of cadavers, men can't help but be fascinated by what's inside. The human body is extremely hard to kill, you know.'

'I know.' Kelly got to the point. 'If it's just the odd meal out, why did you avoid telling me about it?'

'I didn't avoid it. I don't see very much of you, that's all. Besides, I'm old, Kelly, I don't go around announcing my social plans to just anyone.'

Kelly glared at him. He held her gaze but she knew he was uncomfortable.

'Do you interview suspects like this? I'm sure it never takes you long to get a confession,' he joked, but Kelly didn't laugh.

'So you find yourself in town, you get her address, when you could have asked me – all the while telling me snippets of a life that existed in a different time at Wasdale Hall, the place you met my mother – and you arrange to pop in for a friendly catch-up chat after, what? Forty years?' she said.

Ted shifted in his seat. 'Erm, well, I... yes, you could see it like that, Kelly, but not once did I evade the truth or purposely try to conceal anything.' He coughed and looked away as he drained his whisky.

Kelly wrapped her cold fingers around her coffee cup.

'If it really is a problem, then I'll tell Wendy—' he said.

'Stop it,' she said.

'What?' he asked.

'Why do men do that?'

'What?' he repeated.

'You turn everything round to women. When you feel cornered and on the defensive, you strike back even more venomously and make it sound like we're the aggressor. I hate it,' she said. The only man she'd ever met who didn't do that was Johnny. 'You're behaving like a toddler, Ted Wallis. You'll tell Wendy... Go on then. Tell her. Ask her why she didn't bother telling me either while you're at it. What are you two hiding? Did you have a love affair with my mother, Ted?' There, it was out.

Ted got up from his seat and went to the bar. When he came back with another whisky, Kelly had her arms folded across the table.

'Do you ever meet yourself coming backwards?' he asked.

'What?' she asked.

'Nothing gets past you, does it? But I'm afraid it's not for me to divulge anything about your mother. I don't know what her relationship was like with your father. I was there as a shoulder to cry on, on occasion, but I am not going to discuss her behind her back. I'll leave it up to her what she tells you, but don't push her, Kelly, not now.'

Kelly bit her lip. She could cause a fuss, she could sulk and demand an answer. Or she could be a grown-up, and accept that everybody made mistakes, even John and Wendy Porter. She could choose to leave it in the past. She didn't divulge the details of every relationship she'd ever had, so why should she assume that her mother had to do so? She couldn't.

'I hope it doesn't change our working relationship, Kelly. I would miss you terribly, and our little clandestine meetings in the public houses of Penrith and Carlisle,' Ted said, attempting a smile.

'Ah, Ted. Since I got back, a few things have caught me off guard, and they're things I never expected. This is one of them. Of course it's none of my business,' she said. 'And of course it won't affect us. I thought I'd ask, though. I'm inquisitive like that.'

'Oh, I know you bloody well are.'

Chapter 49

Kelly had spent the rest of their half-hour in the pub telling Ted about the contents of the earl's safe. It would appear that Ted Wallis, as well as her own mother, knew more about the earl than they'd let on. She was desperate to challenge her mother, but she was also scared to. It was the thought of hearing something that she could never unhear that made her pause. Because the more she thought about it, the more she became convinced that there was a chance Ted Wallis was her biological father.

The photographs, the arguments, the void between her and Nikki and the need to get away because she felt different. It was too much to consider. Never before had she shied away from what was in front of her, yet she toyed with burying the whole thing right now, never to unearth it again.

But she was curious. Johnny had told her to follow her heart and not her head, because hearts told the truth.

As she drove towards the outskirts of Penrith, she called Will and told him that she was on her way back to Eden House but stuck in traffic. He was to meet her there with photographs of all the documents found inside the safe. He was also tasked with finding Dominic Cairns.

Identity. Everybody craved it, from an earl's son to the daughter of a Penrith housewife.

She parked outside the small terrace where she'd grown up and turned off the engine, steeling herself for an unpleasant exchange. It wasn't every day that a daughter demanded to know who her mother had slept with; it was usually the other way around. If push came to shove, she was prepared to stand her ground. No, she didn't fit in, but that no longer need be a thorn in her side. Perhaps it was something that could be explained.

She thought back to the arguments between her parents, keeping both girls up long into the night when they should have been asleep. Kelly had assumed they'd been about John's hours, or that age-old bugbear between married couples: money. But maybe they were about something else entirely.

She knocked on the door. Unlike Nikki, who still barged in on Mum whenever she liked, Kelly preferred to respect her privacy. She had a key, but she'd only use it in an emergency. Wendy opened the door.

'Kelly! How lovely. I was just telling Nikki that she should come and see you to tell you that she's better.'

'What?'

'Nikki's here. Come in! Why aren't you at work? Day off?'

'No, I came to talk to you, but if you're busy, I'll come back tonight.'

'No you will not! Come in and tell me all about Wasdale Hall. Johnny told Nikki that you've been spending a lot of time there.'

Kelly rolled her eyes and stepped inside. Nikki sat in an armchair in the front room, smiling threateningly. Kelly stared at her.

'Miraculous recovery?'

Nikki raised her middle finger.

'Charming.'

'You wouldn't understand recovery from trauma if it hit you in the face, Kelly.'

'And you wouldn't recognise integrity if Mum served it on your chips.' Kelly smiled.

'What was that?' Wendy shouted from the kitchen.

'Hot boyfriend, wasted on you,' Nikki said.

'Isn't he just?' Kelly said.

Wendy came in. Nikki stood up. 'Right, Mum, I'm off. I need to get my five miles in.' She looked at Kelly. 'Johnny's idea. He said I'm fit but it will still be good for my energy.'

'Isn't that fantastic, Kelly?' Wendy waited for a reply that never came. Kelly walked to the window and faced outwards, willing her sister to leave. For a moment, she wished so badly that she wasn't related to her.

Wendy saw Nikki out, then came back, no doubt to admonish her other daughter. But to Kelly's surprise, her mother's expression wasn't at all belligerent.

'Now, what did you want to talk to me about?'

'Ted Wallis.' Kelly blurted it out without thinking, but it was for the best; she had no idea how else to do it.

'Ah yes, your friend the coroner. He thinks very highly of you. I didn't know you worked so closely with him.' Wendy sat down with her cup of tea and closed her eyes. Her skin looked healthy and she appeared to have put some weight back on.

'You don't seem concerned about me knowing that you've been seeing him.'

'Why would I be?'

'Because you've kept it a secret.'

'No I haven't.'

'You have! Why didn't you tell me that he came here?'

'Do I have to?'

Kelly was stuck. Of course Wendy didn't have to tell her daughter anything about her private life. She tried a different approach.

'How long have you known him?'

'A long time.'

'Did you have an affair with him?'

'What?' Wendy opened her eyes, but instead of the indignation that Kelly expected to see, she saw panic instead.

'You met at Wasdale Hall. Did you have an affair with him?'

Wendy's mouth opened and closed and the skin around her throat turned pink. Kelly felt mean-spirited. Her mother had been so happy when she'd turned up, and now she'd made her feel what she could only see as shame.

'Did he tell you that? My God, you are close,' Wendy said. Kelly wasn't sure if she wanted to hear any more. She had enough to fit together a few more pieces of the puzzle.

'No, he refused to tell me. You just did. Is he my father?'

Wendy put her hand to her chest, but it was a futile gesture: she wasn't affronted at all, just caught out.

'He is, isn't he? Does he know?'

'Kelly, now that isn't fair. You have no right to come in here and accuse me of—'

'Of what? Screwing around because you were unhappy with Dad? I don't blame you for that! Christ, I'm glad that you had sex with more than one man.'

'It was four, actually.'

'What?'

'Four men. There was one before your father, and one after he died. That makes four.'

'Congratulations.' Kelly didn't know what else to say. She decided to head back to the office. In the doorway, she stopped and turned around.

'That's why I don't fit in,' she said. Tears welled in her eyes and Wendy softened. She stood up and went to her. 'Oh, Kelly love. Your dad is your dad, plain and simple.'

'Which one?'

Wendy put her hands over her eyes and sighed. She sat down and looked at her daughter squarely.

'Tell me,' Kelly said.

'I never knew. I wanted it to be Ted's. I wanted *you* to be Ted's. I hated your father by then, Kelly. I'd had enough. Oh, we got through it all in the end, we stayed together like all good old robots do, and we planned to grow old as corpses, in our rabbit cages, never truly going after what we wanted.'

'What do you think in your heart, Mum? Look at me. Look at my chin and my hair and my eyes, for God's sake. What do you see?'

'I see Ted.'

'Does he know?'

'No.'

Chapter 50

Jack Sentry left the Sunnyside Guest House and walked towards the steamer landing. It wasn't his first outing since being in hiding and wanted by the police. He wore sunglasses, but then so did everyone else. The little room was stifling and the joy of fresh air was worth the risk. It had been the right decision, choosing Cheryl. But she wasn't the pushover she'd once been. Gone was the timid little dot he'd first employed at the Peak's Bay, all trembles and tears, willing to do anything for him; in her place was a sulky killjoy who daren't let him out of her sight. She was jumpy as hell and wouldn't let him near her. She'd also told the detective everything – well, almost everything.

He needed to get out of her room. He'd ventured out for the first time three days ago, and he was getting braver. His hair had grown quickly, and Cheryl had dyed it for him; it actually made him look younger. Where there'd once been a neat brown crop, dotted with substantial grey, there was now a shaggy blonde mess, and he liked it. Cheryl had also trimmed his beard. He'd been clean-shaven for most of his life, but he liked that too. He handed wads of cash over to her to keep her quiet. Like all women, she loved money; that was her language. It always had been. She went out on shopping trips and came back with trinkets; but most of it she saved, dreaming that one day she'd leave the hotel industry and make something of herself. Sentry had laughed inwardly at the thought. Annoyingly, she refused to have sex with him, and he couldn't push it because he needed her. For now.

The previous times he'd ventured out, he'd been watching for signs of anyone looking at him a little too long, or acting nervously around him. He also looked for public appeals for his whereabouts. The fuss had died down, and he was in luck: no one paid him any attention at all, apart from a few middle-aged women who were probably just fantasising about a bit of rough. He'd swapped his Jack Wolfskin sweaters, his Crew trousers, and his Ted Baker loafers for casual shorts, flip-flops, and baggy jumpers. He looked like a mountain man rather than the proprietor of hotels and campsites.

He made his way the short distance to the jetty and bought a ticket for the steamer. It wasn't crowded. He pretended to read a book. No one took any notice of him.

The steamer pulled away from the jetty and eased into the middle of Ullswater for the forty-minute journey to Glenridding, stopping halfway at Howtown. The lake was still — apart from the wake caused by the steamer itself — and the travellers were quiet, each busy in their own narrative, watching the water and the fells. For twenty minutes, Jack felt safe. Until they approached Howtown and he wished he'd hitched along the A592 instead.

Police cars were parked at the campsite, and it was clear that there was some activity there. He'd expected it, of course, but to come face to face with it was another matter. A few passengers got off, and several more got on. Jack buried his face in his book again, sitting with his back to the ramp. Soon they were off again, and he breathed a little easier. He'd left nothing for the police to find.

He was relieved when they finally docked at Glenridding, and he made his way quickly out of the car park, turning left onto the main road to Patterdale. He could do this every day of his life, until things died down and he could set up somewhere else. He needed a plan, and that took time. If it meant hiking the fells and lying low all summer, then so be it.

Cheryl had been mad at him last night when he'd come in soaking. She'd made him strip off his dripping gear in the tiny bedroom, and he'd hoped his luck was in, but she'd told him to fuck off, and demanded more cash. He was an easy lodger, and no one was any the wiser as to his presence. Cheryl looked after him, and brought him food and beer whenever he wanted it. But he was bored. Being outside was his only refuge, and so far, it was going well.

He walked past the White Lion, sticking to the line of the wall. There were few hikers about, and by the time he reached the bottom of the climb, he was totally alone. The gradient was steep, and he stopped to drink water and take off his jumper. His tan was coming on nicely and he reckoned that not even the nosy detective would recognise him now. He was getting stronger, too. He must have cleared a thousand feet in under half an hour, and he stopped to rest again. He was nearly there.

He'd taken loads of girls up here, with the promise of booze and drugs and a night of fun. Sometimes they stayed for several nights and still saw nobody. He'd found it by accident: an abandoned stone cottage, vacated long ago, tucked away out of sight just below the crag line. He marvelled at how, centuries ago, men must have hauled the stone up here to build it. It was probably originally intended for shepherds, to break their long shifts guarding their flocks from wild dogs and poachers. He imagined them with crude shotguns, looking for signs of trouble. The amenities were basic: there was a free-standing cooker, which looked as though it had been bought fifty years ago but still worked, and a table and chairs. There was no heating, but the lights still worked, so someone must pay for the electricity.

At the top of Place Fell, he'd still seen no one, and he breathed easily. Each step convinced him of his cleverness at evading the police. But at the back of his mind, he still wondered what he'd return to at the Sunnyside Guest House. He'd found a back route through hedges and gardens that led directly to Cheryl's window, and she left it open if she was out. The space underneath it was covered in brambles; no one would venture round there unless they were breaking in, and no one would break in to a run-down, half-baked establishment like the Sunnyside. It had seen better days. He missed his time at the Peak's Bay, with its white tablecloths, and snooty guests, and rich women wanting extra assistance.

He dropped below the crag line and made his way along a stony path, long disused and grown over.

There it was.

He was hanging onto the slimmest of chances that the door wouldn't be bolted and barred like the last time he'd come. But he was out of luck. The door was indeed closed, as were the curtains, and Jack swore under his breath. Someone had beaten him to it. Again.

He walked around the property and found that there was no other way in. He daren't knock, just in case he disturbed whoever was inside. Maybe he'd have to move on to somewhere else: someone obviously knew about this secret haven in the middle of nowhere, and had decided to stay. He'd have to find another place to pass the time.

Irked, he made his way back to Place Fell and sat at the trig point. A group of walkers came towards him, and he quickly assessed them. They were harmless, chatting amongst themselves, saying hello to him. They were southerners.

After a while, he decided to carry on along the spine of the fells, towards Howtown. From Hallin Fell, he'd be able to watch the police activity. He had nothing else to do, and it was a beautiful day to be outside.

Chapter 51

Kelly left her mother's and headed to the office. Their search had been concentrated around Martindale, where Freya had been found. Their profile was coming together, and Kelly had tasked Emma to focus on the lone-wolf angle, acting out fantasies on vulnerable girls deep in the Lakes. The young DC had an eye for such details and had come up with a few theories.

Firstly, the suspect had transport. The Land Rover lead was their best hope so far. Of the 135 registered in the Lake District, 98 were built before 2000 and they'd ruled out 72 of those. He also needed a base from which to work, and to keep young women away from prying eyes. Kelly referred back to the aerial journey she'd taken with Johnny, and looked at the map. Most of the addresses had been checked out, including the ruin on Place Fell, thanks to Johnny, but there were a couple that had yet to be ticked off their list. The other option was a private residence, and that could be anywhere. But with no physical evidence, she felt as though they were going around in circles.

They'd had a development: Sentry's DNA had been confirmed all over the inside of Sophie and Hannah's tent. So he'd either been in there to collect the arrears the records confirmed they owed, or he was up to no good. He certainly hadn't mentioned being invited for tea. However, as the owner of the site, the fact that he'd been inside the tent wasn't enough to prove he had caused them harm. But it did prove he'd lied to police.

And now Jack Sentry was nowhere to be found. No one had seen him leave the campsite. There was no CCTV or ANPR in the dark lanes surrounding it, but his car had been found at Manchester airport. So far, he hadn't been confirmed on any flights leaving Manchester in the last few days. Kelly had officers combing CCTV of the M6 between Junctions 40 and 20, and his registration had pinged up on the ANPR three times. Photos confirmed he'd been driving.

The details were drip-fed to the media. Each time, more journalists gathered, and they were cooking up a storm. Jack Sentry drove a 2001 Land Rover, close to their window but not in it; the tyres were being checked as she drove towards Eden House. She had enough to arrest, but little hard evidence to charge him. First she needed to speak to him, and for that, they needed to find him. The public's interest had been roused, and they were getting a hundred calls a day. But Sentry was still only a person of interest. If she could go public and say that he was wanted for murder, and that he was highly dangerous, she knew more calls would come in, but that was out of the question. It was inaccurate, illegal and could well result in an inquiry into codes of practice.

Back in her office, she looked at the photos of the interior of the girls' tent. He'd been in there, but when? Her hypothesis was that it was after he'd abducted them, to rearrange vital evidence. She toyed with the idea of passing a few tasty morsels to a national newspaper, to pique public interest, but it would always be traced to her eventually.

The case was frustrating the hell out of her.

She turned her attention to the contents of the safe and the inquiry into the earl's death. There had been no suicide note in the safe, but then if he'd left one, he'd have meant for someone to find it and not ordered it sunk to the bottom of a lake.

The safe had been opened in a sterile environment, under Will Phillips' supervision, and the contents photographed, packaged in protective sleeves and sent off to a lab specialising in lifting prints from paper. That was all that was in there: documents, and aged photographs. That and three medals from World War II. Xavier Paulus Fitzgerald had been decorated for his campaigns mostly in the Middle East, and Kelly was impressed.

She laid all the copies across her desk. There were three death certificates: Delilah's, Oliver's and Trinity's. Delilah and Trinity had died together in a fatal road traffic accident in 2004. Trinity had been driving and she was four times the legal alcohol limit, as well as having significant quantities of benzodiazepine; a prescription downer. Neither had been wearing their seat belt. Oliver's was marked as the boating accident that Kelly had discussed at length with Ted.

She turned to the photographs and made a note to ensure that Zac received the originals when the print service was done. The one that caught her eye was that of the earl with his two children sitting either side of him. They were happy times. The earl looked dashingly handsome, and with what Kelly knew about his sexual exploits, she could see how the ladies might fall for him easily. She studied the faces: Oliver and Trinity beamed on either side of their father, looking relaxed. Most of the other photos were black and white or sepia, and showed the earl in his tuxedo, Delilah in ball gowns, or the twins in an old-fashioned pram, before the era of foldaway buggies. Trinity had the wider features of her mother, and Oliver the narrower, hawk-like ones of his father. Just like Zac.

Zachary.

She picked up a photo of him as a baby. His mother and uncle cradled him closely, laughing into the camera; Trinity sat in bed with Oliver on the edge. Something drew Kelly's eyes to the way brother and sister leaned against one another. She studied the pose and their limbs, a sense telling her something was off. She wasn't mistaken. When she looked closely, she could see Oliver's finger nestled against Trinity's neck. The body language, the protective way that Oliver guarded his sister hinted at a secret between them.

She put the photos down, and turned to the letters. She scanned them and put them in date order. It was laborious, but from experience, she'd be glad of it later. The first was dated 25 September 2001. It was from Oliver Fitzgerald to his father, written six months before his death.

> *Dear Father,*
>
> *I know I've let you and Mother down. I accept that I'm no longer your son. This isn't about me, this is about Trin. It wasn't her fault. I take all the blame.*
>
> *If you would allow me to explain? But how can I if you won't even discuss it?*
>
> *I'm sorry that you found out in the manner that you did. It's unforgivable, but I beg you not to punish Trin. Let her and Mother return home.*
>
> *I will leave Wasdale, as agreed, and you will never have to see me again. With me gone, perhaps you can at least have some kind of normality. Please don't let Trin lose her father as well.*

I will forever pay for what I've done to you and mother.

Thank you for offering to look after Zachary as your own. That gives me some relief. May he never have to pay for my mistakes.

Always,
Oli

The next one was from Delilah to Xavier.

4 June 2003

My dear Xavier,

How is little Zac? I think about him every day, and you, my love, having to carry the burden. Trinity is still quite poorly, but we take each day one step at a time.

London doesn't offer the same allure as it did when I was here with you.

Perhaps we could meet? No one need ever know. Or perhaps your love for me has diminished?

Please let me know soon. I could easily hire a nurse to take care of Trin for a little while. I love your idea. I too think we need a break.

I think you are the strongest and most loving man to forgive your son, my love. May God forgive his soul and may he rest in peace.

And of course I forgive you. I have questioned myself a thousand times, and I should have been there for you when you turned to another.

None of it matters any more.

I am so proud of you.

Much excitement!

Boo X

Kelly was touched that in the twenty-first century, people were still writing letters. It was a dying art form, and one that she mourned. She felt voyeuristic, peering into a private world of love, lust and secrecy, but gradually she was piecing together the reasons for the demise of this once great family. There was no doubt in her mind that Oliver and Trinity had committed incest. The question was whether to tell Zachary.

Progeny. The earl was a virile old bastard. She fingered the birth certificate of Dominic Cairns – found amongst the letters and photographs in the safe – who still kept his mother's name, and stared at the box containing the name of the father: Xavier-Paulus Fitzgerald, 7th Earl of Lowesdale. What a mess. It explained a lot: Dominic's school fees, Linda's secrecy, and yet another letter, which she turned to again.

It was from Linda Cairns to the earl, dated seven years ago, and was badly written. Kelly guessed that propriety had prevented her from tackling the issue head on, in person. Two things stood out, apart from the terrible grammar: Linda's desperate plea for the earl to have more than a financial role in his son's life, and the reference to Dominic's worsening behaviour at school. In it, she apologised for her inadequate mothering and her son's manipulative nature, putting it all down to the absence of a father figure. It was pathos in its purest form, and Kelly felt sorry for the housekeeper. These nobles simply couldn't keep their trousers up, but then plenty of ordinary people couldn't either.

Chapter 52

'Where have you been?' Linda asked.

Dominic looked as though he hadn't slept. He went straight to the pantry and took a sausage roll, stuffing it into his mouth. 'Why are the pigs up at Wasdale?' he asked.

'Please don't call them that. The police have warrants for all the earl's cars. They're searching them and God knows what else.'

She busied herself with ironing a shirt for Zachary, and the steam puffed out in clouds, hissing as it escaped. She hadn't seen Zac since their falling-out and she fretted constantly over what to do. She prayed that he would come round and forgive them their indiscretions. They hadn't meant to be disrespectful, and they hadn't known he'd been listening. She longed to cycle up to Wasdale and see him, but when she'd gone there this morning, she'd been faced with the police and hadn't stayed.

'What have you been up to? That's a nasty bruise,' she said.

Dominic touched his hand to his head, spilling pastry flakes all over the floor. Linda tutted.

'I dropped a kayak on my head, putting it on the roof.'

'Where's your car?' she asked, peering out of the window.

'I walked.'

'You look awful.'

'Thanks, Ma.'

Linda pursed her lips.

'I need some money.'

'You always need money. I've got none. What about your allowance?'

'It's pathetic, a scrubber in the back streets of Cockermouth couldn't survive on that.'

His words stung. He loved referring to those less privileged as if he was somehow above them; it was a trait that had got worse since he found out who his father was. She'd always meant to keep it from him, but in a way she was glad that he knew.

There had been a blazing row; she'd never seen Xavier so cross. It had scared her. His eyes had burned into her with fury and… hate. One thing was for sure: he had enough money to go around, and it was high time he started sharing it. But she couldn't blame Zachary, it wasn't his fault.

'It's a thousand pounds every month! More than I ever earned!' She turned on her son.

'You're a glorified cleaner. I'm the son of an earl. When do I get my money?'

'There is none. If you'd done as I said, it might have been different.'

Dominic walked towards her; Linda raised the iron in front of her and held her breath.

'I'll have what's mine,' he said. She could see the remnants of his snack inside his mouth and it made her dislike him even more. Such a small, irrelevant detail, but in Dominic's mouth, mixed with bare aggression, it was a warning.

He smiled and left the room, and she heard him turn on the shower. She rested the iron on the board and clenched her fists. Brian was out. She seemed to be surrounded by men who came and went as they pleased, not giving a hoot about what they left behind, and she felt powerless to change what had already passed.

She switched off the iron and looked at her handbag. She had several twenty-pound notes in her purse, and if she stayed around long enough, her son would likely lift them. She grabbed her coat and left the house. Brian had taken the Land Rover that she used back to Wasdale for the police, so she got her bicycle from the shed and headed up there again.

She'd cycled these lanes all her life, and as she passed the church, she looked behind her to see if she was alone. Her fears were not unfounded; it wasn't the first time she'd been scared of her little boy. He'd been there that night in the garden, and she hadn't seen him in the dying light. He was angry, as well he might be. Xavier wouldn't budge, and she found herself caught between two stubborn men, each bent on delivering the last stinging blow. But her son had youth on his side. What she hadn't predicted was how full of vengeance he was, and how much he knew. Her priority was to protect Zachary, and stupidly, she'd allowed Dominic inside. The pair had missed each other by seconds.

She pedalled harder as she searched her mind trying to pinpoint when it had started, when the two boys had begun to hate one another. They'd played together as youngsters, eaten at the same table and slept in the same bed. Tears ran down Linda's cheeks as she turned down the lane that led to Wasdale. She didn't know why she'd come, just that she wanted to be away from the house with her son in it. She no longer trusted him. She no longer knew him.

As she reached the driveway, she was stopped by a policewoman in uniform and she got off her bicycle, identifying herself. The officer went across to speak to another, who nodded in her direction, allowing her into the grounds. She parked her bike and tried the back door. Zachary hadn't carried out his threat, and it was open, as she'd expected. She went into the kitchen and sat down heavily on a chair. Here she was safe at least. She realised that with no role at Wasdale, her life was empty, and she put her head in her hands and tried not to think of how it had come to this.

'You've raised a deviant, Linda.' The earl's words came back to her. He was cruel and it was inaccurate. If Dominic had had his father in his life, it wouldn't have been such a struggle. What did she know of raising a child by herself? Of course, there was the money, the allowance, the school, the cottage in Watermillock, but that was all just things. Things didn't make a story, only people. Deviant. She'd had to look it up.

But it was too late. By the time she'd sorted in her head what to say to him, he was dead. Being cut down from his noose by Brian. They both knew that a man like Xavier would never take his own life. He was far too arrogant.

But they knew who could do it.

Linda thought about calling the detective to try to find out what was in the safe. It was her only hope. DI Porter was an intelligent woman, and if Xavier had left anything damning, she'd have worked it out.

Zachary startled her.

'Linda?'

'Zachary! I…'

'Don't worry. It's your house too. I didn't mean what I said.'

'You had every right to be angry,' she said.

He shook his head.

'Why does everyone think I'm just a stupid little boy?' His face was tormented.

Linda didn't answer.

'Why did they leave? Tell me the truth, Linda,' he said. He was shaking. She'd only come back to check on him, she told herself. She'd come back to escape what was in her head.

'I can't,' she said.

'You mean you won't.' He stared at her. 'Was she mentally ill or something? Is that why?'

'Zachary, I promised a long time ago that I wouldn't be the one who told you why they left. I've kept that promise.'

'So break it. It doesn't matter any more, does it? They're all dead. Who made you promise?'

'Your grandfather.'

'So now you're free from that burden.'

'It's not that easy.'

'Bullshit! You're a coward. Why are you protecting them?'

'I'm not protecting them, Zachary, I'm protecting you. If she'd stayed, she would've hurt you. You were an… accident. She didn't want a baby. I'm sorry.' Linda's voice cracked and her heart thudded in her chest.

'You're lying!' he screamed at her. 'In the photos she's holding me, and laughing, and playing with me and…' He sobbed. Linda's heart ached; she'd give anything to make this boy's pain go away. Apart from the truth.

Zac's shoulders sagged, and tears ran down his face. He stood against the Aga and the dogs looked up at him from their baskets with doleful eyes, disquieted by their master's behaviour. They followed the exchange from Zac to Linda and back again.

'Why didn't she want me, Linda? Why?' he pleaded.

She went to him and held him, and he allowed it. They sank to the floor, and he let the pain flow out of him in great heaves. The noise of the searching police officers outside and a distant chirp of late-spring birds penetrated the silence.

'I'm sorry, Zac. I'm so sorry. Your grandmother didn't think your mother would be able to cope on her own, and that's why she went too. They loved you so very much, darling child.' She rocked him.

'I miss him.' Zac's words came between sobs, and he wiped his nose on his sleeve. 'I'm sorry, Linda,' he said.

'Hush, Zac. You've got nothing to be sorry about,' Linda comforted him, wishing that her own son had a fraction of the boy's humility.

'So she went a bit crazy?' It seemed so long ago, and so irrelevant, but to Zac, Linda knew, it was everything.

'Yes, my love. There was nothing anyone could do,' she said.

'Did they really die in a car crash?'

'Yes, my love. When we got the news, your grandfather locked himself away for days; you were the only one he'd let in. No one knows who was driving, but it doesn't matter now.' She lied again, easily, as she'd learned.

'It's all my fault!' He buried his head again.

'No! You must never think that. Zac, look at me.' She forced his head up. 'If there's one thing your grandfather would want you to do, it is to live! Do what none of them could ever do. Lead a proper life, find a wife, have a beautiful family. That's how to make it count, my love. You have to live. You need to take the money and leave this place. Spread your wings, and experience something different. Come back when you're ready, but not before.'

She meant every word.

'But the lake, the fells; I could never leave.' His voice wasn't totally convincing.

'You can. These hills are going nowhere, and that lake has been there since God was a lad.' She cuddled him, and he rested in her arms. He was over six feet tall, but he'd needed to be held, to be wanted and, yes, babied. She'd seen with her own eyes that his grandmother hadn't wanted to go. She was simply doing her duty and looking after her daughter. It would've been easier to stay, but would have resulted in more harm in the end. They'd all done it for him. Out of love and protection.

'Why don't you go out fishing, love?' Linda smiled. 'Bring me a couple of trout, and I'll do them with buttered potatoes.'

He tried to smile, but it was half-hearted. 'I'm sorry I was rude to you and Brian.'

'Oh, don't be daft. You've been through more than most, young Zachary. I just wish it'd been me that found him rather than you.' She looked away and tears stung her eyes.

They sat in silence on the kitchen floor for a long time, each in their own thoughts. It was a curious sight: an elderly woman and a strapping teen resting amiably, propped up against the warm Aga.

'I think I will go fishing, Linda,' he said finally. 'Maybe the police will be gone when I get back. I'm sick and tired of them.'

'Good lad. I'll make you a packed lunch,' she said, and went to get up. She was stiff, and Zac helped her.

'Will you take your key back?' he asked.

'With pleasure, my love,' she replied.

She fetched bread from the larder and carved it generously, spreading it with butter and home-made chicken liver pâté. She wrapped the sandwiches in foil, picked an orange and an apple out of the fruit bowl, and then made a flask of tea. She yearned for an end to the heartache. She'd watched it for twenty years, and it'd taken its toll. It had destroyed her own marriage, and cut dead any relationships she'd tried since, except with Brian. But that was different: he was shackled to the Fitzgeralds as much as she. It needed to end, but not with Zachary. She'd die before that happened. He had to be set free at all costs. She'd promised. Zachary mustn't be tainted; he was too pure, too innocent, and enough sacrifices had been made. She'd tolerate no more. It was too late for Dominic, she knew that more than anything.

Zachary took the lunch from her. They embraced.

'You'll have to take your bike.'

'I know,' he said. 'See you later.' His face was less tense than before, and Linda felt as though she'd helped the lad.

She waved him off, and watched as the police stopped him at the gate. As she turned to go back inside, she stopped. Somebody was in the kitchen.

'Brian? Is that you?' she called.

Chapter 53

Zachary felt more relaxed than he had since before Grandpa died. His conversation with Linda had cleared the air, and his head. Grandpa's death had brought back his anxiety borne of abandonment. He'd been plagued by it for most of his life, but had only articulated it recently with the help of a psychiatrist. Grandpa had picked up the bill, but they'd never discussed it. That would have been insensitive to his grandfather.

He pushed the boat out onto the lake and hopped in. The surface was calm, but there was a breeze, so the trout might still be biting. The storm had kicked up the mineral-rich silt, and a frenzy of renewed life had ensued. He pulled the outboard motor to get her going and made his way to his favourite spot. The lake was busy, and he navigated around kayakers, anglers, rowing boats and steamers. Word was it would be closed again for the weekend, so people were making the most of it while they could. They must be looking for those girls again, Zac thought. He stopped near a shady patch, close to the far shore. There was no access to the shoreline by car, so the day trippers stayed away. Rocks created a swirl below, which the trout loved.

He cast his first line, and waited. He thought about Linda, and what she'd said. He'd made his mind up to drop out of college. Too many people asked too many questions and no one respected his space. He learned more when he took himself off alone to paint. Maybe he should travel somewhere remote. The thoughts came and went as he pulled his line in and cast again. A bite. He was accomplished enough to know a bite from a tangle, and he got ready to do battle. Sure enough, after about a minute, the head of a brown trout popped up. The tail flapped about at the surface, creating ripples that travelled under the boat and all about it. Zac smiled broadly as he pitted his wits against the beast.

He won, and it was a beauty. It must be four pounds in weight, he thought. He held the slippery catch with his left hand as he threaded the hook back out, without hurting the fish too much. He threw it into his bag, where it wriggled and fought for air. It'd make a great meal, and Linda would be thrilled. He smiled, and pulled his hat up to wipe his brow.

At one o'clock, Zac reeled in, placed his rod on the bottom of the boat beside him and opened his rucksack. He chomped on Linda's pâté sandwiches and washed them down with tea from the flask.

By the time his engine delivered him back to shore, he had a booty of three fish. He'd invite Brian tonight; he was owed an apology too. As he cycled back to the house and through the gates, he was relieved that the police had gone. Linda's bike was still propped up against the shed.

The door was open, but the kitchen was full of smoke. The Aga kettle had ceased to whistle, and instead was throwing out ugly thick geysers of black air. Zac grabbed a towel, pulled the kettle off the hotplate and threw it noisily into the sink, where it smashed against the ceramic. He opened the windows and started wafting the toxic air outside.

'Linda!' he shouted.

He heard nothing. Perhaps the events of this morning had got to her too, and she'd suffered a rare moment of forgetfulness. Either that, or she was getting old. They'd laugh about it later. He set about emptying his rucksack. He'd already gutted the fish and so they went straight into the fridge. The thick air hadn't yet cleared, and it smelled caustic and oily.

He realised he was tired, and ran his fingers through his hair. He yawned. He'd run himself a bath, and by then, Linda should be back, ready to make supper. She must have gone shopping, walking for the exercise, forgetting about the kettle.

She wasn't back after his bath, so he flicked on the TV and browsed the channels for something decent to watch. His tummy rumbled.

He had no idea what time it was when he woke up, but it was dark. He must've been asleep for a good few hours. His neck ached and the TV flashed colours that confused him, until he remembered where he was. He focused and sat up. His watch said 7.45 p.m. He got up lazily, still weary, and ventured into the kitchen. The windows and doors were still open, and it was freezing. He quickly shut them and looked in the fridge; the fish hadn't been touched.

'Linda!' Still no answer.

He found Grandpa's tattered old list of phone numbers, still in the kitchen drawer where he'd kept it, and dialled Linda's home phone number. No answer. Next he tried Brian's mobile. It was answered straight away.

'Linda?' Brian said.

'No, Brian, it's Zac.'

'Oh. How can I help?' Brian asked. Their last meeting sat heavily between them.

'I can't find Linda anywhere, I went fishing and we were going to have tea together, but her bike's still here and she hasn't been back. There's no answer at her cottage either.' Zac's voice was pinched with panic.

'I know. I've been trying all afternoon,' Brian said.

'That's odd. She was absolutely adamant that we were going to eat together. I… I apologised to her, Brian, and I owe the same to you,' said Zac.

'Nah, don't worry, lad. You've a lot on. I'll come and do your garden when you're good and ready.'

'Thank you. Have you seen her at all today? Did she have an appointment that she might have forgotten about?' Zac was concerned, and it was odd for Brian not to have seen her either.

'No, I haven't seen her. It's not like her to break a promise, though,' Brian added.

'Do you think we should be worried?' Zac asked.

'Look,' Brian said. 'I tell you what I'll do. I'll walk around the village and check the shop. Leave it with me, she'll turn up.'

But Zac thought Brian's confidence was a brave facade; he sounded worried too. He hung up and paced up and down.

Abandonment.

She didn't mean any of what she said to you today. It was all lies and now she's gone and you'll never see her again, just like all the others who hated you.

Anxiety returned.

When the phone rang again, he was biting his nails and peering out into the night.

'Brian?'

'Yes, lad, it's me. I haven't found her yet.'

'Should we call the police?'

'Slow down. I'll ring them and ask their advice. They might have, you know, a minimum time that you have to wait before reporting someone missing. She could've gone to see a friend.' Brian was unconvincing.

'But she would've told you, Brian. I know what's going on between you two, I'm not stupid.'

'I'll call you back,' Brian said, hanging up.

Zac sat by the phone in the kitchen with the lights out. When the phone rang again, he answered it before it had a chance to go to second ring.

'Brian?'

'Yes, it's me, lad. I've reported her missing. A police officer will be round in the morning to see you. I'll come over at eight so I'm with you when they arrive.'

'Is that it? No one goes and looks now?' Zac felt close to tears.

'No, lad, that's not how it works. Linda's a responsible adult. There's no reason to panic at this stage. Go to bed. She'll be fine. You'll see.'

But Zac didn't go to bed.

Instead he called Detective Kelly Porter.

Chapter 54

'I can't, Johnny, I'm busy,' Kelly said into her mobile phone, which was under her chin. He'd asked to meet up, but she had a million and one things to do, not least working out how to break the news to Zac. She was outside Eden House and the noise of the traffic made the phone call more irritating.

'Kelly, just turn around.'

She stopped walking and looked up, and there on the other side of the road, holding a bunch of flowers and a bag that she could see contained something with a cork, was Johnny. He walked towards her. Kelly put her phone into her bag and waited, completely thrown.

'Johnny, what are you doing?' she asked when he'd crossed the road.

'Desperate times call for desperate measures, Kelly. I'm kidnapping you, just for the evening. Don't look so scared, it's called a date,' he said. She rolled her eyes.

'I can't,' she said.

'Why? What have you got to do at eight o'clock in the evening?'

She didn't know what to say. She had data to input, she had results to wait for, she had phone calls to make to people who wouldn't be in their offices, she had emails to write to people who would also not be in their offices, and she had brooding to do. It was lame. Her mouth opened and shut. Sentry was still out there. Dominic was nowhere to be found and no new leads on the girls had been forthcoming. Eden House was empty at her instruction. There was nothing more to do for the day and she had to accept it.

'Look, will you just spend a couple of hours with me? You've been distant lately. I don't know why; I hope it's not me. I know your office is empty – yes, I've been stalking you – and I know that everyone has gone home. I know you want to find those girls, Kelly, and you will. But not tonight.'

Kelly lowered her head and pushed her ponytail around. Her jaw jutted to one side. She looked up at him.

'I love that face. It makes me more determined.'

'All right, but only for a couple of hours. Where are we going?'

'It's a secret.'

They walked to her car and got in. He directed her to the Penrith and Lakes Hospital. It wasn't the romantic destination she'd hoped for, but he told her to bear with him. She parked in the car park, and they got out. Johnny waved his hand and Kelly looked behind her. A rescue helicopter was sitting on the tarmac, its blades whirring, as if ready for flight.

'Come on,' he said.

'What have you done?' she asked.

'I'm owed a few favours. I like to save them up.' He took her hand and led her to the chopper. They got in. On the floor was a basket, and Johnny told her to strap in. The pilot turned around and smiled. Kelly was floored.

They flew north at first, and Kelly could see Carlisle and further still to Scotland. Then they took a sharp left and circled back to Cumbria. The sky was turning a deep red, and she held her breath. Johnny popped a cork and told her to hold two glasses. She did so, and allowed herself to relax. The pilot didn't speak. They flew south-west, and she could see Blencathra and Skiddaw, framed by a deep purple sky. They sipped the champagne, then Johnny opened the basket and produced smoked salmon bagels. They sat close together and Kelly felt the fizz get into her bloodstream. It loosened her up, and she thought less of her fear and more of the moment.

'What will I do with the car?' she asked.

'There is such a thing as cabs, Kelly. I've got one booked to take us to my place afterwards – if you want to, of course,' he added. She smiled. She didn't really know why she'd pushed him away, but she found it silly now.

They flew over Derwent Water and Bassenthwaite. From the air, they were staggeringly beautiful. A warm feeling spread through her, and Johnny said they should open the second bottle. She agreed. Still the pilot didn't say a word; it was as if he wasn't there. Johnny had briefed him well.

'Have you ever done this before, Johnny?'

'Never.' She moved closer to him, and they looked out of the window. Grey sky was descending quickly, casting shadows and making the colours deeper. Silver sunlight poked over the horizon, fighting for a chance to last just a little bit longer. The Irish Sea looked like a cloud, and they could make out rain coming down in sheets over the water. Closer, to the south, the mountains rolled away beneath them like a crumpled tablecloth, dotted with slivers of dark blue.

As the helicopter swung left, Kelly caught a glimpse of the horizon again, and the sun disappearing beneath it. Dark blue and black sat above them, and she listened to the sounds of the blades fighting through the air and felt the warmth of Johnny's body next to her. She let go of everything that constricted her from the shoulders down and leant her head against his chest. She smelled his scent and allowed him to kiss her forehead. She stared out of the window and felt the tension leave her body.

When they landed, they were silent. The pilot shut down the chopper and they packed up reluctantly. As Johnny had promised, a cab waited for them in the car park, and they were driven back towards Pooley Bridge.

'Thank you,' Kelly said.

The roads were quiet, and in ten minutes they were outside Johnny's house. Kelly had almost been asleep. Johnny paid the driver and they carried everything to his doorstep.

Once inside, he stopped. Something wasn't right.

Josie was sitting watching TV.

'Josie! What are you doing here?' he said. Kelly looked at him, and back to his daughter.

'I've left home, Dad, I'm moving in with you,' said the girl, eyeing Kelly.

'Aren't you going to say hello to Kelly?'

'Hello, Kelly.' It was dripping with defiance. She was a handful.

Kelly didn't hear much more after that. She backed away towards the door, and Johnny spread his hands open in a shrug. He wanted her help, but she was the last person to look to for advice on stroppy teenagers. He folded his arms and rubbed his chin. Kelly felt for him, but she wasn't about to get embroiled in the problems of a thirteen-year-old. Josie had clearly fallen out with her mother, or wanted money, else she wouldn't be here; and that wasn't

Kelly's brief. She wanted no part of that particular jigsaw puzzle. She was adamant that she was leaving.

'I'm sorry, Kelly,' Johnny said.

She smiled weakly and left. What had started out as a perfect antidote to her frustrations had ended up with deflation. It was a nice evening to walk the short distance through Pooley Bridge to her own house. She reckoned she'd go straight to bed.

Her mobile phone rang. It was Zac. She shut her eyes, knowing that she couldn't avoid the truth any longer. But it wasn't a barrage of questions about his grandfather this time.

It was about Linda.

Chapter 55

'Zac, I'm sorry, I've had a drink. Can you come to mine?' she asked. He sounded frantic. So much for not dealing with emotional teenagers, she thought ironically. However, given the choice between Josie and Zac, Zac won hands down. She gave him her address and resigned herself to the fact that her bed would have to wait.

He was at her door in under ten minutes. The Land Rovers had been processed, and it felt strange seeing one of them sitting outside her own house. She was merry from the champagne, and the flight over the lakes and fells. Zac's face was pained, and he came in babbling about Linda. Kelly stood back and let him pass.

'Zac, you look terrible, can I get you a drink? Perhaps a beer?'

He looked at her strangely. 'Kelly, haven't you listened to me? Linda has gone, and she wouldn't do that. Brian hasn't seen her either. She's gone, and it's my fault.'

'I have been listening, Zac. Of course I have. Look, Linda is a mature adult and might not want to be found. People go missing all the time. She's had a lot on, like you all have. People find themselves all over the place emotionally after trauma. I'm getting us a beer.' She closed the front door and went into the kitchen. He followed her.

'No, you're wrong, she wouldn't do this,' he said again.

Kelly opened two bottles of beer. She handed him one, and he took it, draining it in one gulp.

'Better?' she asked.

'Kind of,' he said.

She got another from the fridge and handed it to him, dropping the empty in the recycling bin. She opened the terrace doors. It was pitch black, but the air wasn't too cold. She went to the box she kept at the side of the decking for evenings just like this, and gave him a blanket. He took it, but still paced about. He was making Kelly dizzy. She sat down on a lounger.

'Tell me what happened,' she said. She wrapped her own blanket around her and cosied into it. The boy needed listening to, that was all. He had no one else, she figured. And it was buying her time before she had to tell him what she'd found – *if* she decided that was what she was going to do. But she could let him find out another way. That was even more brutal, and he'd never speak to her again if he found out like that. She had to tell him.

He took a sip of his second beer, and Kelly could tell that the alcohol was settling him. He sat down heavily and put the blanket across his knees. She studied him. He looked worse than the day she'd first met him. He was the product of a damaged family – that much she knew – and she'd seen plenty. Her own was far from perfect, and she still hadn't processed what her mother had told her. It was pushed firmly to the back of her mind; she hadn't even decided if she would tell Johnny just yet.

'I know she wouldn't do it, Kelly, just disappear without a word; she promised me she was coming back. She…' He looked away.

Kelly thought about the safe. She'd hoped to show him a suicide note, or at least an apology. Selfish old bastard.

She wanted to hold him, but she knew that wasn't what he needed; and he could – at his age – take it the wrong way. The boy was handsome just like his father, beautiful even, with his chiselled chin, strong nose and floppy hair. His skin was golden and smooth, and Kelly marvelled at how the young could be so insouciant about their power. She felt old.

'You're busy.' It was a statement rather than a question and she realised that her mind had wandered. 'You found that girl?'

'Yes.' Freya hadn't been much older than Zac.

'What happened to her?'

'Beyond being murdered, I can't really tell you any more.'

He nodded. He understood.

'Have you looked in the safe yet?' he asked.

'It's been opened, yes. I'm afraid it was full of old photos and letters, and not much else, though we did find your Grandfather's war medals and I thought you might like them?'

Zac nodded and took something out of his pocket. 'I found some letters too,' he said. 'They were in a box in Grandpa's wardrobe.' He blushed, clearly ashamed of sneaking around his own home.

Kelly's heart sank. He must already know. But she needed to be sure first. She took the envelope he handed her and read the contents.

'Your grandmother loved you very much. That must make you feel better,' she said.

He nodded.

She changed the subject and admonished herself for being a coward.

'Is there anywhere that Linda might have gone? You said you've spoken to Brian?'

'Yes, we've already thought of everywhere, and he's checked all the places we know,' he said.

'Have you got Brian's number? I'd like to talk to him,' she said.

Linda had never left the Lakes. According to Zac, she'd been shopping to Kendal once and hated it. Zac got out his phone and read out Brian's mobile number.

'Tell me exactly when you realised that she'd gone for more than shopping, Zac,' Kelly said.

He told her about the argument and of his rash decision to order Linda and Brian away from Wasdale Hall. He mentioned the smoking kettle, and that Linda had left her bike. Wasdale was flanked on all sides by hills, lakes and sheep. Zac was growing drowsy from the drink, and he unwrapped the blanket and put it round himself. He looked exhausted.

'Zac, do you have any friends that you could call to come and stay with you? Just for distraction, I mean. It's no good you pacing up and down waiting for news,' Kelly said.

'I'll be all right, I prefer my own company.'

She supposed that he was used to it. She remembered her own childhood, and how busy she'd been with friends, and she wondered if Zac had any at all. The company of his grandfather had made him mature in many ways, but in others he was terribly innocent. She wondered what it must have been like, growing up in Wasdale Hall, all those rooms and gardens to play in but without a companion. She couldn't help thinking that they could all have made it work for him. Trinity was a spineless coward, as well as, judging by the toxicology report, a junkie.

'How long will I have to wait?' Zac asked.

'If you've reported her missing, the police response will be the same as mine. It might save time and energy if we try all the options ourselves. In the eyes of the law, she's an adult. Look, in the morning, we can check her house out and get a contact list of her friends from Brian.' Kelly was convinced that Linda was somewhere close by, sharing her regrets. The woman had lived here all her life; she must have a confidante, someone she shared gossip with, someone to give all that trout to that Zac caught and they couldn't eat.

'Zac, it's late, I'm knackered. You're welcome to stay here. The spare bed is made up, and you look like you need some decent sleep. I'm not sure I want you going back to Wasdale on your own.'

He began to speak, and she held up her hand. 'I know you're used to it, you've told me a thousand times, but sometimes it's nice to have company.'

He drained his beer. 'Do you mind?'

'Of course not. I'm away early tomorrow, so make yourself at home and leave when you're ready – and please try to relax. Linda will be fine.'

She got up and went to the kitchen to throw away her bottle. She peered round the door; Zac hadn't moved.

'Come on,' she said. He stood up and folded his blanket. The action touched her, and she wished he had a mother at home, instead of a secretive old ice maiden.

She showed him the spare room but didn't linger too long. She went to her own room and fell into bed as soon as she had her clothes off. Within minutes she was asleep.

Chapter 56

As Kelly pulled away from her house in the morning in a cab, Johnny was walking along the road. He had come to apologise, but he stopped short of Kelly's driveway. A Land Rover sat in it, and something made him turn around and retrace his steps. Kelly could do what she wanted; she had before. But it hurt like hell.

He went back home.

After picking up her car from the Penrith and Lakes Hospital, Kelly made her way to Wasdale Hall. It was still early, and she was sure that she'd find Linda there, tidying up the mess, ignorant of the drama that had unfolded last night.

The door was open, as always, and she made her way to the kitchen. The dogs fussed around her, and she opened cupboards looking for food for them. She found some and spooned it into two bowls; they ate hungrily. The house was quiet, and the kettle still lay in the sink, broken and burned. She opened the back door and went outside. As she stepped out, Brian almost knocked her over. He helped her steady herself. The man was rock solid.

'I'm sorry, I didn't know anyone was here,' he said. Kelly shook his hand off her arm.

'I'm looking for Linda, Brian.'

'So was I.'

'Really? I thought you'd know where she was?'

'No, I don't. Where's Zac?' he asked.

'I've no idea,' she lied. 'Maybe he's out looking for her. What's your theory?'

Brian looked away.

'I know all about the family, Brian. There was a lot in that safe.'

'I don't know what you mean,' he said.

'Oh come on, stop with the lying, for God's sake! Aren't you tired of it? I know everything. What I don't know is who Linda has gone to warn, and I was hoping that somewhere in that heart of yours you'd like to share it with me.'

'I swear I don't know where she is,' he said.

'But you know where she might have gone? Can't you give that boy a break? He's desperate to know the truth; that's all he wants. But it takes courage, doesn't it, Brian? And you and Linda have none.'

'Don't you dare,' he said, and took a step closer to her. She stood tall.

'Would you hit a woman, Brian? Maybe you got rid of Linda yourself? Is she at the bottom of Ullswater too?' She wasn't scared of him, though she knew she ought to be. If Brian Walker cleaned things up for the earl, maybe he'd got rid of a few things besides a safe over the years.

Brian clenched his fists. A flash of mania passed over his eyes and he blinked; it had only been a fraction of a second, but Kelly had seen it, and it made the hairs on her arms stand up. They were at an impasse until he spoke.

'Can I make you a cup of tea?' he asked. His bearing had transformed since that one blink, and the question threw her.

'The kettle's broken,' she said.

'There's another.' He went inside, and she followed warily.

'So what was in the safe?' he asked.

'I thought you'd know,' she said. He was familiar with the kitchen space and moved about it easily. Linda didn't mind, but Kelly suspected that the earl had. 'I'll need your fingerprints, as a member of the household, to compare with those inside the safe. It's routine, nothing to worry about.' Her tone was casual.

He kept his back to her as he made tea. Kelly watched him.

'Why don't you sit down,' he said.

'Do you always come and go as you please, Brian?' she asked, ignoring his invitation.

'Only outside, Detective. I come in here when Linda makes me a brew. Lately, I've been making my own. No one seems to mind,' he said.

'But Zac did. He asked you both to leave him alone.'

'Ah, he apologised for all that. He's a young lad who's had a shock. Of course he says things he doesn't mean.' Brian's back was still turned.

'What's your theory on who killed the earl?' she asked. 'You must have one. You knew him for forty years.'

Brian remained silent, and Kelly didn't know if he was thinking about her question or simply ignoring her.

'It was his time, Detective. Old people get tired of this world,' he said.

'Don't you think it strange that he was able to achieve it physically, though?' she asked. She wanted to goad him.

The earl might have asked Brian to get rid of the safe, and he might also have asked for help with other things, such as tying tight knots.

Brian turned around and looked at her. He walked towards the table and put a cup of tea in front of her, along with a bowl of sugar.

'Ah, don't go getting all fanciful now, Detective. The earl went fishing all his life; he was a strong old fella and never lost his muscle all the time I knew him. It was only recently that he stopped swimming in the lake every morning,' he added. Kelly made a point to herself to confirm this with Zac. 'If you ask me, I think he was lonely. You know. He wanted a woman. He was never the same after his wife left him.'

'They were never married,' Kelly corrected him.

'Might as well have been.'

They held each other's gaze. Kelly knew he was holding out on her, she just knew it. For whatever reason, Brian Walker was staying tight-lipped, and he was proving a tough nut to crack.

'I know that Oliver Fitzgerald was Zac's father,' she said. Brian flinched. He blinked and swallowed; as he brought his cup up to his lips, his hand shook slightly.

'I wouldn't know anything about that,' he said.

'Bullshit, Brian,' she said. He sipped his tea. 'You don't seem overly concerned about Linda,' she pushed him. 'Did the threesome at home not add up to domestic bliss? Were you jealous that the earl had bedded her?'

'Still waters run deep, Detective. Don't presume to know what I'm thinking,' he said.

Kelly thought the room felt cold, and she shivered. Her cell phone buzzed and she jumped, spilling her tea.

'Shit.'

Brian's face never changed. He got a towel and began to wipe up the mess. Kelly looked at her phone. It was a text from Rob. They'd had a tip-off on Jack Sentry.

'Thank you for the tea,' she said. Brian nodded, never taking his eyes off her. 'I'll make sure the missing person case is started and I'll keep you updated.'

'You do that,' was all he said, still sipping from his cup.

Kelly walked out of the back door and headed to her car. She could hardly breathe. As she pulled away, she could see in the rear-view mirror that Brian was standing at one of the grand front windows, watching her leave.

-

On her way to Eden House, Kelly mulled over the rest of Rob's text. The incident desk had taken a call from a colleague of Cheryl Gregory at the Sunnyside Guest House who claimed that Cheryl was acting strangely, and that rumour had it she was keeping a man in her room – a man who no one ever saw. The caller was a waitress called Demi Turner.

As she got onto the A592, her nerves calmed down a touch and she breathed deeply. Rob had included the number for the guest house in his text, and Kelly dialled it on speakerphone. A man answered, and she asked if Demi was on shift. She was told that the girl was serving breakfast; she asked for her to come to the phone. The man tutted. Kelly waited.

'Hello?' said a bright voice.

'Demi Turner?' Kelly asked.

'Yes,' said the young woman. Kelly had known she'd be young; they all were, these piece workers who slaved away in the Lakes, season after season, for pitiful wages.

'I'm returning your call from Penrith police station.' Kelly played down her role.

'Oh yes.' Demi sounded excited. Perhaps she had an axe to grind and it would be a red herring, but Kelly would decide that for herself.

'Do you want to tell me about your concern, Demi?'

'Well, there was an appeal for any information about Jack Sentry,' Demi said.

'Go on.'

'Well, Cheryl – that's the girl across the hall – she's been acting weird, you know? She's been seeing Jack on and off for ages, and I saw them together a few months ago, I thought he was a creep, and I asked her what she was doing with him.'

Kelly listened patiently.

'She's definitely got someone in her room. I've heard them, there's more than one voice, and she won't let anyone in. I used to go round for a chat, but she won't let me any more.'

'And you think she's got Jack Sentry in there? But you haven't seen him?' Kelly asked.

'No, but... well, there's definitely *someone* there,' Demi said.

'All right, Demi, thank you.' Kelly hung up. She remembered her interview with Cheryl Gregory, and how frightened of Sentry she'd appeared. It was unlikely that she'd allow him back into her life. But she could have been pretending.

She tapped the steering wheel, deciding what to do with the new information. They had the DNA evidence, they had Sentry absconding, they had his history, and they had a tip-off. She rang her boss at HQ. It was a long shot, but if she could convince him that she needed just one

ARV, then she had a chance of catching Sentry. If she failed, she would look like an idiot, but she was willing to risk that. If it *was* Sentry in Cheryl's room, he'd be scared and possibly dangerous. If it wasn't him, then they could all go home again.

She could hear the DCI sucking air over his teeth and she rolled her eyes.

One ARV was authorised, and only one. Kelly held onto the steering wheel and willed the traffic to move faster.

Chapter 57

Johnny hung around at the end of the road. He'd probably walked the length of it ten times, waiting for the owner of the Land Rover to leave. Finally, at 10.30, the door opened and he pretended to talk on his phone. A boy walked out of Kelly's house. Jesus! thought Johnny. Surely not. The lad looked barely eighteen. He watched as the boy got into the vehicle and drove away.

He called Kelly. She was busy arranging a raid.

'Johnny, I'm a bit busy right now,' she said.

'And I'm sure you were busy all night,' he said. He hated himself for his childishness, but he couldn't help it.

'What? After I left yours, I went straight to bed,' she said.

'Who with?' he asked. Kelly was puzzled.

'On my own, of course. What the hell is eating you? I'm the one who was the third wheel last night, if you remember,' she said.

'I know someone stayed with you last night, Kelly.' He couldn't believe that he was about to beg a woman to be faithful. She'd got so far under his skin that he was turning into a jealous lover.

He heard her stop what she was doing. A door slammed.

'Johnny, where are you?' she asked.

'I'm... I'm...' he said.

'You've been checking on me!'

'I wanted to see you to say sorry about last night, but the car…'

There was a pause. 'You fucking idiot,' Kelly said. 'That was Zachary Fitzgerald. The earl's grandson. He was upset and I suggested he come over. His housekeeper has gone missing; it's a long story. He's sweet and he's lonely and he's grieving, Johnny. And I was pissed thanks to you, so I couldn't go up to the hall when he called and asked for my help. He was knackered; he needed a good night's sleep.'

Johnny closed his eyes. He'd got the whole thing spectacularly wrong.

'Fuck, sorry,' he said.

'Never mind. I'm impressed that you think I could bag a nineteen-year-old.'

She had no idea, he thought.

'Listen, I need a favour, and I think you owe me one, now,' she said. His heart rate had steadied.

'Go on,' he said.

'Will you go to my place and check on him for me?'

Johnny had arranged to take Josie out – she needed the exercise; city living was making her lazy – but he figured he could check on the Fitzgerald boy if it meant getting back into Kelly's good books.

'He's already left, but I can go to Wasdale Hall. What do you want me to say?' he asked.

'Just tell him I'm busy all day, but he can go back and hang out at mine if he wants, and that I've spoken to missing persons about Linda, the housekeeper.'

'No problem. Will I see you tonight?' he asked.

'You might see me on the news; we're about to bash in a few doors at the Sunnyside Guest House. Keep everything crossed that I've got this right.'

'You're always right, Kelly,' he said.

'That's the problem. Maybe this time I'm going to screw up so big that I won't get a chance at promotion ever again.'

'OK, now that is your shoulder demon talking.' Kelly had once told him about her special friend the shoulder demon, and he'd suggested giving it a name. He'd come up with Dylan, because he was the character in *The Magic Roundabout* who always hung about in a tree bringing everyone down.

'Tell Dylan to go and jump off a cliff,' he said.

Kelly made a noise Johnny couldn't decipher, but hung up before he could ask her about it.

Chapter 58

Like the rest of the country, Cumbria's armed response vehicles were on high alert. It was deemed that the terrorist threat in the Lakes was low – non-existent even – but with the summer season about to bring in eighteen million tourists, one could never rule out an attack. Kelly knew that the resource was a precious one, and she hoped she'd got it right. The last confirmed sighting of Jack Sentry had been from a trucker at Forton Services. Interviews with some of his old climbing buddies had led nowhere. That was until they'd got hold of the CCTV footage from Manchester airport. Sentry's car had been tracked to one of the long stay carparks, and then he'd clearly been seen making his way to the train station and boarding a train back to the Lake District. The car had been impounded.

The adrenalin caused Kelly to doubt herself, and at the same time she was desperate to get going. Cheryl Gregory had fallen off her radar. The girl had merely stated that she'd had a past relationship with Sentry, and that she was scared of him. Now it was a real possibility that she was harbouring a suspect. It made perfect sense that Sentry would target an old flame who was easily manipulated. Other worries gripped Kelly and she told herself that things would be so much worse should Sentry turn out to be their man and she was the one responsible for letting him go. She had no choice. She had to do this. Furthermore, Sentry might know where Sophie and Hannah were.

It would have been simpler in London, with blues on every corner and over two thousand authorised firearms officers at her disposal. Scrutiny was always going to fall on the provinces when force was used. And it added to her apprehension. She had no evidence that Sentry was armed, but it was always a possibility: that was what rules of engagement were for. The ART would decide on that one. If it turned out to be nothing, and a wasted journey, then that was better than someone ending up dead.

They had reasonable grounds for arrest, and the rest was up to her; she just needed a little help, and the boss agreed. She'd filed the risk assessment and suggested full kit for all officers: stab vest, cuffs, baton, and even a rabbit enforcer tool. A map of the premises was stuck to the incident board, and they discussed entry points. There'd already been three separate plain-clothes walk-bys of the hotel. They were ready.

HQ confirmed that she could have an ARV on twenty minutes' notice to move, and that it was on its way, heading to Junction 40 on the M6, ready to take the A66 into Penrith and on to Pooley Bridge. A rapid-entry team would meet them there. They had insisted on a risk assessment for the immediate area around Pooley Bridge as insurance, and she understood why, but it had taken another two hours to complete.

The manager of the Sunnyside Guest House was fully compliant, although understandably nervous. They needed unrestricted access, and they needed the guests out of the way. They'd been informed that Cheryl was not on shift today, and Kelly hoped she'd be in her room, but their main focus was Sentry.

A superintendent would be the officer in command of the ARV on the ground, and would take the final decision to pull any triggers, if it came to that. It was down to Kelly to feed information to the car's commander to determine risk. She felt the pressure. DCI Cane wasn't stupid: he'd left it to her. She and Rob sat in a patrol vehicle, and she spoke to the ARV by radio. Timing was crucial, and they needed to move at the same time, to secure the hotel and evacuate guests.

Kelly's pulse soared as she gave the order to approach the guest house. The two vehicles stopped outside, and she got out. She'd been through the rig many times before, and she'd seen it go tits up. Her biggest fear was getting the wrong man, or someone getting hurt.

She secured a perimeter around the hotel, and three burly uniforms in bulky kit got out of the ARV. Their weapons were on safety. They moved into the hotel, and three more uniforms cleared reception and checked the other downstairs rooms. Happy that they were clear, they proceeded to the room occupied by Cheryl Gregory. Kelly gave the go-ahead to bang on her door.

'POLICE!'

Cheryl wasn't answering.

Kelly felt uneasy. In London, she would never approach a potentially hostile situation without the TSG. But that didn't exist here. The Tactical Support Group was London-based and provided back-up to all potentially dangerous situations involving armed response. Then again, Jack Sentry wasn't an arms dealer surrounded by ten cronies in a warehouse. He was just one man, out of options. She spoke into her radio and communicated with the officer who led the ARV. She needed to decide whether to bash the door in.

'POLICE! OPEN THE DOOR!'

The radio crackled. 'Ma'am: noise from within the room, sounded like a woman's cry.'

'Go, now!' Kelly said.

Dazed guests milled around the car park, and were cajoled towards the front by staff, oblivious to what was happening inside. Some asked why the police were here, and others refused to be hurried. A few stumbled in haste. Some spoke into their mobile phones. Two people recorded the whole thing; it would be on Instagram within the hour.

From inside Cheryl's room, a man shouted, 'I didn't do it!'

But it was too late for negotiation. The door caved in spectacularly, with wood flying everywhere, and three officers shouted, 'GET DOWN! POLICE!' Cheryl kicked backwards, connecting with the man's shin, and he swore. But before the words were out of his throat, he'd been picked up by two men and slammed onto the bed, where he was cuffed. Cheryl cowered in the corner, crying.

'Please turn around with your hands behind your back,' she was instructed. She did as she was told. Her whole body shook.

The officer in charge of the ARV spoke into his radio.

'Ma'am, two suspects apprehended: no resistance,' he said. Kelly closed her eyes and made her way to Cheryl's room. Adrenalin still pumped through her system, and her hands shook. Rob followed her.

'Contained?' she asked.

'Confirmed,' he said.

She walked quicker now, and instinct took over. She just wanted to get there, as she still had no idea if the man she'd just ordered manhandled and cuffed was Jack Sentry.

She approached the room, and assessed the damage: the door and frame would have to be paid for. She saw Cheryl first; the young woman looked terrified, and so she should be, thought Kelly. She had to look twice at the man. His hair was long and blonde, and he had a full beard. By God, he'd done a good job, but there was no doubt in her mind that they had the right man.

'Jack Sentry,' she said. 'Well, well, you have been busy.'

The pair were led to the waiting vehicles outside, and Kelly stayed behind to thank the ARV officers. She hadn't put them in danger, and for that she was thankful. Three years ago, a raid in London had gone horribly wrong and she'd given the command to shoot. Now, she looked into the eyes of the men who were trained to either apprehend or kill with one shot. They were modest and professional. She shook their hands.

A forensic team would search the room, and until then, police would remain on site, but Kelly's first task was to get Jack Sentry and Cheryl Gregory into custody, and keep them up all night until she got some answers.

'I hope you weren't planning a romantic evening, Rob,' she said.

'No, guv.' He was as ready to get stuck in as she was.

Chapter 59

Sophie clung to the bed sheet. She could feel the strength seeping out of her body. After hearing Hannah, she'd been able to find renewed energy and the will to survive. But it was leaving her again.

She was giving up.

She looked in the direction from where she'd heard Hannah's cry for help, and her eyes closed slowly. She had a fever. Her whole body was covered in sweat and she lay shivering, willing the door to open and Hannah to walk in. She dreamt that they were sitting on top of Loadpot Hill, watching the sun rise, having never been tricked into getting into that car. She was no good at cars — all she knew was that they all had four wheels and came in different colours — but she'd never forget his. The smell.

She hadn't really noticed it when she'd climbed in, hoping to get Hannah help for her bleeding head. She'd held Hannah across her knees all the way as he chatted to her about the sunrise, and how he'd come up here to stalk deer.

How stupid they'd been. Now the smell came back to her. She'd smelled it before, when emptying the rubbish from a rancid bin outside her halls of residence at university. Rotting, decaying, sweet and sour.

The door slammed and she froze. He was here. He was coming. She began to shake. She couldn't take any more. Her body couldn't take any more. She wanted to die, and she was ready. Nothing could be done; they were never getting out of here. She had no idea if Hannah was still here. She drifted in and out of wakefulness and jolted into reality countless times, not knowing if the sounds she heard were the same ones from a minute ago, or if days had passed.

The door opened.

Sophie closed her eyes tightly. She had stopped looking. She'd stopped thinking and feeling. A hand shook her and she recoiled, moving as far away as she could and turning to the wall.

'Sophie.'

It was Hannah.

Sophie flipped over and opened her eyes. They were crusted with salt and grime. It could be a dream, or it could be another trick; she didn't know which.

The figure at the edge of her bed looked different. It sounded like Hannah, but she didn't dare trust it. Bruises made the face swollen, and the voice was deeper. Dead. That was it! They were dead already.

The relief!

The hand shook her again. 'Sophie!'

It really was her. Sophie tried to focus. Hannah cupped her face and cried. Slowly, Sophie moved her arm and reached out to touch her face.

'Hannah?'

'Yes, it's me. Sophie, are you OK?'

Sophie shook her head and caught her breath. Hannah stroked her face and held her hand.

'Why?' Sophie wanted to ask what she was doing in here. She wanted to tell her that she didn't understand.

'Shh. It's all right. There's a woman here. He knows her. He put her in my room and then brought me here. I don't understand, but I'm here now.'

'Who is she?'

'I don't know.' They spoke in whispers.

'He knows her. He knows her well. She talked to him, telling him to stop. She said the police are coming.'

'The police?'

'Yes, everything will be over soon. Hang on, Sophie. Don't go to sleep. You need to stay awake.'

'I can't.'

'Yes you can.' Hannah climbed onto the bed and lay next to her. The warmth of her body convinced Sophie that her vision was real, and she leant in towards her. Hannah held her and rocked her, whispering to her that she was safe. Sophie put her hand up to Hannah's face and touched her cheek.

'Are you OK?' Hannah said. 'You're so hot.'

'I have a fever.'

'I can feel it.' She looked around the room. A bottle lay on its side on the floor, and she got off the bed to see if there was any water in it. There was about an inch in the bottom, and she brought it to the bed and poured it over Sophie's face. Sophie opened her eyes.

'Stay with me,' Hannah whispered.

The two girls looked at one another and held hands.

They both jumped when they heard raised voices. One was a man and one was a woman. They recognised the man as their tormentor.

'That's the woman who came.'

'She's arguing with him!'

'Yes, and he's listening.'

They heard a bang, and a scream.

Chapter 60

'You take Cheryl and I'll take Sentry, then we'll swap after about thirty minutes. Ready?' Kelly said to Rob.

'Yup,' he replied.

Kelly entered the interview room. Jack Sentry looked tense. He appeared so different to the last time she'd seen him, and it was a strange sensation. It was as if she was interviewing a completely different person. A uniform stood in the corner and nodded to her.

'Could we have the table removed, please?' she requested.

It was always better to see a suspect's whole body; a table gave them places to hide. Sentry looked worried by this development, and sat up straighter. His hands were in cuffs.

'That's better,' said Kelly. She'd watch his feet and his posture. She sorted various bits of paper at the table, which had been moved to the edge of the room, and took her time.

'Jack, good afternoon,' she said. She sat down opposite him. 'Let's get the housekeeping out of the way, shall we? Please state your full name and date of birth for the record.' He did so. Even his voice had changed.

'So tell me about your climbing.'

'What?' He floundered, which was exactly what she wanted.

'I know you've been hiking these hills for years; tell me about it. Is it a hobby or part of your work?'

'My work?'

'Abducting, torturing and killing young blonde girls.'

'No! I... You've got all of this wrong. I didn't touch them,' he said.

'Them? We've only got one body. Would you like to tell me where the others are?'

'No! I mean... I don't know! I didn't do anything wrong,' he said. He was almost believable.

'Really? OK. Let's just pretend that I believe you for a second.' She let this sink in. 'Why did you run?'

'Because I knew you'd think it was me.'

'What?'

'Killing Freya.'

'Freya? So you knew all along that she was dead?'

'No! I don't know!' He put his head in his hands. 'I didn't kill anyone. I saw it on the news like everyone else,' he said.

'So tell me about Hannah Lawson and Sophie Daker. Did they reject your requests for payment in kind? Which of them did you prefer?'

'It was a joke! I didn't mean it,' he said. He'd begun to sweat, and Kelly could feel his discomfort. His feet tapped and he pushed back hard on his chair.

'It's not a particularly funny joke, though, is it? Did Freya reject you too? Is that why you killed her?'

'I didn't! You have to believe me. I didn't touch her! OK, so I like women, but I never do anything they don't want!' His eyes filled with water, and he tried to spread his hands. In cuffs, it accentuated the gesture.

'Why should I believe you, Jack? I have a dead girl – who you were screwing – and two more missing who stayed at your campsite, and then you go missing. I've got others who've gone on record about your sexual harassment of them at the Peak's Bay. I've also got the cold case of Abi Clarence who turned up dead three years ago having worked with you. Give me another explanation. I'm listening,' she said.

Silence.

'Jack, we know you were seeing Freya when she went missing, and it's looking likely that you were the last person to see her alive. You have put a lot of effort into evading me, and I'd like to know why. Give me an alternative. I need something. If it wasn't you, tell me what you know.'

Silence.

'Where are Hannah and Sophie?' she asked.

'I don't know!' he shouted. The uniform stepped forward, but Kelly indicated for him to stay where he was.

'When was the last time you saw Freya? Because she obviously never made it back home to Humberside, and you knew that, didn't you?'

Sentry looked at his shoes.

'Have you got a bad temper, Jack?' He swallowed hard and his eyes revealed that he was desperately searching for something to tell her. He was tall, athletic and broad-shouldered, and Kelly remembered what Johnny had said about the strength needed to haul bodies around the fells. Jack Sentry was a mountain man: just like Johnny, she thought.

He tapped his foot against the chair, and Kelly let him sweat a bit longer.

'Did you enjoy dominating those girls, like you did Cheryl? But they fought back, is that it?'

'I didn't hurt Cheryl!' But when he said it, he closed his eyes. He was lying. Kelly held his gaze, and he looked away first.

'I'll ask you again. Where did you last see Freya Hamilton?'

He put his head in his hands and let out a sob. Kelly felt on the verge of a confession. He looked up, floundering under her scrutiny. He had a strong brow and she pondered what those eyes liked to watch.

'Place Fell.'

'What did you say?'

'Place Fell; we used to go up there. There's this abandoned cottage; we used to go there to party.' His head went back into his hands. 'I didn't mean to hurt her,' he said.

Kelly was close; any minute now, she thought.

'What happened, Jack?' she asked.

He looked at his feet.

—

Next door, Rob turned on the charm.

'You must feel very used, Cheryl. How on earth did he manage to convince you to hide him?'

'I d-d-don't know,' she stuttered.

'Drink some water. You've had a shock. No doubt you're worried about what your parents will think. You're not used to disappointing them, are you?' Rob had read Kelly's notes on Cheryl very carefully.

'Yes, but why...' The girl's eyes widened.

'Oh, I took the liberty of informing them, Cheryl. They're waiting outside,' he lied.

Her eyes widened further as panic set in, and she looked at the door.

'They'll wait as long as they have to. I just need you to start giving me some answers. When was the last time you saw Freya with Jack Sentry?' he asked.

Cheryl was thrown by the question.

'I can't remember,' she said.

'Did you help him? Did you trick Hannah and Sophie into thinking he was a kind and innocent man?' He'd started softly, but now the gloves were off.

'What? He didn't do it!' Her body shook with the effort of her passion, and it was clear that she was willing it to be true.

'Do what? Kill Freya? Or Abi? Who are you talking about? Or did you mean he didn't abduct Hannah and Sophie?'

'None of it! He promised... he...' Her sentence fell short.

'How did he convince you of that, Cheryl? Did he hurt you again?'

She spilled some water, and her face crumpled.

'No, you don't understand...' she said.

'Maybe you could enlighten me then. Jack Sentry likes depraved sex, is that right?'

She looked like a vulnerable fledgling, isolated from its mother and facing a hungry predator.

'I don't know,' she whimpered.

'Yes you do.' He looked deep into her eyes. 'Perhaps if you were to tell me the truth, we might be able to keep certain details out of the press and away from, say, your mother and father,' he added.

She bent her head and buried it in her hands.

Rob sat back and looked at his watch. He felt wretched at turning the screw on the woman who was barely more than a girl, but she'd harboured a suspect. Their thirty minutes was almost up.

—

Next door, Kelly spread out four photos.

'Pretty, young and blonde. What did you do there, Jack?'

'Drugs, drink... and...' He stopped. His forty-odd years were suddenly resonant on his face.

'Sex?' she said.

'Yes,' he said.

She spread out a map in front of him. 'Show me,' she said.

He looked at the map and traced his finger in circles around Place Fell. 'We found it up here. It's out of the way, hidden really well. You can't see it from the path.' She watched his finger.

'You're lying, Cheryl already told us about it and I've had it checked out.'

'What?' He looked genuinely perplexed.

'Jack, if you're to have any chance, we need to know the truth. In my eyes, you're guilty as hell, and you running away doesn't help. Give me something.' Her patience was wearing thin.

Sentry inhaled and his hands shook.

'I thought she wanted to fool around a bit. We were totally out of it on coke. She liked it... rough,' he said.

God. Kelly hated hearing this from men. *She liked it rough.* What did it mean? It covered so many bases, and disguised so many sins. It was what rapists usually said in their defence.

'You're going to have to be specific, Jack. What did you and Freya do?'

Sentry struggled with his words.

'I thought she'd like to try something new, but I hurt her... OK? I fucking hurt her.' He was sobbing now.

'OK, Jack. Let's stick to facts. You hurt her how? Physically?'

'Yes,' he said.

'Sexually?'

'Yes.'

'Violently?'

'No!'

'So then what?'

'I left. She told me to go, so I did.' His shoulders shook and his face grew purple with the shame. Tears flowed freely down his face.

'You left her in a ruin on Place Fell after you'd had sex that was too rough?' Kelly was gobsmacked.

'Yes!' he screamed.

'Charming,' she said.

'I went back. I swear I went back. But it was all locked up. I banged on the doors and shutters. I...' He broke off.

Kelly thought for a second.

'When was this, Jack?'

'The next day,' he said.

Kelly got up.

Jack Sentry looked at her and shook his head. He was fucked, and he knew it.

—

Kelly met Rob in the corridor.

'Anything?' she asked.

'She's terrified. She swears he didn't do anything,' Rob said.

'He's still banging on about the ruin up on Place Fell. I think we need to take a closer look.'

'Now?'

'They can stay put; we have them for twelve hours. Who's upstairs?'

'Emma.'

'Get a patrol car. There's no access directly, but we can get a car up the Boredale road.'

They went through the door at the end of the corridor and Rob left instructions with the uniforms. He followed Kelly to the lift and they travelled the three floors up to the incident room.

'Can't you chopper it?' Emma asked when they told her.

'I can't justify it. Not at this stage.'

'Is it on the photos we took?'

'No.'

Emma turned to her desk and lifted her phone. She hooked the receiver under her chin and spoke to Kelly. 'We can have two patrol cars up there in twenty minutes. Can I come?'

Kelly looked at Rob and back to Emma. 'Come on then.'

Chapter 61

They hitched a lift with the patrol cars and Kelly spoke to HQ on the drive through Penrith. She always kept a walking bag in her office, and she'd grabbed it before heading downstairs to the waiting vehicles.

It irritated her that she was confined by a car, but she had to do it properly. She couldn't go hiking up from Patterdale, where she felt most comfortable, because she was in the middle of an investigation. She would have been quicker on foot and on her own, and she fretted in the back seat of the patrol car.

'Use blues,' she instructed the driver.

She wished she'd gone up there herself with Johnny. He'd found it locked up too, and he'd said it was empty. Perhaps it wasn't.

They drove in convoy through Penrith, traffic parting for them, and soon they were on their way along the B5320, through Pooley Bridge and then on to the south shore road, heading for Boredale. They passed the campsite, the turning for the Peak's Bay, and Martindale church.

The road only went so far before they were forced to stop. A helicopter could have got them further but it couldn't have landed easily. They'd changed into trainers and sweaters, and they set off with two uniforms, the other three waiting with the vehicles on a closed channel. They walked quickly and discussed their situation. Kelly had years on Rob and Emma, but she didn't break into a sweat as they hiked towards the peak. After twenty minutes, the uniforms were trailing behind, wiping their brows. Their kit probably weighed a good twenty pounds: vest, radio, baton, cuffs and heavy polished shoes utterly unsuitable to the hike.

Kelly looked over her shoulder and caught a glimpse of Ullswater below. She could kick herself for not coming up here with Johnny to check, but she could have done little without backup. Nobody spoke as they neared the top. Kelly had the route scorched into her brain: Sentry had confirmed it and Johnny had showed her on a detailed OS map.

'Guv?' Kelly turned around to where the uniforms had stopped. 'These are fresh vehicle tracks.'

She walked back and looked at the ground where the uniform pointed. He was right. A muddy puddle revealed a clear tyre track heading in the direction of the hill. Straight for where they were going.

'How the hell has anyone got up here?' The wind was her only answer; Rob and Emma stood with their hands on their hips, catching their breath.

'Any farmland up here?' Rob managed eventually.

'Don't think so. It'd take a tank to navigate these rocks.'

They carried on with caution.

The stone dwelling sat hidden between two rocky outcrops, quietly private and untouched for years. It surprised them all. It wasn't quite a ruin – it still had doors and shutters, just like Sentry and Johnny had said – but it had definitely seen better days. It was quaint and pretty, and Kelly couldn't help but admire it. She tried to remember if she and Johnny had spotted it from the helicopter, and she was sure they hadn't. It was always a slightly invigorating moment when one discovered hidden gems in the Lake District, which had been tramped over by millions of boots before them.

They walked around the ancient dwelling and Kelly stopped at the sight of an old Land Rover. She'd never have thought it possible, but somehow it had got up here, its engine no doubt screaming and tyres sinking. The plate was pre-2000, covered in mud and battered around the edges, barely readable. Their group approached the vehicle and looked inside the windows; it was filthy. Kelly took a close up photo of the tyres.

She approached the door of the cottage.

'Ma'am.' A uniform moved in front of her and she had to remind herself of protocol. They'd have to go in first.

'Did we bring anything to break in?' she asked. One of the uniforms nodded and produced a hammer and a long screwdriver. She wondered where he'd hidden them.

He stepped forward and banged on the door. Kelly, Rob and Emma waited, then walked around the sides and tried the shutters.

Nothing.

They stood back. Perhaps Sentry had set them up all along and there was nothing here. Kelly felt a little foolish. She sighed: another wasted venture. She didn't doubt that he had brought girls here, but he was obviously stalling for time, and she'd fallen for it.

Behind her, she heard a lock turning, and looked back at the cottage. The front door was opening and the two uniforms stood in front of the detectives, ready to handle whatever appeared. Not for the first time Kelly wished they weren't so vulnerable, but at least the uniforms were strapping six-footers.

As she stood waiting, Kelly noticed one of the uniforms lower his radio. There in the doorway, with a viciously swollen eye, and sobbing lightly, stood Linda Cairns.

Chapter 62

'Linda?' Kelly said, stepping forward. 'Are you all right? Zac's been worried sick. What on earth are you doing up here?' The last person she had expected to see up a mountainside was Linda Cairns, and it had thrown her somewhat. Maybe Linda owned this place and it was her little retreat. But that didn't explain why Jack Sentry had been able to use it for so long undisturbed. It also didn't explain her wounded eye.

Linda wiped her eyes. She looked different.

'Linda? Are you alone?'

The uniforms caressed their radios and batons, looking around them for answers.

'Linda?' she asked again. The woman stepped back into the cottage, and Kelly nodded to one of the uniforms to follow.

They filed into the dwelling, leaving Rob and the other uniform outside.

'Linda, are you all right? What happened to your eye? Who owns this place?' Again Linda ignored her.

The uniform moved away to look around as Kelly and Emma took in the state of the place. It stank, and was dark and damp; it wasn't somewhere Kelly would link to such a fastidious woman as Linda Cairns. As her eyes adjusted, she noticed rotting food, dirty dishes, stale water in the sink, and a littered table. The room was a kitchenette, as far as she could make out, but the detritus could've disguised anything; it could be a bedroom for all she knew.

'Do you own this place, Linda? Who lives here?' Kelly asked.

'No, it belongs to – belonged to – Xavier. It's been in the family for centuries, but it fell into disuse. I didn't know he still used it until Brian told me.'

'Who still used it? The earl?' Kelly asked.

'Yes,' Linda said.

Kelly laughed. 'Are you kidding me? He couldn't have made it up here.'

Linda looked away and a shadow crossed her face. Kelly didn't know what to make of her strange behaviour; she could've been speaking to the wall. Linda wrung her hands and sat down at the table. She didn't seem to be aware of the smell.

'Ma'am!' The uniform shouted and Kelly and Emma rushed towards his voice. 'In here!'

Kelly went along a dark corridor and Emma followed. A door was open and they approached it. Inside, the uniform knelt beside a bed and spoke into his radio, calling for medics.

'Christ.' Kelly stopped. On the bed lay two girls, huddled together under a blanket like lovers sheltering from Armageddon. 'Emma, help me,' she said. But she needn't have spoken, because Emma was already searching for signs of life. They checked the girls' wrists and nodded to one another. They were still alive.

The stench made Kelly retch. She bent over, and bile burned her throat. Her eyes watered and she coughed. Emma pulled the blanket away slowly.

'Fucking hell,' she whispered, recoiling.

All they could do was wait. They couldn't be more remote, but at least there was partial access. If only the girls could hold on.

'Sophie?' Kelly said gently. The girl didn't respond. 'We're police officers. You're safe now. It's over. Hannah?' There was no response from the other girl either.

'How long?' Kelly asked the uniform.

He shrugged his shoulders. They all knew that getting medics up here might take an hour.

'First aid, in the car!'

Kelly darted out, passing Linda.

'Don't move an inch,' she barked, pointing at her as she ran out of the building.

Rob watched her as she sprinted past him back the way they'd come. She ran as fast as she could, her lungs burning and her thighs heavy as she gathered pace.

'Help me,' she shouted and he followed, sprinting. They reached the car and Kelly went to the boot, grabbing the medical kit.

'Get the water,' she ordered Rob, then she turned and pounded towards the crag once more. Her heart beat through her chest and she tried to go faster, breathing in great heaves.

Back at the cottage, she rushed into the bedroom and opened the bag. Emma rolled up her sleeves and assisted the uniform.

'Stay with us,' she whispered to the girls, who were still unresponsive. Kelly left the room.

In the kitchen, Linda rocked back and forth on her chair.

'Linda, what is going on?' Kelly said. 'Who did this?'

The housekeeper stared at her blankly.

'He's gone.'

'Who?'

No answer.

'Where?'

'To get Zac.'

'Who did this, Linda? Tell me!' Kelly screamed. She was mad as hell, angry that she didn't know how the pieces fitted together; how Zac was involved. Surely he hadn't done this?

She remembered Freya Hamilton's autopsy and ran back to the room.

'Check for petechiae,' she shouted. 'Purple marks. It's a sign of septicaemia.'

Emma nodded and examined the girls' arms. Hannah began to wake and opened her mouth to scream. She struggled and Emma had to restrain her gently.

'It's all right. It's all right! I'm a police officer. It's all over, Hannah. You're safe.'

Chapter 63

'Hey, Zac.'

Zac turned around, wary. He recognised the voice. Dominic stood in the doorway.

'What are you doing here?'

'Well technically I'm your uncle, bro. And technically that means that all this is mine.'

Samson growled and Zac soothed the large dog. The other Labrador cowered in her basket.

'Get that fucking mutt out of my way,' Dominic said.

'You need to leave.'

Dominic laughed. 'No I don't; *you* do.'

'What?'

Dominic curled the thumb and forefinger of one hand into a circle and pushed the forefinger of the other hand through it, in and out.

'Dirty fuckers, your ma and pa.'

Zac swallowed. He didn't want to know what Dominic was talking about. He hadn't seen him for at least six months, and his childhood playmate had been told to stay away from Wasdale. Zac had no idea why Dominic had turned out to be such an arsehole, but he felt sorry for Linda.

'You don't know anything about my parents.'

'Oh, I do. But mine are even more interesting. Notice the resemblance?' Dominic turned sideways, puffed his chest out and mimicked Zac's grandfather. 'Linda! Fetch me my pipe!' he cackled as he waltzed around.

Zac felt nervous. He didn't know where the conversation was going, and he wanted to get out of the house. Dominic was no longer a boy and could inflict much more damage than merely holding him underwater, like he did when Zac was three years old. Zac looked at him. He was pathetic, possibly mentally ill. He looked like a tramp and had bruises on his hands and his head. The earl would have looked after him had he not been such a brat, but that was none of Zac's business.

'We're not related.'

'Zac. The earl was my dad – did Linda never tell you? They fucked on this table.'

Dominic patted the old oak surface. He was enjoying his moment, but Zac didn't want to hear any of it. He went to grab his coat to leave, but Dominic barred the doorway.

'I'm here to take what's mine.'

'You're crazy.'

'I know.' Dominic laughed heartily again.

Zac's mind spun. Dominic was talking like a lunatic, but he knew how it felt to miss a father figure, and it could easily turn you paranoid. The bluster was no doubt as a result of feeling abandoned. They had much in common, though he didn't want to admit it.

'Lad, what you doing here?'

Dominic spun around. Brian filled the doorway that led to the hall. Zac threw him a look and wondered where he'd been.

'Ah, fuck off, big man. Haven't you got errands to run for my mother? I was just explaining to Zac that this house now belongs to me and he needs to fuck off. As do you. I have no need for lackeys.'

Brian stepped forward and stood between the two young men. Dominic laughed again. He clearly wasn't scared of the gardener who gutted deer and heaved weights in his shed. Zac was puzzled and yet fascinated by the exchange and wondered what Brian would do next. He looked between the two.

'I was just telling him that his parents were dirty fuckers. That whore Trinity and her pervert brother, Oliver.'

Brian looked at Zac, who widened his eyes but could think of nothing to do or say; he was rooted to the spot and inanimate.

'Now, lad, you're a liar and a nuisance, and you need to be getting on or I'm calling the police,' Brian cautioned.

'Oh for fuck's sake, Brian. Do me a favour. Why would you want the police around here when we all know that you strung up old Xavier?'

Zac stared at Brian.

'Lad, he's lying. Don't listen. Go through into the hall and I'll be out shortly, after I've got rid of this little wet weekend.' Brian rolled up his sleeves and Zac slipped through into the hallway. Remembering that he'd left his mobile phone in his jacket, he went into the drawing room and walked to the green phone, so unused and alien to him. He lifted the receiver and dialled Kelly's number. His memory for numbers was as good as his ability to predict which direction a trout would swim if cornered amongst the reeds.

Brian had mentioned the police. Whatever he was doing, he wouldn't want them anywhere near here unless he thought there was going to be trouble, and Zac didn't trust Dominic one bit. He waited as the number rang and went to answerphone. He dialled again, his fingers unused to the round plastic dial that he'd watched his grandfather use, mesmerised by the procedure. It took an age.

Kelly answered and he stumbled over his words.

She told him to repeat himself, but slower, and he tried to do what she wanted. This time she understood and told him to get out of the house. She added that she'd found Linda and she was all right.

Zac was puzzled but decided to do as Kelly had told him. As he opened the heavy front door, he heard a shout and a series of bangs, as if bodies were slamming into furniture. But another sound overrode the commotion and grew louder, and it came from the lane.

Police sirens.

Zac watched the patrol cars as they entered the driveway and a dozen officers surrounded him and held him back. They entered the house by the kitchen door and Zac listened as Dominic ranted profanities and stood his ground. Finally he was brought out in cuffs and Zac overheard the charges read against him, growing numb as the officer announced the final charge – the murder of Xavier Fitzgerald.

Chapter 64

Kelly looked at Zac.

He'd taken her out in his fishing boat, and it was something she wasn't used to. The boat was unsteady and she sat in the middle, not daring to move lest she be thrown out. The day was a beauty, and Zac cast his line again and again. Johnny had ridiculed her, referring to the day out as a date. She'd stuck two fingers up at him and he'd kissed her as she started the car.

She and Zac had become friends. Well, if not friends, something of a pairing; a bit like a big sister and a younger brother, spending time doing nothing. She felt calm when she was with him and they'd struck up an unlikely bond, spending time at the lake or finding hidden landscapes for him to paint, as she watched. Zac was a welcome visitor in her life when she needed something to keep her here. For their own separate reasons, both of them had wanted to leave this place. Neither wanted to know any more about how they came to be where they were. They didn't discuss it again after the time Zac had asked her if it was true that his father was his uncle.

'I think that's a story made up by Dominic to hurt you,' she'd said. 'He was jealous of what you had and he didn't.'

She'd confirmed that his grandfather was indeed Dominic's father, but after talking it through with Johnny, she had decided that the rest was unimportant. It was a decision she didn't take lightly, and she'd have to live with it, but for now, she was sure she'd done the right thing.

Zac took the news like he took everything else; like his grandfather had taught him: with dignity. The old man would have been proud. Zac carried the Fitzgerald legacy, and he was a survivor. Like any good big sister, Kelly didn't burden him with the problem of her own paternity. That was for her to mull over in her own time. Similarly, Nikki need never know, but it did release her in some way from the guilt that kept her imprisoned. Now, if she didn't want to see her sister, she no longer felt anguish, resentment or compulsion. If Wendy ever tried to argue the point, Kelly only needed to look at her and her mother backed down.

As for Ted, she hadn't decided what to do.

As far as she was aware, he still didn't know. Johnny said she should take him out on a date too, and she'd punched him playfully in the stomach.

'How's Brian?' Zac asked her. The boat wobbled and Kelly held her breath; she was far more comfortable under the water than on top of it. Zac laughed. 'Sorry, I'll keep her straight.'

'He's improving.' Dominic had brought a Victorian stewing pan down so hard on Brian's head that he'd been concussed. He was lucky it wasn't worse. At least he had landed a few punches before that. The police had arrived in time to split the two up, and overpower Dominic before arresting him for the murder of Freya Hamilton and the kidnap of Sophie Daker and Hannah Lawson. One day they might have a case for the murder of Abi Clarence, but for now, her bones lay stored in a freezer in a lab in Carlisle. No one wanted them.

'Do you think Grandpa suffered, Kelly?' he asked.

'The coroner reckons that he was probably smothered in his bed, and then taken to the study,' she said.

'Why didn't I hear anything?' he asked.

'Because you didn't expect Dominic to be creeping around your house. You trusted everyone, Zac. You weren't listening for noises. He'd been in there plenty of times when you weren't about, just to test how easily it could be done.'

She'd already explained how hard it would be to prove that Dominic Cairns had murdered Xavier. A jury would have to decide. They had a strong circumstantial case but no smoking gun. But he was going to do time anyway.

'Will I have to look at him in court?' Zac asked.

'That's up to you. There are screens available if you can't stomach it,' she said.

'No, I want to look at him.' Again, Zac had caught her by surprise. She smiled. He'd be all right.

'Here,' he said. He tidied his line, pulled his rod in, and collapsed it into four pieces. He got the urn out of its bag and they sat together looking at the water. Eventually he opened the urn and the wind took a few grains. He tipped the rest over the side of the boat and watched as the gritty sand floated away and sank. The lake had been a part of his family for generations; now it had a new job – to look after his grandfather.

On their way back, they needed no words. Zac got as close to the shore as he could, and Kelly jumped out and helped him pull the boat in and anchor her up. She was glad to be on dry land again. They gathered their things and walked back to Wasdale Hall, barefoot, past the stone fountain where her parents had first met.

Her phone pinged and she opened a text. It was from Sophie Daker. She showed Zac. Sophie had taken a selfie of herself and Hannah sitting on a hospital bed. They were smiling. Bandaged and not yet healed, but smiling. Kelly put the phone back in her bag.

'You did that. You saved them,' Zac said.

She put her hand on his shoulder and squeezed it. Maybe she did belong here after all.

Acknowledgements

I would firstly like to thank my agent, Peter Buckman, for his never ending encouragement and faith; also Louise Cullen, Laura McCallen and the team at Canelo for their passion and meticulous attention to detail. For their fascinating insight, Harry Chapfield, Cumbria Constabulary (ret'd), Inspector Paul Redfearn, London Met Police, and DI Rob Burns, Beds Police. I want to thank the Lemons: you know who you are, I love you.

And finally Mike, Tilly and Freddie for being neglected at odd times of the day; I couldn't have done this without you.

CANELO CRIME

Do you love crime fiction and are always on the lookout for brilliant authors?

Canelo Crime is home to some of the most exciting novels around. Thousands of readers are already enjoying our compulsive stories. Are you ready to find your new favourite writer?

Find out more and sign up to our newsletter at canelocrime.com